"Why don't you just respect my emotions, Stace? I may have fallen in love with the wrong man. A man who doesn't love me. But it doesn't change the fact that I am in love with him . . . don't you see?"

"No, I don't. You sound like Eva Braun in the bunker. What can I say to convince you?"

I began to cry heavy, desperate tears. Eloise put her arms around me. Students crossed behind and in front of us on those steps. I wanted to go back to our college years and be smarter, more aware, less selfish. I wanted to be nineteen years old again . . .

TIES that BIND

CINDY BLAKE

A Dell Book

Published by
Dell Publishing
a division of
Bantam Doubleday Dell Publishing Group, Inc.
1540 Broadway
New York, New York 10036

Previously published in the U.K. under the title
BLOOD SUGAR

ISBN: 0-440-21552-8

Printed in the United States of America

Published simultaneously in Canada

December 1993

10 9 8 7 6 5 4 3 2 1
RAD

For Anthony Holden

How comes it, Tony, that, whenever we
play cards together, you invariably,
however the pack parts, still hold the ace of hearts?
                              —Christina Rossetti

Prologue

The ambulance broke down on the way. The driver and the two paramedics couldn't work out what had happened. Was it the generator? The fan belt? They didn't know about cars. They knew a fair amount about how humans worked, but the inside of the vehicle they were driving was a mystery.

"Maybe it's had a heart attack," the young, female paramedic joked as she stood beside the crippled ambulance. "Maybe we should get it to emergency."

Neither of the two men laughed.

"We better radio in and get a replacement pronto," the driver said, looking and sounding fed up. Ambulances weren't supposed to break down. Who was going to get the blame for this one?

So the two policemen arrived first, juggling cups of Dunkin' Donuts coffee while the car sped, careful to put out their cigarettes before they entered the house.

"It's a little early to look at dead bodies, if this is for real and there *are* any dead bodies," Dick, the taller policeman, said. He had tried his best to look like Tom Selleck playing Magnum, but his eyes didn't

1

pierce and he would never get to Hawaii. The shorter one grunted. He didn't come close to looking like any television star and he knew it.

"It's always too early to look at dead bodies, Dick. Where's the damn ambulance anyway?"

The front door of the house was opened by a young woman who looked like a law student on vacation. Short, sensible brown hair, frightened brown eyes.

"They're upstairs. Upstairs on the left. One in the bedroom, one in the bath. I can't go up there again, all right?" she pleaded.

"You the one that called this in?"

"Yes. I'm the one that found them. Please don't make me go up there again." She was looking at Dick when she said this. Barry, the shorter, fatter, flat-faced policeman, had to acknowledge—for the millionth time, it seemed to him—that they always looked at Dick and they always would.

"How about you make us both some coffee—black —we'll go on up and take a look, and then we'll come down and have that coffee and ask you some questions. That okay?" Dick put his hand on her shoulder.

"Yes. Thank you. That's fine. God, I'm glad you guys got here." The relief registered on every part of her face; her shoulders dropped a few inches. "Up there." She pointed at the staircase. "On the left."

"You sure they're both dead? Where in hell is that ambulance?" Barry didn't mean to sound as pissed off as he knew he had.

"They're dead," she replied, turning away from them, trying to focus on getting to the kitchen, making the coffee, anything normal, anything to take her mind off upstairs. The two policemen started up the stairs, wide enough so they took them side by side. They stopped simultaneously as they heard her call after them.

"I didn't touch anything," she yelled, out of sight. "I know enough not to touch anything."

"Good girl," Dick yelled back.

They went into the bedroom first, Barry taking everything in at once: the dead body on the bed, the view of the ocean out of the window which was open a few inches, enough to let some fresh air in, some sea smells. A sky-blue bedroom. Everything matched. The wallpaper, the curtains, the pale blue rug, the pale blue sheets splayed with rust-colored blood. All that closet space, the closet doors covered in material like he'd seen once in a picture of a ritzy hotel room. Very nice-looking gun, too. Dick had leaned over the body then walked off again, into the connecting bathroom.

"Here's the other one," he announced.

"Shit," said Barry when he got there. "Not a pretty sight."

"Well, it's no hoax, anyway." Dick rubbed his mustache.

"Time to call the boss and get the other guys down here. Could be double murder. Double suicide. Or maybe one murder, one suicide. Take your pick."

"I'm not making any guesses. I need that coffee."

"Yeah," Dick smiled. "Cute girl, isn't she?" Barry ignored him.

"Where's that damn ambulance?"

"A little late for paramedics," answered Dick, turning his back on the body in the bathtub.

1

NOVEMBER–DECEMBER 1989

I was intrigued by the invitation. How Eloise had managed to track me down was one question. But that was relatively easy to answer. Eloise had more money than God; and money, in the right places, can find someone faster than a well-trained sniffer dog can find drugs. More puzzling, more exciting, was the fact that the invitation was to a wedding. Eloise was getting married. The engraved Tiffany card in front of me was proof of that. She was going to marry a man named Robert Chappell. A fitting name, I thought, for a bridegroom.

Over the years I had lost track of Eloise. She'd become part of my memory of college days, of a decade I'd been happy to abandon—the seventies. It had been a confused and confusing time for me, and I was relieved when the clock struck midnight signaling the advent of January 1, 1980. Old acquaintances were not entirely forgot; they were occasionally brought to mind; but I'd started a new life in California and I was happy enough not to recall the old days in New York.

Eloise was different, though. I should have known that. She was a special case and I should have tried, at least, to find her. Yet I'd been hesitant the few times I'd thought of it. And that was due to her money. If I contacted her, would she think I was out to take advantage of her wealth, to take another ride on her rich coattails, as I had in college? I was relieved that she'd found me first, and, of course, curious about this wedding.

The image of Eloise in a wedding dress made me laugh—I had never seen her in anything formal, and I couldn't picture it. The really crucial question, however, the one impossible not to ask myself, the one impossible to answer unless I accepted the invitation, was Robert Chappell himself. Was he a man in love with my old college roommate, or was he a fortune hunter who'd struck lucky? With that much money at stake, you had to wonder. Or at least I had to. Which meant that, yes, most definitely, I would be delighted to attend the wedding of Miss Eloise Camille Parker. I wanted to see her again. And I wanted to check out Robert Chappell.

I was a thirty-seven-year-old divorcee managing a B. Dalton bookstore and living in Tiburon, a small San Francisco Bay community, when I received Eloise's invitation. My life had settled into a predictable, easy pattern made up of work, friends, and the occasional lover. I found that even years after my divorce, I couldn't take romance seriously, couldn't stop myself from laughing at the wrong time over a candlelit dinner, or making some cynical crack when a man would talk to me in earnest about our relationship. Whereas once I'd thought domestic arguments with my husband were a bad parody of *I Love Lucy,* now any romantic interludes with other men reminded me of scenes from *The Love Boat*. It wasn't an attitude designed to help the male ego, but it kept me from getting involved; and that, I suppose, was the point.

I wondered whether Eloise had been married before. Was this the second time around for her? The third? What had she done with her life, her money? Two letters—one about her father's death, the other saying she couldn't come to my wedding—were all I'd heard from her since 1974. I hadn't wanted to tell her about my divorce. She'd been in on my romance with Buddy from the beginning, seen how swept away by passion I'd been. She would feel sorry for me, and I didn't want that. I never even bothered to try to find where she was living in all the years that passed. I thought of her occasionally; whenever I saw lilies, or when I'd hear particular classical recordings we'd both loved. But I preferred not to think about New York too often.

The RSVP on the invitation was Eloise's address on Cape Cod. The wedding was to take place there in two weeks time, on December 7.

I booked a flight to Boston and airmailed an acceptance. "You bet I'll be there, Eloise. Keep your socks on." I put my flight number and time of arrival at the bottom. It occurred to me to call her, but I wanted our first real communication after fifteen years to be in person.

When I boarded my flight, I remembered the last time I'd seen her, the way I'd kept waving, even after she'd turned her back and trundled toward the First Class lounge, about to jet off to Paris. I remembered her chauffeur, John: his prediction that she would get herself into trouble, his request that I look after her.

Well, I hadn't looked after her. She wasn't my responsibility, she was simply my friend. But our friendship wasn't simple, not like the friendships I had in California. Eloise's money skewered it for one, as did my protective feelings toward her. Here I was about to check out Robert Chappell, to see whether he was a scheming gigolo, when it was none of my business whom she chose to marry. And what if Robert Chappell *was* a sleazy man on the make? What was I going to do about it? Tell the minister I had grounds to object at the ceremony? Not very likely.

I'd have to be careful not to let my cynical views on romantic bliss be so evident that they'd affect Eloise's happy weekend. I'd have to keep my smart remarks to myself. I knew I was still bitter about the institution of marriage, but I'd have to keep that hidden. For I recognized another danger, another complication to our friendship—my competitive instinct. Eloise and I had both been only children, and we had come close to being sisters in those college years. There was a sense of sibling rivalry lurking between us. I wanted Eloise to be happy, but I wasn't sure I wanted her to be any happier than I was.

That nasty thought made me wish the beverage cart were closer to my row of seats. When it finally arrived, I ordered a Bloody Mary and sat back, trying to relax.

I had a short conversation with a nice elderly man beside me. We discussed Boston, New York, East versus West Coast, and he asked me politely, just before the movie began, whether I needed a lift anywhere from Logan.

"No thanks, there'll be a limo waiting to meet me, I think." I couldn't resist it. His eyebrows arched.

"Lucky you."

"It's my friend's. My old college friend's. Lucky me." I smiled.

The limo, driven not by John, but by a gray-haired man with the name Edwin pinned on his uniform, picked me up at Logan as expected. I collapsed gratefully in the backseat, immersed in memories for the two hours it took us to get to the Cape. The weather was sharp, clear, and cold, with a covering of new snow on the ground, making me momentarily nostalgic for the change of seasons in the Northeast.

"Edwin?" I asked as we started up the familiar driveway. "Could you let me off here? I'd like to walk to the house."

I wanted a pause by myself before seeing Eloise, a few more minutes of reminiscence for the summer I'd spent there between our junior and senior years, playing tennis, swimming, eating lobster, and leading a rich, idle life.

The white Cadillac, mirroring the snow perfectly, went on as I walked up the drive. I heard Edwin slam his door and open the trunk as I walked past the tennis court and remembered the days I gave Eloise lessons. Then I saw someone running toward me.

I'd never seen a person so totally transformed as

9

the woman who was throwing her arms around me in front of the tennis court. This can't be, I thought, as Eloise stepped back and I stepped back. This can't be Eloise.

2

SEPTEMBER 1970

Eloise and I met in the fall of our freshman year, when we were thrown together as roommates during our first term at Barnard. I was shattered before I'd even arrived at our dorm room for that inaugural day. Having flown in to New York from Chicago, I grabbed a taxi with a wild-looking East European driver who had considerable problems understanding my request to be taken to Barnard College on Broadway and West 116th Street. By the time we had got the destination clear we were crossing the Triborough Bridge; and just moments after taking in the magical sight of the New York skyline, I heard a stereo sound of the doors on either side of me being automatically locked. I knew then that I was about to be kidnapped and sold into the white slave trade. My life was up for grabs.

All my mother's fears for her midwestern daughter in the menacing Big Apple seemed now, suddenly, reasonable. Why hadn't I listened to her? I pulled out a cigarette, lit it, and tried to bring back the high points of my eighteen years on mental flash cards. I couldn't come up with any and switched immediately into an escape mode. If I pounded with my fists on the windows, perhaps somebody would recognize my peril and save me. I scanned the street for friendly faces. And that was the moment when I figured out why the cabdriver had locked the doors. We were driving straight through Harlem.

Columbia University and its sister college, Barnard, bordered on Harlem. I knew that, but I'd never seen Harlem before, never been exposed to throngs of black people crowding the street, radios blasting on sidewalks filled with makeshift stalls. I was glad then that I'd been imprisoned, but I was also glad to be, even for a short time and from a distance, a small part of the energy of that street. It didn't look frightening: it looked alive, full of action, full of possibility. Though not, I knew, for a midwestern, white, hick girl like me.

Columbia, famous for its 1968 riots, was still, in 1970, the politically "in" college to attend. I was only mildly politically motivated, but New York City was where I wanted to be. These were the pre–Ed Koch days, but if there had been an "I Love NY" sticker available, I'd have put it up on my bedroom wall in my hometown—Peoria, Illinois. Coming from Peoria is a joke in itself, a nationwide joke I didn't think was remotely funny. Of course, I understood that some people had to be born there, but I couldn't comprehend why I had to be one of them. As an advanced teenager, I was desperate to shed the Peoria tag and take on some East Coast sophistication, as quickly as humanly possible. Barnard seemed the logical choice for a girl with high college-board scores who had no desire to end up playing field hockey in a remote women's college like Smith or Vassar.

So I was startled and disappointed when I finally paid the cab fare, struggled with my bags to my pre-assigned dorm room on the corner of West 116th Street, and opened the door to find a girl standing in front of me who would have been the class oddity even in a Peoria high school. Eloise would have been the one who didn't get invited to the prom, the Sissy Spacek character in *Carrie*—the awkward girl with the crazed mother who is ridiculed by all the cool kids in her high school and finally gets her revenge with paranormal pyrotechnics. Eloise would have been a shoo-in for that part—until the retribution scene, that is. Then the audience would have problems believing in her psychic powers. She looked too harmless, too lost, too gawky standing there in her baggy jeans and ill-fitting T-shirt. It occurred to me even then that short people aren't supposed to look gawky, but that my new roommate had somehow managed it.

We introduced ourselves, shook hands self-consciously, and stood in silence for a moment.

"Is it okay if I have this bed?" Eloise asked, motioning to the one in the right-hand corner of the room. She was biting a piece of skin off a peeling lower lip.

"Sure. You take the right, and I'll take the left. I guess I should start unpacking."

"It's a small room, isn't it?" The skin came off, she took it in her right hand, searched the room for a wastepaper basket, found one in the corner, brushed her hands against each other, came back and began to shift from foot to foot and bite her lip again. Her dark bangs came down over her eyes and the rest of her hair was just a lank mass. Even in those hippie days, people generally made more of an effort with their appearance. She must be on a scholarship, I thought. From a disadvantaged background. But then why would she have thought the room was small? I was curious, but I didn't want to ask. If we were going to get along, we would have to start out by respecting each other's privacy.

"Stacy?" She was now perched on the side of her bed, watching me unpack, chewing on the ends of a piece of that hair. I couldn't believe it. "Are you going to all these orientation parties and things?"

"I thought I would. I mean, it seems a good way to meet people. Except it's so hot. What is it, ninety-five degrees or so? I don't know if I'll have the energy tonight."

"Maybe you and I could go out for a pizza or something?"

My back was to her as I began to unpack, and I cursed under my breath. This roommate was going to be a liability. Shy and unprepossessing, she would need a lot of help to get through the first few weeks. And I already felt responsible for her. I couldn't just leave her alone, not the first night anyway. That would be like abandoning a lost dog.

"Sure. I'm sure if we walk down Broadway . . . Isn't that great, we've made it to Broadway?" I turned around and smiled and she smiled back. "Anyway, I'm sure we'll find a pizza place."

We did, and Eloise spent the entire time questioning me about my past, my family, Peoria, my dreams of New York. I answered her questions in paragraphs.

"I should warn you, since we're going to be living together for the next year, that I'm a hopeless romantic. Those two words sum me up. I daydream, I read books like some people eat chocolate, I listen to operas, I watch old movies. I'm in love with Fred Astaire. I had a lot of friends at high school, but they spent their time grooving to Jimi Hendrix or testing how short they could wear their skirts to class. They thought I had weird tastes. They were into being hippies in a big way and I'm not. That's one of the reasons I chose to come here—I want to be *civilized*, you know—I want to educate myself outside of college as well, go to the opera or the theater sometimes. Live a metropolitan life instead of that shit that passed for culture in Peoria."

Eloise brightened, smiled, discreetly waved my cigarette smoke away from her face.

"I'm a romantic too," she said. "I even dreamed I danced with Fred Astaire once. On a rooftop. It's the only dream I've had when I was disappointed to wake up. Usually I have intense nightmares. Anyway, there's a fabulous movie theater on 86th Street—the Regency —it plays all the great old movies. You'll love it."

The bill came, and I made a point of paying it, conscious that Eloise might be broke. During the summer holidays I had worked as a waitress and saved up enough money for a few months, depending on New York prices.

"Maybe I could get a job on weekends and then I could afford all these grandiose plans of mine." I laughed. We were lingering over our coffee, taking advantage of the air-conditioning.

"Maybe I could help out," Eloise said. She was busy winding a strand of her lifeless hair around her fore-finger. Her lower lip had two raw patches.

"Sure." I caught myself sounding dismissive. I couldn't picture Eloise as capable of holding down any job, although she might be eligible for welfare. "But listen, I haven't asked you anything about your-self. Why did you choose Barnard, anyway? For all I know you might be an SDS member, a romantic revo-lutionary, and here I am talking about the opera."

"Oh, no." She smiled again and then her elbow bumped into her glass of water, almost knocking it over. "I'm not a radical at all. I think most of them are fakes, actually. They have enough money to come to college and protest. The poor people get drafted and can't get out of going to Vietnam, and these left wing students know that. So they feel guilty and go around like little soldiers themselves, occupying build-ings and marching around, trying to prove themselves by getting in combat situations with the police. I'm against the war too, but I'd feel stupid demonstrating. It's all about money in the end. Multinational corpo-rations, the defense industry. It's all about money. Be-sides—" She peered shyly at me through her bangs. "I love opera too."

Well, I thought, leaving—like anyone who has ever waited on tables—a good tip; I've misjudged her. Per-haps the person in charge of putting roommates to-gether looked through our applications and focused on our interests and hobbies. Eloise and I were well matched.

We walked back to our dorm room in the stultifying heat. I lay down on my bed and watched as Eloise pulled out a black bag from her closet. When she picked a syringe out of it, I sat straight up. What had I got myself into here? Rooming with a junkie. I stared at her and felt anger and panic. Could I go to the college authorities and rat on her, get her expelled? Yes, I could, definitely. There was no way I could live with a junkie zombie. No wonder she looked so awful. She probably shot up in the darkness of the Regency movie theater and blissed out on Jimmy Stewart.

Glancing over and seeing my expression of horror, she laughed.

"It's cool, Stacy, don't worry. I'm a diabetic, that's all. I have to shoot up like this every night. Sorry, I should have told you before."

I laughed back with relief.

"Boy, you scared me there. I was just figuring out how quickly I could get rid of you."

"Oh." She stopped laughing abruptly and stared at the floor, needle in hand. "You'll see I'm not as much of a liability as you thought at first."

I looked away, stunned and embarrassed. Had I made it so obvious? But how had she come up with the exact word I had thought of to describe her—a liability? She must have psychic powers. I tried to ignore that thought, tried to ignore the heat, tried to sleep. My attempts, that first night in the Big Apple, were not particularly successful.

* * *

Eloise and I were taking entirely different courses that semester, and went our separate ways the next morning. I was pleased to begin, on my own, to meet other students, to sign up for my one outside activity—the Columbia radio station. I was hoping to be a classical disc jockey in my spare time, and happy to learn that the station was canvassing freshmen. The heat was still as intense as only New York heat can be in an Indian summer, and when I arrived back at the dorm that afternoon I was sweating so much I felt as if I'd been swimming in a sewer. Until, that is, I walked into our room. Then I was hit immediately by a cool breeze and the scent of lilies.

Eloise was nowhere in sight, but a huge air conditioner had miraculously appeared in the window, and there were at least two dozen lilies scattered around the room in small crystal vases. I couldn't believe it. She must have an admirer, a rich admirer. But, I had to ask myself, who would admire Eloise? When she came in I was still sitting in stupefaction, having already, of course, searched the room for a card which would tell me whom these presents were from. And come up with nothing.

"Gosh," she said, throwing an armful of textbooks down on her bed, "I can already tell my physics course is going to be a bummer. The professor is making eyes at some girl named Bunny something who wears see-through blouses. There's no way I can compete with that."

"Eloise—what the hell is this all about?" I motioned to the flowers and air conditioner.

18

"Well. It's hot, isn't it? I could hear you tossing and turning last night. Now we'll be able to sleep."

"Air conditioners are expensive, Eloise."

"I know." She looked out the window, then back at me, her shoulders slumped. Her posture was terrible.

"And, correct me if I'm wrong, but isn't it difficult to get one and have it installed on the same day?"

"Not if you have enough money."

"Which you have?"

"Yes. It's no big deal, Stacy." She stuffed a piece of hair into her mouth. By the way she said it, I knew she must have more than a little money. She must have a lot.

"What about the flowers?"

"I hope you don't mind. I have a thing about lilies, that's all. They were my mother's favorite flowers."

"Is your mother dead?"

"Yes. She drowned when I was three."

"I'm sorry."

This was all too much to take in. Eloise was rich. A rich diabetic with a dead mother who was addicted to lilies and looked like a rag doll.

"Oh, please, don't feel sorry for me. Everyone always feels sorry for me. Poor little rich girl who lost her mother, has diabetes, and is ugly as well. Don't you start. I thought we could be friends."

"We can. But I don't understand why—"

"Just don't try, okay?" Eloise was angry, and in her anger she lost some of her gawkiness. She stood up straight and began to brush the bangs off her forehead with a ferocity.

"I don't want to talk about it. My money. My looks.

19

My family. The diabetes. Any of it. I just don't want to discuss it. Okay?"

I nodded dumbly.

"Besides . . ." She sat down, her shoulders slumping again.

"Do you have a skirt you could wear tonight?"

I nodded again. I'd given up trying to figure out what was happening.

"I thought we could go to the opera. It's *Traviata* at Lincoln Center tonight. Or have you made other plans?"

"No. I haven't. Give me a second, will you? I can't believe all this. The opera?"

"The opera. Look, Stacy—I feel really lucky to have you for a roommate, because I won't have to hide my money, won't have to pretend. You and I can enjoy it together." Her words had speeded up, as if this was a speech she wanted to get over with quickly. "We like the same things, so let's just take advantage of it. If you were some radical you'd be trying to convince me to give it all to a political movement or something. Because eventually you'd find out. Everybody does. And I don't want to give it all away. Not yet, anyway. I'm too young to make such a big decision."

"That sounds sensible." Eloise thought *she* was lucky? I felt like Dorothy being handed the magic slippers in Oz. Lincoln Center—not to mention the blessed air conditioner. My mother couldn't have been more wrong.

"But I've thought about it, and I don't think we should have my limo pick us up here. It's too embarrassing. We'll have to take taxis on our outings."

"No limo?" I gasped in mock horror. "What a bummer."

Eloise laughed as she changed into an oversized brown skirt and top which swamped her short body, then pulled on a pair of white ankle socks and brown loafers. I'd never seen anyone so badly dressed. She looked over at me.

"I know I'm a bad dresser, but I don't particularly care about clothes."

"Eloise?" I don't think I'd moved an inch since she had entered the room. "Are you psychic?"

"Oh no." She picked up a comb, started to pull it through her hair, hit a tangle and abandoned the effort. "I'm just very aware of what I must seem like to other people."

And what *are* you like? I wondered as I began to dress for our night at the opera. She had made it clear that she didn't want to be interrogated, to talk about her family or her money or her looks, but I couldn't help but think that she was making a statement with her appearance—the "Look, I happen to be rich, but I'm a mess" sidestep.

She had described herself as ugly, but she wasn't really; she'd simply made herself look ugly. Her eyes, if you could find them under the bangs, were an attractive dark shade of brown, her nose was short and straight, her mouth petite and full despite the ravaged lower lip. She even had a beauty mark on her left cheekbone. The cheekbones themselves were set low in her face, between the end of her nose and the beginning of her mouth. But her hair, her clothes, and her posture wiped out any possible prettiness in one convincing swoop of awkwardness. I couldn't help but be struck by it, just as I couldn't help but wonder why she was so intent on concealing her past. It was riveting, all this oddness. Her angry flare-up was a peek into a different Eloise. She was cryptic and I wanted to find the key to her coded personality. But perhaps that was the point. Her whole persona was a challenge. She was seeking attention by seeming to shun it.

I had been bluffing slightly the night before with all my talk of cultural life. Aspirations I certainly had, but I'd never even been to an opera before. I had listened to recordings, read the sleeve notes which came with them, but I'd never attended the real thing. Impressed by the sweep of Lincoln Center, busy ogling all the well-heeled patrons, I felt as if I'd been transported to another world, a world of money and power and glittering occasions. The energy of that world was as foreign to me as the street scene in Harlem the day before. How those two could coexist in one city amazed me. But once the overture began and the curtain went up, I forgot any social comparisons and was lifted immediately into Verdi's world—a world in which a woman died for love, coughing her way into oblivion. It didn't matter to me that she was capable of singing her heart out as she faded away, nor the fact that she was pounds over what a consumptive should have looked like; the music made me believe it all.

The intermission annoyed me. I wanted to hear it all sung with no interruption. Smartly dressed opera buffs drinking champagne seemed out of place, interfering with the passion of the scenes we had just witnessed. I wished, when it was over, that I could have stayed there and heard it all again. I was hooked. So was Eloise, but then she'd been hooked, she told me, since she was twelve and her father had taken her to *Rigoletto*.

"I admire Violetta," she said as we filed out with the rest of the crowd. "She was willing to sacrifice everything for love. Everyone talks about free love these days, but there is no such thing. You always have to pay for love, one way or another. Free love isn't love at all. There has to be something at stake for love to exist. I think you have to suffer for it."

"Do you think you have to die for it?" I asked. Now everything she said intrigued me.

"I'm not sure. But I think you have to be *willing* to die for it."

"You really are a true romantic."

"Maybe I am." Eloise paused. "Aren't you?"

"I've always considered myself one. But I have a horrible feeling I might be too selfish to be willing to die for romance. I don't think I'd go that far."

"Dying's not necessarily such a bad thing." Eloise brushed her hair out of her eyes with her hand, then hailed a cab. "It's probably just like getting into a taxi and going someplace you've never been before."

3

DECEMBER 6, 1989

"Stace, what *are* you doing walking up the drive? Come on in, quick, you must be exhausted."

I wasn't. I was stupefied. Eloise was wearing a bright pink wool suit with a white silk blouse. It was tailored, expensive, lovely. The old lank black mess of hair was short and curly, the way I'd always imagined fixing it, swept back off her face. I could discern eyeliner, foundation, rouge. Even her lips were smooth. She was the "After" picture and I couldn't reconcile it with my memory of her "Before."

"Hold on right there." I grabbed her by the shoulders. "Eloise, what's happened to you? I don't think I can take this." I realized that she had grown as well— we were on the same level—then I looked down to see her pink high-heeled suede boots. "You'll ruin those boots in the snow, Eloise. Where are your socks? How was I supposed to recognize you without the socks?"

"Oh, Stace, don't embarrass me, please. Don't remind me of all that. Please, just come in and relax. Meet Robert. And Bobby. They're just getting ready to play tennis." Of course, the court had been swept clean of the snow, I thought, as we walked to the house, as clean a sweep as Eloise had had. I was still trying to take it in. She walked assuredly, gaily, with little trace of the awkwardness that so enveloped her in the old days. The old days, indeed. How could Eloise manage to look so much younger after fifteen years? I felt jealous, then guilty. How could I deny her such obvious happiness? How could I feel jealous after all she'd done for me?

Walking through the front door into the hallway, I was struck much as I had been the day I'd found the air conditioner and lilies in our dorm room, assailed by the cool, clear, crisp aura of the house. Everything from our mutual past, it seemed, had been revolutionized. In my days there the house had been the opposite of a summer vacation home. Furnished with unwieldy fat brocaded sofas and massive leather chairs which would have been fitting in a Sherlock Holmes story, it was heavy-handed. Antique cabinets and wardrobes were splayed around the place seemingly at random. Thick velvet curtains had blocked out light and obscured the view. Going into that house had made me feel, on hot summer days, as if I'd been forced into a winter coat, hat, and scarf.

Now the house radiated light. The walls were white, the furniture light and comfortable. It looked like a Ralph Lauren store of epic proportions. Wrap it up, I thought, or take a picture and put it on a postcard. Better yet, make it the cover of a glossy magazine—complete, as I now noticed, with two men standing in the hallway, clad in white shorts and tennis sweaters. Holding tennis rackets nonchalantly. One arrestingly tall, about six foot five; young, thin, blond, with blue

25

eyes and high American Indian–style cheekbones. The other, an inch or so under the six foot mark; older, broader, with massive shoulders, curly brown hair, and light brown eyes. The older one approached me, smiling, open armed.

"Stacy," he said, giving me a bear hug. I could feel thin, short fingers on my back, a contrast to the wide shoulders against which my face was being crushed.

"Robert," I replied, stepping back as I had from Eloise's embrace. Those bear hugs affected me in much the same way as the friendliness of Southern Californians when I first visited there. The intimacy seemed wonderfully welcoming at the same time as faintly suspicious.

"Come here." Robert motioned to the younger man, who walked forward with a bashful look. He sported a severe crewcut. "This is Bobby, my son. Here's the Stacy we've heard so much about."

Robert turned back to me after Bobby and I had shaken hands. I saw then something odd about his right eye. The pupil had a splotch, as if a shaky-handed painter had slipped a millimeter when coloring it. The tiny slip was a lighter brown than the rest of the pupil. It was an appealing imperfection.

"We're so happy that you could come all this way, Stacy. I want to see you beat the pants off Eloise on the tennis court." He patted Eloise on the bottom and she smiled up at him. Then he made as if to bow to her. She grabbed the back of his head with both hands, ran her fingers through his hair, and released him. Robert had a rugged, handsome face. Any woman spotting him in the background of a friend's vacation photographs would ask: who is *he*?

He straightened up, swinging his tennis racket in the air with a flourish.

"Bobby here and I are sick to death of losing to Eloise. That's why we're going to get in a little practice now."

"I don't beat you often," Eloise protested with the same bashful look as Bobby, who was now standing a pace behind his father. "He's really good, Stace. I just got lucky once or twice."

I remembered the lessons I had given her, her comical inability to hit the ball over the net. Since when had Eloise been able to beat anyone, much less an athletic-looking man, at tennis? I wondered whether I was in the wrong house with the wrong woman—a different Eloise, an imposter.

"You *let* me win, Cat, and don't think I don't know it." Robert looked at his bride-to-be fondly and the jealousy crept back in my heart. It had been a long time since a man had looked at me with that kind of sexual affection. "Now you two girls probably have a lot to catch up on. Come on, Bobby, let's leave the ladies in peace."

"Have you changed everything in this house?" I asked her as the screen door slammed and I heard the scrunch of Robert's and Bobby's sneakers on the snow-topped driveway.

"Just about. Deborah," she called into the kitchen, "could you get us some coffee—or would you like a drink, Stace?"

"Coffee's fine." I followed her from the hall into

27

the living room, now prepared for the new furniture, the modern abstract painting on the white walls, the air of crisp comfort. Everything fit, everything matched, everything looked wonderful and sleek. Like Eloise. Even Deborah, when she entered and put down a tray with coffee and cookies on it, looked far too sophisticated to be a maid.

"Thank you, Deborah. So . . ." Deborah exited and Eloise turned to me. She put her hand up to her hair, started to twirl it, then visibly caught herself and stopped. The gesture reminded me how vulnerable she could be. "What do you think?"

"Let's see." I leaned back in my wicker armchair and gazed out of the picture window to the beach and the ocean. "I think you've done a remarkable job re-decorating this place." My peripheral vision was good and I could see her, sitting on the sofa to my right, staring at her coffee cup. She was disappointed and I knew why. She had wanted me to comment on Robert, not the house.

"Eloise, will you tell me why you never called me? We were friends and I never heard from you after those two letters, until I got the invitation. Why not?"

"I don't know the answer." I was glad she hadn't turned the question on me, asked me why I hadn't contacted her. "I guess I was embarrassed about a lot of things. The fact that I never got a job, never used my physics, never did much of anything except loaf around and live off my money. I didn't want to admit that to you. I felt stupid, I guess."

"You shouldn't have felt stupid with me."

"Oh, shouldn't I?" She stood up and walked over

to the window, her back to me. I noticed the damp patches the snow had made on her boots. "You made me feel stupid at college quite often, you know. I felt stupid about not having other friends, not having a boyfriend, not doing anything about my looks. I guess I wanted to wait to see you until I had something to show for myself."

"Like Robert?"

She turned around to face me and smiled. She was blocking my view of the ocean, but her face was a view in itself.

"Yes, like Robert. But not just Robert, Robert and me. What he's done for me. Our love for each other. I know it sounds corny, but not to put too fine a point on it, it's what I have to live for, what I'm proud of."

"But why was it so important to show *me*? We haven't seen each other in fifteen years. I would have thought you had forgotten about me."

"Did you forget about me?" She sounded disappointed.

"No. How could I? I thought about you every time I saw one of those damn lilies." I motioned to a huge vaseful of them in the corner of the room and she laughed.

"I wanted you here, Stacy, because you are my best friend, you've always been my best friend. And you're also the only friend I have who doesn't care about my money. Oh, I know you liked it, liked all the things we could do with it. The theaters, the operas, the restaurants, all that." I looked away from her. "I never had any problem with that. But you didn't have that money-hungry gleam in your eyes, the expectant look. Robert calls it the sit-up-and-beg look.

"You know, aspiring lovers aren't the only ones who get that look. Women, female friends get it too, I've found. There were a lot of women who were supposed to be my friends who'd spend days trying to *hint* that they needed something, financially speaking. I wouldn't have minded if they'd asked me straight out. But they would try to be so discreet and it was ridiculous. You could see it in their eyes. Needless to say, Robert doesn't get that look either."

"I'm glad," I said, and I was. I might have been jealous of Eloise, her newfound love and fairy-tale transformation, but I couldn't bear the thought of her being tricked or conned by some gigolo.

"So is Robert fabulously wealthy too, or does he simply not care about money?" Judging by my brief run-in with him, I thought that Robert could have been anything: a company chairman, an astronaut, a stylish truck driver, another recipient of inherited wealth.

"He doesn't care about money. Actually he does. I mean, he likes it, but it's not crucial to him or to me and him. He's a lot like you, really."

"I hope he's not as poor as I am."

"Not anymore." Eloise shook her head and we both laughed. "Now, why don't you take a rest? You're in your old room. Tonight Robert's taking us out, and I'll tell you later about what happens tomorrow. You're my matron of honor, Bobby is Robert's best man, but it's a tiny wedding, so don't worry."

My suitcase had already been taken up to my room

and I was pleased to see that Eloise hadn't changed it in the general overhaul of the house. She was right not to, for it was the one room that benefited from what had been her father's antiques mania. I stretched out on the four-poster, overcome by all I'd witnessed and feeling jet lagged.

I pictured Robert standing in the hallway, so perfectly dressed, so seemingly at ease. Was he as straightforward as he appeared? He certainly looked the part of the loving, caring fiancé, and he'd certainly done wonders for Eloise. For I was sure Eloise's emergence into the well-tailored pink butterfly I'd seen was due to him. Only a man, only love could make that kind of impact. If he'd helped her, as he so obviously had, why should I speculate about him? I wasn't being fair. I was back into my old habit of trying to find faults, pick holes. It was a habit unbecoming in a friend, I decided, and promptly fell asleep.

4

1970–1973

We were, at least for our first three years at college, best friends. Eloise and I hung out together, laughed together, discussed books, plays, operas together, wept unabashedly at old movies and once sat through four straight screenings of *It's a Wonderful Life*. We were anomalies in the hippie era. We both had liberal leanings but were unprepared to get involved in political activities on campus. The only area in which we conformed to our college peers was dress. Well, Eloise didn't, but only because she dressed in such a hopeless, absurd way. Eloise defied vanity.

During one student strike in 1971, we watched as a group barricaded themselves into a classroom chanting, "Two, four, six, eight, we remember sixty-eight,"; and we continued watching as one poor girl tried to cross the barricade and was bitten on her arm by a rabid radical.

"Boy!" Eloise turned to me as we watched the girl retreat, wounded. "That says it all."

We read the posted lists of 167 nonnegotiable demands the protestors had made, and giggled at the inanity of it. It was a jumble, including calls for an end to the Vietnam War and the end of any course requirements. Serious political demands were interwoven with demands for free second cups of coffee at the student cafeterias.

"If there are one hundred sixty-seven *non*negotiable demands, how many negotiable ones are there?" I asked as we sat one spring afternoon on the steps of the Columbia quad, looking across at Butler Library.

"It's all about money in the end, you know. When are they going to figure that out?" asked Eloise. "Politicians are irrelevant. There are people out there making money out of Vietnam. They don't care whether it's Communist or not, they just want to keep manufacturing arms and getting paid for it. Those are the people with power. The war may be winding down, but the multinational corporations will find other wars, or they'll keep making the weapons so that other wars become inevitable. It's a sick joke, really."

"Maybe you should give all your money to a peace foundation."

"Maybe I should." She leaned back on the steps, chewing her lip. Students were crisscrossing the quad in front of us, hurrying into classes or out of them. One long-haired boy was chanting, "Ho Ho Ho Chi Minh, NLF are going to win," as he walked up the steps and passed behind us. Eloise watched him until he disappeared, heading toward Amsterdam Avenue. "But then again, maybe I shouldn't. It might end up in the hands of a frustrated cheerleader like that guy. Come on, let's go look at something worthwhile, something money can't spoil."

We got up, walked to Broadway, and hailed a cab to take us to the Museum of Modern Art.

We avoided marches, avoided demonstrations, avoided drugs.

"Insulin is about all I can cope with," Eloise said as we walked through the dorm later that afternoon, assailed by the smoke of reefers in the hall. "I envy these people who fool around with drugs, who can play with them. That's one thing I *can't* afford to do."

I didn't experiment with drugs either. It wasn't that I believed pot would lead to heroin in general, but what if it did in my case? I was, I knew, an addictive personality. I smoked cigarettes despite all health warnings, and loved smoking them. Ten cups of coffee a day was my minimum. I could easily love pot, love LSD, love mescalin, love every drug in the book. I didn't want to find out.

Eloise and I were, all in all, the oddballs, the ones who listened to classical music instead of the Grateful Dead, the ones who journeyed over to the East Side as often as possible, the ones who watched the early seventies from the sidelines.

Not only did we miss the marches on Washington, shun mind-expanding trips on LSD, make fun of communes, but we also let the sexual revolution pass us by. We didn't sleep around. I dated a few boys from classes, but they seemed just that—boys. They wanted to smoke dope and listen to Eric Clapton. For all the supposed energy of the revolution, they seemed lethargic and self-obsessed.

I did have a brief, impractical crush in my sophomore year. Daniel Sterne taught a required course:

Contemporary Civilization. He was a postgraduate student, teaching as he finished his Ph.D., and he taught with an enormous amount of energy, intelligence, and humor. He also looked uncannily like Stalin; short, with thick, black, swept-back hair and dark, dangerous eyes. Daniel Sterne had a streetwise aura, a tough, matter-of-fact, nonacademic way of speaking, as if he'd come into the classroom straight from playing a walk-on part in *The Godfather*. I fantasized that he was a KGB man, a terrorist, a Mafioso—anything connected with secrecy and danger. Certainly not just a college teacher—he was too mysterious for that. He was also the one teacher I knew who never allowed a student to take an incomplete on his course.

"Some of you are going to give me a load of bullshit about not being able to write your term paper," he announced on the first day of class. "But I'm going to tell you right now that if you don't hand it in on time, I'm going to fail you. So tough shit." There was no outcry, as I had expected, but an acceptance of his ultimatum.

"Always remember," he'd told the class one afternoon as he chain-smoked filterless Pall Malls, "when a group of people raise their hands above their shoulders, it's trouble. Whether they are soldiers saluting, Nazis giving the *Heil Hitler*, a mass of hippies marching, hands upraised in the peace sign, or even a group of screaming hockey fans at a game, what you have is a group mentality, a possible lynch mob. The individual has traded his individuality for the comfort of a group. Trouble."

I sat in the back of the classroom and watched his

every movement, took copious notes, tried to think of a fascinating question to ask him after class; but he always hurried away as soon as he'd finished lecturing. Eloise was amazed by how hard I worked at that course.

Toward the end of term, he screened *Triumph of the Will*, the Nazi propaganda film. "You'll be surprised," he'd said, "even knowing the full evil of the Nazis, how powerful this film is. Some part of you may be moved by the images, by the music. Propaganda can be as potent as weapons."

As the lights came up after the film, and we prepared to leave the classroom, Sterne stopped us.

"Right," he said. "Before you go I'm giving you an assignment." We all groaned. "Write me a story tonight. It can be about anything. Cheer me up, depress me, enjoy yourselves. I won't count it in the grade, but I expect it to be done."

I skipped my other classes that afternoon and went to the Viennese coffee shop on Amsterdam Avenue, a dingy basement restaurant full of old waitresses with trembling hands and smudged lipstick. I loved it there because they'd let me sit and work while I smoked packs of cigarettes and sipped at their specialty—iced coffee with coffee-flavored ice cubes and coffee ice cream floating on top. I wanted desperately to entertain Daniel Sterne, started a few times on a story, tore it up and finally settled down to a tale of a bank robber who pulls off huge heists but becomes increasingly frustrated and unsure of his own existence when none of the robberies are ever reported in the newspapers or television. At one point, I looked up from my work and saw Sterne sitting at a table to my left, with a well-known English professor. They had finished their coffee and were about to depart.

"I hope that's for me," he said to me over his shoulder and smiled a smile he must have known I'd adore.

The next morning, when we handed in our stories, Sterne said, "Thank you. As I said, these are for me. I'm not going to grade them and I'm not going to hand them back. They are my little mementos of this class."

I was crestfallen, hoping that I would have received some response from him and knowing I was doomed to be just another student in another class. But a week later, he breezed into the Viennese when I was there, sipping coffee between classes. He pulled out the chair opposite me, twirled it around and sat, his arms embracing the back.

"That was a great story, you know." I don't think I'd ever been so pleased in my life, not even when I'd been accepted at Barnard. "I read it to some of my friends over the weekend. They loved it."

"Thanks," I said. I wanted to ask him to run away with me. The Caribbean, Alaska, Paris, anywhere. Just the two of us. He brushed a hand back through his dark hair, shook his pack of Pall Malls, leaned over and extricated one with his lips. I thought it was the coolest gesture I'd ever seen.

"Do you—?" He stopped, lit his cigarette, inhaled hard.

"Do I what?"

"Do you think I can have a sip of your coffee?"

That hadn't been what he was going to ask, I was sure. I thought I was sure. He was going to ask me out.

"Help yourself."

"Thanks." He took a quick sip, stood up. "You're doing great work in my course, Stacy."

"Thanks. I—" But he was gone, hurrying out as quickly as he did at the end of a class. I haunted that Viennese coffee shop for the next six months but I never saw him again. The rest of the semester, in his class, he would often pick me out in the back row, deliver his lecture to me personally, I thought. But I was beginning to think I was imagining things, that I had imagined that "Do you" was leading somewhere else. Occasionally we'd pass each other on campus and he'd smile that damn smile, then move on without a word. I got an A in Contemporary Civilization, but I would have preferred a date.

Eloise was riveted by my crush; she even came to the Viennese with me as I lay in wait. Every time the door opened, she'd whisper, "Is that him?" until even I got tired of my obsession. "I wish one of my professors was worth some passionate thought," she sighed. "I'd love to be in love, even if it's unrequited."

"It's awful," I warned her. "I'm giving up thinking about him at the end of this year. I can't give up smoking, but I can give up Daniel Sterne."

Eloise wasn't asked out much. When she was, she'd go halfheartedly and come back looking dejected. "They expect me to go to bed with them on the first date, Stace, and then they call me 'frigid' when I don't. I can tell they're not even turned on by me anyway, so I think I'm just another chick to get in the sack or something. When I fall in love, I'm *really* going to fall in love. I can wait a long time for that." She never told any of them about her money.

By 1973, our junior year, the war in Vietnam was no longer an issue. Watergate was *the* issue. And streaking had replaced demonstrations as the "in" form of expression.

"If you can't change the world, take off your clothes and run down the street," laughed Eloise after we'd seen yet another nude male sprint down Broadway. "That's really going to jolt the president of IBM, overthrow apartheid in South Africa, bring prosperity to Harlem."

We were sitting on our usual spot on the quad steps. I had two cups of Chock Full o'Nuts coffee in front of me and a pack of cigarettes in my lap. Eloise was rubbing the ankle she'd just turned.

"But the war did wind down, you know," I said, "and it did have a lot to do with the students. Sometimes I feel guilty about being so removed from it all. As if I hadn't taken part in historic events. We can laugh about the streaking now, but all those demonstrations did accomplish something while we were busy watching Cary Grant."

"Oh, Stacy, please. I've got enough guilt as it is. I know I'm supposed to believe in peace and love and flower power, but I can't. I'm as cynical about politics as I'm romantic about love. Yes, the war is over. So none of these guys is terrified that his number is going to come up in the lottery and he'll get blown away in a Vietcong jungle. So what do they do now? They streak. The immediate threat is over; now they can have fun. Maybe make token efforts about the other world problems, but that's it. And all these rebels will get jobs and start making money.

"Once the salaries start coming in, they'll begin to think that a house in the country would be nice. A house with a pool, preferably, because, you know, it gets so *hot* in the summers it's impossible to think. And the kids really should go to private school to get a good education. Pretty soon, bingo, they become the pigs they'd always hated. Money's insidious. Daddy told me once that he'd been a Communist in his youth. Maybe that's why I've never taken these people seriously. Let them tell me about it when they're forty. Then I'll pay attention."

From what I could gather from occasional snippets Eloise dropped, Daddy had a villa in the South of France, plus a flat in London, an apartment in Paris, a brownstone on East 74th Street, and a house on Cape Cod.

When it came to discussing her past, Eloise was as proficient a stonewaller as Richard Nixon. Three years after we'd met, she was still in many ways a mystery to me. Her perception was so acute that sometimes it spooked me; she would rob thoughts and words from my mind before I'd had a chance to articulate them. She was intelligent, as well as funny, with a self-deprecating sense of humor. She could also be bleak and moody, falling into depressions which made her shoulders slump until they formed a ninety degree angle to her neck. I began to think of these moods as Eloise's "blips." But the blips didn't last long. With a little effort on my part she could be chivvied out of them.

Our conversations followed a fairly predictable pattern over the years. I would pour out my heart and soul at length on any given subject, and she would listen carefully, interjecting a few pungent comments. Only when pressed would she talk of herself, and then only in short, strange bursts.

"Don't you get tired of me talking all the time, Eloise? Don't you want to talk about what *you* want out of life?"

"Not really," she'd replied. We were sitting in the student cafeteria, having Cokes and doughnuts between classes. Much as I'd always enjoyed talking about myself, I felt suddenly tricked by her silence, her inability to share herself. She spent money on me freely, but she wouldn't give me much of herself. It was the first time I had felt really cheap in her company—as if I'd been paid for, was there to perform.

"Fine. Don't talk to me, then. Keep all your secrets to yourself." I lit a cigarette, stared at a group of students laughing at the next table. Eloise was silent while I puffed away.

"Are you angry with me, Stace?" she asked, after I'd stubbed out one butt and lit another.

"*You* tell *me*. You're the one who knows all about me. You're the one who knows what I'm thinking half the time. While you sit there like the Sphinx. No. Like Orson Welles in *Citizen Kane*. Maybe after you're dead I'll find the Rosebud sled somewhere—the key to your inner life. The only fact I know about your past is that your mother died when you were three. What

41

about your father? Is he dead too? Why do you keep avoiding the subject? Don't you trust me? It's demeaning to me, Eloise. I thought we were friends."

"Don't be angry, please. I hate that." Eloise slumped, twisted her hair, pushed half a jelly doughnut around on her plate. "There's not that much to tell, really. He's very rich, my mother was rich too, so —Q.E.D.—I'm rich. Daddy used to pay a lot of attention to me, he took me out to restaurants, operas, galleries, everywhere. And then when I turned thirteen he cut back on the time he spent with me. Before, well, he'd traveled a lot, but he would always come home and visit. He'd be there for me when I needed him. Then it changed. He'd come for Christmas and my birthday. Sometimes his birthday, but that was it. And he sent me to boarding school. He used to call me his best friend, but I turned from best friend into what I guess you'd call an acquaintance. It hurt. I never understood it."

I was silent for a moment.

"I know what you're thinking, Stace. No, he hadn't fallen in love with some woman. He's a loner. He hasn't had any serious relationship since my mother died. That's part of why I find it inexplicable."

"If your mother was dead and your father rarely saw you, who looked after you?"

"A very nice housekeeper. And remember, I went to boarding school, so I spent only vacations at home. The problem was the timing. I mean, I was a teenager, things were happening to my body I didn't understand, and I couldn't ask the housekeeper about. She was too old. I didn't dare. The first time I got my period I was away at school. It was just after a French lesson. I remember because I told my roommate at the time that I'd started bleeding down there and she threw a box of Tampax across the room at me. I locked myself in the bathroom and studied this box and those instructions and I was at a total loss. It took me three hours cramped in this tiny toilet to figure the thing out. What went where and how. I was in floods of tears. I missed the next two classes and had to think up some pathetic excuse.

"There are lots of embarrassing memories like that. One girl looked at me in gym class and told me I should start shaving my legs. It had never even occurred to me, you know. I wasn't a happy teenager, let's leave it at that."

"But your father should have thought about all that. He could have helped. He shouldn't have neglected you."

"It wasn't really neglect. Maybe benign neglect. He came to school to take me out on my birthday every year. We had some nice Christmases. He was a busy man, Stace. Still is. I just missed being his best friend. I'd write lots of letters to him and every so often he'd reply. It's not as if he forgot about me entirely. He distanced himself from me. That's all. What father wants to deal with a teenage girl anyway?"

"Lots," I didn't say. Instead I reached across for her hand and said, "I'm sorry, Eloise."

She snatched her hand away from mine.

"That's exactly the reason I don't talk about it—comments like that." The Eloise anger. She straightened up.

"I'm not allowed to feel sorry for you?"

"No." She shook her head furiously. "Okay, it makes me sad, I admit that. But if I'm not happy sometimes, it's a good thing. I have to redress the balance."

"To redress *what* balance? Eloise . . ." I looked at her curiously. She'd cut her bangs herself that morning, making absolutely no improvement in her appearance. They were still way too long and ragged. She was wearing a pair of bottle-green corduroys two sizes too big for her, a puce-colored T-shirt three sizes too big for her, and socks which had no hope of matching. One was Argyll and ankle-length, the other knee-length and cotton.

"I'm cursed, Stacy," she mumbled.

"Oh, Jesus," I shouted, and the students beside us turned to stare. "What *is* this? Are you going voodoo on me or what? That's the most ridiculous thing you've ever said."

"I knew you wouldn't understand," she said sadly. "That's why I don't talk about it. It's just a knowledge I have that terrible things are going to happen to me. I have to pay. I have to balance things out."

"Pay for what? Is this some Greek tragedy? You don't seem to take in the fact that terrible things have *already* happened to you. You've had your full share. Your mother's death. Your father's neglect. I'm not buying this benign neglect business. Your diabetes. You've paid your dues. I'm not going to pretend I understand what you're saying, but whatever supposed balance you're talking about *has* been redressed. Fate isn't that cruel. Well, maybe to the Kennedys, but then you don't want to be a world leader, do you? You just want to be a simple physics teacher. The gods can't knock you for that."

"Maybe not. Maybe you're right." She got up abruptly, picked up a stack of books and cradled them. "But do you think anyone will ever fall in love with me?"

I was used to feeling like Eloise's older sister; but the way she asked that question made me feel like her mother.

"Of course someone will fall in love with you. You'll get married, have children, tell them about quantum physics, and live happily ever after. You've seen too many operas, you know. This cursed stuff is all very mysterious and romantic but it's a crock of shit. You're right. I don't understand and I never will understand because it's the stupidest thing I've ever heard. Now it's time for you to go to class and get some sense knocked into you, while I hand in my paper on Lenin which is so bad I think *I'll* be cursed forever by the gods of Communism."

She laughed.

"You always make me laugh when I get like this, Stace," she said.

"Well, Christ, Eloise, somebody has to."

5

DECEMBER 6, 1989

When I awoke, I saw on the bedside clock that it was 7 P.M. The winter night had closed in on the house while I was busy sleeping off the jet lag. I took a bath, got dressed, and prepared for the evening ahead. I had expected other arrivals—limos drawing up to the front door disgorging the beautiful and the rich; house guests arriving the night before for the wedding festivities. When I went downstairs into the living room, I was taken aback to see only Eloise, Robert, and Bobby sitting, sipping champagne. Robert leaped up promptly, poured a glass, and offered it to me.

"A little night music, Stacy," he said. "Champagne is not just bubbly, it's also tuneful. Listen." He held the glass close to my ear as if it were a seashell and I should listen for waves. The fizz of the champagne did, indeed, sound musical. I had never noticed it before.

He saw my smile and smiled with me, then we both turned to Eloise. She had changed from the pink into a brown suede skirt and off-white long-sleeved silk blouse with a high collar. It was a revelation to see her eyes after all the years they'd been hidden by her bangs; they were gorgeous, melting-chocolate eyes. I had always thought she could be pretty, but I'd never imagined that she could be as attractive as she was that night: warm, open, and sexy. Anyone meeting Eloise for the first time would have seen a good-look-ing woman; petite, round faced, well made up and well dressed. To me she seemed a movie star, so far had she moved from the Eloise of our past.

"Is it just us tonight or is anyone else coming for dinner? Johnny Carson, maybe? Robert Redford?"

"Sorry, Stace. It's just us for the whole weekend," Eloise replied.

"Aren't we enough for you?" Robert was wearing white linen trousers, a blue Brooks Brothers–style shirt, and dark blue jacket. It may have been cash-mere. He looked tall, when not standing directly be-side his taller son, and assured and somewhere in his early forties. I discarded the notion of the truck driver along with the son of rich parents. Astronaut seemed closer to the mark because of his physical presence, those broad shoulders. Or an admiral in the Navy. He would look great in a uniform, a natural commander.

Sitting down next to Bobby on the sofa, I wondered why Robert didn't have a best man his own age. But then, I thought, it's sweet to have your son as a best man. It said something nice about Robert. I pulled a cigarette out of my bag, which Bobby quickly lit, tak-ing a pack of matches from his pocket. He was dressed identically to his father, except for the jacket; his was a lighter blue. Such civility from a boy possibly still in his teens took me by surprise and I smiled at him. Bobby's cheekbones were as high as Eloise's were low and his eyes were a dull blue. I wondered what, if anything, lay behind them. I'd have a chance to find out, it seemed. He and I were going to be linked for the next two days, the matron of honor and the best man.

"How did you two meet?" I asked. Robert was sitting on the back of Eloise's chair, gently rubbing her shoulder with one hand, sipping his champagne with the other.

"We didn't meet," he answered. "We collided. Isn't that wonderful?"

"Robert rear-ended me on Fifth Avenue, six months ago to this day. Plowed straight into the back of my limo. Edwin got out and I felt so shaken I got out too. And the rest, as they say, is history."

"The rest is future, Cat." He kissed the back of her head. His voice was authoritative, but not overbearing. I noticed the short fingers again, as they dug into Eloise's shoulders. They looked like a child's hands. "And Edwin was driving very badly, I have to say in my own defense. The light had just turned yellow, and he thought he'd run it, and I thought I would too. Then he changed his mind and slammed on the brakes, and I slammed on mine, but to no avail. And that's all she wrote."

"What were you doing in New York? Do you live there?" I asked Robert.

"Now that's a long, boring story. And I want to impress my future wife's best friend, not put you to sleep. We're going for a hot time tonight, Stacy. No stag party, but as much fun as you can find in this

48

backwater." He finished his glass and poured himself another.

"I hope you like country-and-western music. Eloise and I are into it in a big way, and there's a terrific band called Bourbon Renewal playing in a joint down the road. The food's lousy, but the music's a treat." I liked the way he looked straight at me when he spoke. He was including me, welcoming me into their lives.

But Eloise liking country-and-western? I couldn't imagine the combination. Evidently more than her appearance had changed.

After we had polished off the bottle of champagne, Robert took charge, got the coats, and shepherded us all into the waiting limo. He and Eloise sat facing Bobby and me as Edwin rolled off down the driveway, a new layer of snow descending gently around us.

"All right now, here we are, and it's very important to get things off on the right foot." Robert reached down, undid his shoelace and took off his right shoe. Then he push-buttoned down the window and threw the shoe out. "There. That's better, isn't it?" We all laughed. I was amazed. He leaned over to the liquor cabinet on the side and extracted a bottle of Wild Turkey. "We're about to see Bourbon Renewal, so we should indulge ourselves in a little of the aforementioned spirit before we arrive." He poured out four strong shots and handed them around. "Let's toast. No. Let *me* toast. To Eloise. I love you."

She smiled back at him, eyes luminous.

"Almost as much as I love your money."

Eloise's eyes didn't change. I was watching closely.

If anything, they became more luminous as she laughed, as we all laughed yet again.

He had got it right, Robert. He knew exactly how to handle the overwhelming fact of her wealth. Acknowledge it. Joke about it. He had triumphed. And he looked triumphant, swigging back the bourbon.

Eloise downed her shot with him, ruffled his hair, then leaned over and kissed Bobby and me.

"I love you all. This is the happiest moment of my life."

She put down her window and threw the glass out, followed closely by her right shoe.

Bobby and I, of course, took off our right shoes and chucked them out of the window and the ceremony was complete. We laughed our way to the dive Robert had recommended, stunning the locals with our arrival—limping in, through the snow, one shoe each, looking as if we were involved in some crazy fraternity night challenge.

Robert and Bobby took turns twirling Eloise and me around the sawdust-covered dance floor to the twanging of steel guitars; we all chased our bourbon with beer, howled our approval of the band, and behaved like the college students only Bobby was and Eloise and I had never really been. In fact, Bobby was the most restrained of the four of us. I had the sense, occasionally, that he was watching Eloise and his father carefully, studying them, but he danced well and he drank well and he was wonderfully polite, and why wouldn't he be curious about his newfound stepmother? After all, he must have been thinking about his real mother. Where and who was she? Dead or divorced? I guessed divorce, then stopped thinking about it.

"Eloise and I didn't go in for pop music at college," I told Robert as we danced together, both shoeless.

"Ah, but this isn't pop, Stacy, this is country. A whole different proposition."

"I guess so." I was surprised by how much *I* was enjoying the music. "So, Robert, what do you do for a living, if it's not impolite of me to ask?"

"Checking me out, are you?" He took my hand and spun me around once, then pulled me close. "Of course you are. It's nice that Eloise has a protective friend. I always wished there were someone around to protect me." His feet stopped moving for an instant, then caught up with the beat. "I used to be in the music business. Now I've decided to write children's books. Do I pass inspection?" He didn't ask this harshly, but in a bantering tone.

"From what I've seen, yes, definitely, but who knows, you might have hidden secrets. You might be a criminal in disguise."

"Hey, you have a morbid train of thought, don't you? All those years living in New York?" He laughed. "Don't tell me you want to check out my bank balance before the ceremony. There's such a thing as being overprotective too, Stacy. Not all men are monsters masquerading as human beings." He spun me around again. I was beginning to feel dizzy and silly. My hand was on the back of his neck as I steadied myself. I could feel the thick, soft hair. I moved it back to his shoulder.

"I grew up in Brookline, a suburb of Boston. Middle middle class. Went to Brookline High and then Brown University. I got good grades, was good at sports, didn't steal cars or sell dope. Anything else you need to know?"

"Okay. I'm sorry if I seemed nosy. I admit I was curious. Actually, I had pegged you as something in the Navy. That goes to show how wrong first impressions can be. What did you do in the music business?"

"I failed in the music business. Not a very good qualification for a husband, is it?"

We had come to a stop and were standing still on the dance floor, couples whirling around us. His deep voice carried easily over the sound of the music. It was the perfect pitch to do voice-overs for television commercials.

"I really didn't mean to pry, Robert."

"No. Of course not. Don't worry about it, Stacy. Anyway, when you have to switch careers in the middle of your life, you have to examine yourself closely, decide what's important and what you have to give to the world, if anything. I decided to try to turn my own failure into something positive. I want children to come to terms with the concept of failure so they won't be destroyed by it later. I want them to realize that they're not hopeless little things if they can't always succeed."

Looking into his eyes, I saw a gravity there I hadn't seen all evening.

"I think that's wonderful, Robert. Really thoughtful. I remember all the books I used to read seemed to have superhuman children who could solve crimes or win horse races or do all the things normal kids can't."

"Exactly."

"So you're trying to instill confidence in kids who can't do everything perfectly. I like that idea."

"I'm deeply honored, ma'am." He put on a heavy Southern accent. "But your little feet *can* move, so get them started, will you?" We finished the dance, and went back to our table.

Eloise, sitting with Bobby, was radiant, relaxed—as if she'd broken free of restraints which had hampered her for years. I had seen her drunk only once before and recalled the way alcohol had unwound her then as well, revealing an Eloise I hadn't seen before. The Eloise before me now was like a female Clark Kent emerging from the phone box; she could dance and laugh and yell and let loose. Had Robert or the booze unleashed her? I watched her dance to "Don't It Make Your Brown Eyes Blue," locked with Robert in a passionate embrace. Soon I stopped speculating altogether. I was too drunk to think straight.

6

SEPTEMBER 1973–
JUNE 1974

Our senior year started auspiciously when I fell in love. I met him in the West End Bar one evening. Eloise wasn't there. I was sharing a pitcher of beer with some friends from the radio station when I saw him sitting alone at the next booth. I stopped talking and stared at him. He stared back. "Hi," I said as I passed him on a needless trip to the ladies' room. "Hi," he answered. "Why don't you join me?" "Why don't I?" I waited a proper amount of time in the grubby toilet, then returned to make my excuses to my friends. "I've just met an old buddy," I said. "Catch you later."

He turned out to be a law school student named, I thought cosmically, Buddy. I realized within a few minutes that "falling in love" is an apposite phrase to describe what actually happens. You do fall. You take that step off the edge, or something pushes you, and you fall. It could be the way he smiles, or the way he wipes the beer off his mouth with the back of his hand, or the way he sits with his foot up on the seat, or all three put together to form the hand that presses firmly through your back and against your heart and pushes you over. Knowing all the while that you'll crash like another malfunctioning DC-10 if he doesn't ask you out, get broken into pieces of misery if he doesn't say he loves you within two weeks, end up a splattered, unidentifiable corpse if he doesn't ask you to move in within a month.

I'd lusted after a football player in high school and happily lost my virginity to him; I'd had my crush on Daniel Sterne; but that had all been childish play, I was convinced as I looked at Buddy. I'd never fallen in love. What planet did you come from? I wanted to ask him. How did you get here? He was handsome and funny, sometimes shy, sometimes cocky. I was smitten.

Eloise was on the phone when I breezed in the next morning.

"Stacy!" She hung up. She looked worse than usual. "I've just been calling hospitals. I was about to go over to St. Luke's."

"What's the matter, are you sick?" I was free-falling, watching the world revolve beneath me, happily floating through space.

"Am *I* sick? No. I thought you'd been murdered or raped or something. I was terrified. Where were you?"

"I was with Buddy."

"Buddy?"

"Buddy. The man who makes the earth move and time stand still. Buddy . . ." I started to sing and twirl around the room.

"Oh boy." Eloise sat down on her bed, watching my antics. "You've got it bad. Maybe you should be in the hospital after all. Now I see why you forgot about our dinner arrangements."

"I'm sorry." I continued singing, "I'm sorry, I'm sorry."

"That's okay. I've switched the reservation for tonight anyway. We're going to Lutèce. You love it there, remember?"

"I'm sorry." I did a final pirouette and landed on my bed. "I'm going out tonight. With Buddy."

She turned her back to me.

"Oh, good. That's nice. I've got a lot of physics to do, anyway. I'll go to the library."

I was busy figuring out what clothes to wear that evening. And when I should wash my hair. And whether I should wear makeup. He hadn't seen me in makeup—would that be a good idea or not? These were crucial, life-or-death decisions. Eloise gathered her books together.

"Have a great time with Buddy," she mumbled through the clump of hair in her mouth. "See you later." I heard her drop a book in the hallway on her way out. "Shit," she swore, and I realized that it was the first time I'd ever heard her use bad language. She always said words like "gosh" or "gee" or "heck", sounding like a Catholic at a confirmation party. I wondered what had happened to make her say "shit". Then I began to ransack my cupboard for something that would knock Buddy's socks, shirt, and trousers off that night.

In October I moved into Buddy's rent-controlled apartment on West 103rd Street and Riverside Drive. I told my mother I'd fallen in love with a second-year law student, but I didn't tell her about the cohabitation. My parents didn't approve of living in sin; their faces froze whenever the subject came up. They would turn to me and say, "But you wouldn't do that, would you, Stacy?" and I'd let them think I wouldn't. Eloise was gracious and covered for me, fielding the rare phone call from my mother, lying for me adeptly. I didn't consider that I might have been putting her in an awkward position. Nor did I consider what my departure from our room might have meant to her. I just stopped seeing her. Oh, occasionally I would go to visit, when Buddy was immersed in his law books. Then I'd regale her with the joys of adult love. She'd sit and listen over a cup of coffee while I told her how wonderful Buddy was, how amazing his friends were, how great our sex life was, how love was the only thing that mattered. That's what all great music was about in the end, all great literature. I went on mercilessly.

"Is that what *Moby-Dick*'s about, then?" she asked one morning. "That's not what you were saying at the Cape last summer."

"Well . . ." I thought hard for an instant. "I didn't realize then. Yes. It's about love. I mean, you *could* read it as the ultimate love story. Ahab's in love with Moby, and sure, in the end, he's killed by that love. It's tragic. Like Anna Karenina going under the train, though it's not exactly like that. But it is a kind of love. Or love-hate thing."

To her eternal credit, Eloise didn't laugh.

"I'm happy for you, Stace. You know what a romance-junkie I am. Too bad Buddy doesn't have a friend I could harpoon."

"I know, I've thought of that. But they all seem to be spoken for. By first-year law students, mostly. God, I'm lucky he didn't fall in love with Martha. That's his friend Peter's girlfriend. She's disgustingly pretty and bright. They say she's top of the first-year class. They say she's a candidate for the editor of the *Law Review*. But Buddy says she's a really tough cookie and Buddy says . . ." I was off again, and Eloise listened patiently.

She and Buddy met a few times, but it didn't work. She was tongue-tied, shy, unable to relax around him. He treated her money as if she had been born with a deformity; in other words, he didn't mention it. He did everything to avoid mentioning it—for fear, he explained to me, that she would then feel compelled to ask him to the opera and ballet and theater and restaurants.

"I don't want to sponge," he said. "She's your friend, not mine. She's perfectly nice, but I wouldn't choose her as a friend *unless* I did it for the perks and I couldn't do that."

"I didn't do that either, Buddy. We were put together as roommates at the very beginning and we became friends because we had the same interests, not because of the money. She's bright and funny and you'd like her a lot. It just takes a while to break through her shell."

"Maybe." He looked at me carefully, his eyebrows scrunched. "But I bet you miss the jet-set life you two led. Living with me must be a comedown."

"Living with you is perfect." I hugged him and smoothed out the eyebrows. "It's just perfect."

Eloise would call me at first, ask me out to our old haunts, but I didn't want to go without Buddy, and I didn't want to go with Buddy and Eloise. I was too anxious when they were together, tried too hard to make them like each other, and both sensed that, especially Eloise. I knew that she knew I'd be feeling sorry for her, wishing she could find a man of her own, and I knew how she hated being felt sorry for. It was as if we'd been having a wonderful tennis rally those first three years, hitting the ball back and forth smoothly. Then I'd taken my racket and disappeared. I was playing a different game altogether.

She stopped calling after a few awkward refusals on my part, and we saw each other only during the day, for coffee breaks. Even those began to wind down as I finally became self-conscious talking about Buddy, but couldn't summon up much enthusiasm for any other subject.

"You *can* discuss Buddy, you know," she said once as I was talking lamely about my course on twentieth-century American literature. "I don't mind, really. I know you think I feel out of it, but I don't. Don't think you can't mention him to me. That makes me feel really pathetic."

"I don't think that," I said. But I did. I *knew* she felt out of it. She knew I knew. It was a mess, and our friendship became forced, strained. Polite. And intermittent.

Graduation day, when it came, seemed anticlimactic. I'd persuaded my parents that it wasn't worth their while attending the ceremony, hinting to my mother that she might just get mugged while she was in town as the crime rate had accelerated rapidly in the last couple of months. I didn't want them coming to New York, couldn't face the prospect of moving my clothes back to the dorm room and carrying on a sham in which, of course, Eloise would have had to participate. Nor could I face, quite yet, telling them about my living arrangements. I knew I'd have to break the news soon, but I thought I'd do it gently—go home in June, get Buddy to come out for a weekend, tell them I was planning to move in with him and start my job selling books at Doubleday on 53rd and Fifth. It wouldn't be a pretty scene, so I was happy enough to put it off.

At the last minute I decided not to go to the graduation ceremony myself, to have my diploma sent home. That day I wandered around a crowded campus aimlessly. Buddy was busy and I didn't feel like going back to the apartment on my own. On the chance she might be in, I went over to the dorm and knocked on Eloise's door.

"How's it going? Do you feel like a real person now? We're going to be off into the cruel, cruel world."

The air conditioner was humming, the lilies were in their vases. Eloise was in silk pajamas.

"I couldn't be bothered to go to the ceremony," she said. "They can mail me the piece of paper."

"Same here. But unlike me, you'll be getting lots more of them. Are you looking forward to graduate school?" She had been accepted by Columbia Graduate School in physics.

"I don't think I'll go, actually."

"Why not?" I was startled. "You want to be a physics teacher, don't you? What's going on?"

Eloise sipped her coffee, stared out the window, scratched her elbow, bit her lip, then twisted her hair around in knots. Her round little face looked forlorn, then vacant.

"Eloise?" I snapped my finger. "The physics?"

"I don't see myself as a teacher, Stace."

"What *do* you see yourself as?"

"I don't know."

"Well, that's a great start. We've just graduated, you know. What are your plans?"

"I don't have any."

"I suppose you can afford not to."

"That's a cheap shot, Stacy."

"I didn't mean it that way. Really. I just don't understand what's happened, what's changed."

"Do you care?"

"Of course I do."

"Really? You could have fooled me."

"*That's* the cheap shot."

We sat, avoiding each other's eyes. Until she stood up and went over to the phone. As she dialed a number, she turned to me.

"What do you say we take a ride in the limo? We've never done that before. And the hippie days are ending. I don't think any campus radicals would beat us up if they saw us now. What the heck?"

"What the heck," I echoed, strangely excited by the prospect of a ride in a limousine. As we awaited its arrival, I went on the offensive. Her remark about my not caring had affected me. It made me feel guilty and the guilt made me feel angry. Was I supposed to have been her wet nurse, the mother she never had, the father she only briefly had, the boyfriend she may never have all rolled into one? It wasn't a reasonable request, it was an unfair expectation.

"What is this about me not caring, Eloise? If you're pissed off at me, you'd better come out and say it now." I demanded in a very calm, controlled voice, the way Buddy talked when he practiced legal arguments.

"I don't know." She was getting dressed, pulling on an Indian print skirt and a striped short-sleeve shirt. She had her back to me. "Let's not talk about it, okay? If you want to know, it's probably a mood. My blood sugar's out of kilter this morning. I haven't eaten properly. I forgot my snack last night. So I'm feeling depressed. You know I get that way sometimes. I'll eat something quickly and then let's take the limo to Daddy's house. He's not there. He's in Europe somewhere, or so I'm told. And you've never seen it. There'll be some champagne there, of course. We can celebrate in style."

I'd never been in a limo before, had no idea how omnipotent you can feel sitting in plush seats listening to music, watching the crazed street life of New York through tinted windows. It was no accident, I thought, that the new drug of choice was cocaine. Pot and mind-expanding drugs were on the way out. Eloise had been right: students were beginning to get jobs on Wall Street, selling out to the system *en masse*. They were now buying the drug that went with that lifestyle. As it had been described to me by my more adventurous friends, it gave them a rush of power, the sense that they could cope with anything.

It was the same feeling, I decided, you get in a limo —the short, sharp exhilaration. I was ashamed by how easily thrilled I could be.

We got out in front of a huge brick house on East 74th Street, just off Fifth. Eloise started to tip the chauffeur, then stopped.

"You're new, aren't you?" she asked him. "What's your name?"

"John."

He had a pleasant face to go with the neat little cap and the pearl-gray uniform. Aged, I figured, around thirty-five. I watched, bemused.

"Do you want to come in and celebrate with us, John? We've just graduated. Both of us. Come in and have some champagne."

Eloise's invitation to John floored me. I had seen her dealings with waiters, taxi drivers, the Cape Cod housekeeper. She had always been distant. Polite, but never exactly friendly. Why should she want this stranger to join us now?

"I'd love to, madam. Miss, I mean. Thank you very much." He took off his cap, made a little bow, and Eloise laughed. The deed was done and I'd had no say in it. I wondered what she was trying to prove.

Eloise opened the front door, turned off the alarm system with a special key, ushered John and me into the living room, a visual echo of the Cape Cod house —stultifyingly grand, crammed with antiques, lifeless.

"Here we are," she announced. "Home on the

range. Where the deer and the antelope die and get stuffed and mounted on the walls.'' There were, I now noticed, three sets of heads and horns hanging like trophies on one wall. "It's Thursday—maid's day off. I'll go get the champagne."

"So, John," I said, watching him settle easily into one of the chairs. "Does this kind of thing happen to you often?"

"Not often enough," he smiled at me. He had an impish Jimmy Cagney smile. "Most of the time, I'm invisible. People don't see much more of me than the back of my head. I wonder sometimes what the back of my head looks like. I'd hate to have a wart there. I don't, do I?" He turned his back to me.

"No," I reassured him. "You don't."

When Eloise came back, John leaped up to take the bottle and three glasses she was carrying.

"Let me do the honors," he said.

"Certainly, sir!" Eloise made a mock curtsy in her Indian skirt. She went to turn on the stereo system, the only twentieth-century object, aside from the lamps, in the room. Accepting a glass of champagne from John, I relaxed back into one of the not-so-easy chairs and listened to Eloise's favorite—*Rigoletto*.

"Ah, this is the one with the hunchback who kills his daughter by mistake and finds her in the bag at the end." John was studying the album cover, sipping his champagne. "I've always liked that story."

"Why do you like that?" I asked. "It seems an odd story to like."

John turned his attention toward me, looking at me thoughtfully.

"I like it because it's so sad," he said. He didn't look silly in his uniform, I decided, he looked quite elegant. Eloise was staring at him. My gaze shifted between the two of them. We made an odd triangle.

"Are you a sad person, John?" Eloise asked.

"Only when I have the time," he answered, smiling. He had a nice smile, nice kind eyes. I wondered why he took the job, whether he felt belittled by it.

"Are you two ladies best friends, then?" he asked.

"Yes," we both said, and I was immediately glad that Eloise had asked him in. It had been a bizarre whim on her part. But it had enabled me to say what I wanted to say: that she was my best friend, that my relationship with Buddy may have interfered with our friendship, but it hadn't destroyed it.

"I bet you got up to no good in your college days."

"Not exactly," Eloise said.

"But we *were* different," I added, defensively. "Not like the others, really. We were different."

Eloise sat down on a sofa, John beside her, and we started to explain what we had done in college. Having John there helped in a funny way, for our stories became more entertaining, and took on an added glow with his evident interest. We told tales of us versus the hippies, managing to make ourselves sound clever and amusing while the rest of our generation wallowed in drugs, self-pity, and humorlessness. We drank the champagne and Eloise became more expansive than I'd ever seen her—she was having fun, unwinding, looking relaxed sitting on the sofa, her legs curled up beneath her. The awkward, shy Eloise evaporated with the alcohol. I'd never seen her drunk before and found myself wishing she'd got drunk more often. It was, I thought, the perfect way to end our four years, and it dulled whatever anger had arisen between us that morning.

"Non morir, non morir!" Rigoletto sang to his daughter, and Eloise began to cry. Then John began to cry too. Normally I'd have been crying along with them, but I'd just looked at my watch and thought of Buddy, waiting at home. When the opera ended, both of them still had tears streaming down their faces.

"Which way to the men's room?" John asked, and Eloise gave him directions, snuffling away.

"Are you okay?" I asked while he was out of the room.

"I'm fine," she said. "Perfectly fine. I've made a great decision, you know. I'm going to lose it." She stumbled over and sat on the arm of my chair.

"Lose what?"

"My virginity. Now. With John."

"Oh my God." I had no idea what to say. I had always assumed she'd been to bed with a man at some point in her life. We had talked about sex enough over the years. But then maybe it had always been me doing the talking. I turned to face her drunken eyes.

"Don't you think it's a great idea, Stace? It's kind of D.H. Lawrence stuff. The Virgin and the Chauffeur. Or Humphrey Bogart and Audrey Hepburn in that movie—the one where she's the chauffeur's daughter —whatsitsname?" She began to giggle.

"Sabrina."

"Right. *Sabrina.* What a great name. Sabrina. I wish

that was my name. I wish I could be Audrey Hepburn. Or Katharine Hepburn.''

John walked back in the room.

"John—I've got a great idea,'' Eloise announced.

What could I do? I started to put my hand over her mouth, but she pushed it away roughly.

He stopped in the middle of the room, looking quizzically at us.

"John, your employer has had a few cocktails and I think you should—''

"I think you should sleep with her.'' As Eloise said it, it sounded close to a command. John's expression hadn't wavered. He was looking at Eloise.

"Would you like to? Now?'' John had evidently taken this proposal in his stride.

"Now, by all means. Stace, you can stay here while we go upstairs if you'd like. I'll get you some more champagne.'' We had managed to consume two bottles already.

"I think I'll pass on that, Eloise.''

They were staring at each other, John in his uniform, standing perfectly straight, Eloise slumped over the back of my chair. For once I was the odd man out. The protective feeling I had for Eloise was bothering me. I didn't think this was how she should lose her virginity—on a drunken afternoon in her father's house with a chauffeur she didn't know. She had always talked about falling totally, completely in love when she had been so dismissive about her few dates at Barnard. But what could I say to stop her, and should I stop her anyway? She was enjoying herself, she was twenty-two years old, she wasn't my daughter or my younger sister, and I wasn't a Moral Majority matron. Why shouldn't she go to bed with John? And why should I feel so uneasy about it?

"I think I'll leave you guys to it, so to speak." I got up and started heading for the door. "I guess I should say 'Don't do anything I wouldn't do,' or something really stupid like that."

Eloise went up to John, put her arm around him, started waving to me.

"Bye, Stace. Have fun."

"You too, you two. Good-bye, John." I'd never felt so awkward in my life. When I emerged onto 74th Street, back out into the spring light, I walked slowly down Fifth, past the Knickerbocker Club, past the Pierre, past F.A.O. Schwartz, past my future employer, Doubleday, until I got to St. Patrick's Cathedral. I sat down on the steps, remembering all the times I'd sat on the steps at Columbia with Eloise, remembering all the time we'd spent together. I knew I would always associate Barnard with Eloise. Eloise and Buddy. At which point I ran over to Madison to catch the Number 4 bus back home, back to Buddy.

"Sweetheart, that sounds great. What's wrong with Eloise having some fun, for God's sake. She's old enough. It's about time. Maybe it'll relax her."

"But what if he beats her up or something? I mean he looked nice enough, but what if he's a mass murderer masquerading as a chauffeur? You know, there are so many crazies in this city."

On the trip home I'd been besieged by worries, felt

guilt-racked for leaving her like that. As soon as I arrived back I tried to find her father's number, but it was unlisted.

"Come on, Stacy, be sensible. A chauffeur is a lot less likely to beat her up than some depraved Italian count out for her money. The chauffeur's got a job. Presumably he wants to keep it. What's wrong with you? You must be drunk too. Did you get tipsy and try to seduce the butler?"

I laughed. I *had* been drunk, been silly, overprotective of Eloise. I'd reacted as if I were my mother.

Buddy was feeling amorous and his bedroom looked over the Hudson River and it was a warm May evening. Perfect for lovers, perfect for us. An evening to stay in bed and make love and drink wine and talk about the future and declare undying love. An evening to call Eloise's number in the dorm once, get no answer, and give up trying altogether. An evening to throw off guilt and decide that tomorrow would be just as good as today to quell my nagging fear that Eloise might have been hurt or upset. Eloise was okay. I could spend the entire day with Eloise tomorrow, I decided, as Buddy kissed me again. No problem.

The phone woke me at ten the following morning.

"I'm just calling to say good-bye, Stace."

"Good-bye? Where are you going, the Cape?"

"Oh no. Somewhere much more exotic. Paris. I just made my reservation and I'm off tonight."

"Eloise, hold on. Let me make myself a cup of coffee quickly. I'll be right back. Or wait, even better, I'll throw on some clothes and be over there in a second if you get the coffee ready. Are you back at the dorm yet?''

She was in the midst of packing when I arrived, haphazardly tossing all her dowdy clothes into one big suitcase. I sat down on the bed that was technically mine.

''Before we tackle Paris, what happened with John?''

''We made love. I am no longer a virgin.'' I thought I saw a slight grimace. All my worries resurfaced.

''Oh God, Eloise, was it horrible? I shouldn't have let you go through with it. You were drunk. Shit. I shouldn't have walked out like that.''

She stopped tossing her clothes into the case and put her hands on her hips.

''What *are* you talking about, Stace? John was sweet —and very proficient, if I can judge these things, being as inexperienced as I am. I liked it. He liked it. That's all there is to it. I didn't want some young jerk groping me. I wanted John and I got him. What's it got to do with you—even if I was drunk? Can't I have my own sex life?''

''Of course you can. I just thought I saw you were upset. I mean, I thought that maybe you should be in love, or at least know the guy the first time.''

''And what guy am I supposed to know? The jerks around here? Big men on campus who might condescend to ask me out if they knew how much money I have? They would probably start on a pitch to get me to invest in some rinky-dink company before the first course was even over. John's got more class than that, thank God. Of course he's not Buddy, the miraculous Buddy, but then nobody is Buddy except Buddy, right? And you wouldn't have wanted me to go after *him* now, would you? Who knows, even he might be seduced with enough money."

I could have killed her.

"Cut it out, Eloise."

"I'll cut it out when you stop treating me like a tragic little three-year-old."

"Well, get it straight, will you? Yesterday you say I don't care about you, today you say I care about you too much. Why don't you just say it? Admit that you're pissed off at me because of all the time I spend with Buddy. You're jealous."

"Oh, Stacy!" Eloise crumpled, sagged down onto the floor. "I can't stand arguments. Don't make me argue with you." She put her head in her hands. "I am jealous. You're right. You just left me after you met Buddy, disappeared. I know I can't count on anybody. I mean, nobody can count on anybody. We all have our separate lives to lead. It's just that I was so used to leading my life with you. And you disappeared.

"There was this gap in my life. I felt deprived, the way you might feel if someone took away your cigarettes. I was going cold turkey without you, Stace. I couldn't call you up because I didn't want to interfere. I couldn't come around to your apartment. I'd feel like an intruder. I *knew* Buddy was more important than I was, but it hurt. Do you understand?"

I nodded.

"You'd drop by sometimes like a visiting dignitary and sometimes you'd let slip about people you'd had

71

over, Buddy's friends, people Buddy liked, approved of. I didn't seem to be on that list. It was like my father, Stace. All over again. Like my father."

"I'm sorry," I said quietly.

"I had to learn to be by myself again. It wasn't easy. Then I finally do something with somebody else—I mean go off with John, and you give me a hard time about that. I didn't think you had a right to waltz in and suddenly act concerned. I'm sorry. It's my fault. People have their own lives to lead and you're not responsible for mine. Nobody is. I just don't know what I'm going to do with it, that's all."

I sat down beside her on the floor and put my arm around her shoulder.

"Except be rich."

"Except be rich." She smiled.

"And wear socks."

"And wear socks." She hugged me. "I really have missed you, Stace. You're the only friend I have. I know that's a burden on you, but it's the truth."

"It's not a burden. I missed you too. But I fell in love. I couldn't help it. I got swept away into another world and I felt guilty about not being here, and then I felt angry about feeling guilty. I guess you and I have a complicated friendship. We've never really talked about it before. If it had happened the other way around—if *you* had gone off with a guy, moved in, I'd have felt miserable and left out.

"And I *was* worried about you and John. But I'd never seen you drunk before. You were on a real trip. How are you feeling now?"

"In desperate need of a candy bar." She stood up,

picked a Milky Way off her bureau and devoured it in two bites. "I'm really sorry for saying that about Buddy. That he could be bought. I know it's not true. I was trying to hurt you."

"You succeeded. But I know it's not true too, so that's okay."

"It was a terrible thing to say. I hate arguing. I hate it when I get angry. I feel so out of control. I can't stand it. It makes me feel violent, sick."

"Well, we've stopped arguing now. And one big fight in four years is a pretty good track record," I said. "But you haven't told me why you're going to Paris. Are you going to elope with John?"

"Look there." She got a newspaper off the floor and handed it to me. "Daddy's had a heart attack. He's in a hospital in Paris. The lawyers called me a few minutes after I'd read it."

"God, I'm sorry. You should have told me right away. I don't know what to say."

"Don't worry about it. Daddy's indestructible. He won't die. And this may give us a good chance to be together again. Like the old days, you know. I'm looking forward to it. Really. It could be a new start."

"Maybe you'll find some devastating Frenchman when you're over there. You know, I have to say, John was cute-looking." I mentally slapped myself for saying that then. Her father had just had a heart attack and I was talking like a teen magazine. But I had never liked the sound of her father, blamed him, in fact, for most of Eloise's insecurities. If anyone deserved to have a heart attack, I thought, Daddy did. Eloise's loyalty to him irritated me.

But she didn't pick me up on my insensitivity.

"John's a nice man. He's someone I could really care about. But he's also married with two children, so it's just as well I'm going to Paris. Listen, he's taking me to the airport in the limo tonight. Do you want to come see me off?"

"I'm supposed to—"

"Please?"

"Sure. Great." I suddenly realized how much I would miss Eloise. "I wish you weren't going."

"Thanks." She tore off a piece of skin from her lower lip and I winced.

John and I waved good-bye to a nervous Eloise at JFK that night.

"She's a nice girl, you know," John said as we headed back to the limousine. "A little mixed up, but nice. Most of these rich women, well, I have to be paid to be civil to them. Money talks and I listen, but sometimes I could use ear plugs."

"She liked you too, John," I said.

"Did she now?" He looked wistful for a moment, then put his cap on his head and opened the door for me. We cruised along in silence for the next hour until he stopped in front of Buddy's building. Leaping out, he opened the door again, then stopped me, his hand on my arm. "She'd better be careful, you know. She needs love so bad you can taste it. She needs love the way most people need money. You can feel it in her skin. That girl's gonna get in a shitload of trouble, what with the money and all. Watch out for her, will you?"

"I'll try," I said.

Fifteen years later I found the invitation to Eloise's wedding in my mailbox.

7

DECEMBER 7, 1989

Eloise woke me at eleven the next morning, bringing me a breakfast tray complete with Alka-Seltzer, for which I was very grateful. I dimly remembered being deposited on my bed in the early hours. Whose arms had carried me, I wondered, the groom's or the best man's?

"Robert and Bobby are out playing tennis. Can you believe it?" Eloise looked awful, with bags under her eyes. "Thank God I've got a woman coming to do my hair and makeup. I think Robert wouldn't go through with it if I looked like this." She sat down on the end of my bed, and I struggled to sit up straight. "He's got so much stamina, Stace. I've never met a man so physically impressive. He can drink all day and all night and keep going without any ill effects. He's amazing."

"Mmm hmm." I nodded. Lucky Eloise. I took the Alka-Seltzer and looked at the scrambled eggs and bacon with loathing. "Did we eat last night?"

"No. I don't think so. I forget. I wasn't even sure whether I'd taken my insulin until I saw the needle on my bedside table this morning. Force of habit, even when I'm dead drunk."

"Well, last night was a good send-off for married life, anyway." I managed a weak smile.

"Stace, I'm sorry that you and Buddy split up. I found out when I had you tracked down. That must have been awful."

"It was."

She pulled her dressing-gown tight around her.

"I couldn't imagine divorce. I mean I couldn't imagine divorcing Robert. I'd rather die."

"Well, I should hope so. That's the right attitude to have going into it. Things happen sometimes, that's all." I looked at her. "But I'm sure it won't happen to you." I lit a cigarette, drank another glass of water, and began to feel a little better.

"I haven't shown you my ring yet. Look . . ." She held out the fourth finger of her left hand and I saw a heart-shaped sapphire ring, encircled with tiny diamonds.

"Nice," I commented. "Very pretty." What else can you say about an engagement ring?

"You won't believe how he gave it to me."

"Then tell me. I'll try to believe."

"I was taking a bath. This was three months ago, three months after I had first met Robert. He came upstairs with a glass of champagne. Handed it to me in the bathtub. And this—this ring was at the bottom of the glass. Isn't that the most romantic thing you've ever heard?"

"Yes. To tell you the truth, it is. I could kill you."

Eloise's laugh rang out. It was a lovely sound to hear.

"I knew you'd appreciate it. You're the only other

person I know who appreciates romance. Anybody else would make a comment like 'Lucky you didn't swallow it.'"

The thought had crossed my mind, but it was my jaded side thinking. I kept my mouth shut.

"Listen—back to the old days—I wanted to ask you: what happened to John? Did you ever see him again?"

"John?"

"Come on, Eloise. John. You know. The chauffeur you lost your virginity to."

"John!" Eloise brightened. "Gosh, I'd forgotten about John. He was nice, wasn't he? John. No, I never saw him again. I stayed in Europe, you know. I lived in Paris for a couple of years, then London, then the South of France. Like I said yesterday, I loafed around, not doing much of anything. Except I learned how to play tennis. I had a boyfriend for a while who was a tennis coach, and he taught me. He was useless otherwise, having affairs on the side the whole time, but I didn't really care because I didn't love him. He was using me for my money and I was using him for someone to have around. It was a waste of time, but I was wasting my time generally. My whole life seems a waste of time until I came back to New York and met Robert. Can you believe how lucky I am that he bumped into me?"

"Chance is the fool's name for fate, Eloise." I remembered that line from a Fred Astaire movie. *The Gay Divorcee.*

"Tell me one more thing, though, while we have the time to talk alone. I'm not sure I know how to put this. But did you get your act together—I mean with the clothes and the hair and stuff—before or after you met Robert?"

"Does it matter?"

"Probably not."

"After. Why, do I look like a rich bitch? The kind we used to see in restaurants, the kind you never wanted me to turn into?"

"No. Obviously you look rich, but you don't look like a bitch. You look great, really. I'm jealous. When you get sick of the clothes, pass them my way, will you?" I leaned across the tray and grabbed her hands. "Seriously, I'm really happy for you. And last night was fun. Robert's incredible. He's a dynamo. And he's in love with you. It's terrific. You deserve it all. And I think the children's books are a fantastic idea."

"Did he tell you about that?" She looked surprised. "I know it's good. He just has to start to write, which shouldn't be too difficult, but he hasn't had the time. He's been spending too much time on me, really. You know, Robert is like a Renaissance man. You wouldn't believe everything he knows—all sorts of subjects. And he has amazing talent."

I realized how Eloise must have felt when I spouted off about Buddy nonstop. Were women doomed to talk about men whenever they were alone together?

"So when's the big event? When is the ceremony?"

"Oh my gosh. I've got to start getting ready. It's at one o'clock. In the living room. Wear what you had on last night—that looked terrific and it will go with my dress. All you have to do is stand beside me and hold some flowers."

"And find another pair of shoes."

Eloise rushed off, and I decided to take a quick walk before getting ready. I pulled on some jeans and a shirt and went down to the beach. The weather was cloudy and cold enough to be bracing and helpful for a hangover. As I pondered Eloise's happiness and debated whether it would be possible for me, at least the kind of happiness that included a man, I looked up and saw Bobby coming toward me.

"Oh, good," I said as he reached me. "I've run out of matches again. Can I have a light?" He stood close to me, so as to block off the little wind there was, and lit my cigarette. His hands were large, he was much taller than his father. The pupils of his eyes were faultlessly round. But there was a definite resemblance in one feature—the nose. Both had wide-nostriled, broad noses, not the classic Roman nose, but handsome nonetheless.

"How old are you, Bobby?"

"Twenty."

"God, you're tall."

"I know."

"And you're a good dancer."

"Thank you." He proceeded to do a quick Michael Jackson moonwalk on the sand. Then he stood, hands in the pockets of his corduroys, looking out to sea. I wasn't sure what to say to a twenty-year-old on the morning of his father's wedding.

"Do you like Eloise?" I asked after a long silence.

"Yes, I do like Eloise. This is only the first time I've met her, though. I mean I got here last weekend. So I've only known her for a week. She's nice." He didn't

80

move, still stared at the water. I put out my cigarette, buried it in the sand with my foot.

"You must have had a perfect childhood with a father like Robert."

"Must I? Why do you say that?" The tide was coming in, so was the anger in his voice.

"Well, I meant that he seems to have a natural feeling for children."

I thought I heard him mumble, "Tell that to my shrink." But I wasn't sure I'd heard right, as he was in the act of pulling his sweater over his head.

"What did you say?"

"I said, 'Take this, you're shivering.' " He handed me his sweater. There was something impenetrable about Bobby Chappell. He looked like a well-plastered wall, a smooth surface with no chinks, no place to get a grip on. I felt that if I'd thrown tennis balls at him, they would have bounced back the way they do when propelled from machines, each one landing on the same spot as the one before. Even his anger had sounded controlled.

"Thanks, I was a little chilly. This thing swamps me, though." His sweater hung down like a dress on me. Our conversation about Robert's merits as a father had not pleased him, I could tell, but what was I supposed to ask? Which courses he was taking at college? He may have been seventeen years younger but I was the one who felt silly. "I'm going to take a quick walk, Bobby. Try to shake this hangover. Do you want to join me?"

"No thank you, Stacy. I better have a shower and get changed. It was nice to talk to you."

Robert had taught his son manners. Or someone had.

The wedding itself was uneventful. Eloise eschewed the traditional wedding white, wearing instead a pale yellow silk dress. Robert looked more formal in a gray flannel suit and conservative tie. Bobby and I wore what we had the night before. Whoever had come to do Eloise's makeup and hair had done the trick, and she looked as lovely as every bride is supposed to. The vows were simple, the minister perfectly nice and pleasant. I was holding a bouquet of yellow and white tulips. I was glad for some reason that they weren't lilies.

After they'd been pronounced man and wife, and the kiss was over, Robert ushered the minister out and the four of us sat down to a lunch of lobster salad and smoked salmon sandwiches in the dining room. We were on our own—no Deborah, maid, or butler hovering—a nice touch, and a touch I assumed belonging to Eloise.

Two years previously I had been in a short-term lover's apartment, browsing through his magazines as he was changing for dinner and I found a copy of *Forbes*, the issue that lists the richest people in the United States. Eloise's name was halfway down that list and I found myself calling the man over to my side, pointing and saying, "I know that woman. We were college roommates." He was fascinated and asked me all about her as we ate, but while I told my stories his face took on the look of a disappointed voyeur.

"A summer in Cape Cod, an air conditioner, opera tickets, and one limo ride? That's all you got out of one of the richest women in America? She sounds like a cheapskate to me."

"What are you talking about? We went to expensive restaurants all the time, she paid for all that. She paid for everything. Eloise wasn't a cheapskate by any means—she was unbelievably generous."

"Well, your standards and mine are different, then. If I were best friends with someone that loaded I would have thought we'd be cruising around the Mediterranean every spring break, skiing in Gstaad over the winter—shit, we're talking about serious money here. Air conditioner—Christ. Why didn't you move out of the dorm sophomore year and into an air-conditioned penthouse suite on Fifth Avenue? Come to think of it, why was she living in a dorm to begin with? I thought you said her father had a huge house."

"He did. I went there for champagne on graduation day."

"Wow. Generous to a fault. Champagne on your graduation day. Move over, big spenders; Stacy's roommate is something else."

Eloise *was* something else, I decided when I went to sleep on my own that night. She wasn't tacky. She used her money without flaunting it. It had never occurred to me before that she could have avoided dorm life. Of course she could have lived in Daddy's house. But she didn't want to, she wanted to be as anonymous as possible. The paintings in the Cape house weren't Warhol or Lichtenstein, they weren't the obvious choices of a wealthy New York lady. They were what Eloise actually liked. The fact that she hadn't sold the Cape house and bought something in Vail or some other hotshot hideaway for the rich and famous said a lot about her. She had never been the type to go on luxurious cruises with other billionaires —what would she have worn for a start? I laughed to myself, imagining Eloise on board the Onassis yacht in her Argyle socks.

Perhaps she had lived the jet-set life in Europe during the years we hadn't seen each other, but it didn't seem to have left any traces. Eloise looked different now, but she wasn't behaving differently. Our wedding lunch was proof of that.

"You know, Stacy . . ." Robert's voice interrupted my thoughts. He was pouring me a glass of champagne. "We have an interesting group at this table. All of us are only children, am I right? Not a sibling to be found.

"I think that's unusual. But then I think only children are unusual. We have to spend our childhoods entertaining ourselves, so we end up being more creative, more imaginative. I'd like to do a study of famous people sometime, see how many were only children."

"I wonder," I mused. "Was Shakespeare an only child?"

"Well, that's exactly what I need to find out. Did George Washington have a brother who egged him on to cut down the cherry tree? This could be an historic work. And, of course, I can start with the most famous only child of all."

"Who is that?" Eloise asked.

"Sit up straight, Cat." He put his hand on her head and she bolted upright, threw her shoulders back.

"Jesus Christ." Robert finished pouring the champagne and sat down. Bobby was staring at a painting over the dining-room fireplace. He didn't seem very keen on entering into the conversation.

"I suppose Mary couldn't have *two* Immaculate Conceptions," I said. "That would be stretching credibility."

"The Immaculate Conception refers to the birth of Mary, not Jesus, Stacy." Robert smiled.

"Robert? What are you talking about? The Immaculate Conception means that Jesus was born without Mary and Joseph having sex."

What a strange topic, I reflected, to be discussing at a wedding lunch.

"Do you want a bet on that?" Robert asked, with his triumphant look. "That's what most people think. But it's not the case."

"Come on, Robert. That's what we were brought up on. Not that I'm a Roman Catholic, I'm Episcopalian, if I'm anything, but there can't be something *that* basic that's different."

"It's not different, Stacy. In both cases, Roman Catholic and Episcopalian, in any Christian religion, the Immaculate Conception refers to Mary's birth."

"I don't believe you."

"Well, good for you. Stacy and I are going to argue. I'm really enjoying this." Robert reached over and refilled my glass. "Do you believe me, Eloise?" Eloise nodded. "Bobby?"

"Yes, Dad, I believe you." Bobby's gaze stayed fixed on the painting.

"So that leaves Stacy. Well, Stacy, why don't we settle this? Eloise, where have you hidden the telephone book?"

"I'll get it, darling. And the mobile phone."

"Thanks, Cat."

"Who are you going to call?" I asked. "God?"

Robert laughed.

"God and I aren't on speaking terms. But I'll do the next best thing." Eloise returned with the phone and the directory. Robert quickly leafed through it. "Here we go, Stacy. The Carmelite Discalced Monastery. Right up our street, monks without shoes. Here's the number. You call, ask any monk who answers the phone. He'll tell you."

I sensed he had already won. Of course he had, or he wouldn't have made me make this call. But I dialled the number anyway. The kindly voice of the monk informed me that Robert was right.

"Well, Robert," I said, hanging up. "I guess I'd believe you now if you said Santa Claus is a transvestite."

"Now, where's the number for the North Pole?" Robert began leafing through the book again. We all laughed. Eloise beamed at me.

"Robert knows everything, Stace. I've been finding that out these last six months."

"But I don't know if I can beat you at tennis. What do you say, Stacy. A little game? The fresh air would be good for us."

"Now?"

"Why not?"

"Because I don't feel like changing."

"Then don't," Robert boomed. "That's not a tight dress. I'll play in my suit. Come on, it will be fun. We'll just put some sneakers on."

"Okay." I didn't feel like playing, but I found it hard to say no.

"You can borrow my sweater again," said Bobby. "It's cold out there."

"Again?" Robert arched his eyebrows. "What have you two been up to?"

I felt like a teenager who has been caught smoking —a strange sensation, as I hadn't done anything.

"Bobby and I were on the beach for a few minutes this morning and he lent me his sweater."

"And what were you discussing down on the beach?"

"Dancing," Bobby answered quickly. "Stacy said I was a good dancer."

"But not as good as I am, I hope. It's very unnerving when your son becomes a man, you know. I doubt that I'll ever get used to it. Come on then, Stacy. Finish eating and then let's hit the court."

We must have made an unusual sight, bashing the ball back and forth in our wedding gear. Robert was a decent player, but his energy worked against him when it came to tennis. He'd take a swing and hit the ball way out, yards over the base line; or, on an overhead smash, he'd get so excited that he'd bash it with all his force into the net. He had taken his jacket off and looked old-fashioned in his long gray trousers, but he charged with childlike energy all over the court, yelling various epithets at the ball, obviously enjoying himself. The spirit was infectious, and I began to have fun as well; serving underhand occasionally to send him off balance, hitting the ball as hard as I could, straight at him whenever possible, and laughing when he ducked. Eloise, standing on the side of the court, enveloped in a fur coat, cheered for both of us. Bobby watched silently.

When I finally won, 6-4, Robert took a running leap over the net and gave me one of his bear hugs. I could feel his heart racing with the exercise as he crushed me against his chest.

"Well done, Stacy. Next time I'll get you, though." He released me, bowed. I almost copied Eloise; I almost ran my hands through that hair. Instead I bowed back and saw my breath form a tiny cloud as I exhaled hard into the December air. Then he ran over to Eloise and kissed her.

"I hope you're not disappointed in me, Cat."

"I couldn't be," she said, pulling him to her. "And I'm glad you two get along."

"We couldn't not get along, now, could we? Could we, Stacy?"

"Not a chance, Robert." We were facing each other as I walked toward them. The brown wavy hair was disheveled; he was panting slightly; his eyes looked mischievous as he smiled.

"I need a cigarette after all that exertion," I said, changing course and walking over to Bobby on the other side of the net. "Why don't we take a walk and leave the newlyweds on their own for a while?"

"We wouldn't hear of it, would we, Cat? Come back

inside and let's relax and have some more champagne. We haven't celebrated enough.'' Robert threw his racket up in the air, caught it, twirled it as if it were a dancing partner.

Eloise came over to me, grabbed my arm, and started walking me back toward the house, Bobby and his father trailing behind us.

"Thanks for playing, Stace."

"My pleasure. Besides, it's not easy to say no to Robert. He's a truly forceful character. I can see how you were swept away by him."

"I just hope he was swept away by me."

"Of course he was—I didn't mean that. You look stunning today, and you're an original too. And, though I've said it before, he obviously loves you."

"Do you really think so?"

"Eloise! For Christ's sake, his face lights up whenever he looks at you. He's incredibly attentive. He said his vows with a straight face. You've hit the emotional jackpot—and, believe me, I'm usually cynical about these things. I'll even admit that I've been looking for faults, and the only one I can come up with is his telling you to sit up straight."

"That's for my own good." I could feel Eloise's arm stiffen under the fur.

"Whatever. Anyway, how do you like your new stepson?"

Before she could answer, Robert had run up behind us and thrown his arms around our shoulders.

"Come on, girls, let's get changed into some relaxed clothes and sit around that beautiful fireplace and listen to some beautiful music and sip some beautiful wine and end a beautiful day with a beautiful evening.''

We separated, went to our rooms for what Eloise referred to as an ''afternoon siesta,'' before we reconvened in the living room at six. The beautiful music was *La Traviata*. We listened to it right through without speaking, all four of us in various poses of relaxation. Bobby stretched his long legs out on the floor, his back against a radiator for support. I was surprised that he didn't seem bored, but sat seemingly happily, surrounded by Placido Domingo's voice. I was also surprised that Robert could remain calm for that period of time, that he could be as placid as he was energetic, a complete switch from the evening before.

Deborah and an anonymous butler then served us dinner, with three different wines, while I talked about what it was like to live in California. Eloise and I reminisced about Barnard in much the same way as we had that afternoon with John—managing not to mention either his name or, for that matter, Buddy's.

''I miss the spirit of the sixties and seventies sometimes,'' Robert interjected. ''I'm glad all those boring little yuppies scrounging around Wall Street in their suits and BMWs are finally getting their come-uppance. I'm convinced that Monopoly was at the root of all that greed.''

Would Robert have thought Eloise and I little yuppies in our college years? Probably.

''Monopoly? Whose monopoly of what?'' I asked him.

''Monopoly the game. From an early age, children

were being turned into venture capitalists. Buying, selling, making fortunes, going bankrupt. The yuppie invasion was all Parker Brothers' fault.''

"Did you play Monopoly, Bobby?'' Eloise asked.

Bobby glanced at his father as if seeking permission to reply. Robert tilted his head slightly.

"I wasn't any good at it,'' Bobby answered flatly. "Could I have a cigarette please, Stacy?''

"Of course.'' I stole a quick glance at Robert, but didn't see any disapproval on his face. He motioned for the butler to fill Eloise's wineglass.

"The game I like is Clue,'' I said. "You know, Miss White in the study with a wrench. Does that make me a frustrated detective?''

"You like to ask questions, don't you, Stacy? I'd say you're a detective.'' Robert smiled. I wondered whether he'd told Eloise about our conversation the night before, all the questions I had asked him.

"So where are you two going to live?''

"In New York. The same house. It's been redecorated too. Do you know, Stace, the roof was in an awful state, and the wiring was antediluvian. You wouldn't believe the amount of work that's had to be done. The plumbers alone——'' She stopped abruptly, took a sip of wine and turned to her husband.

"Why don't we play that game you like, Robert? The one where you pick a character in fiction you would like to be and everyone has to guess each other's choices.''

"That's a great idea. Well chosen, Cat. Let's play that one.'' He leaned over and kissed her on the back of the neck.

91

The game was on and ended up being very entertaining. Bobby chose Huck Finn, I chose Jane Eyre, Eloise chose Cathy in *Wuthering Heights*, and Robert chose Lolita, which led to a lot of laughs.

"I'm sorry, but I think the bride had better retire," Eloise said as the game finished. "I hate to spoil the party."

Robert stood up immediately and put his arm around her.

"I have two words to say to you, Mrs. Chappell."

Eloise looked at him quizzically.

"Conjugal rights."

The newlyweds giggled together.

"Eloise and I are going to put this night to bed. How about you, Bobby, are you tired?" Robert sounded solicitous.

Bobby put out another of my cigarettes and stood up.

"I'm going for a walk. Then I'll go straight to bed."

"I'll go straight to bed now," I said, standing up as well.

Robert came over and shook my hand formally.

"Good night, Stacy."

"Good night, Robert. It was nice to—"

Before I had finished, he tightened his grip on my right hand, forced me into a twirl, yanked me back, and planted a hard, closed-lip, explosive kiss on my mouth.

"Of course it was nice to meet me," he laughed, releasing me and throwing his hands up in the air. "Everyone should love me. I'm Lolita, remember?"

Robert left me standing, winded, and charged over to Eloise, swooping her into his arms.

"Come on, Scarlett, honey. Time for me to carry you up the stairs of Tara. Good night, everybody." I could hear Eloise's muffled laugh against his shoulder as he bounded from the dining room.

Bobby and I stood like two extras on a movie set, unsure whether the director had truly finished for the day.

"Jesus, Bobby—your father . . ." I began, but couldn't end. I ran my tongue over my lips, then reached for a cigarette.

"Yeah." Bobby struck a match for me.

"Do you want one?" I offered.

"No thank you, Stacy. I think I'll take that walk."

As I climbed the stairs to my room, I could hear a man's voice singing along to an acoustic guitar. Passing by Eloise and Robert's bedroom door, I stopped guiltily for a moment, listening. It wasn't the radio, as I had thought originally. Robert was singing. He was serenading Eloise. "I'm putting all my eggs in one basket . . ." he sang. "I'm betting everything I have on you." The scene could have been too cute for words—instead, it was too beautiful for words. Robert had an amazing, pure voice, quiet and intimate—not the booming voice he used for making his points. A real singer's voice, sure of itself and almost unbearably tender. I found myself leaning against the wall, knowing I shouldn't be there, but not wanting to leave. He finished the song and I heard the sound of Eloise clapping. I stood still, listening. He was saying something to Eloise I couldn't make out, then strummed a chord and started in with "I've got you under my skin."

I walked away slowly, his voice following me halfway down the hall. He'd been a failure in the music business, that's what he had said. And I hadn't pushed him for fear of sounding too inquisitive. Robert was a singer, no doubt of that, but what kind of singer? And why wasn't he famous? With a voice like that, he should have been. Robert Chappell was as much of a mystery as Eloise used to be. And there they were in their bedroom together, sharing their love and their secrets, united against the world. Under each other's skin. Until death did them part. Or, I corrected myself, divorce.

8

1974–1978

The indestructible daddy did die. A week after Eloise had flown to Paris. I saw it in the papers, read his obituaries, studied his face. The only resemblance to Eloise I could make out was in the low cheekbones. Otherwise he came close to Ernest Hemingway in looks: a mane of white hair, a gruff face, a hint of bullying superiority. His death, however, unlocked one of Eloise's most secret doors—her mother.

Time magazine traced Daddy's life from its humble beginnings. Paul Parker was the son of a gas station manager in New Jersey, worked his way through high school, then college at Haverford. Flirted with Communism briefly before making an about-face and embracing the Republican Party wholeheartedly. He'd amassed his fortune in the commodities market, having what *Time* called "an amazing gift for making the right deal at the right time, an almost supernatural perception of the ups and downs in the markets."

At age thirty, he had married a New England blue blood, Eloise's mother—Frances Spaulding. She had been a debutante and was reported to be a renowned society hostess of her day. She was also fabulously rich.

I wished there had been a picture, but she rated only a few lines.

> Frances Parker's tragic death by drowning in Long Island Sound was attributed to her severe postnatal depression for which she had been briefly hospitalized in 1953. Although Mrs. Parker's death was not officially reported as suicide, friends suspected that she drowned herself during another bout of depression. Mr. Parker himself refused to comment. He never remarried. His daughter and sole heir, Eloise Camille Parker, 22, was at his deathbed in Paris.

I wished that I'd known it all before, that Eloise had trusted me enough to tell me, instead of continually backing off the subject of her mother's death. It didn't take a degree in psychoanalysis to guess that her feeling that she was cursed, her need to "redress the balance," was engendered by her guilt—her belief that her mother's death may have been her fault, that her own birth precipitated a deluge of evil hormones responsible, finally, for her mother's drowning. Poor Eloise. I knew she hated to be pitied, but I found myself in tears thinking about her. A victim of the most tragic of circumstances.

She had told me that her father cut back his relationship with her when she turned thirteen. Was he threatened by her burgeoning teenage hormones, terrified that she'd be at their mercy, like her mother? Did he feel guilty for not looking after his wife better, perhaps letting her out of the hospital too soon? Or did he subconsciously blame Eloise for his wife's suicide? Whatever the answers, Eloise was carrying a burden, that much was certain. All those lilies. I could still smell them, remember their overpowering aroma which swamped our room with every new delivery.

Our letters crossed each other somewhere over the Atlantic. I received one from her two days after sending mine, a day before I was due to fly back to Peoria.

Dear Stace,

Maybe you've read already that my father died. He didn't regain consciousness, didn't know I was there beside him. Or maybe he did, because I talked to him all the time and they say that sometimes people can hear even when you think they can't. All I could think of to talk to him about was physics, so if he did hear me, maybe I bored him to death. Or maybe he'll explain the theory of relativity to God.

They put so much makeup on him before they buried him, he looked like a ventriloquist's dummy. Or a cartoon character. I prefer my childhood memories of him and find myself wishing that I'd let him die alone. Promise me that if I die you won't look at my corpse. It wouldn't help me and it certainly wouldn't help you.

All these French people are flapping around and none of them wear berets. It's very disappointing, though I felt better after seeing *La Bohème* at the Paris Opera.

I have to stay here and sort things out with lawyers flown in from New York. It would appear that I'll be richer than God, as you used to say. Richer than God and the devil put together since I now have my father's money on top of my mother's. I suppose you've read all about my mother's death by now. Nice to have it blazoned across the pages of *Time*. My little secret no more. You understand me, Stace, so you'll understand why I didn't want to talk about it. Now or in the future.

I've just reread this letter. It sounds offhand, doesn't it? Absolutely nothing about my father's death is offhand. But I can't bear to think about it. I always had the hope that we could get back to being as close as we once were and now that hope is gone. I'm an orphan. Being an orphan is worse than being a teenager.

It turns out that he had been having a passionate affair with a married woman in Paris for almost ten years. So you see I was wrong. There *was* another woman. I met her one day at the hospital. She was crying so much it was clear that she'd loved him. I asked her why he'd never told me. She said it was their secret. I would have been more upset, but she looked so tremendously glamorous. Straight out of a thirties movie. She couldn't marry him because she was a Catholic and wouldn't divorce her husband. She told me she had lived for the last ten years in a perpetual state of guilt. And now that he was dead she didn't know whether she was destroyed or relieved.

I just wish he'd trusted me. I might have been

jealous, but even at thirteen, I was a romantic. We could have talked about it. I could have shared it with him. Why didn't he give me more credit? It's such a waste because I really loved him, Stace. I always will.

I hope all is going well with Buddy. Maybe you two could come over here sometime.

Love,
Eloise

My letter to her expressed as much sympathy as I could for a man I considered to be a lousy father. Although tempted, I hadn't mentioned her mother. Eloise had a private cell in her soul; she had locked the key on herself and her mother. I'd be happy to be there if she chose to open it, but I couldn't force her. I believed that I had to respect her instinct not to talk.

My thoughts left Eloise in Paris and concentrated on my upcoming battle with my own father. He couldn't stop me from living with Buddy; I'd be self-supporting in my job at Doubleday, even if pitifully so. But he could make my life miserable with his disapproval. Buddy planned to join me in Peoria the following weekend.

"Don't tell them we're going to live together until after I get there, okay, Stacy?"

"Okay," I answered, relieved to be able to wait a week, to have Buddy at my side when I dropped the bombshell.

I talked Buddy up during that week, told my parents how well he was doing at law school, what a polite man he was, what a nice family he came from. I'd met his parents and sister once, a liberal, laid-back family from Connecticut. They'd had no objections to me, even seemed to prefer me to Buddy's old flames. I hoped my parents would be as pleasant and welcoming to him.

In the event, what I'd been dreading turned out to be a piece of cake. Thanks to Buddy's decision that we should get married. He asked me about five seconds after I'd met him at the airport, and I was in such a state of shock I don't remember much else about the day. Except that I said yes immediately, that Buddy asked my father for my hand and my father said yes after a brief conversation. My mother cried happily. We all drank a lot of champagne. Buddy made a great impression on them and I was euphoric.

I hadn't realized how hidebound by convention I actually was, how much I really wanted to get married and settle into domestic bliss straight out of college. I'd been lucky to get the job at Doubleday, been the recipient of a combination of good timing and old school ties, for the assistant manager at their 53rd Street branch was a friend from my Russian literature course and had recommended me to the personnel department. The prospect of working with books, even at such a low level, delighted me. Meanwhile Buddy would be in his last year at law school. According to my game plan, we'd have an unbelievably wonderful time. We would live out a life of eternal bliss. We'd be a romantic opera without the tragedy. The perfect couple living in the perfect city. That's how I saw it.

We decided to get married in September, in New

York. A small, tasteful ceremony; mostly family, a few friends. I wrote to Eloise in Paris, asking her. She replied:

Dear Stace,

I'd love to come, of course, but I can't, I'm afraid. Would you believe I am still ensconced with lawyers to the point of ultimate tedium? It all has to do with taxes, Daddy's residency, boring things like that, and it seems that they need me here continuously until it gets cleared up. The first time I shot up during a late night meeting, they all practically fainted. Like you that first night, they thought I was a junkie. Honestly, that's the only laugh I've had here.

I'm so happy for you. You know how jealous I was of you before? Well, I'd feel even worse now, except dealing with all these male lawyers makes me worried for you. They are an awful species.

Not Buddy, though, I know. You two deserve the best and you've got it.

Love,
Eloise

I wish I could pinpoint the exact moment when things started to go wrong in my marriage, because then I might be able to understand better how and why a relationship unravels. There wasn't one big, all-out fight, one watershed moment of mutual destruction, just a steady wearing away of love. Like when you find a thread hanging out from the bottom of your dress, and you pull it and gradually the whole hem falls down.

Why do people lie to each other when they're first in love? Not lie maliciously, but treat the truth like Play-Doh, molding it into whatever shape is convenient. Buddy had claimed to be interested in classical music, and yes, I had claimed to be interested in pop. I listened to his Motown while he listened to my Mozart. We were both, so we said, enchanted by each other's different tastes.

Those particular little lies lasted about a year. Then Buddy started to accuse me of being a prematurely old fogie and I started accusing him of being an overgrown teenybopper. It should have been funny, but it wasn't. The stereo system became a battleground. Who got to it first, what was played, at what volume were all little skirmishes we engaged in.

Those were less debilitating, however, than the laundry question. During my college days, I'd gladly done Buddy's laundry for him, lugging it down to the basement with no sense of resentment—with pride, rather. I was taking care of him. But once I was working, fighting my way back on the subway every evening, I was not so thrilled by the prospect of washing his socks at night. And he wasn't thrilled by that prospect either. We let the dirty laundry pile up in the closet until it looked like a health hazard.

At first that *was* funny. We both thought so. But as it accumulated beyond the closet, onto the bedroom floor, we both had a sense of humor failure. I ended up doing it. The rising feminist feeling in me took a backseat to the deeply entrenched instinct that this was my job. But now it was a job I hated. I would do the washing, the cooking and cleaning, but I'd make sure he knew I was doing it under protest. Buddy thought this was unfair because, at the beginning, I'd seemed to enjoy it. And the truth was, I had enjoyed it; what I enjoyed, though, were not the tasks themselves, but the setting up of a domain, the symbolic significance of "looking after" him, of staking out my territory.

And I was afraid that, had I gone on strike, had I refused to do all the household work, he might easily find another woman who would do it eagerly, as his previous girlfriends no doubt had.

When we gave brunch parties on Sunday mornings, I'd look at the female law students who came and be bowled over by them. I'd assume they were fascinating, clever women who could not only wash socks cheerfully but also study hard for the stupendous careers in front of them. Meanwhile I toiled away in the lower echelons of Doubleday, ringing up sales, pointing customers searching for *Jaws* or *Fear of Flying* in the right direction. Sometimes after work I'd go with one of my colleagues to the bar across the street and see a group of French waiters sharing a bottle of wine, the same waiters who used to attend to Eloise and me at the Côte Basque.

I'd come home, tired after being on my feet all day, and resentfully do my chores.

These are the kind of hurdles I suspect most married people clear, if not always easily. But I was running up against one with spikes on the top, and that was Buddy's continual bad mood. He was immersed in his law books, struggling to succeed, to do well at interviews and be hired by a top firm. And the work got to him. The year before our wedding, when we'd been living together, he'd have moody times, but I coped with them in much the same way as I'd coped with Eloise's blips. I'd kid him out of them, make jokes—or do what was far easier, but not an option with Eloise—drag him into bed.

Those remedies began to fail. He'd become immune, or was too tired to want to play. He'd wake up in the morning grouchy, complaining of lack of sleep, complaining of the smell of my stale cigarette smoke, complaining about cockroaches. They were all legitimate complaints, but I couldn't help him sleep more, couldn't stop smoking, couldn't control the invasion of bugs. Then I'd go off to work and come back to more complaints. The jerks who were doing better than he was in his courses, the asshole professors, the sheer weight of work. Even after he'd graduated, when he'd found a decent job with a good firm and started working himself, the pressure continued. Lawyers work fourteen hours a day, sometimes more, and the heat is on to become a partner in your chosen firm within a couple of years. If not, if you're passed by, you're doomed, you've been branded an also-ran.

I couldn't help him, I couldn't ease the tension. I'd mess things up. My friends would invariably call on a Saturday morning just as he was getting his much-needed sleep. Once I bought an illegal, highly recommended cockroach-killing bomb, set it off in the kitchen, and came back after work to find the apartment uninhabitable. It stunk. We were forced to clear out and camp with friends for three days and when we came back were faced with thousands of cockroach corpses littering the place. Another time I washed all his shirts with a pink sweatshirt of mine and it ran. Of course. All those stupid things that would make great episodes for a situation comedy, but lousy moments in real life.

His work was his obsession, he was mine. But the more obsessed I became with making things right, with getting back to the beginning again when everything was wonderful, the more nervous I became, the more mistakes I'd make. I'd remind him of a romantic evening we'd had in our courtship and feel devastated at his lack of interest in resurrecting it, cherishing the memory. His thoughts were elsewhere. They always were.

He would send me flowers on my birthday and our anniversary. Each time I received them, I would think of Eloise and her father. How despairing it is to be acknowledged only on the obvious days.

One Sunday morning when a few people were due over to brunch, I went out early to do some shopping, came back, put *La Bohème* on the tape player in the kitchen, and started to unload the groceries. Buddy came in half dressed, and smiling. I hadn't seen him smile in the morning for ages. He looked just like he had that first night at the West End, but I was smart enough not to mention it.

"Let me help you with that," he said. I smiled back at him. He hadn't even made a snide comment about the opera.

"My sister and I used to do this when we were

kids," he went on. "We made it into a game, so it would be fun, instead of a drag." What game? I wondered. Why hadn't he told me before? We could have made games up for all the work. We could have had fun doing the laundry. Why hadn't he mentioned it before? I didn't dare ask.

"Look. You go over to the fridge, and I'll toss you the stuff. Fast. And you put it away as fast as I throw it."

He was right, it was fun. He hurled cans, and bread loaves and mayonnaise jars and I was sweating with the excitement of catching them and putting them away fast enough to have my hands free for the next item. We were both laughing.

"Okay, here we come to the tough part, Stacy. The eggs. One by one into their little plastic holes on the shelf of the fridge there. You ready?"

"Sure," I said.

I caught the first, put it away, and the second was flying toward me. I dropped it.

"Shit." The third one was on its way.

"Shit, Buddy, I'm not—" It broke. "That's enough."

But the fourth one came, and the fifth and the sixth. They were all splattered, gooey on the floor.

"Jesus, you're uncoordinated," he said.

"I'm supposed to clean this up, aren't I?" I shouted at him. "Some fucking game. Some fun. And then I have to go out again and buy some more, right?"

I didn't stop. I yelled at him and started to cry and then yelled some more. About everything. He stood there calmly and I became more hysterical. When I finally finished, he said: "I *would* have helped you with the eggs if you hadn't gone berserk like that. Why don't you make a list of my faults and pin it up on your side of the bed, Stacy? In case you forget, for a moment, how awful I am. What you really want is someone in an opera, someone like the guy singing his heart out right now. You accuse me of having teenage tastes. Well, your expectations are like a lovesick teenager's. You want me to take you out to dinner, wine and dine you, stare into your eyes, talk about 'us' all the time. I'm sorry, I can't. I'm not Rudolfus or Rudolfo or whatever his name is, holding some woman's tiny little frozen hand, for Christ's sake. I have to work. I know that's very pedestrian of me, but it's necessary. You've got to learn to live in the real world. You're not junketing around town with Eloise anymore."

"You didn't have to call me uncoordinated. I'm not. And Eloise doesn't have anything to do with this."

"Whatever you say. I've got to get dressed." Buddy shrugged and disappeared. I began to clean up the mess.

Our marriage tottered on for another two years, full of bad moods, silences, arguments. I became wary around Buddy, stifling any romantic expectations, making sure that I wasn't getting in his way, or interrupting what was important—his work. I never called him at the office, never dropped by, made myself scarce and performed my wifely duties as efficiently as possible. But I was always waiting for the day when our lives would get back to what they had been before, when we'd spent nights sitting up and talking, making love, making each other laugh. When I wasn't working, I'd spend hours daydreaming about the couple we once were. I couldn't let go of images from the past and I was silently furious at him for what I considered his betrayal of our love, his choice of work over me.

It could have gone on that way forever, I'm convinced. I would have continued waiting for the real Buddy to come back from the office one day and sweep me away into passion again. Meanwhile we could have had children, worried about the right schools when the time came. We could have been a family. But Buddy walked in one night and said he wanted a divorce.

"I'm sorry, Stacy, but we don't have anything in common anymore. We don't talk, we don't have fun, we don't have sex."

"That's because you're too tired all the time," I said. "It's because of your work."

"Maybe. I know that's the way you see it, and it's the way I saw it for a while. But the work is just an excuse. I don't love you anymore. I don't know how else to say it."

"I should have caught the eggs."

"What are you talking about, Stacy?"

"I should have caught the eggs that morning. Our lives would have been different."

"I know this is going to be a difficult time for you," he said, backing away. "Maybe you should try therapy."

"Is there another woman?"

"No. But sometimes I think there's been another man. I mean that you married some idea you had of me, not the real me. I know I'm not easy to live with, but you make it harder because you expect me to be easy. I know I haven't fulfilled your expectations and I know you're only pretending you don't have those expectations anymore. It hasn't worked. Maybe it's because I let you think that I was something I wasn't at the beginning. I made a mistake."

"I'm a mistake?"

"Let's put it this way, okay? We're both mistakes for each other. And it's pointless not to admit that."

That was the end of my marriage. I found a new apartment, continued working, managed a promotion to the Customer Service department, and tried extremely hard to pretend my heart hadn't been irreparably damaged. When I'd see seemingly happy couples together, I'd wonder what was going on really, what was beneath the façade. How long it would take for the cracks in the relationship to appear. I distrusted people, was brittle, defensive, on the lookout for possible slights. And I began to hate Manhattan with the same passion I had once loved it. I thought it was phony, slick—a glittering neon moon hiding a welter of misery. I hated the crowds, the crazies hanging out on street corners, hated the way the wind swept up the streets from the river, scattering trash. And I loathed the subways. The morning when a man in a jam-packed subway undid his fly and masturbated in front of me was the day I decided to leave the city for good.

I didn't want to go back to Peoria. My parents had

made it clear that they felt the failure of my marriage was somehow all my fault. Buddy hadn't been an alcoholic or a wife beater. True, he'd been the one to walk out, but I knew my mother felt that any woman worth her salt could keep a man if she tried. I hadn't tried hard enough, obviously. I was lacking.

So I applied for a job as assistant manager at B. Dalton's in San Francisco. I decided to do what Americans did in the old days when they were at the end of their rope—go West. Get the hell out.

9

DECEMBER 8, 1989

Robert, dressed in jeans and a flannel shirt, was sitting in the living room, his hands wrapped around a mug of coffee, when I went downstairs the morning after the wedding.

"It would appear that we're the early risers in this household, hmm, Stacy? Some coffee?" he greeted me.

"Yes, please," I said and sat down as he disappeared into the kitchen. No sign of Deborah or the butler from the previous evening. I had just lit my first cigarette of the day when Robert returned with a tray.

"Milk?" he asked.

"Yes please, no sugar, though."

"Fine. Here you go." He handed me a mug, sat back, and watched as I took a long sip.

"That's the wonderful thing about caffeine—it kicks in right away. Nicotine, too. You'll be raring to go in a few seconds. What about some tennis?"

"Oh, Robert, please. No more exercise." I groaned.

"I used to smoke. When I stopped a few years back, I couldn't keep still. I can't now either. Poor Eloise is stuck with a jumpy husband. No wonder she sleeps late in the morning—I wear her out."

"I'm sure she loves it. Listen, Robert, I heard you singing last night as I went to bed. You have a spectacular voice. Is that what you meant when you said you were in the music business? Were you a singer of some kind?"

"Of some kind. Yes."

"Am I being very stupid? Should I know your name? You know Eloise and I were pretty perverse about not joining the rock 'n roll generation. I've always been ignorant of popular stars."

Robert put his mug on the table, picked up one of my cigarettes, put it in his mouth, but didn't light it.

"I was one half of a reasonably popular duo. The other half went on to fame and glory. I tried to scale those heights myself, but couldn't. It's a very boring story, Stacy." He waved the cigarette in the air, then replaced it in my pack.

"So I guess that means you're not one of the Everly Brothers."

"Phil and Don. Nope." He laughed. *"Someday when my crying's done, I'm gonna wear a smile and walk in the sun, I may be a fool, But till then, darling, you'll never see me complain. I'll do my crying in the rain."* His unaccompanied voice sounded even more beautiful than the night before. Whoever the other half of his duo had been must have sung like a blazing meteor to eclipse him.

"Come on, Robert. I'll find out from Eloise, even if you don't want to tell me. Remember, I liked to play Clue when I was a kid. Who was your other half?"

"My other half was my other half. My first other half. My ex-wife. Sapphire Shannon. You could say my better half."

"Sapphire Shannon!" I saw Robert wince and regretted my outburst.

Sapphire Shannon. No wonder Bobby had those basketball player's legs. Sapphire Shannon must be his mother. There aren't many six-foot-tall women around, and the ones there are get noticed. Especially one who happens to be a phenomenally successful pop star. Sapphire Shannon stood out from the crowd in more ways than one. She had her height going for her and a powerful voice as well as an unusual appearance. She looked as if someone had poured a bottle of bleach on her at birth: transluscent skin, pure white blond short hair, and unnaturally pale blue eyes. By all rights, she should have looked androgynous; instead she came across as undeniably female. One of those sex symbols normal women sometimes admire, sometimes envy, and very often hate.

But Robert's first wife? I couldn't imagine it. She was so unlike Eloise—every other word Sapphire spoke was "fuck" or "shit." She paraded around in omnipresent skin-hugging blue jeans and raunchy tops. She was crass. Famous, successful, and tacky. I remembered wondering once if her whole act was a gigantic effort to give herself the color she had been genetically robbed of.

No husband, ex-husband, or children had been mentioned in any of the articles I'd read about her, and I'd read quite a few. She was classic fodder for the magazines they give you at the hairdresser's. Toy-boys were her scene, or so the press claimed and the paparazzi proved.

Where had Robert fit in and how? The image of him as a discarded husband didn't fit with his looks, his energetic behavior, and aura of power. But then I hadn't imagined him as a singer, either. I wished again that I hadn't shouted her name out as I had. He must be sick to death of that reaction.

"Well, I'll tell you something, Robert. Marrying someone called Sapphire was your big mistake. Honestly. How could you?"

He chuckled.

"Eloise told me you were funny, Stacy. But her name wasn't Sapphire—it was Amy. She changed it on her solo climb to the big time."

"Maybe you should have changed yours to Platinum or Gold."

"Maybe." He shrugged and chuckled again. "Only in America, right? I make my wife into a star and she turns her back on me at the first possible opportunity. 'Go for It'—that's the slogan these days, isn't it? Amy went for it and she got it. More power to her, I say." He smiled at me and poured me another cup of coffee. "Why are we sitting inside on such a beautiful morning? Come on, up, Stacy. We're taking a walk on the beach now." He stood, pulled me up from my chair. I couldn't say no to him. "Bring your coffee, there. And take this—" He grabbed a tan sweater off the sofa beside him and threw it at me. "I won't be needing it. And it will fit you better than my son's did. Out. Out." He was pushing me now toward the door.

"I've got your cigarettes and I'll ration them for you. One. That's all you get. Doctor's orders."

"Okay, okay, slow down, Robert. I'm coming." He was out the door first into the bright December morning, moving so fast across the snow-covered lawn, I felt like Good King Wencelas's page, treading in my master's steps, trotting to keep up with him. We reached the beach and set off to the left, toward a group of sand dunes. We didn't speak for fifteen minutes or so, while I struggled to keep pace without spilling all my coffee, coughing occasionally into the ocean air. At the first dune, he stopped, climbed up, and sat on the top, beckoning me to join him, pulling my cigarette from behind his ear. Lighting it himself, he passed it to me as I sank onto the wet sand.

"Robert?" I took a moment to catch my breath, then inhaled. "I'm not sure I understand. You've got a gorgeous voice. Why didn't you make it on your own? Even if Sapphire—Amy, I mean—split with you, you could have had your own career."

"Oh, I thought so too at first, Stacy. But once you're labeled as a loser in the music business, you're a loser. You don't get second chances. I was Mr. Shannon, a clichéd phrase, but a true one, and that's all I was. Sorry—Mr. Shannon who had been left behind. A figure of some fun and speculation. Yes, I put out one album after our breakup, but the press was interested only insofar as I was Mr. Shannon. Not Robert Chappell. And I can't say that Amy helped very much. When asked to comment about my album, she said I had a, quote—nice and pleasant voice—unquote. That's what's generally referred to as damning with

faint praise. I had Bobby to bring up too, don't forget.
Sapphire left me three months after Bobby was born.
I had responsibilities which I met. End of story."

"Are you bitter about it? Angry?"

I had stretched his sweater over my knees, and
crouched over the steam rising from my coffee. We
were both watching a group of sea gulls shrieking and
diving for bait in front of us. We could have been
fellow shipwreckees waiting for a boat, so intent were
both pairs of eyes on the horizon.

"Stacy. I'm going to tell you a story. Okay?"

I nodded. Robert grabbed a piece of grass from a
stray clump on the dune, put it in his mouth. The
rustic, sea-blown look suited him.

"When I was a boy, all I wanted to do was fly. I
don't know if the desire stemmed from childhood stories of Peter Pan or not, but I wanted to fly. I knew I
couldn't do it just flapping my arms. But, as in the
famous Peggy Lee song 'Is That All There Is?' a circus
came to town, and when that circus came to town,
they brought hundreds, thousands of helium balloons
along with them. So I had a bright idea. Right? I was
seven years old and I convinced all my friends and all
the kids in the neighborhood, from seven down, to
buy as many helium balloons as they could. Steal from
their mothers' purses if necessary, but buy those balloons.

"And I told them to meet me early Sunday morning in the field back of our house and I would show
them that I could fly. I'd made a basket, you see. One
that I could stand in. Just. The kids came in throngs
with masses of balloons and I told them to stand back

and watch. God, they were excited. So was I. I tied all those balloons on to my basket very very carefully. Then I got in the basket and waited for it to take off. It didn't. It didn't even budge. The other kids looked at me and I could see them thinking of how much money they'd spent. For nothing.

"I had to do something. I had to save face and I didn't know what to do. But I was old enough to figure out that maybe I was too heavy, maybe that's why the basket didn't take off. I told those kids to hold on to the basket for dear life—I'd be back in a second. And I ran like a demon to my house and I raced upstairs and into my bedroom and I took my hamster out of its cage. This hamster was my best friend, you have to understand. I talked to him, told him my secrets every night. He protected me from the bad guys. He was *everything* to me, Stacy. But I grabbed him and ran back out to the field and I put him in that basket while all the others watched and then I watched and all the others cheered as the basket lifted. It not only lifted from the ground, it flew. I promise you, I could see my hamster's face over the edge of that basket as it floated away and I thought I saw tears in his eyes."

Robert paused, threw away his piece of grass.

"So if you ask me whether I'm angry about what happened with Amy, that's my answer. I understand ambition."

"Now—" He stood up, brushed the sand from his jeans, offered me a hand. "Let's get back and wake up that lazy, good-for-nothing wife and son of mine."

* * *

Eloise, Robert, Bobby, and I played croquet on the lawn the rest of that morning. Organized by Robert, it was a hysterical game with lots of cheating and laughter. We'd come in from the cold for Bloody Mary breaks, then troop out again to wage war in the snow. Bobby and I had been teamed together and I could tell that he was more serious about winning than the rest of us, but he was polite about my pathetic attempts to get my ball through the hoops and made up for my inadequacies whenever he got a chance to knock Eloise's or Robert's ball out of play. Eloise was in heaven—bouncy, ebullient, more lively than I could have ever imagined her. Dressed in bright pink and green ski pants and sweater.

I caught myself wondering whether it was an incredible sex life with Robert which had changed her outlook, relaxed her, made her forget all her childhood angst. But it was more than sex. It was sex, romance, love—the perfect combination. Robert didn't just organize wonderful croquet games in December, he also sang romantic ballads, put jewelry in glasses of champagne, danced to country-and-western music, listened to opera happily, told amazing stories, won bets about the Immaculate Conception, and most probably made wild, passionate love. How could Sapphire Shannon have left him? I asked myself as I watched him, propped against his croquet mallet, considering a shot.

"Hey, Robert," I called out to him. "Do you have a brother on the West Coast?"

"Sorry, Stace." Eloise laughed. "There's only one of him. And he's spoken for." She hugged him from

118

behind, he lost his balance, and they toppled over into the snow, kissing. I couldn't take my eyes off their happiness.

"He's got a son," Bobby said from behind me. I turned around to smile at him and caught an angry glare. "I think this game is finished now," Bobby announced, not looking at his father and stepmother, but heading toward the house. "I need another drink."

My flight was leaving early that afternoon, so I left Bobby to his Bloody Mary in the living room and went back to my bedroom to pack. Looking through my balcony window, I saw Eloise and Robert still cavorting, throwing measly snowballs at each other. The rich lovers at play—a wonderful sight. Eloise would never have to worry about washing Robert's socks, she would never have to schlepp around supermarkets after a hard day's work and come back to cook for him. Romance could last forever if you had enough money. The only potential cloud I could see on their horizon was Bobby, the mysterious son with a flashing temper. But Bobby was twenty years old, not a child who had to be looked after constantly. He wouldn't be able to interfere. I watched as Eloise and Robert came back toward the house, sodden, their arms around each other's waist.

Eloise could spend her days furnishing her New York house the way she had furnished this one, while Robert wrote his children's books. They could meet for lunch and dinner and discuss art. They could have beautiful babies.

I turned from the window, zipped up my bag. It was time to get back to my own life. I'd had my share of living vicariously. Eloise and Robert should be left on their own.

10

FEBRUARY 1990

I didn't recognize Bobby's voice at first. Two months had passed since Eloise's wedding, and I had gone back to my normal routine with only an occasional thought for the newlyweds.

"Stacy?"

"Mark, I'm sorry about the—"

"This isn't Mark, Stacy, this is Bobby. Bobby Chappell."

"Oh, Bobby, hi! Nice to hear from you. How are you? *Where* are you?"

"I'm in San Francisco. You never asked, but I go to UCLA. I've just come up here for the weekend. Eloise gave me your number. I was wondering whether you were free for dinner tonight?"

It was a Sunday evening. He'd probably had a raucous weekend and wanted a quiet dinner with an old friend of the family to recover, or else it was a duty call and he'd put it off until the last moment. Either way, I felt ancient.

"As it happens, I *am* free tonight. There's a restaurant called Sam's here in Tiburon. Can you get yourself there by eight o'clock?"

"Yes. Thank you, Stacy. I'll look forward to seeing you."

The same old polite Bobby, or rather the same young, polite Bobby. Would he be more forthcoming over a dinner *à deux,* or would he be that bricklike structure with the occasional flash of anger I'd observed over the wedding weekend? I was curious, and also chagrined that I had never asked him what college he attended. We had virtually ignored him, even though he took part in all the activities. He'd been more like a floating attendant—there, but a negligible presence. I wouldn't mind finding out more about him; or to be honest, I wouldn't mind finding out more about his mother.

Bobby had arrived before me and ordered a bottle of Chablis. He stood up when I came to the table, pulled out my chair for me, kissed me on the cheek. He was as tall as I remembered.

"It's nice to see you again, Stacy."

"It's nice to see you too." He lit my cigarette, then one for himself. Neither of us was sure how to start the conversation.

"So, Bobby, what do young men do these days? For fun, I mean."

"We have dinner with attractive older women."

"Oh, good," I said. Oh, bad, I thought. He wasn't like his father at all. He was too young to be interesting.

"Actually, Eloise and I have fun together. God, the money she has is awesome, isn't it?"

"You could say that." He was wearing a Hugo Boss suit and tie. Had Eloise funded the clothes? Or had

Sapphire? Sapphire must have an awesome amount of money as well. Had she entirely deserted Bobby? Did she ever see him?

"Wouldn't anybody say that?" As he looked at me, his eyes narrowed, signaling that the question was a challenge. We were on to the subject of money within seconds. A *sine qua non*, I supposed, for being involved with Eloise.

"Yes, I suppose you're right. Eloise is massively rich. But . . ." I stopped self-consciously. "*And*, I mean, Eloise is a lovely person. I assume she's making your father happy. I could tell from the wedding weekend that he's making her very happy."

"Oh, Dad's making her happy, all right." He frowned. I was disturbed by the tone he used as well as the frown.

"Bobby, is something wrong?"

"No." The frown turned into a half smile. He took a sip of wine. "My father is a very strong man, you know."

"I know. I could see that. And from what I've read about your mother, she's a very strong woman too."

"I wouldn't know about that." The voice was trying hard to be expressionless, but a bitterness sliced through it.

"I guess you don't see her that often, then?"

"I guess I don't see her at all. Can we please change the subject, Stacy?"

"Sure," I retreated quickly. Like Eloise, Bobby didn't want to discuss the past, and that was his right. Having such a famous mother must be a burden, especially if they weren't close. He looked tense, edgy,

123

and I was grateful when the waiter came. We both ordered hamburgers and another bottle of wine.

"So how is college, Bobby? What's it like at UCLA? What are you studying?"

Political science, it transpired. And we were off on to other, safer subjects. He told me about his studies, I told him about the mechanics of being a bookstore manager. We had polished off the second bottle of wine with no problem when he looked at me in the way his father had, the straight stare into my eyes.

"The food's excellent here."

I looked down at his hamburger and salad.

"That's a strange thing to say when you haven't eaten any of it, Bobby."

"If I say something strange, Stacy, it's because I want to sleep with you and I don't know how to ask, or I didn't know how to ask until now." He leaned forward, left elbow on the table, chin resting in the palm of his hand.

The proposition startled me. I honestly hadn't expected it. There had been none of the usual vibes aspiring lovers send out. Sex hadn't been in the air; but now, abruptly, it was, and I had to think about it. He was, or would be called, a toy-boy. It wasn't an option I had ever considered before, but then I'd never been offered it before. A younger man. A tall, young, lean body after years of run-ins with older men, or men my own age. What would it be like? I found myself thinking, and once I'd found myself thinking about it I knew I'd decided. I could remember how nice and clean his sweater had smelled that day in December.

"Do you want to be a toy-boy, then?" I laughed.

"No." Bobby glanced quickly around the restaurant, then back at me. "I want to be a man, Stacy. I've never done it."

"Done what? Slept with an older woman? That doesn't necessarily make you a man, does it?"

"Done *it*. Slept with an older woman, or a younger woman, or any woman at all. Not any man, either, I'd better say. I'm a virgin."

"Jesus." I'd been as dense as I was the afternoon Eloise talked about "losing it" with John. Now I was cast in the John role. A twenty-year-old virginal man— I didn't think they existed. Bobby's eyes were pleading with me. The stepson of my former roommate— the whole scene took on a ludicrous, soap-opera quality, and I'd had enough to drink to enjoy it. John the chauffeur had done his stuff for Eloise, I could do mine with Bobby. Help him over the first hurdle and he'd be on his way. I could teach him things that would be beneficial for the coming close encounters of his life. By proxy, I could make a lot of young women happy. There would be no complications. He could go back to UCLA and that would be that. A one night stand. Why not? That was the kind of mood I thought I was in.

"All right, Bobby," I said. "Come on, let's pay up and get out of here."

By the time we got back to my apartment I was regretting my decision. If I was supposed to be Anne Bancroft to his Dustin Hoffman, how exactly was I expected to go about it? I couldn't remember how she'd done it in *The Graduate*. I didn't know how to go about setting the scene. Should I pounce on him? Should I change into a negligee and loll seductively on the bed? How could I overcome his nerves when mine were beginning to jangle?

As it turned out, Robert Chappell, Jr., didn't need any help, not a bit of it. There were no preliminaries, no romantic scenes set out, no discussions. Once we'd closed the door behind us, he quickly stripped me, stripped himself, and carried me into the bedroom and slipped on a condom effortlessly. He didn't need to be guided, didn't rush things or, ejaculate prematurely with the thrill of the first time. On the contrary, he made slow, considered love to me for what must have been over an hour before we both climaxed. I'd been had in more ways than one.

"Bobby." I sat up and turned on the bedside light. "You've done this before."

He didn't answer. I slapped him hard on the rear end.

"You've done this before, you bastard."

He raised himself on to his elbow, rubbing his bum. "So?"

"So? So why the deceit?"

"You might not have slept with me otherwise."

"For your information, I would have."

"Call it an insurance policy, then."

"That sucks."

"Yup." He smiled and I could have killed him.

"Stacy, don't get angry. It's a waste of time. We've had a great time anyway. What does it matter how it happened? Do you have a beer?"

I was dumbfounded.

"There's one in the fridge. And get one for me too while you're at it. The kitchen's down the hall on your left."

As I put on my dressing gown, I closed my eyes. There had been an instant, just an instant when he'd begun to kiss me. My hands were wrapped around his neck, touching his bristly crewcut hair and I had thought of his father. I would have preferred his father. I opened my eyes, lit a cigarette, watched cross-legged from my bed as Bobby returned with two beers. He flipped off the tops, then stretched himself out on my bed.

"You know, Stacy, there was a case here in California. A woman hitchhiker was picked up by a married couple. The husband kidnapped her and put her in a box in his basement. He tortured and abused her. But she lived with this couple for seven years. Most of the time she was shut up, imprisoned in this box. A kind of coffin. As time went by, though, the man would occasionally let her out. And you know something? When she had the chance, she didn't run away or call the police or try to get help. She would baby-sit for the couple's kids and talk to the neighbors and everything, and then he'd shut her back in the box every night. Underneath their bed. This tiny box. Like a coffin."

"Jesus, Bobby."

"The wife knew her husband was doing this. I mean, she just stood by and let it happen. At first the hitchhiker girl used to scream and cry to be let out, but then she got used to it. And the wife *knew*. That's what gets to me. The wife knew and she didn't stop it. Seven years."

"I really don't think I want to hear this story."

"I don't know how he was caught eventually. I remember hearing that the girl, the hitchhiker, used to call him up and talk to him for hours while they were waiting for the trial to start. And his defense used that as part of their case. The fact that she was still calling him. Plus the fact that she hadn't escaped despite plenty of opportunities." He swigged his beer. "I'd like to meet her. And him. And the wife. You know they had the box she'd been shut up in as an exhibit at the trial."

He was more engaged in this subject than he had ever been, even when we'd been having sex. The excited look on his face frightened me.

"Bobby. This is seriously creepy. This is not postcoital conversation."

"Do you think I could get to meet them, though? Could I pretend that I was writing a book on the case or something?"

"I don't think it's a great idea to keep pretending you are someone you're not, Bobby. And I don't really understand why you want to meet them. This fascination doesn't sound very healthy to me."

"I guess not." He finished his beer, swung his long legs over the side of the bed. "Maybe I should take off. Can you call me a cab?"

After he had put his clothes back on, we waited for the cab in silence. I was put off by his lie and by that story. I had absolutely nothing to say to him. He seemed to be somewhere else anyway; he certainly wasn't making any effort to have a civilized conversation. When the cab arrived and I had closed the door behind him, I cursed myself for getting involved with such an inappropriate person. He was odd. And a little scary. I had made a very stupid mistake.

11
FEBRUARY 1990

The next morning I woke up shaking from a series of particularly unpleasant nightmares, one of which featured me being locked into a medicine cabinet. I got up and made myself a cup of coffee, pacing the kitchen. Before I was aware of what I was doing, I found myself looking up and dialing the number Eloise had given me for the New York house.

"Stacy, hi! How great to hear from you." Eloise sounded bubbly and my shakes began to recede.

"I called to find out how you are. I mean, how's everything going? How's wedded bliss? Blissful?"

"Totally. This is amazing. You know I was just going to call you, invite you here next weekend. You're the psychic one now. What about it? Will you come? Please?"

"Oh, Eloise, I'd love to. But—"

"But what? No excuse, unless it's a man. And if it is, bring him."

"No. There's no man in my life." A video of Bobby in bed played on fast speed in my mind. I could feel myself blushing. "I hate to say it, but it's cash. I really can't afford to jet around the country. Bookstores aren't the highest paying employers."

"The TWA ticket will be waiting for you at the airport for the Friday afternoon plane, okay? You know I hate to argue, so don't even start."

"Eloise, I—"

"Don't even try, Stace. If you don't use the ticket, the money will be wasted. Edwin will be waiting for you. I think it gets in around nine P.M., our time. Robert is looking forward to seeing you again."

"Well, thanks. And I'm looking forward to seeing both of you. By the way, speaking of Robert, I had dinner with Bobby last night."

"Oh, that was sweet of you, Stace. How is he?"

"He's fine. But I wanted to ask you. Have you ever found him to be strange? I mean, a little mixed-up, maybe?"

Eloise didn't even pause to consider the question.

"No. Did you? How bizarre. He's always been so polite and nice around me. We had a good time together over Christmas. What did he do? Should I talk to Robert about it?"

"No. No. He didn't do anything, really. Maybe it was me. I was in a strange mood myself. Forget it."

"Okay, I will. See you Friday. And bring warm clothes—it's cold out here."

Bobby Chappell left two messages on my answering machine that week, but I didn't return his calls. What was the point of becoming involved with a troubled twenty-year-old? I suspected that Bobby's strange behavior could be attributed to the famous mother who had abandoned him. I couldn't help but be curious about Sapphire. She had ditched her husband, ditched her son, made it to the top of a cutthroat business. A tough woman indeed. A survivor. How long had Sapphire and Robert's partnership lasted? What had precipitated the breakup? I might easily find the answers to those questions, I knew, with just a little digging. So dig I did.

A friend of mine who worked on women's features for the *San Francisco Chronicle* arranged for me to visit the paper's clipping library, where I was presented with a huge file marked "Sapphire Shannon." There was an abundance of articles on Sapphire, so many that I didn't know where to begin. Deciding to work backward, I started with the *People* magazine profile of six months back. It was full of predictable stuff—the requisite picture of Sapphire in the tighter-than-tight blue jeans, this time straddling a motorcycle. She resembled a tall, female version of James Dean, with her short white hair and brooding pale eyes. She had a remarkably youthful face as well. Plastic surgery? I wondered. Then I studied it more closely and saw the wide, open smile—not the kind a woman can manage when her skin has been stretched and tucked.

The T-shirt she had on with the jeans was outrageous. One word was written large: SLUT. The article centered on her forthcoming tour and her toy-boy of the moment. A twenty-two-year-old heavy metal drummer who was pictured in an inset with an attractive scowl, his ears a garden of tiny studs.

Most of the articles throughout the eighties and the last half of the seventies were similar. Raunchy clothes, conversation with expletives deleted, except in *Rolling Stone* or magazines which were willing to print them, and a propensity to talk about sex. "I like having men at my mercy, and the best way to get them begging is to get them in bed," she was quoted in *Esquire*. "They don't fuck around with you then. They just fuck."

I stopped reading and pictured Eloise and Robert playing in the snow together, the innocence of their tumbling and their snowball fights. What a contrast she must be for Robert. Only once had I heard Eloise say "shit": that time when she had dropped her books in the hall. I flipped impatiently back in time to the late sixties and finally found what I had been looking for. A small piece on a duo who called themselves "Boy Meets Girl"—Robert and Amy Chappell—newcomers who had made a mark in Boston and were preparing to play clubs in the Haight-Ashbury area.

The caption under the heads-only photograph said, "Coming to San Francisco with flowers in their hair." And there was Amy Sapphire, her short hair hidden by a crown of daisies, smiling the same smile from *People;* staring straight at the camera. Her eyes, even at that young age, looked knowing. In the language of the sixties, she would have been called groovy. Far out.

The boy beside her was an entirely different proposition. For starters, his head was an inch or so below hers. The photograph must have been taken when they were standing. He was smiling also, but it was a dumb smile. Robert looked like a dolt. His hair was so long and so unruly it could have been a particularly hideous mushroom fungus. It had carnations stuffed randomly on the top, presumably for the caption. His eyes seemed zonked out and I thought that he must have been on dope. That would explain the dumb smile. The camera didn't portray him warts and all, it portrayed him zits and all. One side of his face showed a bad case of acne. I zeroed in on his picture and kept comparing it to my last visual memory of him, waving good-bye to me in the Cape Cod driveway. His face had recovered from the war raging on it in this picture; clearly he was one of those people who needed time to grow into his looks. But how he must have suffered. Especially with this vision of unconventional beauty standing beside him.

Certainly he could have wooed Amy with his voice, his personality. They could have set out to conquer the world together. But I could sense what happened as if I'd been there. Club dates, this unlikely duo crooning away on the margins of the recording industry, just making it pay, waiting for the big break. But some record company executive must have gone to see them and seen *her*, only her. Offered her a lucrative contract with one proviso: "Get rid of the geek with the spots, baby, and I'll make you a star."

What a clichéd scenario, and how absolutely likely to have occurred. If they had been part of a group, if there had been four or five people playing instruments and singing, Robert might have made it. The attention could be diverted from him—he could be the stupid-looking guy in the back. But, no, there were only the two of them, and even worse, they were married. All the male fans would be pissed off that Sapphire was married and none of the female fans would have posters of Robert up on their bedroom walls. Now, maybe, sure. But now, as he himself said, was too late. He had been branded a cast-off, a failure. He had overhauled his appearance as totally as Eloise had, but it was simply too late. I felt so sorry for him, my heart clenched. I didn't want to read anymore. Sapphire had been heartless and ambitious and she had got exactly what she wanted, but not what she deserved. As I put the articles back in the file, I looked once again at the *People* picture. I would have liked to wipe that smile off her face.

The New York City skyline was no longer a miraculous sight to my eyes, but I couldn't turn away from it as Edwin drove me into town the next Friday evening. I stared at the lights and remembered things I didn't want to remember, wishing I had never accepted Eloise's invitation. Cape Cod was fine, but Manhattan was a direct threat. The looming buildings, the honking horns, the loonies performing antics on the street corners, all the myriad signposts of the Big Apple made me think only of my own failure there. I was relieved that we were driving along the East River Drive, avoiding all the West Side routes of my past. Barnard, the West End Bar, Riverside Drive, were half a city away. If I stuck to the East Side Eloise inhabitated, I could limit the memories. I could pretend, as I did reasonably successfully in San Francisco, that Buddy had never existed.

This time I was prepared for the redecorated house and the revamped Eloise that greeted me. She was wearing a white Chanel wool suit with a pearl necklace and pearl earrings, looking as dignified and serene as an ice carving. After we embraced with a hug, she led me into the living room, where Robert was standing with a bottle of champagne in his hands, pouring me a glass. That pose was now a familiar sight.

"It's wonderful to see you two," I said. Taking the champagne from Robert, I quickly gave him a kiss on the cheek. I was half expecting to feel the rough texture of skin that has been scraped, a process I'd heard doctors used to rid people of bad acne, but his cheek felt normal. Not soft, but normal. He looked so unlike his picture that I suddenly wondered whether it *had* been him, then remembered his name had been printed. The eyebrows were the same, also. The awful bushy long hair had made the photograph even more appalling, but, I reminded myself, long hair was *de rigueur* in the sixties, whether it suited the man or not. Now, luckily, Robert was living in a decade which allowed him to wear his hair the way that looked best on him. Sapphire's short cut had managed to look stylish through the passing years; she had got away with it. But she was a woman who could probably get away with anything.

"How are you?"

"I couldn't be better, Stacy." Robert beamed. "How's my favorite bridesmaid?"

"Matron of honor," I corrected him.

"Ah, but are you a matron and are you honorable?"

"No comment."

I went over to the fireplace and surveyed the room. Whoever had decorated it had done a beautiful job. All traces of animal heads and horns had vanished.

The macho atmosphere had been superceded by pale pink and white fabrics. The two sofas and armchairs were covered with silk cushions, the tables all had vases full of lilies and silver-framed photographs. But the paintings were of the modern variety which cause people to think: "I could have done that. How can anyone charge so much for a splotch on a white canvas?" In that setting, though, they worked. The bold colors added a shock of modern liveliness to what was otherwise a traditional drawing room and counterbalanced the feminine pink. Robert, I noticed, was sitting down on a pink-and-white striped sofa which had replaced the old one John the chauffeur had occupied all those years before. He looked thoroughly at home.

"We thought we'd have a light dinner here tonight, Stacy, since you must be tired. And tomorrow we can paint the town. Is that all right with you?" Eloise asked.

"Fine. That's perfect. I need to readjust to New York City gradually."

"You've come to the right place. We'll ease you into orbit." Robert refilled my glass, then Eloise's. She was sitting up with her back as straight as a soldier's standing for inspection, her legs crossed demurely, but her eyes looked slightly unfocused. I wondered how much they'd been drinking before I arrived.

"How is the writing going, Robert?" I saw, as I asked this, that Eloise looked down at the floor.

"It isn't, Stacy. I have writer's block and I'm not even a writer yet. Neat trick, isn't it?"

"It's hard for him to work because there's been so

much going on with redoing the house. It's been difficult for him to get any peace and quiet." Eloise put
her hand on Robert's thigh and he grabbed it in his.

"My wife is my number one fan, aren't you, Cat?
Isn't that great? And I'm hers. Aren't you jealous,
Stacy?"

Caught off guard by the question, I took a large
gulp of champagne.

"Of course I'm jealous. Who wouldn't be? You two
are the perfect couple."

"And you'll be half of a perfect couple soon,
Stace." Eloise was rushing her words. "Robert didn't
mean to be insensitive, he just likes to show off." Robert put his palms up in the air and smiled at me.

"I can't help myself sometimes. Come on, honorable matron, I'm starving. Let's go in to dinner."

As I walked with them into the dining room, my
face flushed, I wished again that I had never come
back to New York. Why did being half of a happy
couple have to be the apex of a woman's life, especially in the 1990s? It wasn't supposed to be like that
anymore. Work was supposed to count for something;
a career was supposed to make up for any emotional
deficits. I was happy in my job, even if it wasn't financially the most rewarding career I could have chosen.
But I enjoyed it. Why, after all feminism had accom-
plished, did the presence of a man in my life, or
rather the absence of one, still matter so much? I was
angry at myself for reacting so to Robert's question.

The dining room was a shock and made me forget
my irritation. It was dominated by a bright-red lacquered round table surrounded by highly glossed

black lacquered chairs. The entire motif of the room was black and red.

"It looks like hell in here," I said to Eloise "I mean hell literally. Where's the devil with the pitchfork?"

"We're buying him," Eloise said. "I mean we're buying a picture of one Robert found in a gallery downtown. Don't you like it?"

"Yes, actually. I do. I guess I associate the devil with food and drink. It's an interesting concept for a dining room. And it's kind of spooky."

A butler began to serve us the first course of watercress soup. Robert, Eloise, and I were grouped at one end of the circular table. It could have easily seated ten. I wondered how many dinner parties they hosted with the chic and the rich of Manhattan discussing whatever the chic and rich discuss. It was all a long way from our room at Barnard, the regulation matching beds and dressers shoved into the tiny square space.

"Why do you think people are more frightened at night than in daylight?" Robert asked, not directing the question specifically to Eloise or me.

Eloise answered first.

"I guess because you can't see in the dark. It's a fear of the unknown, especially for children. I remember being terrified of monsters when it was bedtime and the housekeeper turned off the lights."

Robert rubbed his hands, clasped them together, then put two fists down on either side of his place setting.

"But that's just what doesn't make sense. Children come from the dark. The womb is pitch black and the womb is supposed to be the greatest place on earth. Being born is traumatic. That's why all these pregnant women deliver in low-lit labor rooms these days. The light is what's spooky, as Stacy says. Children, all of us, should welcome the dark. We should imagine heaven as a place of overwhelming darkness and hell a prison of bright light.''

"That's certainly an original thought, Robert. But the fetus doesn't know it's in the dark.'' I was getting caught up in the discussion. It reminded me of ones Eloise and I used to have. "A fetus doesn't know it can't see anything. A child or even an adult *knows* when the lights are out that he can't see, that he's vulnerable.''

"I'm glad to hear you choose the masculine pronoun, Stacy. We don't want any raving feminists in this house. It's bad enough already—we have a mailwoman who insists on referring to herself as a mailperson.'' Robert chuckled. "But are you saying that what you don't know can't hurt you? Being a fetus was wonderful because we weren't conscious of anything? Ignorance is bliss?''

Robert leaned back in his chair. He looked like he was having fun. I was struck by how long it had taken me to notice that he often talked in questions. Tagged on to the end of sentences would be the phrases "don't you think?" or "isn't that great?"; a technique which always put the burden on the other person. You felt compelled to answer, and often, in my own case, to agree.

"Ignorance is bliss as long as it doesn't end up hurting you,'' Eloise said. "What you don't know *can* hurt

140

you. Anything can hurt you. That's the problem." She looked as sad and vulnerable as she must have when a child terrified of monsters. Robert shot a meaningful glance at me, saying, in effect, that we both knew Eloise's predeliction for unhappiness.

"Lighten up, Cat. There you are, dressed in white, looking like an angel in hell. You should be as happy as an angel. Doesn't she look like an angel, Stacy?"

"You do, Eloise. Robert's right." Eloise had a touchingly innocent aura that night. Despite the designer suit and pearls, she looked otherwordly set against the black and red of the dining room. As if we had summoned her in a séance.

"Of course I'm right," cried Robert. "Misery doesn't suit you, angel. Have another drink." He poured her a glass of red wine.

"I'm sorry." Her shoulders sagged as she drank, but she immediately collected herself into the drill sergeant's posture and looked over at her husband. "Stacy had dinner with Bobby last weekend, did I tell you?"

"You did. How was he? I hope my son behaved himself."

"He did."

"And I most certainly hope that he made a pass at you. He'd be a fool not to."

Eloise choked on her wine. "Robert! Bobby's only twenty!" she managed to say between coughs. Robert's eyes now felt like X rays. I crossed my legs, uncrossed them, tried to meet his stare head-on, and was grateful for a moment's reprieve as the butler cleared the soup.

* * *

"So, Stacy," Robert persisted. "Did you teach my son a thing or two about the facts of life?"

"You really are outrageous, darling." Eloise laughed.

"I didn't teach him a thing. We talked about his studies at UCLA," I said.

"What a thoroughly boring evening that must have been. I'll have to teach Bobby more about entertaining women." Putting his wineglass down, Robert smiled at me. "I apologize on his behalf."

"No apologies necessary, Robert. Bobby is an interesting young man. Honestly."

"Good. I'm glad to hear that. It's so difficult being a one-parent family, you know. You worry, you're never sure if you're doing the right thing. A boy growing up without his mother is deprived. I tried to make up for that, but how can I tell if I succeeded? It's reassuring to get positive feedback."

"I bet it's hard," I replied. "I see so many customers browsing through the Child Care section in my store. What they're looking for is a book that will tell them how to be a perfect parent. And there's no such book."

Robert and I discussed various books I knew of relating to child care; which titles were the big sellers and which ones disappeared without a trace. I looked over at Eloise occasionally, but she didn't join in. She was visibly sagging.

"I don't know about you, Stacy, but I'm exhausted." Eloise finally spoke up. She looked like an angel about to drop its harp.

142

"Cat—what about dinner?"

"I can't eat anything else, Robert. I think I've had too much to drink. The excitement of Stacy's arrival and everything. I better go to bed. I'm sorry, Stace."

"Don't be. I had some food on the plane. I think I might crash out now too, if the cook wouldn't be insulted."

"The cook is used to it," sighed Eloise, getting up and leaning against her chair.

"Used to what?" I was confused.

"Oh, she's used to people not eating every single thing she cooks. So many people are on diets these days," Robert answered, patting his stomach. "Although, as you can see, I'm not. I'll take Eloise up to bed. Frederick—" He motioned to the butler. "Can you get Sarah to show our guest up to her room, please? And arrange for a tray with the rest of my dinner to be sent up."

"Certainly, Mr. Chappell."

I'd had too much to drink, too, I thought, as I followed Sarah up the grand white marble spiral staircase to my room. And I'd had it in a very short time.

I had been lucky to avoid more cross-examination on Bobby, though. I could still hear Eloise choking on the thought of her stepson and me in bed together. On the whole it was much safer in life, I decided, to sleep alone.

My bedroom made me feel as if I'd taken a trip to Paris, not New York. A red velvet chaise longue was in the corner; the bed itself was vast, with linen sheets and square pillows. The paintings all displayed women emerging from bathtubs or standing naked in front of sinks. It looked like a high-class bordello, or at least it gave me the feeling that it would be the perfect room to have sex in.

The bathroom was no surprise, for there stood an immense white bathtub on four feet, a mirror image of the bathtubs in the paintings. Ditto the sink. While the bedroom was ostentatiously voluptuous, the bathroom was rustic, with a plain white tiled floor. The ultimate items of luxury were there, though, hanging from hooks on the wall. White fluffy towels so large they could have accommodated a seven-foot-tall Sumo wrestler. And the kind of bathrobe I'd read about in travel magazines. The one that the Georges V Hotel manager assumes his customers will steal.

After I had indulged myself with a long, hot bath, I climbed into bed and found a hot water bottle waiting for me. It wasn't just easy to go to sleep, it was a true pleasure. No sooner had I woken up the next morning than Sarah appeared, asking me what I'd like for breakfast. Being pampered like that made me wonder what Eloise's life was like. What could she possibly do all day? Relax and enjoy it all, I supposed, like anybody normal would in the same circumstances.

Finishing my breakfast in bed, I dressed and went downstairs to find Eloise, but failed. She wasn't in the living room, so I wandered down a hallway to the right of the staircase. The first door off it opened into a high-tech room catering to television, video, and compact disc playing, painted in dove gray, lit by recessed bulbs. An entire wall was given over to storing long-playing albums, arranged alphabetically by singer, every pop singer I'd ever heard of—except, I was interested to notice, Sapphire Shannon. Plus a large selection of the older singers like Fred Astaire and Bing Crosby. There were fewer CDs, and they were a mixture of classical, opera, and country-and-western. These must be Robert's new passion, I decided. Eloise must have introduced him to the pleasures of opera while he introduced her to the likes of Tammy Wynette.

I went back to the album section, remembering that Robert had recorded a solo album. I found it in with the rest of the CDs and pulled out the jacket sleeve, only to find that it had no record inside. Just the sleeve with the title "Because It Was There" and a picture of Mount Everest. Robert's name was at the bottom in blood red type. I turned it over—no picture of Robert on the back either—and scanned the song titles. Side A: "Love It or Leave It"; "Play Fair"; "Burning Sands"; "Why Not?"; "I Tried." Side B: "Because It Was There"; "Think Again"; "If You Don't Live It Up, You'll Never Live It Down"; "Half a Mile"; "What You Want."

All written by Robert Chappell. The absence of the actual record frustrated me. I would have liked to hear that voice recorded, find out whether it was merely "nice and pleasant" as Sapphire had described it, or better than that. I wanted to know exactly how bad a hand Robert had been dealt by fate in the form of his ex-wife.

Replacing it, I went across the hall and popped my head into a small sitting room. It looked like the perfect place to read the morning papers and have a leisurely cup of coffee. Decorated with Regency-striped wallpaper, the room was furnished with a standing lamp, two big easy chairs, and a fireplace surrounded by a marble frieze on which was carved what looked like an Italian hillside town. There was a cozy window seat covered in material matching the wallpaper, and the inevitable mass of white lilies. I went back into the living room and studied the silver-framed photographs I'd noticed the previous evening. What I wanted was to find one of Eloise's mother. I'd snooped around the Cape house with that purpose as well, but never found one. I was out of luck here, too. Most of them were of Robert and Eloise smiling at each other or the camera, though there was one of Bobby in tennis clothes and one of Eloise's father dressed in hunting gear.

Deciding to continue my exploration of the house, I went back into the hall, retracing my route past the little sitting room and music room and continuing down a corridor to the left. I opened a door into a study—Robert's study, it transpired. He was sitting, feet up on the desk, playing the guitar.

"Good morning, Stacy. We early risers always find each other, don't we? Have a seat." He motioned to the leather chair facing him and I settled in. "Have a drink. Bloody Mary, Screwdriver, gin and tonic—you name it." It seemed early to be drinking, but it also seemed silly not to. "Bloody Mary, please." I got out a cigarette. Robert put his guitar on the floor, lit my cigarette for me, then went to the bar at the side of the desk and fixed me my drink.

"Don't let me stop you. What were you playing?"

He reached down for the guitar, slung the strap

over his shoulder, perched on the edge of the desk, facing me. Our knees were touching.

"On the good ship Lollipop—" he started in, and I laughed immediately.

"Stacy, Stacy. This is not a laughing matter. Shirley Temple had a magnificent voice, an uncanny voice. She could switch keys like Ella Fitzgerald. I love this song. Sit back and listen."

He sang it as a plaintive ballad; his voice sad, lamenting. It was as affecting as "Somewhere Over the Rainbow," more so, because I was so used to hearing it as an upbeat little kids' song.

"Robert," I said a moment after he had finished, "you haven't given up, have you? You can't really give up singing. You're too good."

"I certainly can give up. And I have given up." His voice boomed out, a startling switch after the singing. Then it softened again. "Now. If you can find me a teacher to make me into an opera star at this advanced age, sure. But I don't have the range for that, do I?"

"I don't know. I haven't heard enough. You might, with training."

"No. I'm too old. Life does begin at forty. It begins to fade away. And I don't like the idea of competing with the divas, all those pushy, pushy fat women."

He smiled at me, unhooked his guitar, placing it carefully in its case by the side of the desk.

"Did you like those Shirley Temple movies?" I asked.

"Sure. Doesn't everyone? They were the perfect stories. She was usually this cute little orphan who

147

would find the perfect parents by the end. Loving parents who would stop the rot of a potentially miserable childhood. So she could end up with that big smile and that happy voice and dance away. I used to fantasize that the same thing would happen to me. You know, most kids have a big fear that they've been adopted. My fear was that I wasn't adopted. That my parents were actually my parents and no wonderful figure could then come to reclaim me and get me out of it all.''

"Get you out of what?''

"Well, to be precise, get me away from my mother.'

"Why?''

"To tell the story properly I'd have to lie down on a couch.'' He laughed. "Look. A lot of people have miserable childhoods. We all know that and most of us are bored by that unless it happens to be our own miserable childhood.''

"I'd like to hear, Robert.''

"Would you?'' He looked thoughtful, as if he were weighing up the pros and cons of telling a painful story to a stranger. "Well, you have to remember that I grew up in the fifties, a time when Mom was supposed to be Mom and Dad was supposed to take you to football games. Also a time when polio was on the rampage. It didn't get me, though. It got my father. He became a cripple and my mother became the breadwinner.

"So the roles were reversed. She went out to work and he stayed home watching television. All of which might have been fine, except my mother became a mini-executive. She worked her way up from being a secretary in the head office of a supermarket chain to being in charge of a supermarket herself. She had no time at all for my father. She treated him like a cripple. And as far as I was concerned, well, I was just in the way. She never came to my schools, never showed up for parents' day or drove carpools or came to any of my sports meets. When I would ask her, she'd just shake her head and say she was too busy.

"My father and I ate spaghetti out of cans and Campbell's Minestrone soup. My mother couldn't be bothered to cook. My father's bedroom was on the ground floor, of course. My mother's was upstairs. She would breeze in and out and we'd have to watch out for her moods. If she'd had a bad day at the office, there was all hell to pay. We hadn't kept the house tidy enough. We didn't appreciate how hard she worked. We were leeches, clinging on to her, sucking her blood.

"The best way to handle her was to avoid her. My father stayed glued to the television in his bedroom. I stayed in my room upstairs doing my homework and practicing on my guitar—a Christmas present from my father, by the way. My mother gave him an allowance and he saved it up. Like a kid. When my mother got vacation time, she'd take a trip on her own and leave me to take care of my father."

As he was telling me all this, I noticed that the little imperfection in his right eye looked like a teardrop falling from his pupil. A constant tear that could never be wiped away. The rest of his face, though, appeared nonchalant.

"But what did your mother do in the evenings if

your father was watching TV and you were in your room?''

Robert didn't reply.

"She sounds cruel, Robert. Didn't she have *any* redeeming features?"

"She was good at her job. She paid my way through college. A debt which she liked to remind me of. They're both dead now. He basically wasted away and she had a heart attack."

"What a grim childhood."

"Oh, come on. It's not that bad. Children have been physically abused by their parents, you know. I learned to keep myself to myself. I survived. I'd dream about other mothers, of course. Real mothers, the ones you saw on television shows."

"What about your father, though? Didn't you two have a good relationship?"

"Like I said before, I always wanted someone to protect me. My father never did. Now I know that I should have protected *him*."

"What do you mean?"

The telephone on his desk rang. I jumped and saw him smile as he picked it up. "Yes. Fine. I'll be right there," he said and hung up.

"Eloise has woken up. I'm going to go have some coffee with her. Now listen, Stacy. I'm not sure why I told you that story. I seem to be making a habit of telling you stories from the past. You shouldn't be such a good listener."

"Don't be silly," I protested. He came around the back of my chair and began to rub my neck gently.

"You should try acupuncture, you know."

"What?"

"The smoking. You're a bundle of nerves. Your neck is like a squeaky voice. You need sorting out."

On that pronouncement, he left. I stayed seated, pondering on Robert's childhood and how well he seemed to have emerged from a sad start. Saddled with such an insensitive mother and then finding himself married to a woman like Sapphire Shannon, he had still managed to retain a sense of humor and perspective. Eloise, I thought, was even luckier than I had imagined. She'd had an absent father, he'd had an absent mother. They were well matched. Robert would never mock her frailty.

The study was as stacked full of books as the music room had been with records and CDs. I began to examine them, trying to gain insight into Robert Chappell's character from his choice of reading. They were alphabetically arranged by author—Robert, among his many other qualities, must have appreciated order —and split into sections. Fiction, nonfiction, art, history, travel and finally, a tiny section on psychology. The novels ranged from the classics to Elmore Leonard. The nonfiction was biography and autobiography, covering famous figures as diverse as Laurence Olivier and Ed Koch. The history centered mainly on the Civil War. Art was reserved for twentieth-century artists. I wondered who had chosen the paintings in my bedroom.

The psychology section was what struck me the most. It was full of popular junk. *When You Say No, Do You Feel Guilty?*, *How to Feel Better About Yourself*, *What Do Women Really Want?*: titles I would have thought

Robert Chappell would laugh at, not buy. The last book of the section made me stop and pull it out. *Love —The Ultimate Brainwash* was the title, a slim paperback. I recognized the author, though. Daniel Sterne. Why hadn't I seen it before? Books were my business, but I'd never been made aware of this one. If I had, I would have given it a huge display in the front window of Dalton's. I checked the date it had been published —1987. How had I managed to miss it? Just seeing his name brought an instant rush of nostalgia. I could see the old ladies in the Viennese coffee shop, their hands shaking, their crooked lipstick and kind eyes. Iced coffee with coffee ice cream floating in it. Rain-drenched afternoons I'd spent there writing term papers. And that one afternoon when I had been so positive Daniel Sterne would ask me out.

Skimming through the book quickly, I could see that it would make a good read. I would like to know more about love and brainwashing, I thought, then smiled at my little self-deception. I would like to talk to Daniel Sterne again. I would very much like to see Daniel Sterne again. I put the book back, picked up the phone and called information. There was, indeed, a listing for Sterne, Daniel. On West 93rd Street. I dialed the number.

Eloise came in just as I'd hung up.

"Robert told me you were in here," she said. "Are you ready for a tour of the art galleries and maybe a little shopping? We can have a quick lunch at Mortimer's, if you'd like."

She had regained the color she'd lost the night before and looked exotic in a flowing silk kimono. "I'll get changed in a flash. It will be like the old days, won't it? The culture vultures are back in town." She smiled.

"That sounds great, but I'm afraid I can't have lunch. On the spur of the moment I called an old teacher of mine—remember Daniel Sterne? Anyway, we're having lunch."

"Oh. Okay." Eloise went over to the bar and poured herself a Bloody Mary from the jug. "Wait a minute. Daniel Sterne? He's the one you had the crush on, isn't he? Oh, Stace, don't blush. Listen—if you have a good lunch, invite him to dinner tonight. Eight o'clock. I'd like to meet this man."

"He's probably married."

"Did he say he was?"

"No. He didn't even sound surprised to hear from me. All he said was 'Of course I remember you, numbskull. The Viennese coffee shop is closed, but meet me at The Balcony at one for lunch.' "

"That sounds promising."

"It doesn't mean he's not married."

"Stace—look at you. You can't hide the excitement. You're hooked already. I love it. Isn't romance great?"

"He's definitely married. Or gay."

"You are hopeless." Eloise shook her head and laughed. "Come on, I'll hurry up and get ready—we'll squeeze the Museum of Modern Art in before lunch. But you better put some makeup on."

"Eloise? You telling me to wear makeup—that's a joke."

"Not anymore, Stace. We're getting older, you

know. We need all the help we can get. It's important to look your best."

"Okay, okay, I just never thought I'd hear you say that."

"Things change," she said. Her tone was deadly serious. "People change."

Daniel Sterne hadn't changed much; he was still short and bulky with dark, swept-back hair and that Stalinesque—thanks to the mustache—face. Even now in his forties, he didn't look like a professor, he looked dark and dangerous and a candidate for an old-fashioned rum smuggler on a pirate ship. I was pleased that he recognized me and waved as soon as I came into the restaurant, and pleased to see that he hadn't given up smoking. He was puffing on a nonfilter Pall Mall.

"That's impressive," I said, sitting down across from him. "I was afraid you'd joined the ranks of health freaks or switched to Marlboro Lights."

"Nope," he said. "There are a lot of people out there waiting for me to drop dead. I don't want to disappoint them."

"Who wants you to die?"

"One ex-wife. A couple of old girlfriends. A lot of students I failed. My brother, because he'll inherit my season ticket to the Yankees. They've all been real patient with me. They send me cartons of Pall Malls for my birthday, Christmas, but I haven't even come down with the flu yet. The least I can do is smoke two packs a day."

I hoped I hadn't betrayed a look of relief when

he'd said "ex-wife." We were sitting in The Balcony, an Upper West Side restaurant with polished wood floors, and a purely decorative balcony running the length of the floor above us. It was a sedate, comfortable setting and I remembered having gone there once before, with Buddy. The music was the same as it had been fifteen years before—Chopin piano music. I'd had an argument that evening with Buddy. About my smoking.

"Why did the Viennese close down?" I asked.

"Take a guess. Batty old waitresses, a management that thought it was cute for students to sit chatting or writing papers all afternoon, ordering maybe a total of two cups of coffee. It's an economic miracle they lasted as long as they did."

"That's sad. It was a part of my past." Unexpectedly, I thought of Robert singing "The Good Ship Lollipop," in his woeful style. "But I'm glad you're still teaching. You must be a fully fledged professor by now."

"I'm not glad. Teaching stinks. It's the next worse thing to writing." He laughed. His voice sounded as if it were always on the edge of laughter.

"I just saw your book: *Love—The Ultimate Brainwash.* I haven't read it yet, only glanced at it. It looks fascinating. I can't figure out why I haven't seen it before —I manage a bookstore now in San Francisco. I could have sold a lot of copies for you."

"It sucks, Stacy. Please. Do me a favor and don't mention it. My dipshit publisher didn't put a lot of faith in it and it died a quick, unnatural death on the few shelves it temporarily graced. I have to write all sorts of crap, even now that I'm tenured, and, of course, none of it makes money. It's academic jerking off. So I tried to cash in on the pop psychology market and that was a waste of time too. Now I'm on my sabbatical and I'm supposed to be writing the definitive book on Hofstadter, but I'm cheating and churning out the ultimate money maker: *You Need Never Have Backache Again*—that's going to be the best seller. Do you know how many people in America, Europe, Nicaragua, Papau New Guinea have bad backs? I'll be famous, I'll be rich, I'll be on *Oprah Winfrey*. You're lunching with a future superstar.''

"Do you know anything about backs?"

"Not a thing. But I'm good at making up easy exercises and reading medical textbooks and if I throw in a chapter on the greenhouse effect as applied to the lower spine, I'm golden.''

I laughed. We both laughed. We were sitting in a West Side restaurant, right in the midst of Buddy territory, and I was laughing. I decided I liked the way Sterne laughed at his own jokes.

"You know,''—he leaned across the table conspiratorially—"I hate the food at this place, but I keep coming here because one of the waiters or waitresses never fails to spill something. It's like the old days at the Viennese, but the difference is, these are young people. The odds are they won't fuck up, right? I mean, they're young, coordinated; they're supposed to be trained, they do this day in day out. But, boom, you hear a crash and there's a plate of French fries on the floor or a drink spilled over a customer's dress.

It's great, but it's bankrupting me. Maybe today they won't. Then I won't have to come anymore."

I knew then that I'd split the bill with Sterne. Strangely, I'd gotten used to men paying for meals out in California. When I had first arrived there and gone on dates, I'd always tried to pay my share and always been very firmly rebuffed. And my feminist instincts had subsided quickly on that issue. But he'd made his financial position clear, and I was grateful. I'd forgotten the relief of being on equal terms with a man. I wouldn't have to worry that I owed him anything. Not, I had to admit, that I'd have much objection to a physical relationship with him. He was a physical man, often grabbing my arm as he spoke. And he wasn't doing it, as some do, to be purposefully "touching," a conscious tactic many people used to force immediate intimacy. It was an inherent mannerism, I could tell. He couldn't *not* make physical contact. If I were a man, he'd do the same. But I felt a distinct sexual response to him, his movements, his laugh, and I remembered sitting in his class feeling an overwhelming yearning.

"Would you have dinner with some friends and me tonight? I'd really like it if you could," I asked.

We heard the crash of falling glass and a loud "Shit!" from a waiter near the bar at the back. Sterne put his head in his hands in dismay. Then he looked up, took another drag on his cigarette.

"Dinner. That depends."

"On what?" I asked.

"Who are these friends and what are we going to eat?"

I did my best to explain Eloise and Robert as we ate our lunch. Daniel sat, smoking more than eating, listening, occasionally asking a question.

"You've got a nice transformation here, haven't you?" he commented. "The Prince kisses Sleeping Beauty and she turns from a spoiled, ugly, rich girl into a spoiled, pretty, rich girl."

"No. That's not it. Eloise isn't spoiled. It's hard to explain if you haven't met her, but she's not spoiled. She has the limo and the houses and the servants and the fur—"

"Uh huh, and she's not spoiled? I want to hear this one, Stacy. What doesn't she have? Her own professional pedicurist on twenty-four-hour call?" His hand was on my forearm.

"What she doesn't have is arrogance. And she's not ostentatious. She looks well off, all her possessions are beautiful; but she doesn't reek of money. She's nice. She's always been nice. And somehow defenseless."

"I should be so defenseless." Sterne smiled at me and took my hand in his. "Stacy, I'm already dying to come to dinner and meet these two. We'll forget what the food is—some nouvelle cuisine trash, I'm sure. But right now I'm also dying to take a leak. Save my place, will you?"

His acceptance of my invitation thrilled me; not only because I would see more of him, and so soon, but also because I wasn't exactly looking forward to another night as the lone spectator of Robert and Eloise's profound happiness. I was beginning to feel, when I was around the two of them, like the last unadopted child in an orphanage. Shirley Temple waiting for the perfect parents. And my one-on-one meetings with Robert were beginning to affect me. I had caught myself wondering more than once what would have happened if I had met him before Eloise came on the scene. A dangerous thought. I was pleased to have Daniel Sterne spring back into my life at this precise moment.

When he returned, I was thrown off balance by his silence. He sat back in his chair, smoking, but didn't speak. I didn't know what was supposed to happen next; whether I was supposed to ask a question or whether we were supposed to sit in companionable silence for a while. As the silence continued, my foot began to bob up and down. Luckily it was under the table. If I could tell him a story, I thought, a story like the one Robert told me about the hamster, anything to get his attention, to make an impact. I began to panic, the whole scene was too reminiscent of our last meeting and I didn't want it to be like that. Yes, he was coming to dinner, but probably just to check out my massively rich friends, see the fairy tale in action.

I stubbed a cigarette out, lit another. And then I found myself telling him about Bobby, everything about our meeting in San Francisco. I didn't stop talking until I'd finished with Bobby's grim tale of the hitchhiker in the box. My motives for choosing that story were so jumbled they could have been run through a food processor. Bobby's blatant lie about being a virgin—that was good for psychological discussion. His choice of that particular story to tell after we'd made love had to be worth ten minutes of talk at least. But the kicker, the real reason I blurted out the anecdote of that night, was a desperate, pathetic desire to let Daniel Sterne know I was fanciable. A twenty-year-old wanted to go to bed with me.

As soon as I had finished, I felt foolish. I wanted to slink away from The Balcony and never see Daniel again. I longed for an erase button, something to cancel out what I'd just said.

"Stacy—" Daniel leaned forward, crossed his arms on the table. "You are some strange lady. Palling around with an heiress and Sapphire Shannon's ex-hubby. Hitting the sack with a boy who is just dying to meet up with three raving psychos." He laughed. "I don't like the idea of leaving you alone, you know. You're the kind of person who opens closet doors and dead bodies fall out. Some taxi driver will feed you a line on the way back to the East Side and you'll believe he's a deposed crown prince planning a revolution. Shit—he probably will be, and you'll be queen of fucking Ruritania before the month's out. So just watch your step before I see you tonight. And plan on brunch here again tomorrow morning. Then we can listen to some more plates crashing and I can fall in love with you and you can leave me to go back to your delirious toy-boy or some other loony tune on the West Coast."

"You certainly have an unorthodox way with women, Professor Sterne."

"Yeah, well." He looked at me, then up at the ceiling. "I guess I better smoke another cigarette."

12

FEBRUARY 1990

Eloise and Robert were talking in the living room when I returned from lunch. I could hear Eloise, as I entered, say: "I think it's a good idea, really I do. At least until I get—" Robert, seeing me, stood up, cutting off the end of Eloise's sentence.

"The prodigal returns. Nice lunch?"

"Yes, thanks."

Eloise raised her eyebrows expectantly and I had an urgent desire to get out of the room. I felt like a teenager back from a date and I found their presence cloying. But I didn't want to be impolite and I could hardly rush out again as soon as I arrived. Robert had already poured me a glass of champagne.

"So what's this good idea I heard you talking about when I came in, Eloise?"

"We'd rather hear about your lunch, Stacy," Robert said.

"Daniel's coming to dinner, Eloise. I hope you meant it when you told me to ask him."

"Of course I did," she said, grabbing Robert's hand. "We won't cross-examine you, Stace. You must have had fun if you invited him. Not gay, I take it?"

"No."

"Married?"

"Not anymore."

"See. I told you not to worry. I can't wait to meet him. I remember hanging around that dingy coffee shop for hours."

"So what's your good idea, Eloise?" I sat down. "Tell me about it."

"Oh, I was just saying to Robert that I'd like to go to graduate school. You know, be a mature student or whatever they call it. Get back into physics. I'm tired of not doing anything day after day."

As if to emphasize Eloise's point, Sarah the maid came in quietly to draw the curtains across the two back windows. Neither Robert nor Eloise acknowledged her presence and she slipped out wordlessly. I looked at Eloise, wearing another one of her perfectly tailored designer suits with Paloma Picasso jewelry and Charles Jourdan heels, and I felt deprived. She looked like a human incarnation of the Trump Tower. I missed the shambolic Eloise, her mismatched socks and her dumpy clothes and her messy hair and her ability to explain physics. I wanted to grab her, haul her into the street and into the back of a taxi and take her to the Columbia quad, sit her down on the steps and talk about what was really happening in our lives.

"What do you mean, you don't do anything? You take care of me, Cat. Doesn't that count?" Robert put his hand on her neck, started to rub it. I took a sip of champagne.

Eloise turned to him. I could see those melting eyes again.

"Looking after you is the most important thing in the world, Robert, you know that. I just thought—"

"You just thought you'd leave me alone every day and forget about me, did you? Now, that's not nice, is it, Stacy?"

"I don't know, Robert. I mean, Eloise was really good at physics. Maybe she could go back. I'm sure she could be a student and a wonderful wife at the same time. Most women work now—it's important for them." I looked at Eloise and smiled encouragement.

"It's important for me that she stay at home," Robert said evenly. "Women need everything now, don't they? They need the whole damn lot. Love's not enough, a home is not enough—they have to fulfill themselves. And it is always at someone's expense. Their children's expense, their husband's expense. It's all so damn unnecessary."

A raw nerve. His mother. Sapphire. I held back rising arguments about equality, respect, women's rights. Robert had been badly burned by two career women; he was allowed to be a little irrational on the subject. And, I was certain, Robert was more important to Eloise than physics was. I didn't like giving up my support for Eloise's fledgling independence, but I didn't want to put any wedge into their happiness. I didn't want to abet them in what might well be their first disagreement.

"You're right, Robert," Eloise glanced over at me, then back at her husband. "Some women *have* to work, of course. Like Stacy. But it would be absurd for

me to pretend I need a job, to take a physics degree
and then find work. I don't need to. And I'd be de-
priving someone who *did* need to. It wouldn't be fair.
Besides, I'm glad you want me at home so much. I
love being at home with you.''

A fairly spurious argument, I thought—the corporate heads of America would have to resign *en masse* if
being rich disqualified you from working—but a good
way to diffuse the tension. Of course Eloise knew
about Robert's past; she would be aware of his vulner-
ability. Having a painful past herself, she must have
empathized with him. I wanted to talk to Eloise about
Sapphire; I wanted to get her alone and have a heart-
to-heart. Not at that moment, though. Her capitula-
tion had sparked off a torrid embrace between the
two, another public display of sizzling affection.

"I think I'll go to my room and take a nap," I said.
"Jet lag." I doubt whether they heard me, they were
so engrossed in their kiss. I trudged up the marble
staircase thanking God for the fortuitous appearance
of Daniel Sterne.

He arrived on time that evening, at eight sharp,
wearing a parka so voluminous he looked for an instant like the Michelin tire man, but once he'd had it
removed by Sarah, he returned to his normal bulky
size. He was wearing dark blue corduroys, a white
shirt, and a lively Liberty print tie. He winked at me as
I greeted him in the hall.

"Nice pad," he said. "Do you think they might like
to adopt a struggling professor? Anyone here got back
problems?"

"Shut up, will you, Daniel?" I took him by the arm and led him into the living room.

Eloise and Robert seemed intent on making Daniel the center of conversation. Robert peppered him with questions about college teaching, asking how the students' values had changed over the years and what qualities he thought were needed in a good professor. Daniel fielded the questions easily. Eloise, sitting beside me on the sofa, nudged me once and whispered, "He's terrific, Stace," and I felt pleased and proud of her seal of approval.

Dinner was, as Daniel had predicted, a concoction of nouvelle cuisine dishes. I could see the disdain on his face when tiny portions of duck arrived, arranged skillfully over the plates, accompanied by a raspberry sauce and a few color coordinated vegetables. He was obviously a steak and potatoes man, but he was making up for his appetite by piling three bread rolls and a mound of butter on his side plate. He hadn't commented on the hellish aspect of the dining room, taken it in his stride. I decided he didn't care much about physical surroundings, would have been entirely uninspired by a country idyll or a Venetian palace. I imagined his apartment was a mess, with books and papers flung far and wide, cigarette butts which looked like they'd been reproducing in ashtrays.

"What is the most difficult part of teaching, Daniel?" Eloise asked.

"Selling myself. The students have to think you're smarter than they are, which is not always the case. And you have to sell them on the subject they're studying, catch their attention and keep it. I'm acting when I get up there and deliver a lecture. They have a preconceived idea of what a good professor sounds like, how he or she delivers the material. I can't walk in and fumble around for words, I have to convince them that what I'm saying is worthwhile and what they're learning is interesting. It's not easy. I have off days when I wish I could give them a spelling test.

"But I had practice. I used to sell encyclopedias door-to-door. Then I moved on to vacuum cleaners. You know what we were trained to do as vacuum cleaner salesmen? Get into somebody's apartment by whatever means possible. The favorite method was to ring the bell and say, 'Western Union,' and when the lady buzzed you in and opened the door, waiting for her telegram, you say, 'I'm terribly sorry—you must have misunderstood—my name is *Wesley* Union and I'm here to sell vacuum cleaners.' "

Robert, Eloise, and I burst out laughing.

"Then," continued Daniel, "we were supposed to take a bag of dirt and dump it all over her rug. She would start to go hysterical, but we would find a plug and vacuum it up and show how well the machine cleaned. Great technique. Better than sitting talking earnestly about little Johnny's education and the value of the encyclopedia. Much more fun. I got a big kick out of it."

"Did you sell a lot of vacuum cleaners?" Eloise asked.

"Sure," he replied.

"I would buy one from you."

"Listen, Eloise, if I had come to *this* house, I'd expect you to buy five hundred."

166

Daniel then switched the topic of conversation from himself to politics. It was deft timing, for he was threatening to monopolize the evening with his anecdotes.

We had all hit the wine pretty hard and raised our voices while talking about world affairs, but it wasn't a contentious evening. The four of us were of the liberal persuasion—any disagreements between us only shadings on the issues. I was beginning to wish I didn't have to leave the next day when Eloise suddenly stood up. I thought she was going to make a toast, but she wasn't. She was going to go to bed, she announced. She wasn't feeling well.

"What's wrong, Cat? Too much talk about nuclear threats or do you think you have the flu? You walked out on us last night too, remember." Robert looked concerned.

"Maybe I do. I'm sorry. This has been wonderful, but I have to go to bed." She was clutching at her chair for support. "I'm so sorry, Stacy. Daniel. I just feel awful."

"Don't apologize on my account." Daniel stood up as well, went over and put his hand on her shoulder. "It was a pleasure meeting you and I appreciate your hospitality. I'm not good at thank-you letters, so I'll do the next best thing. I'll send you a copy of my book, *Love—The Ultimate Brainwash*. If you have to stay in bed, it might give you a few laughs."

"Oh, thank you." Eloise closed her eyes. "That sounds great, just great."

"What a title," Robert chimed in. "I'd like to read that too. Now I better put Eloise to bed and then I'll come down and we'll have some coffee in the living room.''

"I'll come see you tomorrow morning and bring you some soup or something," I told Eloise as Robert ushered her out of the dining room. "I hope you feel better." She mumbled something I couldn't hear and was gone.

"She did almost exactly the same thing last night," I said. "I think she's had too much to drink." Daniel was sitting down again, staring at the untouched sorbet in front of him.

"Mmm." He didn't seem to be paying attention to what I was saying, he was back in his silent mode. I told myself not to panic again.

"That was fun. I haven't had a discussion like that in ages. I don't know why. It just hasn't happened."

"Mmm." He played with the sorbet, cutting it up into little melting slices.

I couldn't stand his quick retreats into himself, couldn't understand them either.

"No offense, but I thought you were embarrassed by that book—why mention it to Eloise?"

"Just for kicks," he replied. "I wonder when the dessert wine is coming. We've had champagne, white wine, red wine, and there's a glass here for what must be dessert wine. But I guess we're not having any dessert wine. Straight to the coffee in the living room. Too bad."

"You greedy pig." I laughed. "You're a real old-fashioned guy when it comes to eating and drinking, aren't you? Come on, let's let them clear up in here and go back to the living room."

We returned to our predinner positions. I was on the sofa, Daniel stood with his back to me, looking into the fire.

"You know it's strange seeing you in these circumstances, outside of a classroom, even after all these years. I'm glad I called you." Daniel didn't turn around or say anything. This was becoming embarrassing. Had I misinterpreted his flirtatious manner at lunch? Was he glad that I'd be leaving the next day? I wondered whether I'd made a fool of myself. An ex-student bugging him was doubtless the last thing he wanted.

"Like I said, I called you because of the book. I mean, it seemed such a coincidence that Robert would have a book by someone who had taught me." I was floundering, trying to make excuses for myself, convey to him if he wanted to renege on our brunch date the next day, he shouldn't feel beholden or guilty. Our meeting could be a coincidence. The last thing I wanted was for him to pity me. Daniel turned around to face me, lit a Pall Mall.

"But Robert didn't know anything about my book, did he?"

"No, I guess not." He was right. Robert hadn't recognized the title; in my tipsy state, I hadn't picked up on that. I felt idiotic. I wasn't sure what Daniel thought I wanted from him, why he was playing this distant scene. The sooner I got back to California, the better. New York City was my nemesis.

Robert swept in and collapsed in a chair by the sofa. I was grateful for his presence.

"Poor Cat," he said. "She's not feeling at all well. She went to sleep as soon as her head hit the pillow."

"My head better hit the pillow soon too," Daniel said. "I should start my trek to the West Side. Thanks for a great evening, Robert." He made a rapid exit toward the hall. Robert and I got up and trailed after him.

"Don't forget to send that book you told Eloise about. We'd both love to see it." Robert was shaking his hand. He was a few inches taller than Daniel. Bobby would have made Daniel look like a dwarf.

"No problem." Daniel hefted himself into the parka. It appeared that he couldn't get away quickly enough. "And Stacy," he turned to me, one arm struggling into the jacket sleeve—"do you have time for that brunch before you go tomorrow? Same place? Around eleven?"

"Sure," I answered, amazed by the reinvitation. I had assumed from his behavior during the last ten minutes that he wanted to cancel.

"Good." His arm shot through the sleeve and his hand appeared on the other side. He zipped the coat up, kissed me on the cheek. "See you then. Night, all." He bustled out the door.

"Interesting man," said Robert as soon as the door had closed. "I bet he's a good teacher."

"He is."

Robert and I went back to the living room, settled back into armchairs.

"We're the early birds *and* the night owls, Stace." The shortened form of my name jolted me; Eloise had been the only one who had ever called me Stace. "Do you want some brandy?"

"No thanks. Have you ever worn a beard, Robert?"

"Whew! Where did that question come from?" He stroked his cheeks with his hands. "Didn't I shave well today?"

"No. It's not that. No designer stubble showing. I was just curious."

"I thought about it. Often. I thought I'd grow a beard to hide my eczema. I had a terrible case of eczema when I was younger. Everyone thought it was acne, which made things even worse. It was very painful. Psychologically speaking, I mean. I tried everything—I won't bore you with the details. In the end, though, one skin specialist told me it was nerves, pure and simple, told me to meditate, do yoga. Very sixties." He laughed. "Although it was the mid-seventies by then. So it was a simple question of mind over matter, eczema matter. I had to learn to control my mind, my thoughts, my nerves. It worked."

"And you think I'm a bundle of nerves?"

"Aren't you?"

I laughed—nervously, I realized.

"Tell me about your father. Why did *he* need protection?"

"No, I don't think I will. It's not the appropriate time, Stace."

His response said that I had pried into his life quite enough as it was. I felt chastened.

"Maybe it's time for me to go to bed."

"Ah ha. Beauty sleep? Your brunch with lover boy tomorrow?"

171

"You could say that." I stood up and yawned on purpose, trying to hide a rising blush. "But listen, I've been meaning to ask you. I saw Daniel's book on brainwashing in your study this morning. That's why I called him actually. Didn't you know it was there?"

"Is it really? How strange. No, I'd never heard of it before. I wonder how it got there. Life is full of bizarre coincidences, isn't it? Now you better get along and go to bed. Beauty sleep, right? Makeup. Hairdos. Clothes. I don't know how you women have the time for it all."

"It's supposed to be for the benefit of you men, you know. Night, Robert."

"Sweet, sexy dreams, Stace."

Eloise woke me the next morning wearing another intricately designed silk kimono. She was holding two mugs of coffee.

"Room service," she announced. "For once I'm up early."

"How are you feeling?"

"Not great," she answered, placing the coffee on the bedside table and sitting down beside me.

"Do you think you have the flu?"

"No. I *know* I have a hangover. I drank too much last night, that's all."

"It's hard *not* to drink around here." I sat up and had a sip of coffee. "But do you think it's a good idea to drink so much if it has that effect on you? That was the second night running you crashed out. I mean, you never drank at Barnard—apart from that one day with John. It can't be good for you with the diabetes and everything."

"Oh please, don't go puritanical on me, Stace. There are thousands of things that aren't good for me. I can handle it, really. Believe it or not, I'm a fully grown woman."

The anger I remembered from moments at Barnard flashed out.

"Okay, okay. Sorry. Maybe I don't like the idea that we've *both* grown up. Anyway, I'm glad you woke me up. I feel like I've hardly seen you this weekend and I have to fly off this afternoon. We haven't had a chance to talk."

"I know. That's why I *did* wake you. I need to talk. You're the only person I can talk to about this."

"About what?"

She had relapsed into her old habit and was trying to find a piece of her hair long enough to stuff in her mouth. Unable to, she tossed her head back, sat down on the bed, and crossed her legs underneath her. We could have been two girls the night after a pajama party.

"Well, about sex, actually." A self-conscious smile appeared. "This is going to sound pathetic, but I have to know."

Was she going to ask me whether I *had* been to bed with Bobby? No. I was being paranoid. This wasn't about Bobby. This was about Eloise.

"Come on, Eloise. Cut to the chase, as they say. This sounds riveting."

"All right. I just need to know. How do you know if you're good in bed?"

173

My immediate reflex in a tricky situation sprung into action. I lit a cigarette.

"Let me think about that for a second," I said. How did a woman know if she was "good" in bed? One answer could be that if you didn't know you were, then you weren't. But that would be a glib response and an unfair one for Eloise. I wasn't even sure whether it was a true one. We could have a philosophical discussion as to what "good" in bed actually meant.

"Stacy?"

"I'm thinking, Eloise. Hold on."

A man could tell you that you were good in bed; that was one way of finding out. But men's notions of what was good might differ wildly from individual to individual. The term was meaningless, I was about to say. Then I thought of sexual encounters I'd had in San Francisco, nights I'd been lying underneath a man thinking: He doesn't have a clue. This man is lousy. What had made them "not good"?

"This might sound strange, but I think that if you *enjoy* making love, if it's not a duty, but a treat, a pleasure—then you're good in bed."

"I enjoy it." Eloise was concentrating on the bedclothes, her eyes cast down as she plucked at the sheet with nervous fingers. "But I don't think I'm good at it. I don't know, I'm not—I'm not *abandoned* enough. That's the word."

"You seem pretty abandoned to me. I've seen some heavy-duty making out with Robert, Eloise." I laughed.

"That's just kissing. It's not the same. That's easy.

174

Sex is different. I'm not sexy. I don't do anything *different* in bed. I'm not as good as—I mean, I'm useless. You know, sometimes I don't even know if Robert has —I mean I don't think he always—''

"Hold on a second. As good as who? It's Sapphire, isn't it? You're comparing yourself to Sapphire?"

"You know about her?"

I nodded.

"Well, what am I supposed to do? She was *wild*, Stace. Robert—she and Robert—used to spend whole *days* together in bed. I wouldn't know what to do. I don't know what to do."

"They were probably stoned out of their minds. But why did Robert tell you all this? It's not exactly fair to you to set up some kind of competition with Sapphire. Besides, I didn't think he liked her. I was under the impression he disliked her, actually."

"He doesn't like her. But he has told me about their relationship. And he told me that he had to be honest with me, he never wanted to lie to me. So he *had* to tell me how dynamic she was in bed. It was the big part of their marriage, the most important thing."

Eloise started to cry, and I thought how vicious honesty can be. Robert wouldn't know the effect his truthfulness had on Eloise; he was a man, and men were, on the whole, dumb when it came to female emotions.

"Don't cry, Eloise. Listen to me for a second. You've been married for what? Three months? You knew him for six months before that. These things take time, sex gets better the more you know some-one, the more used to each other you get. It's better to start slow and build up than to burn out the passion quickly. Sapphire's not a threat to you. Robert loves you. Just give it time.''

Eloise sniffed, wiped away her tears with the palms of her hands, then reached for the coffee mug.

''I guess you're right. And it is improving. A few drinks can relax me now, and I'm less inhibited.''

''You don't need to drink to relax, you just have to have a little more self-confidence.''

''Do you know how difficult it is to relax when you know you're *supposed* to relax? Robert keeps telling me how tense I am. I don't suppose Sapphire was ever tense about anything.''

''Forget Sapphire, will you? She's a bitch. She left her husband and child, she ran off so that she could go on an endless ego trip. She's not worth your tears, Eloise. Forget her.''

I felt helpless, for I couldn't think of a way to give her more confidence about her lovemaking. The subject was a minefield of fear and insecurity. How was I to know what she did right or wrong in bed? How could I reassure her? Tell her to find her first lover John and get a good reference from him? All I could do was change the subject.

''The sex thing will be fine. Stop worrying and give it some time. Really. But you've got to help *me* now, Eloise. I've got brunch with Daniel and I'm counting on you to lend me something to wear. Knockout stuff.''

Eloise clapped her hands together like a child in front of a birthday cake and I was relieved.

''This is going to be fun. It's finally my turn to play

the older sister. Come on. Let's go to my dressing room."

We acted like schoolgirls for the next two hours, ransacking her many cupboards, trying things on, discarding them, trying them on again, giggling the whole time. It was amazing, after her total disinterest in college, that she'd managed to learn so much about clothes; but she had, and by the time I left the house I was looking casual but chic. She had stage-managed my appearance perfectly. We had had a wonderful female morning together, a women's equivalent, I supposed, of a boys' night out.

It was 11 A.M. when I walked into The Balcony. I wasn't tired. I hadn't had any alcohol. There was no excuse for falling in love. I saw Sterne before he saw me; he was sitting, his elbows on the table, a Pall Mall hanging from his mouth, reading a section of the Sunday *Times*. He had a bright blue sweater on, the same shade of blue I had painted my first bicycle. I wanted to walk out of the restaurant and fly out of New York and get away from him as fast as possible. At the same time I wanted, in the words of a country song I'd heard that night before Eloise's wedding, to be glue on his shoe. I was in big trouble. More trouble than I'd been in with Buddy, because this time I knew what trouble with love was all about. It was the color of his sweater, I convinced myself. I was confusing my old love for my bicycle with a new love for a man. He looked up, saw me, raised his hand and waved.

"Never put your hand above your shoulder, Professor Sterne," I said as I sat down. "It's dangerous."

"Only in crowds, Stacy. You should remember that." He cleared the papers off the table and dropped them with a thump on the floor. I lit a cigarette and ordered a Screwdriver. I didn't feel half as composed as I knew Eloise's clothes made me look.

"So. What a swell party that was. Mr. And Mrs. Chappell make an interesting study."

"What did you think of them? Did you like them?"

"I liked her. I have to admit it, you were right; she's not spoiled, even with all the trinkets and the serfs around."

"And Robert?"

Daniel pulled his chair closer to the table, swept his hands through his hair.

"Robert. I don't know. I have some problems with Robert."

"Why?"

"There's something you should know about me, Stacy. I play poker. I'm a good player. To be a good player you have to study people's faces. Try and look into their characters. The way I do it is this—I look at their faces and I pretend they're on a jury and I'm an innocent guy standing accused of manslaughter. Your friend Eloise—now there's an open, no-holds-barred face. It's sweet, a little confused, and eager to please. She never wants to read out a guilty verdict. I'm safe with her.

"You—well, you like to think you're in control, but your emotions dance all over your face while you're unaware of it. They sweep on and off like tangoing hurricanes. Your face is very twitchy, very expressive. You'd nail me to the wall if I were guilty, but I'd want you in my jury because you would bend over backward to be fair. You'd listen. If you had one tiny doubt you'd hold out against all the others. You believe in something—what it is, I'm not sure. But I can see it in your face.

"Now Robert's face is deceptive. The eyes are twinkling, but it's an angry twinkle if you look closely. That weirdo right eye of his is the one to watch. It's the one that shows the anger. He smiles and laughs, but it's a hard smile, a pissed-off laugh underneath. The guy would vote guilty for the fun of it. And I'll tell you something else. He doesn't love his wife."

"You're wrong there, Daniel. Dead wrong. I've seen them together enough now. Maybe he's been bruised a bit, but he's not hard or nasty. You're reading him wrong. He's a sensitive man. You should hear him sing."

"Maybe." Daniel looked up at the ceiling as he used to do in the classroom—a quirky habit of his I'd forgotten. I always wondered whether he was looking for signs of cracks or searching the heavens for inspiration. Often he would talk to the ceiling as if it were a student who had asked a difficult question.

"Maybe I'm just jealous of all that cash he has access to. Who wouldn't want to play Aristotle Onassis for a few years? Or maybe I'm jealous of anybody who has slept with Sapphire Shannon. Shit, I admit to being jealous of that."

"What's so great about Sapphire Shannon? I'm really getting sick of hearing about how amazing she is. Is every man in the world attracted to her?"

Dumb move, I told myself. Never trash a woman in front of a man.

"Stacy—come on, she's hot. Have you ever seen her onstage?"

"I don't go to pop concerts. I think pop music is trivial."

"Oh, I like the dismissive tone. It's cute." Daniel laughed, pushed his leg against mine under the table. The waitress appeared at our side, and he ordered coffee and scrambled eggs. I wasn't hungry. I had already smoked too many cigarettes that morning to contemplate food.

"Anyway, I think we've exhausted the Chappells as a subject of conversation. You know I still have that story you wrote in my class. I reread it this morning. It still works. It's good."

"Thanks."

The waitress returned and put a coffee cup in front of him. I could sense that Daniel was hoping she might spill something, but she managed to pour successfully. He smiled up at her and said, "Thank you." I couldn't wait for her to move away. When she did, I was glad to see that his eyes hadn't followed her retreating bum.

"So—" I started, then stopped. I didn't know what to say. I was dreading one of those silences of his and terrified I'd tell another silly story to fill the vacuum. "So—" I lit a cigarette. "Nobody has spilled anything or dropped any dishes yet." I wished I could evaporate, join the steam rising from his coffee cup.

"Nope." He grabbed my arm and squeezed it. "This may be our lucky day. We may never have to eat here again. The eggs are bound to be a mistake. I think McDonald's could do better.''

We both laughed. I tried to force my muscles to relax.

"Still. It should be better than that shit last night." He pushed his coffee away. "And I like the Chopin, even if it does get repetitive."

He started to talk about his favorite composer— Bruckner—but I wasn't concentrating on his words. I had fallen in love when I'd walked in that morning with the same rush of feeling I'd had on my first glimpse of Buddy. That had to make me suspicious of myself. And now I was experiencing all those desperate feelings I thought I'd never have again.

Every time he touched me, I felt an intense physical reaction that translated into pure pleasure. When he removed his hand, I felt bereft. I was like a lovesick adolescent again, waiting on a man's whims. I hadn't progressed in California, I'd merely been treading water, waiting for another killer shark. I studied Daniel Sterne carefully, trying to keep my head above my heart, trying to pretend that *he* was a juror at *my* trial. He caught me staring and chuckled.

"I know," he said. "It's scary, isn't it?"

"What's scary?" I looked away quickly. "I would never call Bruckner scary."

"Come off it, turkey. Not Bruckner. You and me."

I didn't say anything and Daniel smiled.

"Okay, keep your mouth shut if you want to. I figure we've both got enough mileage on us to be wary. But I want to tell you something. This isn't out of the blue for me. I was attracted to you when you were in

181

my class. Very attracted. And in case you're wondering, that's unusual. In fact, I've never felt that way before or since with a student. Still, it's not a good idea to get involved with a student. A very dubious proposition. So I steered clear. That morning at the Viennese, I almost blew it, asked you out, but I knew it wouldn't have been smart.

"I kept tabs on you, though, Stacy. I found out you got married to some preppie lawyer and I found out later that you and he divorced. I have my spies. I also knew you had moved to California.

"I wasn't obsessed with you. I've been married and divorced myself meanwhile. I've had enough romantic liaisons to keep me busy." He shrugged. "But I was always interested. When you called yesterday, I cancelled my date for lunch. Now, I figure, you were also interested in me."

"How do you figure that?" I was trying to keep my face from being as expressive as he'd said it was.

"You wouldn't have worked so fucking hard in my course otherwise."

"Did I earn my A, fair and square?"

"You earned your A, Stacy." He leaned across the table to kiss me and knocked my Screwdriver glass on to the floor, breaking it.

"You should apply for a job in this place." I laughed. His kiss had tasted of smoke and coffee, the flavors I was already addicted to.

"So." Our waitress came to sweep up the glass. Daniel apologized and ordered another cup of coffee. "Since we're about to conduct a coast-to-coast romance, and we don't have much time, let's telescope a few dinners into a cup of coffee. I want you to tell me your life story right away. Everything you like, hate, envy, dream about. But leave out anything to do with ex-boyfriends or husbands. Toy-boy Bobby was bad enough. I don't need to know that stuff, okay?"

"Okay," I said. "I like your sweater."

"That's all right for starters," Daniel Sterne replied, lighting a Pall Mall.

13
FEBRUARY 1990

Romance was a medieval mountebank performing flips and somersaults in my heart.

I hadn't allowed myself to fall in love with anyone after my divorce, had nipped potentially serious boyfriends in the bud—an apposite phrase, given my history—and been glad to do so. But then I hadn't been particularly tempted. I'd been able to find fault within minutes of meeting a man. After hours of talking to Daniel Sterne, I knew I couldn't dismiss him, nor did I want to. I was ready to gamble with my emotions again, but this time I hoped that I wasn't going to lose. The distance between us would help, I decided. Daniel and I could get to know each other gradually. Write letters, talk on the phone. And the fact that we hadn't slept together yet was a bonus as well. I could keep the passion at bay, make sure I knew what I was doing. I was going to be practical and rational this time.

I paid off the cabdriver outside Eloise's front door, rang the bell, and began to laugh. I could make a living out of kidding myself. All I wanted at that moment was to stay in New York, climb into Daniel's bed, and not leave it for days. I would have to get used to being out of control again. As long as I kept those feelings hidden, though, I'd be safe. The most aggravating aspect of life, I'd found in my thirties, was that all the old how-to-get-a-man clichés you're force-fed as a girl are true. The less interest you show, the more attention he pays. He may want to be sure of your love, but he doesn't want to be absolutely sure. If you make too many demands on his affections, as I had with Buddy, he feels cornered. I couldn't believe that such a simple formula worked, especially in the 1990s, but I had seen it in action with friends as well as myself so many times it seemed a scientific certainty. My mother used to call it playing hard to get.

It was perfectly permissible for Daniel to tell me he had been attracted to me in class, had kept tabs on me. But what if I had said the same to him first? Women had bumped up against the double standard and all its ramifications in the seventies and eighties, but they had succeeded only in giving it a nudge. They hadn't dislodged it. Some of them even liked it.

During the taxi ride, I had contemplated postponing my flight, calling in sick to work, telephoning Daniel to tell him I was still in town. But I couldn't. I wouldn't allow myself.

After Sarah let me in, I took a quick look around the house before I found Eloise in the small sitting room. The Eloise I found was a wreck. Her face looked like a water slide with blobs of mascara taking a ride for free. She was hunched up, huddled in her chair, sobbing; sobbing when she drew breath, sobbing when she let it out.

"Eloise, Eloise. God what's happened?"

Had Robert died? Had muggers come into the house, raped her, knifed him? I had slid back effortlessly into a New York City frame of mind.

"I can't do it," was all she managed to get out.

"Eloise, Jesus. You can't do what?" I went to her, knelt beside her chair.

"I just can't."

"Can't what?" I shook her shoulders. "Can't *what*?"

Her reply was to pick up a book on the table beside her and throw it across the room. When it landed, I saw the cover—*Parachutes & Kisses*—an Erica Jong novel.

"You can't read Erica Jong? Eloise? I don't get it. What's so awful about that? I can't read Proust. So what?"

She was trying to stop crying now, but it took a few minutes before the sobs were under control. I waited, mystified.

"Robert gave it to me this morning. A present."

"And? Eloise, come on. Your husband gives you a book and you have a nervous breakdown. Can you please try to make sense?"

"Sex. It's all about sex. *Another* uninhibited woman. Why? Why is sex so important? Why did he have to give me that book? He's trying to tell me something, he's telling me how unsatisfying I am. I know it. Stace —what am I going to do? I'm going to lose him. I know I am. I love him so much and I'm going to lose him. I need a drink. Can you get me a drink, please?

There's a pitcher of Bloody Marys in the corner there. Can you pour me one?"

"Of course." I did, pouring one for myself as well. I handed hers to her, sat down again at her feet.

"Eloise, listen to me. First of all, sex is *not* the most important thing in the world—"

"Oh, sure. Sure. Tell me about it. It's everywhere, Stacy. All the movies, TV shows, books, they're all full of people making wild and passionate love to each other all the time. If it's not the most important thing in the world, why is everyone so obsessed with it? Answer me that."

"Maybe it's so wonderful and wild in films and books and TV because it's not in real life. Have you thought of that? Maybe the whole world likes to fantasize."

"Nice try, Stace." Eloise shook her head, bit her lip.

"Well, I think I may be right about that. But we'll forget it for the moment, okay? Sex is not the most important thing in the world because love is the most important thing in the world. Look—would you still love Robert if he were paralysed from the waist down?"

"Of course I would." She sounded offended.

"Right. And he'd still love you if for some reason you couldn't have sex. Eloise—you're getting hysterical. You're getting back into your old doomed, negative ways of thinking. Now you've found happiness, you think you're going to lose it. A shrink wouldn't even deserve to be paid to say that your mother's death and your father's treatment of you have warped your outlook on love. It's so damn obvious.

"Robert gives you a book that has sex scenes in it and you draw the absolute worst conclusion. Maybe he thought it was funny. Erica Jong can be funny, she can be enlightening about male-female relationships. It's not just *sex*. You're seeing everything that way because it's a sensitive subject at the moment. You have to calm down."

"Oh Stace—" Eloise sniffled, attempted a smile. "I'm so glad you're here. I guess I did overreact. I was doing fine at first, reading that book. I even liked it. But then I got up to go to the bathroom and there was this . . ." The tears started to come again. "This magazine on the floor. I don't know, I guess one of the maids left it there. If I knew which one, I'd fire her." She pulled out a copy of *Vanity Fair* which had been scrunched down into the side of the chair and handed it to me. Cover photo—Sapphire Shannon. All six feet of her leaning against a palm tree with her blue jeans, an off-the-shoulder bodice-hugging sky-blue top, and mirrored sunglasses. Cool, sexy, stunning. I looked back at Eloise's ravaged face.

"See? I saw this and I tried to forget about it, go back to the book, but then I came across another heavy sex scene and I lost it." She finished her Bloody Mary in one gulp, held the glass out to me, and I helped us both to a second round. Sapphire's mirrored eyes stared up at us as we drank.

"Daniel thinks she's hot," I said. "The bitch. She's enough to turn a woman into a misogynist."

"I wish she'd disappear," Eloise groaned.

"Not much chance of that. Robert doesn't love her, though, Eloise. Hold on to that."

"I'll try. But it's hard. I keep finding these magazines around with articles about her. Maybe our butler has a crush on her. But I can't exactly ban magazines from the house, now, can I?"

"No. You're above all that. Don't think about her. She's irrelevant. If you keep thinking about her, you'll get even more uptight. From what I've heard, her voice isn't that great anyway. She's certainly not an Elisabeth Schwarzkopf or Joan Sutherland."

The words sounded lame as I looked at those legs, that face, that smile which lay on the floor like an evil spirit. I decided to gratify a childish desire.

"Stace!" Eloise yelped, then laughed through her tears. I had found a pen in my bag and was busy drawing a mustache on Sapphire Shannon. I added a goatee. I put a pitchfork in her hand and horns on her head. She looked like an albino devil in drag. Eloise went into a fit of giggles, almost as manic as the fit of crying had been. I handed the pen to her. It was her turn to improvize on Sapphire.

"What's so funny, you two?" Robert asked as he walked into the room. "I could hear you from the stairs."

Immediately, Eloise turned the magazine over, and I stood up, blocking Robert's view.

"I was just showing Eloise a hysterical review of an opera. They've done an all male version of *The Barber of Seville* and the critics have gone for the throat."

I took the *Vanity Fair* away from Eloise and was able to shove it into my capacious purse.

189

"Cat—your face. What's happened?" he asked, staring at her.

"We were laughing so hard, we were crying. God!" I looked at my watch. "I've got to get packed. Will you come up and help me, Eloise?"

"Sure. Right away. I'll fix my face while I'm up there." Eloise stood up, anxious as I was to get away from the scene of the crime.

"Well, come down again quickly, girls." Robert kissed Eloise on her mascara-speckled cheek. "I've hardly seen you today, Cat. You've been hiding. Shall I tell Edwin to get the limo ready, Stace?"

"Yes, please," I said, hustling to get Eloise and me out of the room as quickly as possible.

Upstairs, we had another laugh about the *Vanity Fair* cover—the naughty girls who had gotten away with something behind the teacher's back. Robert may well have laughed along with us at Sapphire's defaced picture, but I didn't want to take the chance, nor, I could tell, did Eloise. I threw the magazine into the bottom of my suitcase and finished packing while I told Eloise about my brunch with Daniel, all the emotions he had reawakened in me and all the fears.

"I think it's wonderful. Love *is* the most important thing in life, Stace. You were right downstairs. I'm sorry I got so out of control. Thank God you were here. It won't happen again, though."

"Promise?"

"I promise. He *does* love me, I know he does. And things will get better—I mean, physically—you're right. I just have to relax. And I will. I promise. Now you promise me you'll keep that outfit of mine. It suits you better than it does me. And it will remind you of Daniel when you're back in San Francisco.''

"Eloise—"

"Stace—I hate arguments, remember?"

"Yes, I remember."

"Good." Eloise was sitting on the chaise longue, winding her hair around her forefinger. "Listen, I want to say something before you go. You know me so well—you know how to get me out of my moods, you know what to say and do to calm me down, you know how I sometimes lose belief in myself. I know you too. And I know you've got a fierce pride. Whatever happened between you and Buddy has scarred you. You'll be looking for ways to get out of this relationship with Daniel, I can tell already. You won't want to allow him to get to you. You'd prefer to keep it the way it was at Barnard—a crush, a dream. Distant. That way your pride can't get hurt. But you *have* to take the chance, Stace. We were good spectators in college days, but we have to be players now. We have to get involved. And we've never been the types to get involved in politics, we've been the crazy people who get involved with love. Don't back off.

"That's my speech for the day. Now I'll get myself together and come see you off. No tearful farewells this time, though. I think I've cried myself out."

I gave Eloise a long, warm hug before I got into the limo. Our friendship was back on track—we were as close as we'd been at Barnard, and I didn't want time, money, or distance to separate us again. I'd missed her. We had shared a room and our lives for three years, had been closer emotionally than most married couples. If I were in trouble, anytime or anywhere, I knew Eloise would come bail me out. And I'd do the same for her.

Robert enfolded me in his bear hug and I whispered: "Take care of her," to him. We all needed looking after, I reflected as Edwin closed the car door. Though few of us wanted to admit to that.

Daniel called me the evening after my return to San Francisco, and we had a funny, relaxed conversation that lasted an hour. As soon as I hung up, all I could think of was when I could see him again. Neither of us could afford many transcontinental flights or marathon long-distance phone calls. And despite Eloise's command to "get involved" I was still intent on remaining somewhat distant emotionally, at least pretending to have some control. I wasn't going to beg him to come out and visit, I wasn't going to alter any aspect of my life. If I spent most of my time daydreaming about him, well, that was entirely my own business. I dug out an old family album from my closet and found a picture I had taken of my blue bicycle, the one that matched Daniel's sweater. I carefully cut it out and propped it up against my bedside lamp. Desperate people do unbelievable things.

The following afternoon I was teased mercilessly at the store when three dozen flowers were delivered to me. As I signed for them, I found myself thinking that this was not something I would have expected from Daniel. Such an obvious romantic gesture seemed out of character, but I couldn't have been more pleased. While my coworkers gathered around oohing and aahing, I wondered how I should respond. At least I would have a legitimate excuse to call him that night.

Then, peeling away the protective paper, I saw what I should have expected anyway. White lilies. Eloise, not Daniel, was responsible. The note attached read: "Do you need an air conditioner?" and I would have laughed if I hadn't been so disappointed. The rising joy I felt when those flowers had been delivered reminded me that I was falling into the same behavior pattern I had been in with Buddy, expecting life to be full of romance. The fact that Daniel hadn't sent the flowers now irritated me, even though I hadn't originally expected it. I was a mess, I would always be a mess when it came to relationships with men. I would always want more than anyone was capable of giving.

I carted the flowers home that night and arranged them around the apartment. They struck me, when I stood back and looked at them, as funereal and I almost tossed all thirty-six of them into the trash can. Instead, I put on a Beethoven tape, sat down and concentrated on the music. Before I went to bed, I wrote a one-line note to Eloise: "What I need is an air-conditioned mind. Thanks."

The word "obsession" had become a verb in the California culture, and I was trapped in it. I was "obsessing" over the fact that Daniel didn't call me the rest of that week. I obsessed when, the times I tried to call him, there was no answer. I obsessed about my own obsession. *Love—The Ultimate Brainwash* was not listed in *Books in Print,* so I put out calls to all the secondhand-book people I knew, desperate to get a copy as quickly as possible, and thoroughly angry at myself for not borrowing it from Robert's shelf.

I couldn't eat. I smoked nonstop. Work was just another place to sit and freak out. I knew what I needed was to write off the relationship until I had managed to get my feelings back in control. Much as I had enjoyed that rush of passion springing up again, I would have to wait until it receded before I could deal with Daniel on a sane basis. Still, I kept that picture of the bicycle by my bed.

On Fridays I liked to leave my Honda Prelude at home and take the boat across the bay to and from work. Even in bad weather I enjoyed that trip, loved to look at the Golden Gate Bridge from the water and stare at the now empty Alcatraz in its inescapable glory. Even though I had lived in San Francisco for over ten years, I still felt like a tourist. Walking from the dock back to my apartment was the only exercise I got all week and if I stopped myself from lighting a cigarette for the entire journey I felt absurdly healthy when I arrived home.

The Friday after my weekend in New York, I chain-smoked on the walk back. I had just paused to light another when I saw Daniel Sterne sitting outside my apartment, in his blue sweater. Neither of us spoke as I opened the door. We didn't speak once I had closed it either. He hugged me, held me close for a long time before he began to kiss me, and we continued to kiss while we undressed each other. There was a brief interruption to our activities as he fished a packet of condoms out of his trousers, but we didn't move to my bedroom. We made love on the living-room rug. It was as intense and as passionate as any sex I'd ever had, but there was a different element to it as well, something I had never experienced before. It was like the first time I had gone up in an airplane and seen the clouds from above. The clouds were still the clouds I'd looked up at all my life, but they seemed alive and enticing; they looked like they were beckoning me to open the plane window, jump in, and play. Which is exactly what Daniel and I were doing. Some serious playing.

After we had finished, I put on a pair of jeans and a T-shirt, poured two glasses of white wine, and brought them into the living room. Daniel was sitting on the floor, his back propped against the sofa. He was dressed in a pair of white Levi's and a blue striped cotton shirt, the sleeves rolled up above his elbow. The blue sweater was lying on the floor where I had dropped it. I sat down beside him and handed him the wine.

"Why do you think people get dressed after they've just undressed?" I asked.

"Because they're looking forward to getting undressed again, I suppose." Daniel reached over and brushed my hair back from my face. "I don't know about you, but I like taking clothes off. I like the whole process. I like your apartment too."

"Why? I didn't think you noticed your surroundings. What do you like about it?"

"I don't notice surroundings, I notice atmospheres. This is cozy without being suffocating and it's feminine without being cutesy. Although I think you've overdone it with the lilies."

I was about to tell them that they were from Eloise, but thought better of it.

I looked around, trying to see my own place through Daniel's eyes. I'd kept the walls white, and polished the hardwood floors. I'd bought the furniture gradually, piece by piece. All of it secondhand, but in reasonable shape. Then I'd had the large sofa and two armchairs covered in an apricot-colored cotton material. The place had a well-worn air. My bookshelves sagged comfortably in the middle, like a much used double bed.

Daniel stood up and walked over to the upright piano I'd inherited from my grandfather. I had never been sure where to put it and settled finally for the corner of the living room. Its presence reminded me that I couldn't play at the same time as reminding me of my grandfather, my favorite relative, so I had ambivalent feelings about it.

"Do you play?" he asked. "No, you don't," he interrupted as I was about to answer. "You told me at brunch. This is your grandfather's, right?"

"Right."

I was glad to see that he didn't bash out "Chopsticks" as some men in my life had done.

"How long were you prepared to wait outside my door?" I asked him.

"Who knows?" He lit a cigarette. "I'm in love with you. I might have waited all night. On the other hand, I was getting pretty bored."

My phone rang, but I didn't answer, let the machine answer for me. After the beep I heard a male voice say: "Stacy, this is Bobby. I'm in town again this weekend. I'd like to talk to you. Really. I'd appreciate it if you would call me. My number is 423-9764. Thank you.''

Daniel arched his eyebrows and shook his head. I laughed. He walked over to me, stood above me, and began to tug my T-shirt out of my jeans. Thank *you*, Bobby, I thought.

This time we ended up in my bedroom, and I didn't bother to get dressed again afterward. We sat up in bed smoking and laughing, Daniel with his arm around my shoulders. I felt at home with him, relaxed and happy. There were, I knew, perfect people for certain activities. I had once gone ice skating with a man who came into his own soul on the ice. Anyplace else, in restaurants, movie theaters, bed, he was his normal nice, timid self. But on the ice he was the platonic ideal of a skater. He was entirely at ease, un-self-conscious, powerful.

Other people could come into their own in the most unlikely of places—buying groceries at an out-door market, watching television on a Sunday evening, sitting in a diner over a two-dollar-special breakfast. I had tended to compartmentalize people I knew, male and female, into the activities that most suited them. I'd go to the movies with one, go to concerts with another, drink in a bar with someone else. They rarely overlapped.

As far as I was concerned, Daniel came into his own whenever he opened his mouth or he touched me. He wasn't conventionally good-looking—he was too short for that and too stocky; physically he was shaped like an inverted triangle, with large, broad shoulders and a barrel chest that tapered down to surprisingly thin hips and legs. But he was comfortable, funny, and curious. He liked to ask questions, and unlike most men I'd known, liked to listen to the answers. Just as I was about to ask him what he wanted for dinner, he squeezed my shoulder hard.

"Colorless green ideas sleep furiously," he said.

"What?"

"Just a little Chomsky. Livens up any evening."

"You're hopeless," I sighed.

"No. I'm hungry."

I phoned up a home-delivery pizza service. There was no food in my fridge and no way I was going to let him out of my bedroom.

Daniel Sterne had grown up in Brooklyn in an apartment building composed of people who, he said, talked about the holocaust day in, day out.

"We're talking about an eight-year-old kid here, stopped in the hall, on the stairs and forced to listen to these gruesome stories. I know it's my heritage, I know as a Jew I have to pay attention. But I'm eight years old. I want to go out and play stickball. I can hear other kids my age out on the street, whacking the ball around while some little old lady is feeding me details of gas chambers. It's nineteen fifty-two, the war is over, and I feel like telling everyone, 'Hey, *I* can't change history. I'm a Jew, I'm proud to be a Jew, but leave off.'

"My parents, all their friends, they saw themselves as victims. Of course they were victims. I'm aware of that, I was aware of that then. But I didn't like identifying with victims. I didn't want to be one myself. So I picked fights with kids when I knew I could win and was a general pain in the ass. A streetwise pain in the ass, though. I hung out with the toughest guys around. Learned how to gamble, how to shoot pool. At the same time I studied like crazy. Furtively. I spent my days hitting the streets and my nights hitting the books. That way I didn't look like a wimp. Nobody thought I was a candy-assed bookworm, they thought I was naturally smart. They thought I was pulling one over on the teachers because I got great grades without studying. They didn't see the bags under my eyes. It was a nice trick.''

''A con man,'' I said.

''Sure. Aren't we all, in one way or another?''

''Maybe.''

I was so entranced by this man that I was beginning to panic. He had come for the weekend and it was already verging on Saturday. How many hours did that leave us? I veered back to my insane college fantasies about Caribbean islands; rum drinks, palm trees, sex on a moonlit beach as he continued telling me about his college career. You've lost it, Stacy, I cautioned myself as I studied my pepperoni pizza. You're way out on a limb with this guy. Back off.

After we had finished eating, I went into my living room and put *The Marriage of Figaro* on the CD player, hoping it would help to reel my emotions back in. Mozart and Da Ponte knew about romance. Count Almaviva had once been madly in love with the Countess, but he was soon intent on exercising his droit de seigneur with his wife's maid. Passion never lasts. Love is fickle. I made a mental note to reread

Anna Kerenina. And then I skipped back to the bedroom with a second bottle of wine.

"So tell me about *Love—The Ultimate Brainwash*."

We were sitting cross-legged on the bed, facing each other, both dressed in shirts only, an ashtray and the remains of the pizza between us. Another pajama party, but a male-female one this time.

"Well, I've always been interested in brainwashing, as you know. Brainwashing and propaganda techniques. I'd read all the studies on Korea, China, Vietnam, the classic methods, the innovations. What happens to prisoners of war. What happens on Madison Avenue, advertising. How you go about changing someone's mind, or persuading a person to do exactly what you want that person to do. Manipulation, if you will.

"Did you know that the first printed use in any language of the term 'brainwashing' was in September nineteen fifty? A man named Edward Hunter wrote an article for the *Miami News* entitled: 'Brainwashing Tactics Force Chinese into Ranks of Communist Party.' Hunter was a CIA propaganda operator who worked undercover as a journalist. He made up the term 'brainwashing' from the Chinese *hsi-nao*, meaning, literally, 'to cleanse the mind.'

"By the end of the Korean War, seventy percent of the seven thousand one hundred ninety U.S. prisoners held in China had either made confessions or signed petitions calling for an end to the American war effort in Asia. Fifteen percent collaborated fully with the Chinese, and only five percent steadfastly refused.

"So the CIA have got to start wondering what the hell is going on there and how they can get a slice of the action. How can they alter basic beliefs and behavioral patterns? How can they capture people's hearts and minds? That's when they start testing LSD on unsuspecting victims, that's when they lead field trips into Mexico for magic mushrooms. The head honchos are convinced that a drug will do the trick. Find the right drug and you can brainwash anyone, anywhere. They believe this even after two of their top guys come up with a comprehensive report stating that the Commies didn't have any magic drugs, that their technique rested on the cumulative weight of intense psychological pressure and human weakness.

"That's what gets us in the end, you know. Not our susceptibility to any drug like LSD, but our human flaws, our weak characters. Our desperation to be accepted and loved. Look at Jonestown. Nine hundred and thirteen people convinced to kill themselves.

"You have to ask yourself: how did Jim Jones get nine hundred and thirteen people to commit suicide *en masse*? That's not an easy one to pull off, if you think about it. He isolated them in Guyana, he instilled fear into them, but he also gave them a vision, a vision of a promised land. Acceptance, love. He was offering something to these people that they had been unable to find on their own. It was a short step from Jim Jones to Charlie Manson in my mind. Those kids who latched on to Manson were lost and lonely, searching for acceptance and Charlie gave it to them. So much so that they were willing to kill for him.

"In the end what motivates cultists, what motivates

zealous fundamentalists of any kind? The desire to belong, to be accepted, to be given self-definition. To believe.

"I'm thinking about all this when I pass a church one day and see a bride and groom coming out. Boy, do they look like they believe. In marriage, in each other, mostly in *love*. So my slightly twisted mind which is on the prowl for a commercial book idea starts to vibrate. These kids coming out of the church must know that one out of every two marriages ends in divorce, but they're grinning inanely at each other, rapt.

"Before, I had focused on the power of groups, people's willingness to lose their identity in a group, but you don't need a group ethos to lose your identity, you can lose it like that—" He snapped his fingers. "When you fall in love."

Daniel tapped a Pall Mall on his wrist, stuck it in his mouth, and lit it.

"You don't have to, not necessarily," I protested. "You can have an equal relationship where you don't give yourself up." I felt strange being the less cynical person in a discussion on love.

"Equality? I'm not so sure. It's like international relations. The balance of power might shift occasionally from one country to the other, particularly after a conflict, but it's rarely equal. One country has a few thousand more rockets to its name, or one country has more ground troops."

I was struggling to assimilate everything he had said, but I had the feeling that I was back in his classroom and should be taking notes.

202

He stood up, walked over to the bedroom window, peered out into the night.

"Nice curtains," he commented, fingering the cotton.

I sat shaking my head. Daniel turned around, saw my disbelief, and grinned.

"Right now, Stacy, *you're* in the position of power. I've told you I love you, you haven't said the same to me. You're one up on me. I've flown out here to see you. That makes you two up. I'm looking for your approval so I try to entertain you with stories of my past. You ask me to go waterskiing with you tomorrow and I might just do it to show you what a great guy I am. I have to weigh that factor against the fact that I can't water-ski and you might laugh at my failure. Then you'd be three up."

"Daniel—this isn't a game of tennis. Or chess. We're talking about emotions, not scoring points off each other. Besides, I have the distinct feeling that telling me *I've* got power over you actually gives *you* power over me."

He came back to the bed, leaned over, and kissed me.

"Like I said, Stacy, you earned your A in my course." He began to tickle my bare foot.

"Stop it, Daniel. This isn't funny. Is that the premise of your book—that love is actually just a psychological war game, that by making someone fall in love with you, you can brainwash her into doing what you want?"

"Her or him." He grinned again, jumped onto the bed, and lay across from me. "Here's a hypothetical.

Let's say, just for the hell of it, that you've fallen desperately in love with me. You are a quivering wreck of emotions, totally in my power—"

"Thanks a lot." I tried to kick him in the shins but missed.

"No problem. My pleasure. Anyway, stop interrupting me. If I want to control you, what I do now is give you positive reinforcement, build you up, tell you how wonderful you are, how much I love you, how nobody else has ever really appreciated you before. You can trust me, depend on me for approval. I am mother, father, brother, friend, shrink, lover all wrapped up in one cute package. You're hooked."

"And you're doing this on purpose?" I asked quietly.

Daniel shrugged.

"Once you're hooked, what I do is withdraw my approval gradually, in, of course, a reasonably subtle way. I drop little hints about your inadequacies, play on your weak spots. You won't know what has hit you. What have you done wrong? How can you win my love back?"

I looked at him. He had a splash of what must have been dried paint on his left shirtsleeve, above his elbow.

"Then, presuming you haven't told me to take a hike, I institute the behavioral patterns I want you to follow by dispensing or withholding my approval as I see fit."

"Daniel—" I stood up, began to pace around the room. My stomach was tight, my hands clenched. "Let me get this straight. Let's forget about you and me as an example, okay? Are you saying that in every love relationship one person, the person who has the so-called power, consciously victimizes the other in order to get whatever he or she wants? That's sick.''

"Whether it's conscious or not is irrelevant, and, no, I'm not saying this happens in every relationship. What I *am* saying is that it happens sometimes. Couples can get involved in power plays. Every aspect of the relationship can turn into power politics. Who washes the dishes. Who initiates sex. Who makes the little decisions, not to mention the big ones. And the person who wins the power struggle will always be the person with fewer needs.''

I stopped pacing, lit a cigarette, poured myself another glass of wine.

"Don't you think it's simply a question of compromise?''

"Sure. But I was interested in the dynamic. Who compromises on what issues and why? As I said, as far as I'm concerned, it's down to who needs to be loved and accepted the most.

"But listen, I'll be honest here. I wrote the book right after my divorce, so I wasn't what you'd call an unbiased observer. I was getting out a lot of my own frustrations. That's why I said it sucks. The publishers didn't push it because it was too downbeat about love. And now I have to say I agree with them. I've seen couples who work, who don't smother each other. People who have great relationships. Those are the people who are *really* interesting.'' He sighed, shrugged again, blew smoke at the ceiling. "Still, I believe some of my conclusions. If you want to get someone to do something they have been trained not to do, or something that is not normally in their character, don't put bamboo shoots under their fingertips or imprison them in cages. Make them fall in love.''

"Physical torture would work better on me. If someone came near me with a knife, I'd spill any beans I had.''

"Yes, sure. But I'm talking about a long-lasting effect. *Converting* a person. Those POWs in Korea or Vietnam, most of them who had been supposedly brainwashed, reversed themselves as soon as they got home. As soon as the threat was over. Love is long term. Those Manson girls still believe in Charlie, you know.''

"Tell me, why did you say you'd send the book to Eloise?''

"Because I don't think Robert, even if he had read it himself, *especially* if he had read it himself, would give it to her. And I think it's an appropriate book for Eloise to read. She strikes me as a woman who has given herself away. The way she looks at him is abject. That worries me because I like her. I think she needs to be educated.''

"Do I need to be educated?''

"What *you* need is to admit that you love me. Then we'll be even. For a while, anyway.'' His dark eyes zeroed in on mine, unblinking.

"You think I'm going to tell you I love you after all that brainwashing business? You scare the shit out of me.''

"Good.'' He laughed and began to unbutton his shirt.

"You really are a jerk, Daniel. And stupid, too," I said. "You shouldn't be allowed to teach."

"I'm an asshole, a pain in the ass, stupid, poor, jealous."

He took my hand, pulled me down to the bed, threw the pizza on the floor.

"And those are my *good* points. Do you still want to make love with me?"

I nodded.

"Fine. It's my turn to be on top."

14

FEBRUARY–MARCH 1990

Falling asleep was not simple that night. No amount of wine or sex or nicotine had managed to erase Daniel's perceptions on love from my racing brain. I couldn't lie peacefully beside him as he snored into the approaching dawn. I couldn't relax. He could throw his theories around as if they were Frisbees sailing gracefully through the air, but I felt as if they had winged me, dented the most exposed parts of my pitiful hopes. I sat in the chair by my dressing table, watching him sleep, wishing that I could continue doing just that. I didn't want to talk to him, make love with him, have any more interaction. I wanted him unconscious.

Daniel could claim to know happy couples. He could say he'd changed his mind about the possibility of good relationships, but I was fixated on my own debacle with Buddy. Daniel had moved on from his divorce, I hadn't. I'd be qualified to write *Love—The Ultimate Brainwash, Part Two*. I pretended that I didn't buy his notions on power politics in relationships, but I'd not only bought them, I'd already wrapped them myself. I could have handed them out as Christmas presents to every couple I knew. Yes, there was always a dominant partner in a relationship. No, equality did not exist. Even in couples where both partners worked, shared the household chores, had a supposedly modern, perfect relationship. One of them always had the upper hand, while the other was trying desperately to please. Accommodating. Compromising. Sacrificing.

I would have liked to blame men for the failure of relationships, attribute it all to their inability to come to terms with women on an equal basis, but I couldn't. The common belief that men were less interested in love than women, that they defined themselves by their careers whereas women defined themselves by their men, was not always the case. I'd seen men emotionally maimed, too. Hopeless men doing everything in their power to keep their women happy, but not able to fulfill the dreams, to meet the expectations. There were plenty of Othellos and Leontes out there, driven mad by jealousy; men who killed their wives' lovers or their wives; men who became obsessed. The John Hinkleys of this world who would do anything, including trying to assassinate the President, to prove themselves to a woman. Passion was an equal opportunity employer.

If Daniel could joke about going waterskiing with me, I could be all too serious about placing myself, lock, stock, and heartbeat at his whim. I could easily envision taking up mountain climbing if that happened to be his passion, or cutting my hair if he fancied his women *à la* Audrey Hepburn. During our pizza dinner I had already thought of ruses to go out on my own for a quick shopping trip the next day in order to buy a stunning new dress. Oh, and yes, in all my obsessed daydreams, I had cheerfully thrown in my job, moved back to New York, into his apartment; seen myself sitting comfortably in an armchair, pregnant and barefoot, a short step from the kitchen. Jesus. I was a natural victim of love.

Careful not to make any noise and disturb him, I went into my kitchen and made myself a cup of coffee. I had watched too many soap operas as a child and, like Eloise, too many operas as an adult. I believed in love, in passion, in abandoning myself to a man. At the same time, I wanted to retain my dignity, my self-respect, a large degree of control. A difficult trick to pull off.

As the word "abandoned" reverberated in my mind, I remembered Eloise; her terror of being thought inadequate in bed, not *abandoned* enough. Poor Eloise had taken a quantum leap into the abyss of love while I was still trying to stay on the tightrope. She would put herself through flaming hoops for Robert and sit sobbing if she didn't perform correctly. John the chauffeur had said she wanted love so bad you could taste it.

Exactly how bad did I want it?

I dragged so hard on my cigarette, I could feel the smoke in my toes.

The rest of the weekend, I played guide to Daniel's tourist in San Francisco. We rode the cable cars, strolled around Fisherman's Wharf, did all the sightseeing we could fit in during the few hours we didn't spend in bed. I was continually surprised by Daniel's apparent ease with himself—a quality many people spend years searching for in therapy. He never made any excuses for himself, would admit to fucking up as readily as he'd give himself credit for succeeding when he talked about his past. He laughed at his own jokes, laughed even more when they were against himself. He didn't seem to feel the need to prove anything, either physically or intellectually. Making love, he could be either slow and relaxed or hurried and intense, depending on the mood. Worried was what he never was.

As we talked, I was at first astounded by little comments he'd make. He could attach as much importance to an episode of *Leave It to Beaver* he had seen thirty years ago as any ground-breaking academic work getting rave reviews in The Sunday *Times*. He was pan-cultural, as at home with rock as he was with classical music, as interested in baseball as he was in art. I knew that I had a lot to learn from him, the first and most important lesson being not to be a snob. I had been a closet TV watcher all my life, not daring to admit to it until someone else did first, afraid that I'd lose any credibility I had if I confessed to my secret delight in junk TV. I saw television watching as an admission of failure. Daniel saw it as a necessary and often enjoyable occupation.

"If you're smart, you can learn things from the dumbest shows," he said. "Do you believe that de Tocqueville, if he came back to study America, would dismiss television? Don't you think he'd devote *chapters* to it?"

All the while, as we lay in bed, as we roamed the city, as we faced each other over dinner and lunch and breakfast, I plotted. I laid plans. I was going to be a Green Beret of emotion. Rule number one—be mysterious. I had already told him too much about my life over our brunch in New York, given him too many clues. Well-timed silences were important, the kind of silence he used so effectively. Retreat in order better to ambush. Challenge him whenever possible, but in a dispassionate, clinical, cool way. Rule number two—don't expect anything. Don't expect terms of endearment, romantic gestures, any form of commitment. Rule three—make plans for the rest of my life without him. This weekend would be an interlude only. As soon as he boarded his plane back to New York, I would erase the thought of him. Stop obsessing. He wasn't going to pull his brainwashing act on me. I'd give him name, rank, serial number, and a huge amount of pleasure in bed. Full stop. If I was prepared for the worst, the best might just happen. Driving him to the airport on Sunday afternoon, I remained preternaturally calm, my mind doing the mental equivalent of a thousand fast push-ups. He had tuned the car radio to an oldies pop station and was singing along with John Lennon to "Hey, You've Got to Hide Your Love Away." I was beginning to believe in Jung's concept of synchronicity as I listened to the lyrics, but I kept my hands rigidly on the wheel, at the ten to two position, eyes straight on the road before me.

"Stacy," he said after the song had ended. "You're

doing a great job of hiding yourself away, but you're wasting your time. Our time."

"I don't know what you're talking about, Daniel." I stepped on the accelerator, switched from the middle to the passing lane. He laughed. I pushed the pedal down farther.

"Of course you know what I'm talking about." He began to sing along to Buddy Holly's "Everyday." His voice was the voice of a heavy smoker. When we reached the airport, he put his hand on my thigh, kissed me on the cheek. "Don't bother to come in with me. I'll jump out here." I turned my face away, scrambled in my bag for a cigarette. He reached over and grabbed it from my hand. "Now don't be a lame-brain, Stacy. I can be cynical about love and still be *in* love with you. How can I not be in love with a woman who keeps a picture of a bicycle by her bed?" Daniel chuckled, shrugged. "So we can play whatever games you want for however long you want to play them, but we're going to end up together. If one of us gets hurt, one of us gets hurt. I'm willing to be the one who makes the running jump for the moment, but you're going to have to come across too sometime. I want to see tears on your cheeks when I leave you next time, not this stony, rigid face I'm seeing now. And I'll cry too, okay? We're worth a try. Who knows, maybe we can buck the odds. We can be the interesting people, not the predictable fuck-ups." He retrieved his over-night bag from the backseat, climbed out of my Honda, and disappeared into the terminal. If he had come back, he would have seen the tears.

I returned to rumpled sheets, full ashtrays, and an

empty answering machine. Sunday afternoon blues with a vengeance. I took a shower, washed my hair, dried it, put on makeup for no one, scrubbed it off, tried to listen to Beethoven, turned him off, sat on my sofa and attempted to lose myself in a mental exercise. I tried to remember all the bathtubs I'd ever been in.

When the phone rang I was in my grandfather's tub: long, deep, hot. Practicing a trick with a washcloth he'd taught me. Right hand outstretched under the cloth, you lower it slowly into the water, catching the air before removing your hand and forming a closed circle with the cloth. Submerge it and squeeze the balloon the washcloth has formed and bubbles burst out like underwater fireworks.

"Stace—hi, how are you?" Eloise sounded like a weatherman predicting a sunny weekend.

"Fine. I'm fine. Well, no. To be honest, I'm not fine. I'm sitting here feeling sorry for myself."

"Why? What's happened?"

"Daniel came for the weekend and I'm even more in love than I was before and I don't know when I'm going to see him again and I don't think it's going to work out."

"Stacy!" Eloise laughed, which irritated the hell out of me. I was tired of people laughing at me. "What you need is a romantic agent. Like movie stars and authors have agents, you know. You need someone to take charge of your romantic life. And I'm the one. I called because Robert and I are going to Las Vegas next weekend to see Kenny Rogers in concert and I wanted you to come too. You and Daniel. Now don't tell me you're both broke, because I'm paying. I'll call Daniel tomorrow and fix it. So there—you'll see him next weekend. No problem. I get ten percent of your happiness, that's all.''

"Eloise—you're drunk.''

"Maybe I am. It's almost midnight here and I've had a few drinks and I'm in a great mood and I've come up with this perfect plan. The four of us in Las Vegas. I'll be your agent. It's perfect, Stace. You two can get married in one of those chapels. This is so perfect I can't believe it. Maybe I could buy Kenny Rogers—get him to sing at the ceremony.''

"Eloise, I think you should go to bed. Get some sleep.''

"I will, I will. Don't be so bossy. You should thank me, you know.''

"Thank you. Now go to bed.''

"All right. Robert wants me to go to bed too.'' I could hear her take a deep breath. "I may be a little tipsy, but I'm serious about next weekend. I'll book you two a room at the Golden Nugget. I'll call Daniel tomorrow. He's listed in the telephone book, right?''

"Don't call him, Eloise. I'd love to come. Sure. I want to see you again, but don't pressure Daniel.''

"Just show up at the hotel Friday, Stace. I'm your fairy godmother. Fairy godmothers don't pressure. They wave their wands.'' She hung up.

A plane trip to Las Vegas is different from a plane trip to any other city in the United States. All the passengers looked expectant, like children on Halloween night, confident of filling their bags with candy. People talked to each other across aisles, giving advice on which shows were worth seeing, which slot machines in which hotels had the biggest payoffs, which poker rooms had the most action. I eavesdropped, wondering whether they would all be so happy on the flight back. And how would I be feeling on my return trip? I was taking a big gamble myself. Eloise had left a message on my machine mid-week exhorting me to meet Robert and her at the Golden Nugget on Friday evening, but she hadn't mentioned Daniel. Nor had Daniel called himself. Would he be there? The suspense wasn't killing me, but it was certainly affecting my nerves. I thumbed through the in-flight magazine at least five times, never able to concentrate on any one article. I pulled out Hunter S. Thompson's book *Fear and Loathing in Las Vegas* and attempted to lose myself in his madness and humor. Instead, I found myself uncharacteristically wishing I had drugs on me, any drug which might put me on the same plateau as my fellow passengers.

Las Vegas as a city didn't interest me. The slot machines greeting arriving passengers at the airport, the limos waiting to pick up heavy rollers, all the garish colors and tacky paraphernalia left me cold in the desert heat. All I cared about was finding a cab as quickly as possible.

Every cabdriver has a story to tell and mine was no exception. He claimed to have been a millionaire who had lost it all at the roulette tables and was applying himself to recapture his booty. He had a system now. A system at the roulette table that would bring him back his fortune. I decided that he was lying about the amount of money he had had and deceiving himself about the amount of money he would have. And I didn't like the "Thank You for Not Smoking" placard with little happy faces surrounding a request which was, in fact, a command.

Giant neon-lit billboards were planted along the highway leading downtown like massive trees from a science fiction planet, a forest of advertisement for upcoming "acts." Tom Jones smiled down on us, Kenny Rogers smiled down on us, gods in the heavens who had condescended to show up for a weekend and give the mortals a show. Gods and one goddess.

"Get a load of that, will you?" The ex-millionaire pointed to a billboard higher, wider, almost double the size of the others.

Sapphire Shannon. Her publicity people must have been given a big pay raise for this picture. The blue jeans were as tight as ever, but from her crotch to her knees they were covered by what appeared to be palomino ponyskin. The animal rights people wouldn't let her get away with that, I decided. It must be fake. Real or not, it was a sexy touch. Her hands were on her hips, her legs spread. The eyes flashed, literally flashed, for they were sapphire blue bulbs flashing on and off rhythmically. But that little trick wasn't attention-grabbing enough, no. Instead of an off-the-shoulder blouse or ripped T-shirt, Sapphire Shannon was wearing a tank top around her considerable bust and a real live snake around her waist. Coiled like a tightly fitting belt, head coming straight out from her belly button, showing its fangs to anyone who dared look. This perfect Western cowgirl with the white hair was set against an entirely black background. A pale ghost leaping out from the dark, looking like a mixture of Annie Oakley, Ann-Margret, and Eve: tough, sexy, but also strangely pure.

Eloise must have driven by the same billboard, been assailed by the same specter. I sighed in sympathy. No one could draw a goatee or a mustache on that picture. We had driven by before I registered that the billboard had announced Sapphire's gig at Caesar's Palace.

"Isn't she something?" The cabdriver turned around to face me with the question.

"Mmm hmm." I closed my eyes and nodded. "When is she playing here? I missed the dates."

"Lots more to look at than the dates, huh?" He shifted his gaze from me back to the road. "Next weekend. All sold out."

Next weekend. That was a relief. At least she wouldn't be in the same town at the same time. Still, it was bad luck for Eloise, not what she needed on this jaunt. Whether Daniel showed up or not, I was now glad that I had come. Eloise would need me.

The lobby of the Golden Nugget hotel looked like a shopping mall the week before Christmas. Queues of people checking in or checking out, desperate to get into the action or away from it. A stupendously fat man stood in front of me, clad in a red Hawaiian shirt which matched his bloodshot eyes. He was clutching his American Express card as if it were a life support system. An equally fat woman wearing a see-through white blouse over a black bra appeared at his side and nudged him in the belly with her elbow, motioning for him to follow her away from the lobby. He wouldn't go. She grabbed his elbow, pulling him. A tug-of-war between two pro wrestlers. The woman finally won and the man followed her meekly. The story behind that couple, I suspected, would be more interesting than my cabdriver's.

There was a note for me at the desk.

> Get settled in your room, Stace, then come to our suite for a drink.
>
> Love,
> Eloise
>
> P.S. You'll notice your room has a king-size bed. Your Agent.

So Daniel had shown up, had accepted Eloise's invitation. When the receptionist threw me a wary look, I realized that I'd jumped up in delight.

"Have a nice stay," she said in a monotone. No doubt she'd seen plenty of people jump for joy and subsequently fall flat on their faces.

Daniel's bag was already in the room, the ashtray was littered, and a note lay on the pillow.

> About time, ace. Welcome to Las Vegas. Eloise has adopted me. Lady Bountiful. Now get your ass up to her suite. I get nervous with rich people.

I sat on the bed, collecting my thoughts, garnering my emotions. I wouldn't be able to keep my Green Beret persona intact for much longer, I knew that. Sooner

219

or later I would abandon my tightrope and leap into his arms. And then what? Rational brain cells maliciously went into overdrive. I would move to New York, give up my job, my careful life in San Francisco, live with Daniel, watch as we grew overaccustomed to each other, watch as all the romance drained from our relationship, leaving us a colorless, dreary couple, resentful and brooding. Is that what I really wanted?

I stubbed those thoughts out, fixed my face, and made my way to the Chappell's suite.

Robert opened the door to my knock, bowed and ushered me into the high-rolling splendor. Leather chairs and sofas, deep pile white carpet, two TVs, mirrored bar, sleek, slimline telephones, glass tables, a fax machine in the corner. Modern living *à la Miami Vice.*

"Welcome, Stace." Robert, his arm around my shoulder, gave me a kiss on the cheek. "A little cocktail?"

"Yes, please. A Screwdriver."

"Fine. Eloise is getting dressed, she'll be right out."

Daniel, seated on the sofa, wearing jeans, a Golden Nugget T-shirt, and a NY Yankees baseball cap, patted the seat beside him.

"Glad you could make it." He raised his eyebrows, smiled. "Robert just beat me on a bet and I'm feeling very stupid."

"What was the bet?" I sat down beside him, he took my hand.

"What the Immaculate Conception means."

"He beat *me* on that one, too. Robert"—I looked

up as he handed me my drink—"you could make a living on that bet."

"I know. It's a good one, isn't it?" He settled down into the chair at a right angle to the sofa, put his feet up on the glass tabletop. A pair of sunglasses perched on his head. He was dressed in blue jeans as well, with cowboy boots and a cowboy shirt, every inch a country-and-western afficionado. "Now, I've already filled Daniel in on the schedule, Stace. We have a couple of hours before the show starts and I think we should do a little gambling. Daniel's anxious to hit the poker tables, and Eloise and I plan to go to the baccarat room. We'll meet up for a drink before the show. How's that?"

"Sounds perfect."

Eloise swept in, crying, "Stace! Welcome!" looking like Robert's double. Matching boots, jeans, shirt, the only variation being an outrageous rhinestone-studded leather waistcoat. They looked like they should be the ones on stage. I leaped up and hugged her, noticing, at close quarters, bags under her eyes the makeup she wore couldn't quite disguise.

"It's wonderful to see you. How was your flight?" she asked.

"Fine."

Eloise stumbled as she made her way to the bar, but regained her balance and poured herself a glass of champagne.

"I would have gotten that for you, Cat." Robert half rose from his chair, decided to settle back down.

"No, no. I'll do it. I want to make a toast." She lifted her glass, waved it in turn at the three of us.

"Viva Las Vegas. I'm so glad we could all be here together. To friends. And lovers."

"To friends and lovers," we echoed, and drank. Daniel kept my hand in his. I couldn't decide whether Eloise looked silly or terrific in her outfit—it was a close call and probably depended on the mood of the moment. But I questioned her wisdom in wearing jeans. Jeans on Eloise did not match up to jeans on Sapphire. That was a comparison she'd be better off avoiding. She was evidently a few drinks ahead of me. She swayed over to Robert, arranged herself on his lap, one arm over his shoulder, the other still holding the champagne.

"Sometimes it's hard to be a woman," she sang, "Giving all your love to just one man, You'll have bad times, He'll have good times, Doing things that you don't understand." Eloise had never sung, never even hummed a tune in our college days. Now I knew why. She was off key, out of tune, awful. Taking a gulp of champagne, she continued in her grating voice. "But if you love him, be proud of him, Cause after all, he's just a man. Boom, boom, boom. Stand by your man, Give him two arms to cling to . . ."

She was into the chorus now, singing at full volume as the three of us sat and listened. I wanted to stop her, wished I knew the words so I could join in and dilute the sound, wondered why Robert didn't take over, silence her. It wasn't cute, it was embarrassing. She must have been plastered. Finally, thank God, she finished.

"Great, Cat." Robert hugged her to his chest,

looked over her shoulder at Daniel and me with a "what else can I do?" expression.

"Should I sing another?" Eloise struggled to her original position, began to wind her hair around her finger with a vacuous smile on her face.

"Eloise." Daniel leaned over, grabbed her arm. "I love you. Your voice is even worse than mine, and that's saying something, believe me. Grand Ole Opry contenders, we're not. Either you and I practice on our own, out of everyone's hearing, or we'll get slapped with a legal suit for inflicting cruel and unusual suffering."

"Am I really that bad?" Eloise asked Daniel in a girlish voice.

"You're worse." Daniel laughed, keeping his eyes locked on hers. "Stick to what you're good at, as my father used to say."

"But what am I good at. What *am* I good at?" Her eyes were pleading with Daniel. I sat rooted, unable to help, unsure why Robert didn't move or say anything either.

"I'm taking a guess here, Eloise, because I don't know you very well, but I'd say you're good at being honest. And that's a rare talent. More important than singing. Stick to that."

"You're good at everything, Cat." Robert finally spoke, gave her a bear hug from behind.

"Daniel's right," she said, more to herself than to the rest of us. "At least I'm good at *something*. I used to be good at physics, you know. Did you know that, Daniel?" She hadn't appeared to notice Robert's embrace, she was concentrating on Daniel.

"Yes, I know that. I also know you need some coffee or you'll pass out in the middle of Kenny Rogers. Coffee and mineral water. Any chance of that, Robert?" Daniel released Eloise's arm, stood up, took Eloise by the shoulders, lifted her from Robert's lap and placed her in his seat beside me.

"Of course." Robert immediately stood as well, went over to the bar, and poured a large glass of Perrier, then a cup of coffee from a thermos. "I guess she had a few too many—the excitement of Las Vegas. It's her first trip here."

"It's my first trip here," Eloise repeated dully. "Don't you just love the billboards?" I flinched when she said it, then turned to face her.

"They're tacky," I said firmly. "Low rent. Obvious. The shallow selling the lowest common denominator. How do you suppose they'd do with Pavarotti? Domingo? Now that would be a challenge." Dig yourself out of the pit, I wanted to say. Don't drown in self-pity, in your insecurities. Forget Sapphire. Fucking Sapphire. Robert handed her the coffee and water, glancing to me as if asking for help. She drank both in alternate sips while Robert launched into an anecdote about seeing Pavarotti on the street in Manhattan, his famous bulk barely able to fit through the door of a restaurant. We filled the next half an hour with opera stories, waiting for Eloise to sober up a little. After three glasses of Perrier and four cups of coffee, she had regained her composure enough to announce that she was ready for the casino.

"Cat, honey, are you sure?" Robert asked in a solicitous voice.

"Positive," she replied, standing up. "Let's go win some money."

Down in the bustling casino, Robert and Eloise went into a private baccarat room, while Daniel and I walked over to the section reserved for poker playing. Everywhere I looked I saw frenzied people, pale figures hunched over slot machines, sweating beside roulette wheels, shoving each other to get closer to the craps tables. Zombie faces intent on winning, some probably even more intent on losing. They reminded me of the cockroaches in New York, teeming, swarming, ugly insects scurrying along the casino floor. The fear and the hope were both tangible, omnipresent backdrops to the noise, the end-of-the-world atmosphere. Daniel, oblivious, was homing in on a low-stakes poker table, relieved to find a seat open. I stood and watched him from the rails.

There were eight people at his table. Three ancient men, hands covered in liver spots, beady eyes, thin, unsmiling faces. An old woman eating a banana with a bag lady aura and two-inch, red-painted nails. Be careful of her Daniel, I thought. She's a toughie, she's one to watch out for. A jumpy, heavily bejeweled black man sat beside the dealer and two middle-aged, puffy-faced guys with Texan hats flanked Daniel. I followed the game simply by seeing who pulled in the pots each time, and proved my hunch right. The bag lady was winning. Daniel was faring all right, though, occasionally reaching out to haul in the chips. The Texan hats were seemingly throwing away their money, losing hand after hand, scowling, pushing back their hats, mopping their brows, muttering at the dealer.

After an hour, I felt I was watching underworld figures. Not mobsters, but dead people who had crossed the river Styx, never to return. A hellish concoction of soul-sellers, ready to trade in their last drop of humanity for a full house. I went and tapped Daniel on the shoulder. He looked up, annoyed.

"It's time to meet Eloise and Robert," I reminded him.

"Okay. Right." He counted his chips, excused himself from the table, allowed himself a smile. "Twenty dollars. Not bad."

"It looks like very hard work," I commented. "Not much fun."

"Oh, it is fun, Stacy. A lot of fun. If you win."

We went to the appointed bar, an evident pit stop where gamblers could recharge before taking off into the action again. The Chappells hadn't yet appeared.

"Mineral water, please," I asked the waitress when Daniel ordered a scotch for himself. "After seeing Eloise, I think I'll avoid booze for a while."

"She was in bad shape." Daniel lit a cigarette, looked thoughtful. "We flew here together, you know. In a private jet she'd rented. Very fancy. I was very impressed. I was so impressed I wasn't paying enough attention to her."

"I think that poster of Sapphire must have set her off. I think I'd get drunk if Sapphire were your ex-wife."

"She is."

"Very funny."

"Actually, Roseanne Barr is my ex-wife."

"Even funnier."

"You know, Robert didn't say a word when we passed that thing. We were all riveted, all three of us were staring at it and no one was saying a word. Very awkward. So I made a crack. As is my wont. I said, 'Shit, I was expecting an alligator around her tummy. Doesn't she know snakeskin's out this season?' "

I didn't laugh.

"Yeah, I know it wasn't that hysterical, but what could I do? The tension was so high in that limo, I thought the air-conditioning had gone off. Someone had to defuse things and that asshole Robert just sat there staring up at his ex."

"He's not an asshole, Daniel. I'm sure he was taken by surprise, thrown off balance. What was he supposed to say?"

"Well, Stacy, he's been married to Eloise for six months, yes? He must know that Sapphire's a hard act to follow for anyone, Queen Midas or whoever. He should have dealt with that by now, put Eloise at ease on that subject. That's his job. If he loves her, that is."

"You keep questioning their love. It seems obvious to me."

"*Her* love seems obvious to me. You should have heard him on the plane. He kept telling her to sit up straight, not to fiddle with her hair, fix her makeup, the eyeliner wasn't quite right. *Heil* Robert. A Nazi schmuck."

"You're overreacting. Now watch it, here they come."

They were threading their way past the blackjack tables, hand in hand, an updated Roy Rogers and Dale Evans, looking pleased as punch with themselves and each other. Daniel's way off on this one, I said to myself. I know mutual love when I see it. Eloise stopped a waitress by our table and ordered a mineral water. Considering what was about to happen that evening, she should have had a real drink.

The rich don't have to stand in lines. Doors are opened, barriers crossed, while the others, the ones who scrimp and save for their Las Vegas vacation, patiently wait for their turn, willing to spend hours and hard-earned money for a chance to see a star perform. Our tickets were "comped," on the house, free because the hotel valued Eloise's patronage and expected that, over the weekend, she'd drop much more in the casino than any tickets might cost. She and Robert had already lost fifty thousand dollars at the baccarat table, so the policy had paid off.

The four of us were ushered into the club room, past the throngs who turned their heads to see if we were stars ourselves and looked disappointed when we weren't. We had, of course, a table up front, all the better to see Kenny Rogers in action. The atmosphere was more intimate than I had expected, the room smaller, darker, friendlier, not a vast concert hall. We settled in to watch the opening act, a male comic who managed a few good jokes, but looked more nervous than he should have. Being a warm-up act for the star turn must be unnerving, I thought. He must know that the audience was hoping he'd finish soon, anxious to see the person they'd paid for, the man with the real clout. Kenny Rogers.

After the comic told his last joke, thanked the audience excessively, a short intermission was announced as Kenny's team set up the stage. Eloise leaned over to tell me the titles of Kenny's most famous songs, but in the middle of her list of hits, a hush fell over the room in a wave. The silence started in the back, I noticed, and swept forward. Row after row of tables suddenly fell quiet, heads swiveled, whispers raced from ear to ear. I thought Kenny Rogers had appeared at the back of the room, a trick entrance, was working his way through the crowd, glad-handing, then would leap on the stage. People were staring, certainly, following a figure as it moved toward the front. A tall figure. In blue jeans.

"Oh, shit," I said. Eloise was straining to see what was the cause of the excitement. I grabbed her hand, squeezed it as Sapphire came closer, a phalanx of what looked like bodyguards in her wake. Wearing blue jeans with sequins running up the sides and a totally transparent white blouse with two sequin-encrusted circles just large enough to cover her nipples. I couldn't not look. She walked regally, as if in a procession, leading her acolytes through the room to a table not far from us.

"Sit the fuck down, you guys," she said, waving to the coterie of men, who did just that. "The show's about to start. Shut the fuck up."

"Where's the snake?" Daniel whispered in my ear. Eloise looked like a woman whose child had just been run over. I pressed her hand harder, glanced over at Robert. He had sucked both cheeks in, had an unlit Pall Mall of Daniel's in his mouth as he watched Sapphire. His head kept nodding back and forth in a "no, no, no" rhythm. Then, abruptly, it stopped nodding. I looked back at Sapphire. She must have been searching the room for other celebrities and found her ex-husband instead.

"Hey," she yelled, "Robbo. Long time no see. Fucking hell. What are you doing here?"

Robert didn't respond, turned his back on her. People at neighboring tables focused on us, the recipients of a star's recognition. Who were we? Sapphire, unfazed by Robert's snub, studied Eloise, Daniel, and myself cooly.

"Robbo—you like dykes now?" I dropped Eloise's hand as if it had been a live grenade, could feel a blush traveling the length of my body, could see Eloise's matching blush, hear laughter at the adjacent tables.

The house lights dimmed.

"Ladies and Gentlemen," the MC announced. "The Golden Nugget is proud to present the one, the only, the all-time greatest country singer—Kenny Rogers." The band began to play, Kenny Rogers strolled on to thunderous applause, wearing a tuxedo, his silver hair shining in the spotlight. The show was on. As far as I was concerned, though, the show was already over. Eloise slumped in her chair, not bothering to look up at the stage. Robert sat rubbing his forehead as if trying to erase his mind, Daniel was the only one paying attention, listening as Kenny belted out, "Ruby, Don't Take Your Love to Town." I kept sneaking looks at Sapphire, wondering how any woman could be such a destructive bitch. Of all the cities in all the world, I thought. Why here? Why now? The song had ended. Kenny sat down on a stool, began to speak to the audience in his low, sexy voice. "I'm so glad to be with y'all tonight . . ."

"I feel sick," Eloise said. "I want to go back to the suite."

"Eloise—don't let her win," Daniel said. Voices raised around us saying, "Shh."

"I want to go back. Please. Now. I feel sick."

"Shh."

Robert stood up, took Eloise by the arm.

"We're going."

Kenny Rogers stopped mid-anecdote, as Daniel, Eloise, and I rose, pushed our chairs away, weaved through the tables to the aisle. "Did I say something wrong?" Rogers asked. We kept our heads down, hurried toward the back, the audience laughing at Kenny's joke. "Did y'all think I was Dolly Parton? Sorry to disappoint you." Howls of laughter. It seemed to take forever to reach the exit; when we finally did, some functionary stopped us, asking what had gone wrong.

"She's sick." I pointed at Eloise. "Nauseous. She didn't want to throw up at the table."

"No, no. Of course not." He looked relieved. "Perhaps you can come back tomorrow night. It's a wonderful show."

"Thank you. We will," said Daniel.

"I need a drink," said Eloise as soon as we entered the suite. She walked to the bar, poured herself a whiskey.

"Make that two, will you?" requested Daniel.

"Three, please," I added. Robert remained silent, crossed the room, and stood by the window overlooking the pool.

"I'm sorry to ruin the show for you." Eloise collapsed into the leather armchair. "Did you see what she was wearing. It was so . . ." She hesitated, looked over at Robert. His back was to us.

"So crass," I finished Eloise's sentence. "So unsubtle."

"I don't think Sapphire Shannon's into subtlety in a big way, Stacy," Daniel chuckled. "Her whole act is a sledgehammer act, she's hitting everyone over the head, clobbering them with sex. That's the gimmick."

"Do *you* think that's sexy, Daniel?" Eloise asked but she was still looking at Robert's back.

"Depends what mood I'm in," he replied. I wanted to hit him. "Madonna's into the same act, you know, all that underwear on display. But Madonna comes across with more control, more humor. Like she is really enjoying putting everyone through the hoops, playing with pop culture. Sapphire has boxed herself into a corner. She's at the mercy of her own image, can't be anything but a vamp. And she's getting older. It won't work for her in a couple of years. She has to make hay while the sun shines."

"You find it sexy, though?" Eloise pressed, never moving her eyes from Robert. Robert could have been a mute hitchhiker the three of us had picked up en route.

"No, to tell you the truth. For the most part, I don't find it sexy. As Stacy said, it's too obvious. I'm not going to sit glued to her tits, praying she'll make a move and those sequins will slither a quarter of an inch and reveal all. That's what she's hoping for, wearing that blouse. No, I'm more partial to the librarian type, the one with hair pinned up in a bun, wearing glasses, the one with smoldering fires only I can unleash." He shrugged, smiled at me. He was lying, I knew and I mouthed a thank-you to him. He'd picked up on what Eloise needed fairly quickly, for I hadn't told him of her fear of sexual inadequacy, but Daniel had realized Eloise needed reassuring. Why wasn't Robert helping out as well? How could he stand there staring out of the window so selfishly? Yet his history with Sapphire must have been so painful that he'd been momentarily paralyzed by her. That "Robbo" was so dismissive, so patronizing, it must have brought back more memories than he could handle.

"Robert, would you like a drink?" Daniel was the one to ask him, to coax him back from his private world.

"Yes, of course." At last he turned to us, ran his hands through his hair, then rubbed the bridge of his nose. "I'll join you in a whiskey."

Eloise smiled at him, gratefully.

"For Christ's sake, Cat, will you sit up straight," he barked. Eloise reacted as if she'd been slapped. Tears leaped from her eyes instantly, her back stiffened.

"Oh, God, I'm sorry," Robert crossed to her, put his hands on her neck and massaged it. "I'm tired. I didn't mean to snap at you."

"No, no, you're right. My posture has always been

terrible. Ask Stacy.'' She was trying to stop the tears, get hold of herself.

What a night, I thought. Thank God Daniel had come. I couldn't have handled it on my own.

"Would you mind terribly if we had an early evening?'' Robert directed the question at Daniel and me as he continued to rub Eloise's neck. She was relaxing under the pressure of his hands. I remembered the soothing feeling, a tonic for tension.

"Of course we wouldn't mind.'' Daniel and I stood up simultaneously, moved to the door.

"Let's meet for coffee tomorrow morning,'' Eloise murmured, her eyes closed. "Around ten? Here?''

"Sure,'' Daniel said. "See you then. Get a good night's sleep.''

"We will,'' Robert said very quietly.

As Daniel and I undressed back in our room, I unleashed a verbal tidal wave of abuse on Sapphire Shannon.

"Stacy,'' he interrupted. "You can't blame Sapphire. She came, she saw, she conquered. She's one of those people. Eloise should have stayed put, not fled. Robert should have defended his wife when she made that dyke quip. The problem doesn't lie in Sapphire, it's entrenched in Robert and Eloise. They have allowed Sapphire to become a part of their relationship. You can't blame Sapphire,'' he repeated.

Oh, can't I? I said to myself.

"Why didn't you defend *me* then, when she called us dykes?''

He slipped off his boxer shorts, threw them into the corner of the room. They landed on the TV set.

"How do I know you're *not* a dyke?"

"Daniel!" I went to punch him in the stomach—he reached out, caught my fist, threw me on to the bed.

"Physical violence solves nothing, Stacy. Why don't you prove your overwhelming heterosexuality right now?" He nipped at my earlobe.

"You asshole," I growled.

"Why do I get the feeling that's going to be your nickname for me?" He laughed. I closed my eyes as he kissed me. Why did the image of Sapphire Shannon in her transparent blouse appear against my eyelids? Why did I believe that Daniel was thinking of her too?

We arrived at the suite just after ten. A vast array of rolls, croissants, bagels were spread out on the table, with pots of coffee and tea. The perfect breakfast. The bags under Eloise's eyes were darker than the day before, but she looked relaxed otherwise, in a pale green Donna Karan skirt and top. It looked better than the cowboy outfit had and I was glad to see Robert had changed as well, into white linen trousers and a purple Yves Saint Laurent short-sleeved shirt. Eloise, as she poured us the coffee, apologized again for wrecking our evening out and told us that she'd managed to arrange tickets for the show that night.

"Robert thinks we should go see Circus, Circus, this afternoon. Apparently it's an amazing place. But you don't have to come," she said to Daniel, handing him his coffee. "If you'd rather play poker."

"I'll think about that," he answered. "I'm not great in the mornings. I have to wake up before I can make any important decisions."

"Stacy and I are the early risers." Robert bit into a croissant, leaned back into the sofa. "We're morning people. I was swimming at seven this morning, Stace. You should have joined me." He winked and chewed. The doorbell rang.

"Who's that?" Eloise asked. "They just brought the food up—they can't want to clear it away so quickly."

"I'll get it," I said, putting my coffee cup down. "You stay here, I'll deal with whoever it is." I opened the door to Sapphire Shannon, who marched right by me followed by two burly young men I recognized from the night before. Bodyguards. "Oh, shit," I said again. "Oh, shit." She must have heard me, for she stopped in midstride, turned around.

"My what a nasty tongue you've got. Worse than mine." Then she continued into the room, took a quick look around to size up the situation, waved her bodyguards over to the window, headed for the bar herself, hoisting herself up into a sitting position on the counter, beside a champagne bottle. Her legs were spread wide apart. She was wearing the blue, off-the-shoulder, *Vanity Fair* cover top. I followed her, took up a standing position beside Eloise's armchair.

Robert, Daniel, Eloise, and I were immobile, waiting as she gave us the same once-over she had the night before, studying us all from head to toe. Her posture, I noticed as I waited for her to speak, was perfect.

"So. Don't tell me, let me guess." Her voice was

low, husky. She tossed her head, the cropped blond hair stayed impeccable. "You're the new wife, right?" Sapphire pointed at Eloise, smiled. Her fingernails were painted a metallic silver. Eloise didn't move. "No offense to you—" Sapphire pointed the same finger in my direction. "But she looks richer than you do, babe. And I figure whoever's running this show" —her hand swept, indicating the suite—"has big bucks. It's better than mine over at Caesar's. I think I should complain to the shit-assed management there. I come here a week early to get ready for this half-assed show and they give me a fucking awful suite. How do you like that?"

"What do you want, Amy?" Robert's forehead was furrowed but his voice sounded calm.

"What do I want, Robbo? So suspicious. I come in peace. I want to congratulate you on your new life, your bride. I was sorry to hear about—"

"All right," Robert cut in, "you've congratulated us. Now leave."

"Hey, slow down. I haven't even been introduced." She put her hands on her thighs. "I mean it, Robbo. I don't see why we can't be civilized here, why we can't be friends now. All the fucking water's gone over the fucking bridge or under the fucking bridge. Anyway, it's fucking gone. Let bygones be bygones. We've got new lives, new loves. No reason not to be on speaking terms."

Robert's jaw visibly tensed, his eyes closed.

"How's Bobby? How's our son?" Sapphire picked up the corkscrew from the bar beside her, twisted it back and forth. "I'm sick of this shit you've laid on him all these years, telling him not to communicate with me. Let it be, Robbo. When your other—"

"He's my son, Amy, not yours. You gave him up, remember?"

"History, history, ancient fucking history." Sapphire jumped down from the bar, threw the corkscrew on the floor. "You've punished me enough, dickhead." She tossed her head again. She looked truly Amazonian. I was surprised to feel physically frightened by a woman. "It's *over*, for fuck's sake. You've punished me enough. You've brainwashed him. He won't answer my letters, take my calls. I'm his *mother*, Robert. Can't you let up now? It's been twenty fucking years!" Her hands were clenched at her side. I saw with my peripheral vision the bodyguards move a step closer, exchange looks.

"*You're* a woman—" Sapphire had turned her wild eyes on Eloise now. "Even if you may be a dyke. You know, people make mistakes. But he's my *son*. Will you reason with this man? Will you tell him? Whatshername tried—"

"Leave Eloise alone, Amy. Leave Bobby alone. And leave *me* alone. You made your choice, you live with it. You've got plenty of other compensations. Bobby is twenty years old. He can make his own decisions. He doesn't *want* to see you." Robert stood up. "This conversation is over. If you don't leave now, I'll call security."

"Call the fucking FBI, see what I care. I'll go, though. You're impossible, a control freak. A fucking bastard. You couldn't be civilized if you tried." Sapphire stomped her foot on the floor like a giant female Rumpelstiltskin, then advanced on Eloise. I thought she was going to hit her or pull a snake from her cleavage and throw it in Eloise's lap. I desperately scanned the room for some object to defend Eloise with, a knife, a paperweight, anything.

"I feel sorry for you, babe." Sapphire loomed over Eloise, glaring down at her. Eloise cringed. "I feel fucking sorry for you. You married a monster. I did too. But at least I got out of it. Come on, boys. We're out of this hellhole."

With that, the hurricane swept out; I found myself clinging to the back of Eloise's chair for support, my legs shaking. Daniel was staring at the ceiling. Eloise's head slumped forward—I couldn't tell but guessed she was crying. Robert paced around the room once, ended up in front of the bar.

"Anyone for a drink?" he asked. He sounded oddly pleased.

"Yes." Eloise lifted her head wearily. "A gin and tonic." When Robert had mixed the drink and handed it to her, Eloise asked in a low voice, "Don't you think you should let her see Bobby? Maybe then she wouldn't bother us again. I never want to see her again."

"The point is Bobby doesn't want to see her. Don't be foolish, Cat." Robert smiled heartily. "She won't be back. She won't bother us again. Don't pay any attention to her."

"But Robert," Eloise sighed, took a large gulp of her gin, "how do you know she won't be back? She might have us followed. Oh, God, I wish she were dead. I wish we'd never come here."

"And miss out on this weekend with Stacy and Daniel? Cat, sweetheart, don't go all paranoid on me. I've dealt with her. End of story. Drink up, it will relax you. You're far too tense."

But Robert had been tense, very tense indeed when Sapphire had barged in. His words had been clipped, his face set like a rock. He hadn't truly dealt with Sapphire, I thought. She had certainly had the last word. Why did he seem so pleased now?

. We didn't go to Circus, Circus, that afternoon. Eloise didn't want to go out, was terrified, I suspect, of running into Sapphire again. It's often said that reality is less threatening than imagination, but in Eloise's case, meeting Sapphire had been much more damaging than thinking about her. In the flesh, Sapphire was every inch as compelling as on magazine covers, more so, for she had an aura of power. Even when asking Eloise for help on the Bobby issue, she'd been commanding, not begging. You didn't look at anyone else when Sapphire was in the room, and Sapphire knew that. The power didn't derive solely from sex appeal, I reflected. Here was a woman who knew what she wanted, got it, held it, a woman who had made it in a man's world, and managed to make it bigger than most men. I should have admired her, looked up to her as a female role model. Instead, I found myself cowed by her and the fear she inspired made me hate her.

Eloise hit the bottle with a vengeance. I tried to stop her, but she wouldn't have any of it. Robert finally pulled me to the side of the room, whispered, "Let her get drunk, Stacy. She needs to relax. You must understand that scene was too much for her. I'll put her to bed this afternoon—she'll be fine by tonight." I nodded, not entirely convinced that another bender was good for her, but, just as on that afternoon when she lost her virginity to John, who was I to stop her? Daniel had apparently absented himself mentally, for he watched Eloise's drinking, my efforts to halt it, and my eventual surrender without saying anything, smoking his cigarettes, staring at the ceiling, immersed in one of his silences. The longest I'd ever encountered. If Eloise's nerves were bad, mine were shot. Like her, I wished now that we'd never come to Vegas. The weekend was fast turning into a disaster.

By noon, as Robert and I made desperate small talk, Eloise sat quietly, the glass never far from her mouth. Daniel's refusal to take any part in this scene began to seem petulant; Robert and I were left to keep up a pretense of conversation while Eloise dissolved in our midst. Robert was waiting until she had drunk herself into enough of a stupor to be put to bed. When the moment finally arrived, when her head lolled forward in a daze, Robert picked her up in his arms. She looked tiny, the rag doll from our first day at Barnard.

"I'll call you when she's slept it off," he whispered. "I'm sure she'll be back in shape by early evening. Sixish, say."

"Okay," I answered for the both of us. "If there's anything I can do, let me know."

"She just had to get it out of her system." Robert hugged her to his chest, kissed her hair. "She's not a particularly strong person sometimes. Doesn't know how to let go of her fears. Liquor was the outlet to-day."

"And yesterday," Daniel put in sharply.

"It's been a difficult weekend, Daniel." Robert's tone was patient. "She'll be fine when it's over. We all need a little outside help occasionally."

15

MARCH 1990

"It's a reasonable request, Stacy. She is his mother. Why shouldn't she see him?"

"Why *should* she? You heard Robert. She gave Bobby up, relinquished him. Now she wants to waltz back into his life, the proud mama. Spare me."

Our room, a jail cell in comparison with the Chappell suite, felt as if it were shrinking further as Daniel and I waged war.

"Calm down. Your arms are waving like a windmill on coke. Why can't you see Sapphire Shannon as a person, too? She did what millions of men do every day—walk out on a marriage, leave a child. There could be any number of reasons—another woman, career, you name it. Does that mean those fathers don't have a right to see their children forever after? Can't you look at it from her point of view?"

"No. I'm looking at it from Robert's point of view. He gets ditched, *his* career ends up in ruins, he's left holding the baby. She's a monster."

"She's a feisty lady—"

"Stop defending her. Look what she did to Eloise, look at the effect she had."

"Stacy, Stacy, Eloise did it to herself. With Robert's help. He encouraged her to drink herself silly. What's the use of that? He's colluding with her, allowing her to get thrown by Sapphire. Why? That's what I'd like to know. All this business about Eloise being a weak person, that's bullshit. He treats her like a weakling, actually sits there and waits for her to pass out. He's the one undermining her strength, not Sapphire. I wonder who the other woman is, the whatshername Sapphire referred to."

"Who cares? She had no right to barge in like that."

"As far as you're concerned, Sapphire Shannon doesn't seem to have any rights. Aren't you being irrational?"

"You're just taking her side because you hate Robert so much. You *are* jealous of him, aren't you?"

"We've established that already, Stacy. I'm jealous of his money, yes. I'll admit it. But are you talking about something else here? Are you asking whether I'm jealous of him in regard to *you*?"

"Jesus. Why would you be jealous of him in regard to me? He's Eloise's husband."

"And that means he couldn't possibly fancy you, you couldn't possibly fancy him?"

"Yes, it means that. Of course. Absolutely."

"Be careful, Stacy. Don't protest too much."

"Well then, don't say such absurd things."

We were standing in the middle of the room. Daniel pulled a cigarette from his pocket, tapped it on his wrist, walked over to the king-size bed and sat down.

"I'll try not to. I'll try to say something profound."

He smiled. I didn't budge from my spot. "I want you to move in with me, Stacy. I want you to quit your job, come to New York, live with me. I realize what I'm asking. I know it's not fair. But this commuting business isn't going to work, even if Eloise funded us every weekend. I've flown out here twice now. I've told you I love you and I've meant it. I can't guarantee happiness, but I'll try my best."

It was all there, all the words I'd dreamed of were floating in the cigarette smoke between us. All I had to do was say yes. But I was still involved in our argument, feeling defensive, competitive.

"Do you expect me to wash your socks, cook for you?"

"Stacy," he sighed heavily. "That sounds like a scene from a bad seventies movie. Sometimes you'll wash the socks, sometimes I will, sometimes you'll cook, sometimes I will. How's that?"

"It won't end up that way. It never does. Read your own book. What about my career, my apartment, my *life*?"

"What about them? Are they that wonderful?"

"Jesus Christ. Don't be so dismissive."

"I'm not being dismissive. I *know* what I'm asking, okay? But I can't, I don't want to transfer to some California college. I'm not a Californian, I'm a New Yorker. I laugh at Woody Allen's California jokes. You have to decide whether it's worth it to you to give up your towards life out here and move in with me. It's your decision."

"Well, it's obviously not worth it to *you* to give up *your* life. Why should it be worth it to me?"

"I don't know why. I'm just asking if it is. That's all."

"It's not." I folded my arms.

"Well, that sounds decisive." Daniel stood up, grabbed his baseball cap off the chair, began to walk past me toward the door. As he came level with me, he reached out, squeezed my shoulder. "I'm going to play poker. To answer your question, I'm not jealous of Robert apropos you, no. I'm jealous of whatever demon inside you made that stupid choice just now."

A good job of self-sabotage. I had stepped on the mine that was my pride and blown myself up. Sure, I could run after him, go down on my knees in the hallway, but I'd have to be able to move, not stand in the middle of the room paralysed. If only I hadn't been so hurt by Buddy, if only Daniel and I hadn't had that argument about Sapphire just before he asked me, if only he hadn't written that damn book.

The entire subject of men and women, what they wanted, how they differed, *if* they differed fundamentally, was a maze. I didn't have a map, was tired of taking wrong turns and running into walls. If only Gloria Steinem and Germaine Greer had kept their big mouths shut twenty years ago. I might be settled in a suburb with five children, a dog, happy as the proverbial clam to give up my individuality for the better good of the family. If only.

I shuffled to the bed, lay down, and cried. Did I love Daniel or was he my last ditch chance as a thirty-something woman? Had I loved Buddy, or, as he claimed, loved the idea of him, the romantic ideal? Just exactly how fucked up was I? Not a question I wanted to answer as I sobbed. If only I could have an accident. Nothing fatal, but bad enough to land me in the hospital. Daniel would come visit me. We could have a tearful reconciliation. I would be looked after by kindly nurses, abrogate responsibility for myself. Let other people take over my life, tell me what to do. Why did *I* have to be the one to decide whether I moved in with Daniel or not? If only he'd swept me up in his arms and carried me away, carried me as Robert had carried Eloise on their wedding night, as he had carried her this morning. If only Daniel had been more persistent. If only.

Could I track Daniel down in the poker room, interrupt his game, announce to the underworld figures that this was the man for me? That would be romantic. That would be histrionic. That would be an option. Something Sapphire Shannon might do, because she was such a "feisty" lady. Would I have to be a feisty lady all my life to please Daniel? If I started to relax, showed my weakness, would he get bored?

I dragged myself out of bed, went into the bathroom, washed my face. It was time to get a grip on myself, but where were the handles? I needed some caffeine, a good hot cup of coffee to go with my cigarettes. After Buddy left me, I went on a caffeine and nicotine binge; cigarettes, Cokes, coffee, and chocolate saw me through the first months of divorce. I was about to call room service when I heard a knock on the door. Daniel. After splashing more water on my red-rimmed eyes, I ran to open it, to throw myself in his arms. The arms I landed in belonged to Robert.

"Hey, Stacy!" He put one arm around me. He was

carrying his guitar in the other hand. "What's wrong? Why the tears?" He guided me into the room, brushed my disheveled hair back from my forehead. "Somebody been beating you up?"

"No. I've been beating myself up." I had recovered quickly from my disappointment. At that point, any human presence was welcome.

"Ah, that's the worst kind of beating to take. I know all about it." He looked around the room quickly. "Hell, it's smoky in here. Where's Daniel?"

"Playing poker, I think. How's Eloise?"

"In Never Never Land still. She'll need a few more hours of sleep before she rejoins the human race." Robert slipped off his loafers, moved to the chair in the corner of the room. "Mind if I play a few tunes? I was afraid I might wake Cat up, so I came down here to see what you two were doing, whether you wanted a little entertainment."

"I'd love it. It might be just the thing to calm me down."

"Nerves again, Stace?" He gave me a sharp look, strummed a few chords. "Listen, if you need to relax, I'll help you."

"I don't think a neck massage will do it this time, Robert."

"No, not that. Remember I said everyone needs some outside help once in a while? We've all had a strange weekend. Why don't you join me in a smoke?" Reaching into his inside jacket pocket, he pulled out what I recognized as two joints. "Cat told me you two never did drugs at college, but one reefer isn't going to hurt you. You should experience it, Stace. It's part of our generation's culture.''

"I don't know—" Either I joined Robert or I kicked him out politely, went down to find Daniel, to tell him I'd changed my mind. But had I? If I told Daniel I would move in with him, would I feel unsure and hysteria-prone the moment after the words were spoken? I wasn't in any shape to make a major decision. "Sure. Why not?"

Robert lit my joint, then his, settled back in his chair, inhaling deeply. I had seen enough movies, knew what I was supposed to do to get the maximum effect of the pot. Inhaling was second nature to me anyway. Fixing the pillows behind me on the bed, I sat against them, stretched my legs out, waited for Robert's show to commence.

The first tune had a calypso beat, a long introduction before Robert began to sing. "Upon arriving at the well-known port of Caypot, All the people come to say, 'Oh, my, oh God, Wipe that silly frown off your face, If you don't live it up you'll never live it down, boy.' " What well-known port of Caypot? I wondered briefly. A rhyming device? I began to laugh, then recognized the words and stopped myself. This was Robert's song, one of the titles on his album. He'd written it. And he was smiling as he sang it; his voice had a West Indian lilt. "Lift your hat, let the wind blow. Let the sun dazzle your mind, And let me tell you of this truth, That the women love the beaches and the breeze, That you've never tasted life with such ease, Take that careworn look off your face, If you don't live it up, You'll never live it down, boy." He segued into "Yellow Bird." Airplane music on a flight to Jamaica, Harry Belafonte in whiteface, but it worked. As with "Good Ship Lollipop," he slowed the pace, turned 'Yellow Bird' into an aching lament. The two songs complemented each other perfectly. I was entranced. And more understanding of why his album hadn't been a success. "If You Don't Live It Up" was not a pop song, it was an entirely different genre, not a tune to disco to or to play at top volume on the car radio. I took another hit of the joint and felt my body relax, my shoulders drop. I would prefer Robert to Kenny Rogers any day. His voice was more subtle, his phrasing more thoughtful. From "Yellow Bird" to "Jamaica, Farewell," then on to "No Woman No Cry." I had been transported to the Caribbean, and sat back peacefully, smoking the joint, picturing the palm trees, feeling the warmth of the air.

"Now." He finished, inhaled his dope. "Enough of that. What would you like to hear, Stace? Any requests?"

"That was beautiful, Robert. God, anything. Anything slow."

"Say it's only a paper moon, Hanging over a cardboard tree, But it wouldn't be make believe, If you believed in me . . ." He was off again, another old favorite. I listened to the lyrics properly for the first time, was affected by them; this was all the great old movies rolled up into one song. He continued along the Cole Porter, Irving Berlin trail, wound up with "A Fine Romance." At its conclusion, I felt cocooned, peaceful. I had almost forgotten about Daniel.

"Stacy." Robert placed his guitar carefully on the floor beside him. "Are you hungry?"

"Now that you mention it, yes. I'm starving."

"Good. Let's order some food up. What would you say to some chocolate ice cream and a platter of French fries?"

I laughed.

"That sounds disgusting. Wonderful. Ketchup. We need ketchup for the French fries." My joint was three quarters finished.

"Ketchup coming up." Robert stood and strolled over to the phone beside the bed to order our frightful concoction of food.

"Robert—" I laughed again. "Where the hell is Caypot? The well-known port of Caypot? I've never heard of it."

"Ah, but Stacy, do you think you have to have heard of a place for it to exist?"

"If it's well known, it should be well known. That makes sense, doesn't it?"

"Not necessarily."

"No? Maybe not. I'll have to think about that one. You wrote that song. I know you did. I saw your album sleeve in New York. Where's the album?"

He lay down across the foot of the bed.

"What a little snoop you are." He laughed. We laughed together. "Miss White in the study with a wrench. The object of this exercise is to get you to relax, not to ferret out all my little secrets. Close your eyes, Stacy." I obeyed, pushed my head back farther into the pillows as I felt his hands remove my shoes, and then begin to massage my feet. It felt too wonderful for me even to consider that it might not be appropriate. "You tell *me* what you were beating yourself up about when I came in."

"Choices. The need to make a choice."

"Between life in New York with Daniel and life in San Francisco by yourself, presumably?"

I nodded dreamily. Daniel's asking me to move in with him seemed a long time ago.

"You women." I felt I could hear him shake his head. "You're all so tense. Because you're all so greedy. You're like a bunch of hyperactive children hunting for Easter eggs."

"Hey," I cried. "That's a tender spot there." Jerking back, I opened my eyes and tried to focus on Robert. "What were you saying about Easter?"

"Never mind." He took my foot back, rubbed it gently, one toe at a time, and I sank back into oblivion again. The doorbell brought me to—I'd been so relaxed I'd fallen asleep. Robert went to answer it. I briefly wondered what to say if it were Daniel. Of course it wouldn't be Daniel, though. He had his own key. I should have thought of that before, when Robert knocked. The fact that Daniel had his own key seemed supremely important and I concentrated on it as Robert helped the waiter put the ice cream and French fries on the bedside table. He produced a wad of bills from his pocket and I saw a waiter's pleased face. Big tipper. That's nice, I thought. But then he can afford to be.

"Should we call Eloise? Get her to join us?" I asked, sufficiently self-aware to realize I hoped he would say no. Why did I want to stretch this time alone with

Robert? Because I didn't have to think about anything, I realized. I didn't have to worry about myself or anyone else. I could postpone anxiety. Robert and I were in a different world, we were taking a break together. Not mentioning Sapphire, not talking about anything crucial. Nothing wrong with that, I assured myself, sat up, and took a handful of French fries as the waiter disappeared.

"Let's let her sleep, Stace. What do you say?"

I nodded, stuffing the fries in my mouth.

"Did *you* have a good sleep?"

"Mmm." I couldn't speak.

We devoured the fries intently, taking turns dipping them in ketchup. I was about to start on the ice cream when Robert went back to his chair, picked up his guitar, strummed with a flourish and began, "It wasn't me who started this old crazy Asian War." Kenny Rogers. "Ruby, Don't Take Your Love to Town." He was doing a perfect impersonation, exaggerating it just enough to have me in total hysterics. Laughing so hard, I could barely catch my breath between paroxysms of mirth. "Ru-uu-uu-uu-beeeee—" He elongated the name so much I was weeping with laughter. "For God's sake turn around." He finished on a high squeak, the opposite of Kenny's low growl, bowed, patted himself on the back. I tried to clap but found it difficult to coordinate my hands.

"I can't move," I gasped out. "Don't make me laugh any more. Please." I didn't know what was happening to me, I felt so weak, so totally abandoned to laughter. Robert came back to my side, leaned over me, licked the tears off my face with his tongue, and kissed me on the lips. That hard, closed-mouth kiss I remembered from the wedding.

"Robert—" Before I could continue, he had taken a spoon of chocolate ice cream and shoved it in my mouth.

"Shh." He put his finger to his lips. "Just be quiet." He fed me three spoons of ice cream, then walked away, toward the door. He's leaving, I thought. He's the strangest man I've ever met. He stopped by the door, reached out, and turned off the lights. "It's nicer in the dark, isn't it, Stacy?" He went over to the window and pulled the curtains shut.

I didn't move, didn't say a word, unsure of what was going to happen next. Trying to decide whether I was frightened. Tasting the cold chocolate still. Think calmly, I told myself. He's not going to rape you. He's Eloise's husband. I could make out his movement in the dark, see his form walk over to his guitar, pick it up. I have no idea what he played; there were no words, just sound, chords and notes wafting around the room. I groped for my cigarettes on the bedside table, found them, lit one. The tip glowed, comforted me. The music stopped; Robert was kneeling beside the bed, his hands suddenly on mine.

"Come here," he said. "Be quiet." This time he kissed me gently, so tentatively it could have been a first kiss. The difference between his commanding tone when he said "be quiet," and this soft, boylike kiss threw me totally. I felt sucked in, as if by an undertow, drawing me out over my head, into the fastest current imaginable. My cigarette was in my hand, I could feel it, see the burning top. That's like my body,

I thought. My body's burning. Robert broke off the kiss, placed my hands on either side of me, his head hovered over my blouse.

"Shh," he said. "Watch me." He undid my buttons with his teeth. I was astounded, amazed, watching him, absorbed in the process; each button slipped out without any struggle whatsoever, as if he'd been using his hands.

"Don't."

"Don't what, Stacy?" he murmured, lifting back each side of my blouse with his teeth, uncovering me, braless to his gaze. "Don't do this?" He brushed my nipple with his tongue. "Or this?" The tongue was on my other nipple now, circling it. "Hmm? What should I not do?" My body was making decisions for me, answering his questions for him. For me. I took a drag of my cigarette, blew out the smoke toward the ceiling. His tongue was running wild over my stomach now. He unsnapped my jeans button with his teeth. In the dark, I groped for an ashtray, found one. Ground my cigarette into it. And then I reached down and ran my hands through his hair.

"Should I not do that?" He had pulled my jeans off me, buried his tongue inside me, treated me to a subtle exploration. Then he had raised his head, asked me that question, the question that was becoming a litany. "Answer me, Stacy. Should I not do that anymore?" I shook my head.

"Talk to me, Stacy. Tell me. Should I do it?"

I raised my hips, pushed myself at him. This had to happen. He couldn't stop. I didn't want him to stop. He was biting me now, gently, arousing bites, nips at my most sensitive part, all the while undoing his belt, pulling his trousers down. Then he raised himself, yanked his shirt off, kneeling naked between my legs, displaying a huge penis. Larger than I'd ever seen. He could kill me with that, I thought, but I was too lust-ridden to let that thought interfere.

"Now," he said, his voice low, menacing. "What do you think I should do now?"

"Just do it, Robert. For God's sake, do it." I didn't know if he'd heard me; my voice was below a whisper. What he proceeded to do was brutish, animal mating. No passion, no fulfillment, just blank, detached thrusting. Hard, deep, in and out motions with no letup, as close to rape as possible with a consenting female. I wasn't a part of it. I wasn't there. I could have been a corpse. He was tearing me, wounding me, and above all not stopping. My head was jolting back and forth, side to side with the force of it. It went on and on and on. When I looked into his face I saw a determined, grim, harsh mouth; I saw bleak black eyes. An avenging devil. But what was I? A whore screwing her best friend's husband. I deserved to suffer. I deserved to die.

He pulled out abruptly, with no hint that he'd finished. He hadn't, at least physically. He hadn't come, of that I was sure. Was he going to do something else? Something even worse? Profound relief swept through me as I saw him reach for his shirt. It was over.

How long had we been there? What was he going to do now? How could this have happened? All the questions jostled in my brain, each one seemed as important as the other. I scanned the room for a clock before I remembered I had my watch on, but I was too intent on Robert's next moves to dare to glance down, away from him.

The way he put his clothes on reminded me of someone. Bobby. Like father, like son. My eyes closed. Perhaps when I opened them, he would *be* Bobby. This could all have been a mistake, a nightmare, a time warp. The lights came on, I opened my eyes. Robert. Sitting in the chair as if nothing had happened, staring at me. I became aware of my nakedness then, leaped up and searched for my clothes, threw them on as if there had been a fire alarm ringing in the corridor.

"Calm down, Stace."

"Robert, please leave." I wanted to cry but didn't feel as if I had any tears left.

"I'll leave. But don't blame yourself. Or me. These things happen. I won't tell Eloise, if that's what you're so het up about."

"Robert"—I shook my head, my neck was aching—"whether you tell Eloise or not, don't you understand what I've just done? What we've just done? I feel sick." I wanted to hide in the closet, I wanted him to leave. At the same time, I dreaded his leaving. I'd be alone with my conscience.

"You certainly do take things to heart." Robert laughed. Looking at him, the broad, open, laughing face, I superimposed the emotionless, scary features of the man on top of me a few minutes ago. An ugly, cruel stranger with massive shoulders. Who was this man? Was he always like that in bed? Poor Eloise.

Jesus Christ. Eloise. How could I ever look at her again? Daniel. Oh, shit, Daniel. "So." Robert stood, stretched, yawned casually. "I'll go upstairs now. Time to wake Eloise up." He reached for his guitar. "A very pleasant interlude, Stace." He approached me, chucked me under the chin. "See you later, alligator."

"Robert—" I didn't want to touch him, but put my hand on his arm to stop him from walking out. "This can never happen again. Do you understand that?"

He tilted his head, screwed his mouth to the side, a look of puzzled amusement.

"Listen, Stacy, everyone in the world has affairs. Everyone screws around sometimes. You should have seen my mother. She'd be out with some guy every other night. Get dressed up, even ask my father how she looked before she went out. Stand in front of his wheelchair, blocking his view of the TV and do a little pirouette.

"What we did isn't going to hurt anyone now, is it? You don't tell Daniel, I don't tell Eloise. No big deal. This little episode never happened."

"But it did," I said more to myself than to him. He was gone anyway, the door had closed. I was left alone to face the walls, the melted ice cream lying in its dish, the joints smoked down to the last breath, the crumpled bedcover. I was left alone to face myself.

What I had done, what I had allowed to occur was unforgivable. Rank betrayal. There were no mitigating circumstances, no excuses possible. Oh, sure, I could say that I was stoned for the first time in my life, screwing under the influence, as it were. But I'd been sufficiently aware of what was happening, I hadn't been given knockout drops. I had participated, at least at the beginning. At the end I'd lain there like a Victorian virgin, but at the beginning I'd been involved. Any jury would find me guilty. The twelve angry men and women in my brain were screaming for punishment.

Eloise. Of all people to betray. Eloise who had trusted me enough to admit that she was insecure about sex. Fucking hell. The perfect words. Fucking hell.

I paced the room. I tidied it up. I took a bath. Changed into a different set of clothes. All the while I could hear Robert's voice. *What shouldn't I do, Stacy? Should I not do this?* I could feel his hair in my hands, feel him inside me, pounding away. My womb ached. I would never be able to erase this afternoon, never feel the same about myself again. In short order I had slept with Bobby, Daniel, Robert. I should be forced to wear a scarlet letter. I should be dressed in Sapphire's T-shirt. SLUT.

The phone rang. I let it continue, sat on the edge of the bathtub smoking. What would happen next? Daniel would come back from playing poker. Stride in in his baseball cap. Smell the lingering marijuana. Ask me questions. What had I done this afternoon? *Oh, I got stoned and slept with Robert.* No. I'd have to lie. Lie to him, lie to Eloise. Be a good actress. Sit there watching Kenny Rogers with a smile on my face. I stood up, looked at myself in the bathroom mirror, practiced a smile. A transparently guilty face stared back at me.

I ran to the closet, dragged my suitcase out, ransacked the room for my clothes. I had to get out. Immediately. I couldn't lie, couldn't carry on a charade. I had to get back home, to my safe, sagging bookshelves, my untouched piano, my sanctuary. I opened the windows, hoping the room would air out. At least there weren't any telltale signs of sex. No stained sheets. I had Robert to thank for that. The phone rang again, making me think faster. I didn't have much time. The people I least wanted to see would be looking for me.

> Dear Daniel,
> I have to go back home. I'm sorry for everything, but it's all impossible. Please make my excuses to Eloise. Tell her I'm not well. Tell her how sorry I am. Don't try to call me. It's useless. I'm not the right person for you. Too many demons.
>
> > Love,
> > Stacy

The plane back to San Francisco was quiet, half empty. The few people on it looked disappointed, had probably had to cut short their weekend because of heavy losses. I stared down at the cover of the book in my lap. *Fear and Loathing in Las Vegas.* Hunter Thompson didn't know the half of it.

16

MARCH 1990

According to a book I once skimmed, there is only a certain amount of space in the human brain for ideas. Therefore all ideas are waging war, competing against each other for room, for a place to sit down in our heads, so to speak. When I walked into my apartment, one idea was king of the castle in my brain—it had driven out all the others and taken over completely. It was sitting back with its feet up, smoking a cigar. The idea was self-disgust.

I tried to ignore the flashing light on my answering machine. Two messages, and I could guess whom they were from. Daniel and Eloise. I threw my bag down in the bedroom, fixed myself a strong gin and tonic, and circled my telephone. I could choose not to listen to the messages, that was one possibility. What would a corporation call that tactic—avoidance management? If there was a truly important message, if one of my parents had died, for example, I would be called back. But that meant I'd have to answer the phone. Whereas if I listened to the messages now . . . The light signaled to me like unopened bills lying on a desk. Better to get it over with quickly.

Beep.

At the sound of Daniel's voice, I flinched, sank down on the sofa, and gulped my gin.

"Stacy, you idiot. What do you think you're doing leaving me here? The least you could have done was stick it out through Kenny Rogers. The note was a touch melodramatic, don't you think? I might have to reconsider that A I gave you. I won some money this afternoon and I was going to buy you something really kitsch. You lose. And so do I. Lucky in poker, unlucky in love."

He hung up. He had sounded amused. What was there to be amused about? Was it so impossible to take me seriously? I had written him a farewell note, walked out of his life, and he had sounded amused.

Beep

"Stace, hi. Sorry you're so sick. I wish you'd told us you weren't feeling well this morning. We could have gotten a doctor for you here. And I wish you'd waited till I'd woken up before you left. We have to go see Kenny Rogers now, but get better soon, I'll call you tomorrow and—" Robert's voice broke in. "And Stace, get lots of rest, drink lots of fluid, and take aspirin. The old remedies always work, don't they? Be a good girl and take care of yourself. We hate to think of you suffering. Good-bye."

I put my head in my hands and rubbed my forehead as hard as I could. Hearing his words made me feel as if I was covered in warts. The gall he had in talking to me that way was revolting. It was a combination of deceit, a condescending attitude, and gross self-confidence. Though he could afford to be self-confident. I wasn't about to tell Eloise of our seedy run-in, and he knew that. *Be a good girl.* A good girl was exactly what I wasn't. I lit a cigarette and leaned back, overcome by a desire to kill Robert, to watch him squirm as I pushed the knife in, even better, to strangle him slowly with one of his own guitar strings. Watch his eyes pop out as he begged for mercy. If his mother had been such an outright bitch to his father, treating him inhumanely, making him watch as she prepared to go out with other men, how could he be so offhand about his conduct to his own wife? He hadn't felt guilty, not in the least; he'd been cavalier and, yes, amused. Why were these cataclysmic events so amusing to those two men? Eloise and I were like pawns being moved square by square across the chessboard while the men, the bishops, the knights, the rooks, swept past us. Why weren't we the queens, though? Why weren't Eloise and I, two supposedly bright, reasonably attractive females, in charge of the game?

Sure, Stacy, I thought. And how could we be in charge when we were busy warring against each other. Female solidarity? Please. I had just had sex with my best friend's husband, and my best friend was terrified of her husband's first wife. Sapphire, Eloise, and I would make a great advertisement for the power of sisterhood.

The phone rang. Terrific. Who now? The IRS? Robert again to remind me to wrap up warm? Daniel to tell me more about his poker games? I answered without answering, in other words I picked up the phone, but didn't say anything.

263

"Hello." I heard a male voice. But not Daniel, not Robert. Familiar, but not instantly placeable. "Stacy? Are you there?" I knew that voice. "Stacy?" I waited, making sure. "Stacy?"

"Yes, I'm here, Buddy." My life was on a downward spiral, the nadir of which was this telephone call. My ex-husband, who was probably calling me to tell me what a lousy wife I'd been. My eyes closed. I sat down on the floor. This had to be some kind of a joke.

"Are you all right? You don't sound very well."

"I've been better."

"Sorry. Should I call again another time? It's just that I was in San Francisco for business yesterday and I stayed over. I thought, well, you know, it's been a long time. It would be nice to get together for a drink."

I reached for my gin and tonic, finished it.

"Water over the bridge."

"What? Stacy? Are you sure you're okay?"

"I'm fine." Opening my eyes, I lit a cigarette from the butt of my last one. "Buddy—do you really think it's a good idea to have a drink? Wouldn't it be too much like a school reunion? Both of us trying to prove to each other how well we've done over the years?"

"That's a very cynical position to take."

"I wasn't always a cynic."

"Uh-oh. Is that a jibe at me? Is everything still all my fault, Stacy?"

"No, Buddy," I sighed. "There's much too much that's my fault. I'll take some responsibility now. Sure. Of course we can have a drink. In fact . . ." In fact, I thought, maybe Buddy's call was the only event capable of diverting my attention away from my monstrous self. I knew that my afternoon with Robert had cut off a piece of my past, had made it impossible now for me to see Eloise again, ever. I would have to make excuses if she called, turn down the plane tickets, plead any engagements I could think of, but I could never be in the same room with her again. I would explode with guilt. And Daniel, well, Daniel was gone too. I'd blown the whole damn thing.

Buddy, at this point, might be a welcome relief. At least I wouldn't be alone. And Buddy, despite all our problems, had never been amused by me. Annoyed, yes, but not amused.

"In fact, why don't you come over here, we can have a drink in peace? I don't think I could face going out right now. I've just gotten back from Las Vegas."

"Las Vegas? You? Things have changed."

"It's a long story, Buddy," I said, then gave him the address. And it's a story, I thought, I'm not about to tell.

He was more distinguished-looking than I would have guessed; he had a calm, competent professional face that had aged well—just enough wrinkles around the eyes to make his smile reassuring, just enough of a bulge around the stomach to suggest an ease with his life. When he sat down on my sofa, having kissed me on both cheeks and handed me a bottle of champagne, he immediately pulled his leg up to his chest, rested his chin on his knee. He'd assumed that I wouldn't mind his shoe on my sofa, and he'd been right to assume that. It was the first-night West End Bar pose and it still worked.

I couldn't decide whether I was more nervous or curious. I'd dressed in jeans and a sweatshirt, not wanting to seem too formal or too eager to please. If I'd put on one of my short skirts, he'd think I was trying to seem young, I decided. And the only really perfect clothes for the occasion were the ones Eloise had lent me, the brunch-with-Daniel outfit. I have to admit that I almost wore them.

Here was the man I'd walked down an aisle with, a man I'd sworn to love forever, sitting with his leg up on my sofa. An intimate stranger. That's what he was. I knew everything and nothing about him. I wished that I was sitting across from Daniel, I wished Daniel would sigh and grin and shrug his shoulders and call me a lamebrain.

"So—" He took the glass of champagne I proffered. "No second marriage, no husband lurking around?" That *would* be the first question he asked. Not how was work, how much money did I make, how successful was I, but where's the man? That question brought a lot of unpleasant memories rushing back.

"No." It was almost nine o'clock at night. What were we doing having drinks in my apartment? What was this person doing here? I'd asked him, I reminded myself. I'd made another major mistake. "How about you?"

"Mmm." He nodded, reaching into his pocket. I was sitting in the armchair at a right angle to him and I knew what was coming with a dreadful certainty. "Would you believe I have two kids now? Look." He passed the pictures over and I flipped as quickly as humanly possible through them. Two smiling, tow-headed children on the beach. I didn't want to see their resemblance to their father, I didn't want to think what could have been.

"They're beautiful, Buddy." I handed them back and watched as he stared down at them.

"You know, I used to make fun of people who thought their children were the most special kids in the universe. But—" He looked up from the pictures and grinned. "I'm one of those people myself now." I smiled back at him. This was torture specifically designed to pay me back for what I'd done that afternoon.

"Jane—their mother—she's the blonde. I don't have a picture of her with me. She's a lawyer too." I shook my head up and down, the smile shook with it.

"That's nice."

"Oh, Stacy, you're not still smoking?" I hadn't even noticed that I'd lit a cigarette. "Listen—how's work? Are you running the store now?"

"Yeah." Buddy—I wanted to say—cut the crap. You don't care about my work, you don't care about me. It's just like I said on the phone. You want to compare notes and see how well you've fared against me. The two kids, the blond, working wife, your clean-cut, still-handsome, if not more so, face—you're chalking them all up against me, scoring points. You'll walk out of here and shake your head and say, "Whew—that was a close call. Glad I got out of that when I did." Go back to your hotel and call Jane and tell her how much you love her. I poured myself a second glass of champagne. "But I'm afraid I won't be working for too much longer, actually."

"Really?" Buddy switched legs, perched his chin on his right knee. "Why's that?"

I felt giddy with the horror of it all, the crazy confluence of events—hours after sleeping with my best friend's husband I was having drinks with my ex, discussing his wife and children. It was so absurd, so dreadful, my head felt as if it were full of helium.

"I'm going to get married soon," I said, smiling.

"Great." He lifted his glass, toasted to me. All those years ago we'd toasted each other in my parents' house, clinked our glasses with locked eyes and interlocked hearts. "To whom, if you don't mind my asking?"

"Placido Domingo."

"What?" His head rose off his chin, his eyebrows scrunched up. Then he settled back down, smiled at me. "Very funny, Stacy. God, you had me there for a second."

All those times we had laughed together in bed, before our marriage. All that innocence. I wanted to cry—not for Buddy, or for me, but for the lost innocence, the dreamy, starry-eyed romantic innocence of a couple first starting out. That could never be recreated. You could find love the second or third or fourth time around, a love you might be able to live with happily for the rest of your life, but you'd never have that untouched innocence. You'd be tainted. That was the word. Tainted.

I felt tired and lost and alone. Homesick, but not for any particular home. An unspecific yearning. Perhaps I was having a nervous breakdown after all. I could be carted off to a hospital screaming that I was going to be Mrs. Domingo.

"So how long have you and Jane been married?"

"Seven years."

"Do you throw the groceries at her?"

"You know, I do that with the kids now. They love it." He laughed. Buddy had always had a nice laugh, a soft, shy laugh. He was boyish despite the professional, competent veneer. He reminded me of Richard Gere in *Pretty Woman*. I wondered whether Jane looked like Julia Roberts. No, she was blond. I pictured him hurling eggs at the little blonds I'd seen in the pictures, Jane standing by watching with a contented maternal happiness. They were all incredibly coordinated and caught the eggs with one hand. They juggled them. That image killed the polite conversation I had intended.

"Well, Buddy, I'll call you a cab. I've had a long, exhausting day."

"Stacy, come on. We've barely started to talk. We've got so much to catch up on. Why don't we go out to dinner?"

"Because I'm tired. Because I lost everything in Las Vegas."

"What do you mean? You gambled away your savings? This doesn't sound like you, Stacy."

"I know, I know. I didn't lose any money, Buddy."

"Are you all right? Can I help? You should come back to New York and visit. We have a great house on Long Island now, you could relax. Jane would love it. We could throw a few dinner parties for you."

269

And introduce me to some eligible men, no doubt.

"Buddy." I shook my head. "Buddy, Jane wouldn't love it. Why would she love an ex-wife hanging around? It's a very civilized thought, but that's not the way people work. She'd be pissed off. I would be in her position." I was thinking of Daniel's ex-wife—the last person in the world I would want to throw a dinner party for.

"You're wrong about that. You don't know her. If I tell her I've seen you, she'll be pleased. She would want us to be friends."

"Bullshit." I was tired of him, of myself, of anything to do with men and women. "I think you should leave now, Buddy."

"Okay. Fine. I'll leave. I'm sorry this didn't work out well." He put his coat on, stood by the door, his hand on the doorknob. "Stacy, I don't want us to be on bad terms. Really. There's no need for it. If you don't want to be friends, fine, I can understand that. But we don't have to be enemies." I could feel my heartbeat slow down as he said those words. I didn't have to hate him anymore. I'd been wrong, he wasn't an intimate stranger, he was simply a stranger. Someone I once knew who was now married to a lawyer named Jane and had two kids. Buddy wasn't a nasty, sadistic, depraved man who had intentionally hurt me; no, I'd been hurt by a failed relationship. In his legal terms, there was no malice aforethought in his actions toward me. He hadn't set out to destroy me. He had believed it when he told me he loved me and he believed it when he told me he didn't. That I preferred the former truth to the latter was my problem.

"No, we don't have to be enemies." I bit my lip, went over and gave him a hug, the good-bye hug you don't get to have in a painful divorce. It was a familiar, comfortable hug and when I stepped back I felt a shadow which had been following me for years slip away. I smiled up at him. He would be a good father, I could tell. "Tonight was just bad timing."

"That's better." He smiled as well. He was halfway out the door when he turned back to me. "Listen, before I go, whatever happened to Eloise?"

"She got married and she's blissfully happy, living in New York."

"Still stinking rich?"

"Mmm hmm." I nodded.

"Lucky man," he said wistfully.

"He's—" I interrupted myself. "He was married once before—to Sapphire Shannon."

Buddy whistled. We should have had all our talks when he was halfway out the door; we were both fine if we saw an end in sight. The infinity of marriage to each other had been the damning element.

"*Seriously* lucky man." He shook his head. "Sapphire Shannon. I don't envy Eloise. Sapphire Shannon would be a hard act to follow. As bad as Placido Domingo." He laughed, now three quarters out the door. "If you change your mind, call us. Good luck, Stacy."

"Thanks," I said. "You too." And that was it. I'd never call him. We wouldn't have any more reunions. Another part of my past disappearing for good. This had been a day James Joyce could have done wonders with.

I didn't turn off any lights, didn't get undressed. Instead I headed fully clothed for my bed with a brief stop for a sleeping pill en route. I turned on the television, wondering if I'd be awake for *Saturday Night Live,* then flipped on the radio as well. My apartment was buzzing with activity, voices and music competing with each other as I waited for the pill to kick in. And they'd be there when I woke up tomorrow as well. I'd leave the TV and radio on all night so I wouldn't be alone. When I woke up, I'd be comforted by Sunday morning preachers, bible bashers.

At least I hadn't slept with my ex-husband. That was one point in my favor. I hadn't made a pass at him to try and get my own back on seraphic Jane and the kids. Bad thought. It led me straight back to Robert.

He hadn't wanted me, that was becoming more and more clear as the hours passed. He hadn't slept with me because he was overcome by lust, he hadn't been temporarily unhinged by passion. There was something calculated about that afternoon. But what? And why?

Nothing. No reason. I had drifted into a conspiracy theory when all the afternoon had been about was sex. Men took it when they could get it, had it off and forgot about it. It was a purely physical act, no different than my tennis game with Robert had been, only a lot less enjoyable. He hadn't ejaculated, he'd been rough, brutish, and uninterested, but maybe that's what appealed to him. Sex had no significance. It was ridiculous. Meaningless. As Robert had pronounced: no big deal. Just something for men and women to do together to while away the time. Nothing special about it. Maybe I hadn't done anything so awful after all.

Ah, but what if Eloise had slept with Buddy all those years ago. Would that have been a big deal? What if Eloise were sleeping with Daniel right now. How would I feel about that? Would I compare it to a tennis match? *There's no such thing as free love*—I heard Eloise's eighteen-year-old voice. *You have to pay for it.* And there's no such thing as a zipless fuck for a woman either. Erica Jong had been off base on that one. Women can't separate emotions from sex, hard as they might try. I could see Eloise's face as she threw that novel across the room. Why is sex so important? she'd asked me and I'd countered with an affirmation of love. But Eloise was right. Sex is a very big deal indeed. For women.

My brain race was showing no signs of stopping. I stood up and weaved back into my bathroom, groped for another sleeping pill. I couldn't successfully rationalize my behavior with Robert. Or his with me. But I could try to blot it out.

17

MARCH–
DECEMBER 1990

When Eloise called the next morning, I let the answering machine do my talking for me. She was exuberant, almost incoherent with praise for Kenny Rogers. "Just call me back, Stace," she said at the end. "We'll be in New York tomorrow. I want to talk to you about Daniel. He misses you. We all miss you. Just call me back tomorrow." I could no more just call her back than a heroin junkie could just say no to drugs. Robert hadn't told her about our afternoon, obviously, given the friendly tone she used, but that didn't make me feel any better. I knew I should call her to allay any suspicions a prolonged silence might arouse, but I couldn't. I didn't want to talk to her. So I wrote to her instead.

Dear Eloise,
Remember that air-conditioned mind I wanted? Well, I've been given a wonderful break. The executives at Dalton's have offered me a year-long world tour of bookstores. Check out the competition in foreign cities, see if we should expand into Europe, Japan. It's a wonderful opportunity

and one I can't pass up on. So I'll be out of touch for quite a while, but I hope all is well with you. I'll contact you when I get back.

All my love,
Stace

I should have said I was going on a world cruise with Placido Domingo. My lies were building me a wonderful life—the truth was less enticing. But the letter would stop Eloise's phone calls and give me the breathing space I needed. I couldn't bear to hear her trusting voice again.

I had all sorts of stories ready to keep Daniel at bay and never got to use one of them. He was incommunicado. I was in a state. Should I call him, apologize, hop on a plane to New York, show up at his apartment as he had at mine? I was too frightened that I'd surprise him with another woman—who was the woman he'd canceled the lunch date with to meet me? Where was she now? In his arms?—and too frightened that he might ask me questions I couldn't answer. What did you do that afternoon in Las Vegas, Stacy? Tell me exactly why you ran away. I don't believe all this bullshit about not being the right person for me—there's something more, isn't there?

So I didn't call, I didn't make a surprise visit—I hunkered down in San Francisco, working, going to the occasional party, watching a lot of movies and a lot of TV. I spent a vast amount of mental energy trying to decide whether *The Cosby Show* was wonderful or whether it sucked. I called up the platonic iceskater and felt better as I watched him whizz around the rink. I considered taking ice-skating lessons my-self, but didn't. I went to a hypnotist to give up smoking and lit up a Merit as soon as I left his office. I made plans for a rip-roaring thirty-eighth birthday party, but never invited anyone.

Eventually I eased back into the life I'd led before Eloise's wedding. The only problems I had were physical. My jaw ached—my teeth were clenched from the moment I woke up in the morning until I went to sleep. My shoulders felt like Quasimodo's after a twenty-four-hour session of bell-ringing. I wrote it off as stress, that most prevalent late twentieth-century condition, so I smoked some more and listened to Alfred Schnittke, the greatest living Soviet composer. My preference in music was now moving to the modern, the jarring, the kaleidoscope of sound. Other music sounded saccharine in comparison—it belonged to a well-ordered world. Schnittke belonged to the real world, he belonged to my world. I liked the fact that his music could be considered irritating.

On a wet Friday in the first week of December, nine months after I'd returned from Las Vegas, I drove back from work, put my key in the lock, stepped into my apartment soaking wet, and screamed like hell when I saw two people sitting on my sofa.

"Stacy, Stacy—" One of the people stood up. A man, an immensely tall, potentially very threatening man. I stopped screaming. It was Bobby Chappell.

"Jesus Christ, Bobby. What the fuck are you doing in my apartment?" I was still shaking, terrified, my sanctuary invaded—worse, invaded by a Chappell.

"Stacy, I'm sorry—we just thought we should talk to you. There are things you should know." He looked as confused as I felt, but older, much older than he had when I'd last seen him.

"Why didn't you call me? How did you get in here? Who is *we*?" I glanced then at the other person sitting on the sofa and saw Sapphire Shannon in a pair of fashionably ripped jeans and Hard Rock Café sweatshirt.

"What's *she* doing here?"

"Stacy, sit down, I'll explain everything." Bobby sounded nervous.

"This isn't your apartment, Bobby. Don't start telling *me* to sit down. You better explain this fast, and it better be good. I'll start screaming again, I swear, if you take even one step toward me." He *did* look like Robert. I shuddered, backed myself against the door, ready to run out and keep running until I found help. Bobby stood in the path between me and the phone in the hall.

"Oh, cut the drama queen scene, will you? He's not about to rape you, sweetheart." Tough-talking Sapphire.

"I don't believe this," I said, attempting to keep my voice calm. "Will you two get out? Now. Just get out."

"Stacy. We need to talk to you. It's about Eloise." Bobby went back and sat down beside his mother. "We're worried about her."

I exhaled hard, laughed in disbelief.

"You're worried about Eloise, Bobby? You should be worried about yourself. You break into my apartment with your mother, make yourself at home, and expect me to listen to you? Please. Spare me. How did you get in here anyway?"

"One of my security men knows a lot about picking locks." Sapphire replied nonchalantly, as if she broke into apartments every day. "Don't worry, he's not lurking in your bedroom—" She had caught me scanning the room for a beefy bodyguard. "Although he'd do you a lot of good."

"Mom—" Bobby pleaded. I was fuming, ready to explode.

"Sorry, hon." Sapphire turned and smiled at him. For a second she looked almost human. "Listen, Stacy, I promise no more cracks. But sit down. We're not going to hurt you. We wouldn't have broken in only Bobby said you never returned his calls and I think you need to hear what we've got to say."

"That's no excuse," I muttered. I could feel my anger dissipating though; it was being vanquished by curiosity. What were Bobby and Sapphire doing together? She'd said in Las Vegas that she hadn't seen him since he was a baby—Bobby had said that as well. How did they get together or had they both been lying all along? And what, exactly, did they want from me?

"I'm sorry, Stacy, I really am." Bobby sounded genuinely contrite, and, I noticed for the first time, he looked scared. His mother, Sapphire, looked wonderful, there was no denying it. The Hard Rock Café sweatshirt which I'd seen on so many tourists seemed as if it had been specially designed for her. There was such a clarity to her face that I found it very difficult not to stare.

"Okay, all right, hold on and I'll get us a bottle of wine. I don't know about you but I need a drink after finding you here." Taking my time opening the bottle of muscadet, I puffed on a cigarette and tried to second guess them. Could they possibly be attempting to enlist my help in an effort to break up Robert and Eloise? Did Sapphire still love Robert? I carried three glasses and the bottle in on a tray, sat down, sipped on my drink, and tried to look intimidating.

"So, what's this all about?" I noted that neither Bobby nor Sapphire took any wine. Those milky blue eyes of hers were huge and unafraid. I thought of Eloise, whose chocolate eyes, from the moment we'd first met, had been frightened. I'd had a postcard from her eight months previously, telling me to call when I got back from my trip, but she hadn't tried to contact me since. At that precise moment, staring at Sapphire and sipping my wine, I knew I loved Eloise with all my heart and I would do whatever was in my power to protect her. All I needed to establish was whether she needed protection and if so, from whom.

Sapphire was staring right back; Bobby seemed like a shadow on the sofa beside her. She held my gaze silently, ran her hand through the short hair, frowned.

"It's like this, Stacy. Your friend, your pal, Eloise, is in trouble. It's a long story and I'm not too hot on telling long stories, but I'll do my best." She settled back. Bobby's eyes darted back and forth from his mother to me.

"I'm going to take it from the top. Robert and I met when he was at college. Brown. In Providence,

Rhode Island. I was a townie, dropped out of high school, couldn't take that academic shit. I was working in a record store on Hope Street, near the Brown campus, right?''

I could tell I was supposed to nod. Sapphire was used to audience reaction.

"Anyway, Robert came in a lot and we used to talk and he impressed me—he had a way of talking, a way of seeming like he knew what he was talking about, knew more than any guy I'd met before. He wasn't good-looking then—he had eczema—the right side of his face was a wreck if you want to know the truth, but he was charming and I was prepared to be charmed. The boys I knew, the men, they were always rushing me, pushing me into bed.'' She glanced at Bobby and I saw the mother in her again, the mother who doesn't want her son to know everything about her past. "Robert was different. Robert took his time. He courted me—you know, that old-fashioned shit. Flowers, candy. What can I say, it worked, right?'' I nodded. Romance—we were all suckers for it, even Sapphire Shannon. "He was wacky sometimes, and fun. Crazy even. And he had a car too—he'd worked odd jobs on weekends through high school, summers too, and saved up. We used to drive around Providence in it—a Mustang—and listen to the radio and sing along. Robert has this voice—it's a fucking amazing voice, actually.''

"I know," I said. "I've heard him sing.''

"Right, so you know.'' Now *she* nodded, looking pleased. "He had his voice and I had my voice and he had plans—for us. We'd get married and be an act as well. Sing together. Become famous. Live in mansions with servants. None of this sixties commune stuff. He didn't care about politics and neither did I. He wanted to get rich. Rich and famous. It sounded great." She shook her head, sighed. "And it *was* great. For a while. My parents—my father's an electrician, my mother's your ordinary housewife—well, they were thrilled. They'd always worried about me, thought I'd get myself into trouble. Especially when I dropped out of high school.

"I think I scared them because I was so fucking tall. And white. They were both normal size you know, and out comes this giantess. They were blonds too, but not like me. I'm as close to a fucking albino as you can get without being one. They thought I was something out of a bad fairy tale. Not quite human. So they were glad when someone else took me over, when Robert —a student at an Ivy League college no less—took charge. And that's exactly what Robert did. Take charge. He told me how to dress, how to behave. He never let me out of his sight. Once I'd put that ring on my finger, I was his. He monitored my phone calls, opened any letters I got; if I told him I was going out to lunch with a girlfriend, he'd ask me where and then show up himself. I had nothing, Stacy—do you understand that? No space, no room, nothing of my own." She looked over at Bobby again. "I mean, it was like that Svengali story except I read it once and Svengali used to put Trilby into a trance. Robert never did that—I was conscious the whole time. He'd keep me up all night talking about things I didn't understand, but the gist was always the same—I was a slut because I'd slept with other guys before I met him. It was—what do you call it?—jealousy of someone's past."

"Retrospective jealousy?"

"Yeah, right. I never slept with anyone else after we started going out, but that didn't count. I was a whore anyway. We'd go to a bar for a drink and I'd ask the bartender for a beer and Robert would haul me out on the street and accuse me of flirting with the guy. And we'd be standing out on the sidewalk in the middle of winter and he'd be telling me what a whore I was and how he would have preferred it if I'd been a heroin addict. That used to really get to me, when he said that.

"The thing is, he was so fucking *sure* of what he said, he was so certain that he was right, that I began to believe him. I'd never run up against anyone who was so self-confident. You know, at three o'clock in the morning when someone's been explaining to you for four hours what a bad person you are, you start to accept it. You start to apologize. Or at least I did. I mean, my parents had always thought I was kind of a freak, so Robert thinking I was another kind of freak wasn't so crazy to me then. I *had* slept with my fair share of guys." This time she didn't look at Bobby. "In those days, you did. You know, free love and all that. I hadn't thought I was a slut, but Robert convinced me.

"My girlfriends began to think I'd gone crazy because I was crying all the time and they kept telling me to leave him when they had a few minutes to get me alone, but I wouldn't leave him because I loved him. I *believed* him. It was a mess. We'd go to gigs and I'd be petrified he'd think I'd looked at some guy in the audience or done something that would get him going on his favorite theme. At the same time he made me dress like a slut. I don't know. I don't understand it. I never did. I never will."

I remembered Robert in bed, the look, the hard nasty look in his eyes, and the slightly jumbled story took on more of a focus.

"Did he hit you?"

"No. He didn't have to hit me. He had a way of looking at me—I can't explain, but it was like getting hit. He'd lecture me all the time. He'd tell me his mother refused to see me because I was such a slut. His friends felt sorry for him because he married a slut. And you see I wasn't old enough. I was nineteen, twenty. I wasn't old enough or smart enough to say, "Listen, honey, if I'm such a slut, such a horrible person, why did you marry me?" I just took it. I believed him. Shit, I was dumb. But I kept thinking he'd go back to being the person I thought he was at the beginning. This charming, crazy, smart guy, this man who was going to take *care* of me. And sometimes he would. He'd bring me flowers. He'd write a romantic song for me. So when he'd go into one of his jealousy fits, I didn't understand what had happened, what had changed.

"When we were first going out, the first month or so, I didn't know why he kept grilling me about my old boyfriends—I thought he was just curious about my life—but everything I'd ever told him—as soon as we were married, he'd throw it back at me. He'd *tor-*

ture me with it, you know? How could I have been so cheap, slept with such disgusting men, humiliated myself? He had me believing I was a nympho and hating myself for it."

I nodded. I tried to imagine a vulnerable Sapphire, a tall young woman who cried with girlfriends.

"So, anyway, I put up with it. And then I got pregnant and had Bobby. At the same time, we started to play better gigs, people were beginning to hear about us. We took Bobby with us everywhere we went and it seemed like Robert had mellowed. He wasn't yelling at me the whole time—he was too busy planning our career, our path to fame. His path to fame, if you want to know the truth. I was supposed to stop singing, settle down, and take care of Bobby. He'd launch out on his own. He was real insistent about that. But we'd been booked for these gigs as a double act, so he decided to phase me out gradually. I wasn't too happy about the plan, but I didn't see what I was going to do to stop it. He was in control. We took a trip to the West Coast—here, actually. San Francisco. And that's when the shit really hit the fan.

"There was a talent scout, you know, a rep from a record company who came to watch us. James Griffin. He bought us a drink after we'd finished, and I tried, I did my damnedest not to look at him because I knew what would happen if I did, but I couldn't *not* look at him. He was gorgeous, you know? Hip, cool, sophisticated. Older, about ten years older than us. Robert was really excited about the whole deal, he was trying to make a big impression on Griffin, talking himself up. Meanwhile I was trying not to look at James and the whole time I knew I was in trouble. I knew he wanted me and I wanted him. I don't have any excuse for what I did, Stacy. Griffin came back the next night, supposedly to clinch the deal for Robert—a solo record contract. Instead, he managed to get me alone for ten minutes and he asked me to go back to New York with him, catch the flight that night. Sneak out then and there. He'd buy me whatever I needed when we got there. He'd make me a star. It was a way out of my life with Robert. My ticket to ride away from what had become a nightmare to me. It seemed like the only way out at the time."

"Bobby wasn't welcome?"

"I wasn't welcome." Bobby's neutral voice cut in. I looked over to him quickly but didn't see the anger I expected. He looked resigned.

"Right. I can't make it up to him." Sapphire took hold of her son's hand and I was interested to see he didn't pull away, but he didn't squeeze it either. "I just had to get away. I had to split. It was my only chance to survive." She waved her hands in the air, ineffectually, I thought. Then the cover girl look, the hard, practiced celebrity face took over. "There was no other fucking way. Robert would have killed me. I'm still surprised he didn't kill me. I can't tell you how much I hate that bastard. He has ruined my fucking life."

It was a difficult story to disentangle as far as fault went. There were other ways to get out of bad marriages, I thought, ways that didn't involve ditching your infant son, even given a maniacally possessive husband. How could she walk out on Bobby? Still, she'd been honest—she'd said there was no excuse. I had to admit to myself that I hated her less, but I wasn't sure if I warmed to her either. The instantaneous change of facial expression from mentally abused young wife to star persona was disconcerting. If Robert's accusations had upset her so, why did she spend the next twenty years behaving like a raunchy vamp in public? Why did she wear a T-shirt with the word SLUT emblazoned across it?

"That's interesting, Sapphire, but what does any of this have to do with Eloise?" I didn't want to be seduced, to concentrate on the story of Sapphire's life when Eloise was the woman we were supposed to be talking about.

"That's just the background, Stacy." She crossed her hands behind her head, settling back into the sofa. "I called Robert a lot over the next few years but he would just hang up, you know? So I kind of gave up." She shrugged. She called him when she was terrified he might murder her? That didn't make a whole lot of sense. Bobby began to fiddle with his watchband. "I kept track of them, of course. You know, I became successful pretty quickly so I had some power, I could keep tabs."

Daniel Sterne had kept tabs on me. Eloise had tracked me to San Francisco. Buddy had called me out of the blue. These days I was too busy trying to forget my past and reinvent myself to wonder what had happened to people in intervening years.

"I sent Bobby presents and shit but I don't think you ever got them, did you, hon?"

He was still playing with his watch as he shook his

head no. At the beginning of this talk he'd looked thirty, now he looked about twelve.

"Then I heard Robert had remarried and I thought —hell, I should steer clear here. I called her once and she sounded really nice, real sweet, so I thought to myself: Bobby's got a mother now, a better mother, probably, than I'd ever make. Someone who would bake him cookies and all that crap."

"Eloise? Making cookies for a college student?" I laughed.

"Eloise? No, not Eloise. Shit, no. Susan—you know, his second wife."

"His second wife?" I looked at Bobby. "What second wife?"

"My first stepmother." Bobby glanced up. "Susan."

"Susan," I repeated dully. "I've never heard of Susan."

"Dad doesn't talk about her," Bobby said matter-of-factly. "That's why we came here, Stacy. Because of Susan."

"Wait a minute. Does Eloise know about Susan?" I was conversing with Bobby now; for once, Sapphire was on the sidelines.

"No, Eloise doesn't know about Susan. Dad didn't tell her. And I couldn't tell her, because if I told her—" He stopped, reached over and grabbed my cigarette pack balancing on the arm of the chair, and helped himself to one. I waited for him to speak, but he didn't. He sat there smoking.

"If Bobby told her," Sapphire continued, tossing her head back, "he'd have to tell her that Robert murdered Susan and Bobby's got a little conflict on that issue."

I snorted and put my head in my hands. This could have been a perverted Mutt and Jeff act, except they were both Mutts.

"Fine," I said. I couldn't stop myself from another derisory snort. "Could one or the other of you please tell me how Robert is supposed to have killed this Susan? How exactly did she die?"

"She died of fucking anorexia nervosa," Sapphire replied. "And I'll have a glass of that wine now, okay?"

"Sure. Why not? Let's all get ripped together. That's the most sensible thing to do when my apartment is invaded by two crazy people. It's all very amusing, you guys, and I'm sure Jessica Fletcher would have a ball with you. Susan died of anorexia and Robert murdered her." If I were smart, I thought, I could sell this story to the *National Enquirer*—famous mother and son reunite after twenty years and both go stark raving mad.

"So tell me—how did he manage to starve her to death? Lock the refrigerator?"

Bobby stopped the sarcasm with an Indian-on-the-warpath look. It came out of nowhere, as quick to register as Sapphire's retreat into celebrity poses. His face made me sit up straight and pay attention.

"Stacy, this isn't a joke. You weren't there—you didn't see it happening. I was and I did and I'm in therapy now because of it." He shot a glance at his mother. "Among other reasons, that is. No, my father did not lock the refrigerator door. Susan was just too weak for him. I was too weak for him. I let it happen. I could have stopped it. That's why I'm trying to stop it now. Eloise isn't Susan. Nobody could be like Susan. But she doesn't deserve to die.''

"Bobby was very fond of Susan, Stacy.'' Sapphire spoke more gently than I'd ever heard her.

"Susan was my *mother*,'' he murmured. He was on the verge of tears. That's where he got the polite demeanor, I thought, from Susan. The nicest parts of Bobby must have been Susan. But who the hell *was* Susan? I looked back and forth between mother and son.

"Will *someone* please tell me what's going on?''

"Dad married Susan when I was five.'' Bobby's face was in profile to me now, staring out my window. "He was working for a record company in Denver, doing PR, and putting out that one album which flopped. I had baby-sitters all the time, when I wasn't at school—baby-sitter after baby-sitter. They were okay, I guess, but I remember feeling lonely. Then one day Dad brought Susan home. And she stayed. She took care of me. She took care of Dad. She was fragile, kind. She *cared*.''

"*And* she was the boss's daughter,'' Sapphire cut in. "Catch this, Stacy. She was the boss's daughter with a history of anorexia, right? She'd been in and out of the hospital as a teenager—obsessed with fat, with not becoming fat. But that'd been dealt with, supposedly, by the time she married Robert. She's twenty-two and she's over all that. Next thing you know, her father gets cancer and dies—Bobby's about ten then, right?''

Bobby nodded. He looked too pained to speak.

"So Susan's father kicks the bucket, and would you believe it, a month or so later, the mother kicks it too. It happens sometimes, you know, with these happy couples. One dies, and bingo, the other pegs out. Weird but true. Anyway, Susan is left with a reasonable-sized inheritance, a fair amount of cash. What happens next is what you've got to hear and you may not believe. Susan starts to go anorexic again. Okay, maybe the fact that both her parents have died has an effect on her, sure. Maybe she doesn't feel like eating. But there's more to it than that. Tell her about the pictures, Bobby."

Bobby stood up—his height was imposing, his face a study of misery.

"Dad took all these pictures of her and he'd put them around the house. I knew, I mean I sensed even then that something was wrong with those pictures, but I was too young to know. I just felt something was wrong. It's taken a year of therapy to figure it out and when I did, I figured out other things as well. Things I'd been hiding from myself."

I looked up at him.

"What was wrong with the pictures, Bobby?"

"They made her look fat. All of them. She wasn't fat—she was a fairly normal size, not exactly thin, but not fat. But those pictures—he'd point the camera up and catch her with a double chin and so there'd be a picture on the mantelpiece of Susan with this double chin sticking out. Or he'd take a picture when she was bending over and her stomach was bulging over her jeans. Those kinds of pictures which any other woman might just tear up but which I'd catch Susan staring at

290

obsessively as she moved around the house. She couldn't stop looking at them and I couldn't stop her from looking at them because I hadn't figured out what was wrong with them.''

"But that wasn't all, was it?" Sapphire coaxed.

"No—it's hard to explain because it was so kind of subtle that it was almost not happening, but I remember Dad staring at her at mealtimes. Watching her eat. She'd catch him looking at her as she had a forkful of mashed potato and she'd say, 'Maybe I shouldn't have this—it's fattening,' and Dad would say, 'Oh, no, Susan, what are a few more pounds here or there?' and then he'd just look at her some more with this *disappointed* look.''

"Shit, do I know that look." Sapphire poured herself another glass of wine.

"So she just stopped eating and the less she ate the nicer Dad was to her, 'You've got great willpower, sweetheart,' he'd say to her and he'd bring home clothes for her. In small sizes. I don't know what sizes women wear but he'd get her some totally tiny cocktail dress—I remember one that was black velvet and beautiful and I caught her crying when she was trying it on. She couldn't quite fit into it. 'Guess I have to lose some more weight, Bob,' she said to me—she always insisted on calling me Bob—she said that Bobby was for little boys and I was already a man. 'Guess I better not eat for a while. I want to wear this beautiful dress, don't I?' Oh, Christ, I don't know how long it all took, but she was in the hospital soon and my father was all solicitous and telling her she should eat more and conferring with doctors, but it was too late. She'd decided she couldn't be thin enough.''

"A woman can never be too rich or too thin," I mumbled.

"Or too dead," Sapphire added.

"But why would Robert want to kill her? Or to encourage her to die, or whatever it is he is supposed to have done?" I asked.

"He got her money, babe. He inherited everything. He could afford to quit his job and live in semiluxury in Denver and screw all the women he wanted to and not have to worry about a wife back home. Deep down he's not too fond of women, Stacy. If it's my fault, well, so be it, but I'll tell you, I don't think he was too fond of women when he married me, either. I didn't know that then, but now I think he hates us. Enough to kill."

"But he didn't actually kill her." I wasn't sure why I was protesting, but I had a very sick feeling in my heart. If Robert was that evil, what would happen to Eloise? "And couldn't he have gotten some money from you? I mean, couldn't he have sued *you* for alimony?"

"Honey, the money he would have spent trying to find out where my money is would have bankrupted him. I know how to duck and dive financially."

I looked up at Bobby. What anger he must have holed up in his heart.

"Robert didn't knife Susan, no. But he fucking persuaded her to kill herself. Same thing, isn't it?" Sapphire smirked. "She was in love with him."

Love—the ultimate brainwash, I thought. I lit a cigarette. Bobby was still standing over the two of us, staring at my piano in the corner.

"She would have done anything for him," he said quietly. "Anything to keep his love. I couldn't have done anything—that's what my analyst says. I was powerless in that situation. And I had all these ambivalent feelings about Dad. He was the one who was bringing me up. He hadn't run off and left me." Sapphire sat up and crossed her blue-jeaned legs. "The thing is, I loved Dad too. Dad—well, you've seen him, Stacy, you know he can be amazing—like that night he threw the shoe out the car window. He always did crazy, fun things. My friends from school all said how cool he was, how they wished he was their dad. He knew about music and he played games with us and he made everything fun." Bobby's voice sounded exhausted. "I loved Susan, but I loved Dad too. I just pushed all the crap to the back of my mind. I didn't think about the pictures or the size-too-small dresses or the looks he gave her at the dining-room table. I thought about the father I loved."

Sapphire patently didn't relish hearing about Bobby's love for Robert.

"God knows what other things he did to her," she said. "The things Bobby didn't pick up—what he said to her in private. I can hear it now. 'Susan, honey, skinny women are so much sexier,' or 'What are those little bumps on your thighs—is *that* what they call cellulite?' Bullshit like that. I can just fucking hear it."

Then *I* stood up and went over to the window. I turned my back on them and stared out into the rain, wishing like hell that they'd never come. I knew what was coming next. I wanted desperately for Daniel to be by my side when it came.

"Stacy—" Sapphire snapped her fingers. I turned around but didn't move away from the window. "Right, now pay attention. Bobby had his reasons for not talking to me or seeing me all those years, right? I understand that, of course. It's a fucking shame, but that's the way it was. But he started to act out at college and his college advisor sent him to a shrink and after he'd spent some time at the shrink he began to put two and two together. When he gets to four, he calls me up, comes to see me, tells me the story. Not just because he wants to bond with me now, but because he's worried and he doesn't know who to go to. He's fucked up about the whole thing, right? He's got a loyalty to Robert, but he's beginning to see that Robert killed Susan. *And* he's beginning to think that maybe Robert's going to kill Eloise too.

"After all, your friend has a lot more money than Susan. Susan's money has just about run out, I'd guess, so he's on the hunt. Who does he manage to trap but one of the richest women in America. Not bad, huh? It's just a shame she's not an anorexic. I mean Susan was more or less easy to deal with—she had a history of anorexia. Not many people die of anorexia, sure, so Robert's taking a chance. But then maybe he just wanted her to suffer and when she does die it's a bonus."

Bobby and I both flinched.

"So Eloise doesn't have a disease like that he can work on, he can use. But Bobby's shrink was worried about her and then Bobby gets worried about her and

I suggest coming to see you to fill you in on all the details because maybe you know something about it we don't. Maybe you know that they're real happy and Eloise is a real strong person and couldn't be hurt in any way by Robert. Or maybe you know that the banister rail in her house is loose at the top of some marble stairs or he keeps a radio plugged in on the edge of her bath. I don't know. We just thought you should know. That's why we broke in. Are you still pissed off?"

I turned back and stared at the rain.

"She has diabetes," I said. "Eloise has diabetes."

18

DECEMBER 1990

Sapphire paced around my living room like the classic expectant father in a labor ward. She looked as if she wanted to hand out cigars, so pleased, so excited was she by my statement.

"That's it—don't you see? He's going to nail her. I mean he's going to shoot her up, overdose her with insulin. Then he puts the needle into her hand and presto, she's ODed on her own, made a fatal mistake. Boom, she's dead and he gets the money. Robbo. Shit. Trust him to find a rich diabetic." She shook her head, laughed to herself. Bobby had collapsed on the sofa, his head in his hands.

"Listen," I said loudly. I moved away from the window, sat down beside Bobby, and put my hand on his shoulder. "Whatever else Robert may be, he's not stupid. *If* he did kill Susan—and Bobby"—I tightened my grip on him—"I'm not saying your memories of that period are wrong, I'm not doubting you, I just don't think we have all the facts, I think we're rushing into things here. Anyway, even if he *did* purposefully turn Susan into an anorexic again, Robert is not about to kill Eloise with an overdose of insulin. I

mean, seriously. Haven't you heard of Claus von Bülow, Sapphire? Do you think Robert wants to be labeled Son of Claus? It's too similar. I shouldn't even
have mentioned the diabetes. I got carried away
there. Forget it."

Sapphire threw her hands up in the air theatrically.

"Stacy, sweetheart, where the fuck have you *been*
lately? Read the book, read *Reversal of Fortune*. Sunny
von Bülow wasn't even a fucking diabetic. I thought
you worked in a bookstore. How come you're so ignorant?"

"How come you're such a bitch?" I hissed. "I don't
read every book in the store. If I did, I wouldn't be
able to keep my job running it. Some of us lesser
mortals have to work hard eight hours a day, you
know. We're not all as supremely talented as you."

"Jesus." Bobby shook his head, raised it in exasper-
ation. "Stop this, will you? It doesn't help. I'm so confused. But I think Stacy's right. I don't think Dad
would actually put a needle into her arm. I mean, if
he'd wanted to do that, he could have by now. He'd
do it differently. I'm the only one in the room who
knows him, really. He'd do it differently. That's what I
was trying to tell you that night, Stacy. You know,
when I was talking about that hitchhiker who got
locked in the box and then chose to stay locked in the
box, I was really thinking about Susan. The way she
chose to let herself die. That's why I wanted to talk to
those people. I wanted to understand what makes
people do things like that.

"Whenever I have sex, I think of death and I think
of murder. I scared the hell out of one of my girl-

friends at college one night. I mean, by what I said, not anything physical. But that's when I got sent to the shrink. And the memories started to come back. When I went out with you that night, I'd been going to the shrink for about five months and things were just starting to surface. Memories. After we'd had sex, I started thinking about Dad and Susan and what really went on between them, but I wasn't ready yet to talk to you about it. You must have thought I was really weird."

"Oh, cute. This is really cute. You two have screwed. Little Miss Prissbody here and my son. I should have figured that one out from the start." Sapphire hit herself on the forehead. "Dumb."

"How do you mean, he'd do it differently with Eloise, Bobby?" I'd taken my hand off his shoulder.

"I'm not sure. I guess I mean he'd do it like he did it to Susan. Get her to kill herself, if you see what I mean."

"I see what you mean."

"You two want to go into the bedroom together? Am I intruding here?" She was pacing, her hands stuffed in her jeans pockets.

"Oh fuck off, Sapphire." I was so fed up with her act I screamed it.

"Okay, okay. I suppose I should approve of my son's taste for older women." She eyed me up and down, then flopped into an armchair. "Bobby's probably right. It's not Robbo's style to commit outright murder. He's too sly for that. Besides, how would he know how much insulin is too much, or even how to inject it? Still—" Sapphire ran her finger over her top lip. "I think the diabetes figures in here somewhere, somehow."

"But how?" I asked.

"Like Bobby said. He gets her to kill herself. Which must be easy for a diabetic. I mean, she has access to that insulin every day. And you know, I read somewhere that diabetes is up there with cancer and heart attacks and stuff in the top ten of killers."

"You seem to read an awful lot for a pop singer," I said wryly.

"You want me to play dumb, Stacy? Is that it? You want me to be an aging bimbo with no brain? Will that make you feel better? You're just like most of the shitty men I meet."

"Jesus." Bobby stood up. "I can't take much more of this."

"I'm sorry," I said quickly. "Sit down, Bobby. Don't go."

"Yeah, Bobby. Don't mind us."

Bobby sat back down, the obedient son. And lover.

"He has to make her feel bad about herself," he said. "So bad she'd—" He stopped, reached for his untouched glass of wine.

"Right. So bad she'd kill herself." Sapphire finished the sentence. "Preferably when he had a watertight alibi. He could do it, too, you know. I really think he's capable of it. Playing her just right. No offense, Stacy, but Eloise didn't look like a tower of strength to me, she looked like a little pushover. Am I right?"

I didn't reply; I was too busy flashing back, recalling various moments. The first day we'd met, the time

299

she'd told me she thought she was cursed, her terrible moods, her statement at the Cape that her love for Robert was what she had to live for. Eloise on the edge of my bed in tears about her sexuality, Eloise in *floods* of tears that same afternoon in the sitting room. Eloise drunk in Las Vegas. Eloise drunk, well, most of the time I'd seen her since her marriage. She'd told me she could handle the booze, but why had I believed her?

I stared at Sapphire, my mind whirling.

"When you read about diabetes, did it say anything about diabetes and alcohol?"

"No." Sapphire stared back. Her skin was the color of an ivory piano key. "Is that an issue here? Drink?"

"She drinks a hell of a lot," Bobby put in. "But then so does Dad."

"Where's your phone, Stacy? I need to make a call."

"There's one in my bedroom—down the hall, second door on the right. You can have some privacy there."

"Thanks." Sapphire disappeared. Bobby and I sat in silence, as if we were always destined to be the bit part players, as we had been at the wedding. I wanted to apologize for not returning his calls, but I was too tense, too wrapped up in wondering about Sapphire's phone call, too busy trying to decide whether this entire scene had been the result of overactive imaginations—Bobby's, Sapphire's, and mine. None of our relationships with Robert were what anyone would call straightforward. So Bobby and I smoked, waiting.

When she returned, she had a piece of paper in her hand, one I recognized as my bedside notepaper.

"Right. Stacy—" She sat down across from us, paper in hand, looking like a journalist trying to piece together a story. "Is Eloise a type one or type two diabetic?"

"I don't know," I replied, embarrassed. I'd never talked to Eloise about the details of her disease. Sapphire was looking down at her notes.

"Well, does she shoot up every day?"

"Yes." I was relieved to know *something*.

"Okay, then. She's a type one. That's the heavy-duty type of diabetes."

Bobby and I both nodded, as if we were in a classroom.

"I called my personal physician and he gave me some quick answers. The gist of it is: if she's a type one diabetic, she shouldn't be drinking period. It's not a good idea for the type twos either, but we don't care about them now. Anyway, he told me all this shit about hyperglycemia and hypoglycemia and blood sugar levels and the caloric load of different alcohols which I didn't understand at all, but the point is, she should not be drinking heavily. It screws up her blood sugar levels. So—let me get this right—wait a sec." She studied the notes again. "One thing that can happen is that she has too much to drink and fucks up the amount of insulin she's supposed to take because she's drunk, and ODs that way, or—"

"Hold on—" I broke in. "I've been with Eloise the morning after a binge. She told me she can take the insulin in her sleep, she's so used to it."

"Okay. But my doc said that if she's a type one, she's got a health problem to begin with. She's not a happy camper medically speaking. And if she continues to abuse her body with large quantities of alcohol, she'll die anyway. Might take a few years, but it'll get her in the end. He said it's like someone who has been diagnosed with lung cancer deciding to take up smoking. She's fooling around with something she's not supposed to fool around with. Robert can afford to wait and let nature take its course. Diabetes *is* in the top ten list of killers. I was right. You can't mess around with it."

"I have to say, this all sounds like a long shot to me." I sighed. "But she *is* drinking heavily."

A few drinks loosen me up, Stacy, I could hear her say. *I can relax more in bed*. Who put that idea into her head? Who told her she was lousy in bed to begin with? Who told her that she'd perform better with a few drinks? Robert Chappell.

"But there's still a big problem with this whole theory." I protested, hanging onto hope. "Why does he *need* to have her dead? Why can't he live happily enough off her money? She's generous. I'm sure she gives him everything he needs. She's always been generous with her money."

"He wants it all. Simple as that. He doesn't want to have to answer to anyone, especially not to a *woman*. Don't you get it yet, Stacy?" Sapphire was clutching the piece of paper as if it held the answers to all the questions in the universe.

Who left the pictures of Sapphire around the New York house? Did the butler do it? Or did Robert Chappell? To goad Eloise, to make her more and more insecure? To send her scurrying for the Bloody Marys to feel better about herself?

Who planned that trip to Vegas to see Kenny Rogers when Sapphire was in town? Could he have known she'd be there a week early? Did he have spies in the music business, old friends who'd let him know Sapphire's whereabouts?

Why had Robert seemed so *pleased* after she'd barged into the suite that morning? The certain effect it would have on Eloise? Was he knocking Eloise's feet out from under her inch by inch? Hacking away at her self-esteem, fueling her jealousy?

Daniel said that Robert didn't love Eloise. Daniel had distrusted Robert from the first.

Robert had Daniel's book in his shelves, but denied having ever seen it. Was he using it as a guide to a do-it-yourself brainwashing course?

Robert hated his mother. Robert's mother had humiliated his father. Robert must think that all women were tramps, out to cheat on their husbands, treat them like dirt, control the purse strings.

Robert had slept with me.

"Do you think Robert could have engineered their meeting?" I asked. "Do you think he looked her up, found her name in the Forbes list, did a little research, *planned* it so that he'd rear-end her limo? Do you really think that?"

Sapphire nodded.

Had he engineered our afternoon too? Would he use that information to push Eloise over a psychic edge? Would he tell her that I was even better than

Sapphire, that she should take some lessons from her friend? From the only friend Eloise had ever really had? I could imagine Eloise lighting into five bottles of vodka with that piece of news. And passing out forever.

"Tell me something, Sapphire. In the years you knew Robert well, did he talk about his parents a lot?"

"No. He did say that his father had died and that his mother was a fine, upstanding, moral woman who would not meet a slut like me. He never went to visit her though. Sometimes I wondered about that, but then I guessed he was so embarrassed about having married me that he steered clear of her."

I stood up.

"Sapphire, you're very rich, right?"

"You better believe it."

"Can you get me a jet? Are you rich enough to order me up a plane at midnight? Fly me to New York?"

"Sure thing, babe."

I was about to thank her.

"But don't do any freebasing on it, will you? It's an expensive piece of machinery. Try not to blow it up."

19

DECEMBER 1990

I sat hunched over my fifth cup of coffee in one of those diners in New York where customers come in and ask for "the regular." People next to me at the counter were discussing whether there would be a war with Iraq, and if so, how quickly we could wipe Saddam out of existence. They seemed hungry for war as they mopped up their fried eggs and hashed brown specials. They had eager, excited voices. "This ain't gonna be no Vietnam," the man next to me announced. "We're gonna wipe those Iraqis off the map." Would the students at Columbia be protesting now that there was no longer a draft? I wondered. Would Volkswagen Beetles with flower power slogans come back onto the streets, with the youth of the country flashing peace signs at each other? Or had the mood turned? Did America need a war we could win, a war against an evil monster this time, not Ho Chi Minh?

My own private war against Robert Chappell was what concerned me now. During the plane trip, I had gone over and over every scene I had been witness to between Robert and Eloise. Robert pouring drink after drink, Robert telling her she should stay at home, not go back to graduate school. Robert controlling her life; the puppeteer.

How could a man most hurt a woman? By telling her she was lousy in bed, by comparing her with another woman. If he had loved her, he would never hurt her like that. If he was calmly sitting back waiting for her to ruin her health with booze, I had to stop him. She had told me she couldn't fool around with drugs because of her diabetes. What made her think she could drink so much?

As I paid my bill, my hands shook. I hadn't slept and I hadn't thought out a reasonable plan of action. I'd have to wing it, decide what to do when I saw the situation. And pray that Eloise and Robert hadn't decamped to the South of France or London.

How do you deprogram a person brainwashed by love? During the seventies, parents of Moonie children had hired professionals, the most famous of whom was a man named Ted Patrick. He kidnapped the kids, spirited them away from their Moonie enclaves, and, I'd heard, offered them all the benefits of the material world they had left. He'd present the boys with classy hookers and the girls with shopping sprees. It worked for some, didn't for others. Not, I thought, a particularly thoughtful technique and certainly not of any help to Eloise, who was, I was now convinced, being brainwashed by Robert. Robert, the father-substitute, the lover, the husband, the friend. What could I come up with to compete against him? Suggest that Eloise and I room together again?

She had no sisters or brothers, no parents, nobody

to fall back on if she left him. Except me. And I had hardly been the most sensitive of friends in the past. I had vanished from her life as soon as I met Buddy. She couldn't trust me not to desert her again. Especially if she knew about Robert and me. If she knew that, though, she would slam the door in my face as soon as she saw me, she wouldn't let me talk to her. I had to pray that she was in New York and I had to pray harder that Robert hadn't told her yet. If he had, I would be useless. Worse than useless. The embodiment of betrayal.

I put on my coat, picked up my bag and walked to 74th Street. I smoked three cigarettes as I walked up and down it, between Fifth and Madison, patrolling like some old-fashioned policeman, summoning my nerve. Sapphire Shannon wouldn't have hesitated; she would have marched right up to the door. Too bad Sapphire was the wrong person for this scene. Too bad Sapphire wasn't Eloise's best friend. They had more in common than Eloise would ever have guessed.

Robert opened the door.

"Hey, hey, what have we here? A blast from the past. The person from Peoria. Come on in, Stace." He winked at me. "Nice to see you again."

"Is Eloise here, Robert?"

"You're not going to say hello to *me*? Uh-oh. Have I done something wrong?"

"Is Eloise here, Robert?"

"Yes, Stacy. Eloise is upstairs. Asleep. Remember me? The early bird who catches the best friend?"

I ignored that dig.

"Is she hungover?"

He arched his eyebrows.

"Maybe. Maybe not. I'll ask her when she wakes up, all right? I think it would be a good idea if you came in, Stace. You're letting in some very chilly wind."

I made up my mind. Confrontation time.

"I want to talk to you. Alone." I said.

"That sounds ominous."

Humming the theme from the *Twilight Zone*, he threw my bag on to a side bench, linked his arm in mine, and walked me down the passageway. "Enter." He swept his arm, ushering me in to the study, then closed the door after him.

"So how's it going, Stace? Good around-the-world trip?" He settled back in his chair and I stood opposite him. The showdown at the OK Corral.

"You're not going to get away with it, Robert."

"Mmm hmm." He grinned.

"I mean it. I know about Susan. I know everything. And I'm not going to let you get away with it." My hands, I noticed, were still shaking, so I hid them in my pockets.

"Glad to hear it." The grin remained. He looked in his element, immensely pleased.

"Robert—" Now my voice was shaking, but I couldn't control it. "I'm going to tell Eloise everything. She's going to leave you. Your game is over. Do you understand me?"

"Stace—" He threw his hands up. "Be my guest. Tell Eloise whatever you want to tell Eloise. And then," he said lightly, as if were were having a friendly conversation, "and then *I'll* tell her a few things too.

I'll tell her you're in love with me, have been from the beginning. I'll tell her you seduced me in Las Vegas. I'll tell her you're a desperate, unmarried, unhappy, jealous woman who wants to ruin her more fortunate friend's life.

"Tell me this, Stacy. Whom do you think she's going to believe? Do you think it is in her interests to believe *you*? To leave the husband she loves? Whatever story you choose to make up about Susan, I can counter. I haven't told her about Susan yet, haven't told her I was married a second time, but I can say I was overcome by grief at her death and I just don't want to talk about it. Which is, of course, the truth."

I was very surprised that he didn't protest his innocence more; his willingness to face my accusations and the perfectly relaxed tone he used with his nasty words unsettled me. It was as if he'd been waiting for me.

"I'll get Sapphire to back me up. I'll get Sapphire to tell her about *your* insane jealousy, the way you treated her."

"And *I'll* tell her how Amy treated me. How she taunted me, humiliated me with other men from the moment we got married. Do you have any idea what it's like to be a constant cuckold? It's a plain fact that Amy ran off with another man, left me with Bobby. Nobody can dispute that. What do you think that feels like, Stacy? The person you love most in life, the woman you have helped launch on a career ups and disappears with another man. Leaves you with a baby and no prospects for the future. A selfish, terrible woman who flaunts herself in public at every opportunity? What do you think it was like to have a wife like that?

"Obviously Amy has been talking to you. Well, it's interesting that you believe her side of the story without hearing mine. Women together against the world, right? Sisterhood is powerful. Well, that just won't work with Eloise. It's Eloise and me against the world now, as far as she's concerned. Go ahead and tell her, Stace. It will only bring us closer together, make her more dependent on me. This is a kamikaze mission you're on. All you'll end up destroying is your friendship."

I sat down, lit a cigarette.

"You've been convincing her to drink. Even though it's bad for her health. I can get a doctor to tell her that."

"And I can get a doctor to tell you smoking's bad for your health. But would you give it up? You must read the warnings on every pack of cigarettes you open. So, evidently not." He sat back in his chair, swiveled from side to side. I should have brought a gun, I thought. I wanted to see some fear on his smug face.

"Robert."

"Yes, Stace?"

"You're trying to push Eloise to the edge. Physically. Mentally. I know all that business about her not performing well in bed. You're trying to hit on every weak spot, and she's got lots of them. We both know that. But why? Why can't you live with her, make her happy—she must give you plenty of money."

He raised himself slowly, came to the back of my

chair, leaned over me as he had before, when he'd told me I was a bundle of nerves. His hands were wrapped around my neck.

"Let's just suppose what you say is true. A big supposition, but I'll indulge you. Suppose I want all the money, not part of it, but all of it. Suppose I had a plan. Suppose I've always had a plan. But I needed a fortune to make that plan work." I tried to free myself from his grasp, but he pushed me back in the chair. Every bone in my body ached in revulsion.

"Let's just say I had enough money to buy out Amy's songwriter. Forever. I bet she didn't tell you all her songs are written by one man—every single song she sings, every single song that goes to the top of the charts—except for her cover versions, of course. Suppose I were to buy him out, let her struggle to find someone else. Not easy. She's worked with the same man for close to twenty years. Like Elton John—but you don't know about pop stars, do you?"

He shook my neck from left to right, forcing me to shake my head no.

"She finds a new writer and puts out her next album. Fine. Now, suppose I were to organize, with all this money I've got, suppose I were to make sure a not-quite-top-notch team were hired to do the videos. A team that used to be hot but was sliding almost imperceptibly downhill. You know how fickle the recording industry is? You know how up-to-date it has to be, how momentary the magic is?

"A few mediocre videos, a mediocre album, and that's all she wrote for Amy. The star begins to fade.

The star begins to doubt herself. Pretty soon the star stops twinkling altogether.

"But—" He straightened up, stopped whispering in my ear, moved back to his seat. "I love Eloise, Stacy. And I'd never do anything to hurt her. You think I'm making her drink too much? *I'm* not forcing the booze down her throat. She happens to like it. Like you like your cigarettes. She's over twenty-one—how am I supposed to stop her? But I'll do my best. I did my best with Susan—if you've heard otherwise, you've been misinformed. I've let you spin this fantasy of yours, but I'm not going to let you destroy my marriage. Eloise and I are happy. There's absolutely nothing you can do to wreck that happiness."

"You're crazy. You really are," I shouted at him. "You can't ruin Sapphire's career. That convoluted plan of yours would never work. *You're* the one living in a fucking fantasy world. This is all because of your mother. You're twisted and bitter, you hate women because of her, what she did to you and your father. But taking revenge on all the women who have loved you isn't going to help you, Robert. You need professional help."

"Oh, so you *believe* those stories I told you? That's nice. Do you think I should see a female shrink or a male one, Ms. Freud?" His voice was quiet, amused. "If you choose to make wild allegations, go ahead. As I said before, be my guest. Pit yourself against me, try to convince Eloise I'm a monster and you're a saint. Do your damnedest, Stacy. It won't work. Love conquers all, sweetheart. Even old college roommates. Do you want a bet on that?"

I leaped up and rushed out of the room. I couldn't stand to look at him, couldn't bear to hear that voice. He hates all women, I realized, loathes and despises us. Whatever part Sapphire had played, whether she'd been the abused or the abuser, he'd come away from that marriage obsessed with her destruction. I took the stairs two at a time, then stopped abruptly at the top and tried to garner my thoughts, tried to calm down. I *had* to see Eloise, but what was I going to say? Robert was probably right, Robert could twist anything I said. He held the ace up his sleeve—our infidelity. But how could he prove it? There was no physical proof—it was his word against mine.

Unless. I was born with three moles directly underneath my belly button—the lower half of my stomach looked like a dotted "i." I never wore a bikini, was so embarrassed I almost had them surgically removed, but decided against it. I could feel Robert's tongue on my stomach. The moles were slightly raised. Eloise knew about them. And now Robert did. And Robert would remember.

I could say he raped me.

Sure.

20
DECEMBER 1990

Eloise was propped up against the pillows, a breakfast tray beside her. She was dressed in pale blue silk pajamas. My heart melted when I saw her.

"Stace!" She jumped up out of bed. "God!" She hugged me tightly. "What are you doing here? How terrific! Sit down, tell me everything."

I sat down at the foot of her bed, she returned to her original position.

"Sorry, I should have called, but I was on a plane all night. This is the last stop for me, so I thought I'd drop by."

She looked fine, perfectly fine, except for one thing. Her lower lip had the two raw patches again. Where was I supposed to go from here, I wondered, realizing as I saw her in the flesh what I hadn't brought myself to realize in my fervor to be the Savior Friend. Robert was right. It would be close to impossible to tell Eloise her husband was trying to kill her. She wouldn't believe me.

"God—I've missed you, Stace." Eloise picked up a glass on her breakfast tray, a glass filled with red liquid. Not blood red orange juice but a Bloody Mary. It

314

was ten o'clock in the morning and she was drinking. Robert deserved to die.

"I've missed you, too. How are you?"

"Fine, fine," she replied, sipping away. "Except I'm—"

"You're what?"

"I'm tired. I get tired a lot. Lethargic. But I don't want to talk about myself. Tell me how you're doing. It's been such a long time. You'll stay here while you're in New York, won't you?"

"Sure." I said. "Absolutely."

"But you might prefer to stay with Daniel. What's happening with you two? Are you getting back together?"

"I haven't seen him. I don't know. Eloise, listen. I've got a crazy idea. Why don't you get dressed and we'll catch a cab and go sit on the steps at Columbia. The way we used to. I know it's cold, but it will be fun. We can talk the way we used to."

She stared at me with sluggish eyes.

"Can't we just stay here and talk?"

"We could, but I'm feeling nostalgic. Come on, it will be fun."

"Okay." She brightened. "Why not? It's so good to see you, Stace."

She took an inordinate amount of time getting dressed and I was nerve racked, listening out for Robert, speculating as to whether he'd try to break us up, or whether he was so sure of himself, he'd let me have as much time alone with her as I wanted. Let me hang myself. After ages spent looking through her closet, she ended up wearing what she'd worn in the old days. Jeans, huge sweater, sneakers, and socks.

"Hey, what happened to the designer outfits?" I laughed feebly.

"This *is* designer, Stace." She smiled. "Do you want to take the limo?"

"No, no. Let's be bums. Let's take a cab."

"Anything you say."

As we went downstairs I kept expecting Robert to rush up to us, but he never appeared. In the hall, she picked up a telephone extension and pushed a button.

"Robert, Stace has just flown in—isn't that terrific? We won't disturb you at your work, we're just going up to Columbia to reminisce. We'll be back for lunch." She made a kissing sound. "Love you too."

We must have looked like real oddballs—two nearly middle-aged women sitting on the steps of a college quad, huddling in the cold, watching students running in and out of classes.

"I was good at physics, wasn't I, Stace?" Eloise asked.

I had been silent when we arrived, nervous about starting the conversation, not sure what I'd say. But I didn't like the tone of her voice, the way she used the past tense so easily. And her demeanor had been uncharacteristically distant in the taxi. Although she'd asked a few questions about my tour, she didn't seem to listen to my improvised answers. She was gazing out of the window, uninvolved.

"Of course you were good. You got into graduate school, remember? Do you wish you had gone?"

"No." She shook her head. "Then I might not have met Robert."

I had been practicing under my breath in the taxi, saying over and over again, Robert wants you dead, Eloise, hoping that with repetition, I'd find it easier to say when the time came. *If* the time came.

"Are you *happy* with him, Eloise?"

"Happy?" she asked. I recognized the vacant look; I'd seen it on her before, the day she'd told me she wasn't going to graduate school. I waited.

"All Americans are entitled to the pursuit of unhappiness," she said.

"What does *that* mean?"

"You lied to me, Stace."

I felt my entire body shrivel. I looked away from her and lit a cigarette.

"You said that someone would fall in love with me. You promised me. That day in the cafeteria." She sounded disembodied, floating. Not angry or bitter. Removed.

I exhaled, swallowed, inhaled again.

"And isn't Robert in love with you?"

"Robert's in love with Sapphire. He always has been and he always will be."

"Are you sure?" I was startled, must have sounded it.

She opened her eyes extremely wide and stared at me.

"I'm sure."

I thought carefully about the next question.

"Then why don't you leave him?"

"Because I love him."

I lost it then.

"Eloise—what has he done to you?" I grabbed her by the shoulders, shook her. "Wake up, for Christ's sake. Why are you drinking in the morning? Why are you drinking all the time? Why are you letting yourself be destroyed? Robert's not worth it. No man is worth it."

She didn't respond. I shook her again.

"I'm going to tell you something you should know. Robert was married before—I mean, a second time. To a woman named Susan. And—"

"Oh, I know all about Susan." Eloise cut in, emotionless. "If you're here to warn me about Robert, Stace—" She laughed dismissively, gently removed my hands from her shoulders. "You can save your breath. Susan died of anorexia and some of her friends think Robert contributed. He may well have." She stopped and I was silent as well, not knowing what to say.

Eloise already knew about Susan?

"Who cares?" she asked, her eyes following the movement of a couple in front of us, walking with their arms entwined around each other's waist.

"Christ, Eloise, *I* care. I'm worried about you. If Robert did contribute to Susan's death, he could—he could—"

"He could be trying to contribute to mine?" The same dismissive laugh. "He could be trying to kill me for my money? Or to make me kill myself? Listen, Stace—" She faced me, the vapor from our last sentences mingling together in the winter air. "I've figured it all out already. I know about Susan because I hired a private investigator to look into Robert's past. After Las Vegas. I'm no fool. Well, I was for a while, but not anymore. The pictures of Sapphire all around the house, the way he kept pouring me booze, even when I said it made me feel lousy, that my doctor advised me against drinking a long time ago. The way his behavior toward me changed. All the little criticisms and the big ones. Why didn't he love me the way he had at first? Was it all my fault?

"You don't know how I agonized, how unhappy I was. I was looking for an answer, any answer that might explain what was happening to us. I decided I needed to know more about his past—he wouldn't talk about those years after Sapphire and before me. He was as silent about his past as I used to be; I figured he had something to hide. Like I did, when I wouldn't answer your questions. When I wouldn't talk about my mother. He'd brush them off. As if they didn't mean anything. So I knew they meant a lot, and I hired an investigator. There are all sorts of corporate spies who'll sell their services to a very rich woman. I felt like JR in *Dallas*. Anyway, the man who was recommended to me did some good work and ended up in Denver and talked to Susan's friends. And reported back to me.

"Oh, yes, and I'd read Daniel's book by that time, too. He'd sent me a copy like he said he was going to. I read it like the Bible. Give someone unconditional love and then withdraw it, bit by bit. Classic. You really should see Daniel, you know. He's a wonderful man."

"Daniel isn't important, Eloise, *you're* important. You need to tell me everything. Keep on talking."

She was still speaking as if this story were about someone else, people she'd met at a party. I wanted to shake her again, but refrained.

"Daniel *is* important, Stace. You two should be together. I snuck out and saw him a few times, you know. On my own. I got very involved for a couple of months in the subject of brainwashing. We talked about it a lot. It's fascinating."

"Eloise—" I tried to sound calm. "If you know Robert's trying to brainwash you, if you know about Susan, why don't you get the hell out? I don't understand."

She looked at me sadly.

"I love him, Stacy."

"Eloise—Jesus! How *can* you love him, how can you be so self-destructive?"

She looked at me with pity.

"Love isn't something you can control. Not the kind of love I feel. If it were, well, nothing would be at stake. Nobody would have broken hearts. We'd all be sensible, rational people. People without souls."

Her voice had woken up finally.

"I know Robert doesn't love me, I know that most probably he wants me dead, but I adore the man, Stace. You don't understand. I couldn't live without him. And don't start with that other fish in the sea business. It's not like when you're a kid and a dog gets run over and your parents buy a new puppy to replace it. It doesn't work like that for me. He's irreplaceable. Do people tell parents to go out and get another baby

320

when their child dies? No, because they know that child is irreplaceable, that you can't substitute love. Robert is the love of my life. I can't afford to lose him."

"Answer me this, Eloise"—I was on the verge of hysteria—"can you afford *not* to lose him?"

"I've made my decision. He doesn't know I know, of course. That wouldn't work. For him to be happy, he has to believe he's controlling me. Actually, it's kind of fun to see what he does next, to see what tricks he uses. For a while he alternated days of being really sweet with days of criticizing every thing I did. It's like being a guinea pig in an experiment. I drink enough to make him happy, but I can handle it. I know more about diabetes than he does. Don't worry, I won't get drunk and overdose on insulin. If I die, it will be my choice. My conscious choice."

"What do you mean *if you die?* You won't die, Eloise. I mean, you won't commit suicide, promise me that. You have to promise me that."

"I can't promise you anything, Stace. I've run out of promises. I'm tired." She bit her lip. "Look at it this way. Men go off to war. What do they die for? Freedom, democracy, their country? Oil prices? Most people accept that. So what's so wrong about dying for love? I mean, love is just as valid a concept as democracy or Communism or oil. If you ask me, it's more valid. You know I love you too. I appreciate your concern, I really do, and I'll do my best. But—"

"Listen—you've just said he doesn't love you. You wouldn't be dying for love then, would you?" Be logical, Stacy, I told myself. Be logical and you'll get through to her.

"I'd be dying for *my* love. Violetta sacrificed her love for Alfredo's happiness, remember. She died for him."

"Eloise—that's an opera. That's *fiction*. You have to distinguish between real life and fiction. Please."

"Why?" was all she asked.

"I'm going to get you committed, Eloise. I'm going to put you in a hospital, get a twenty-four-hour watch on you. I'm not going to let anything happen to you, anything bad."

"I'd call putting me in a hospital pretty bad. I'm not crazy, Stace. Well, maybe everyone in love is a little crazy, but I'm not insane. I made the choice to stay with Robert because I love him. The problem is not that he wants to kill me, it's that he doesn't love me. He feels no passion for me—the only person he feels passionately about is Sapphire. If he were wildly jealous of me and wanted to strangle me, well, that would be different. I would have some hope. As it is, I'm just in his way. Maybe I'll stay in his way for a while, just so I can be with him, see him, listen to him, touch him. Or maybe I'll sacrifice myself, make him truly happy. Bow out."

"Sacrifice yourself? He's not a god, Eloise. Why don't you just give him all your money?" I said quickly. "That's the solution to all this. That's all he wants. He's got some crazy scheme; he thinks if he had all your money he could ruin Sapphire. Give him the money, if you want to make him happy. Give him the money, not yourself."

"Oh, Stace, I've thought of that. But there are lawyers, people who'll want to know why I'm doing it. People who will ask questions. Robert would be disappointed in me, too. A lot of my money is tied up. He wouldn't be able to get his hands on it all at once. Anyway, if he had it, if he had however much he thought was enough, he'd leave. I'd be alone, knowing he was out there somewhere. With someone else. You don't know what that thought does to me. I'd rather be dead."

"Eloise. Robert killed a woman. You don't seem to have taken that on board. How can you possibly love him?"

"Yes, Robert may have killed Susan, and yes, I may have killed my mother. He and I are even."

I stood up, sat down again. Knocked my closed fist against my forehead. Lit another cigarette. Eloise sat composedly, staring at Butler Library.

"You didn't kill your mother, Eloise. It's not the same at all. You need a psychiatrist."

"Stace, please. Listen to *me*. For once. Don't think of your own life, what you want from me, think of *me*. You would like me to live in the real world. Well, my whole life has consisted of people whom I loved unconditionally, who seemed to love me unconditionally, disappearing, making that love vanish. My mother, my father, now Robert. That's *my* real world. No psychiatrist in the world can bring that love back and *that's what I want*. I want my mother, my father, Robert. Those three people. Specifically. Nobody else.

"Do you want me to divorce Robert? Then what? Do a Barbara Hutton and take a string of husbands?

323

Live on my own? I've done that and I don't like it. I hate it. And I don't want some shrink telling me I have to love myself. What good would that do? Honestly?"

"It might help," I said quietly.

"It won't," she shot back. "Why won't you just respect my emotions, Stace? I may have fallen in love with the wrong man. A man who doesn't love me. But it doesn't change the fact that I am in love with him. You can't get me to leave Robert. It's a principled choice, don't you see?"

"No, I don't. You sound like Eva Braun in the bunker. What can I say to convince you?" I began to cry heavy, desperate tears. Eloise put her arms around me. Students crossed behind and in front of us on those steps. I wanted to go back to our college years and be smarter, more aware, less selfish. I wanted to be nineteen years old and intelligent enough to tell Eloise she should get help. Not kid her out of her moods, not joke around, but take them seriously, take *her* seriously. Why had I respected her privacy? Her private thoughts were her hell. I should have intruded. Instead I talked about myself the whole time. I deserted her when Buddy came on the scene. I hadn't been a true friend to her. It was Eloise all along who had been the real friend to me.

"Stace—it's not your fault. You couldn't have done anything back then but be the friend you were." Eloise the psychic. She pulled back from me, put her hand to my cheek, as if I were a small child, "Now go see Daniel. He's not involved with anyone else—he loves you. Go find him and stop being a fool. And stop worrying about me. I won't kill myself, okay? We'll go to the Regency tonight and watch *Notorious*. It's on with *Suspicion,* the perfect double bill. Go see Daniel and then come back to the house and tell me about it. How could I kill myself when there are still Cary Grant movies to be seen?"

I laughed in the midst of my tears. A laugh of temporary relief.

"Good. Now get your ass down to 93rd Street. You see, I'm even getting into streetwise lingo now. Go for it." I sat helplessly as Eloise stood up and walked toward Broadway. I watched her back, watched as she turned and waved, smiled. Then she swung around again and hailed a cab.

21

DECEMBER 1990

Daniel's apartment was as I had imagined; untidy, smoke filled, with books and half-drunk coffee mugs littering the floor. A nice mess. He hadn't sounded surprised when he'd heard my voice over the intercom, didn't hug or kiss me when he opened the door, just motioned to two armchairs in the corner of the room and lit a Pall Mall.

His presence overwhelmed me momentarily. Those sharp black eyes, the swept-back hair, his low voice all paralyzed me. He seemed so easygoing, so at home with himself, so content without being placid. I sat uneasily, torn between the need to help Eloise and the urgent desire to establish myself as a part of his life again.

We talked about Eloise. I told him about everything except my run-in with Robert that afternoon in Vegas. Repeated excerpts of my conversation with Sapphire and Bobby, with Robert that morning, and all of my conversation with Eloise on the steps. Then I asked him for his advice and help.

"I don't know what to say." He leaned forward, elbows on his knees, chin resting in his hands. "As she told you, I've seen her a few times myself. We've had some good talks. I would have liked to discuss her with you, her emotional well-being, but I figured you'd opted out. From me and from her both.

"As you know, I was always suspicious of Robert. I didn't like those eyes. And I was curious from the beginning about the amount of booze he handed out. We all like a drink, but there's a limit. I wasn't sure what he was heading for, or why he kept her tanked up. But then she called me after I sent the book and she came over here and we talked. She would say things like: 'If someone were trying to brainwash someone would he attack all her weak spots at once, or gradually, one at a time?' She's an intelligent woman, and, of course, I knew she was talking about her relationship with Robert—why else would she be so interested? But I thought I should play a waiting game for a while, not confront her, just give her the information she wanted. Talk hypothetically.

"Finally, after about her fourth visit, I came out with it. I said: 'We're talking about you and Robert here, aren't we, Eloise?' and she said, 'Yes, we are.' She looks great when she's telling the truth, you know. She has such an honest face. Anyway, I said: 'If he's playing mind games with you, you should be very careful indeed. You don't want to end up being a victim.' She answered: 'Isn't everyone a victim of their own emotions?' Then she went into a monologue about love. How love is like a political cause for her. Robert is her belief system, or rather, what she feels for him constitutes a religion. She won't abandon him. She was fervent about that. And surprisingly articulate and coherent. She almost had me signing up for the love brigade, I'll tell you. It was interesting."

"It's terrifying."

"You know, Sonia stuck with Raskolnikov, even knowing he had murdered two women. Followed him to Siberia. And if you reread *Crime and Punishment* enough times, you come to realize more and more how unsympathetic Raskolnikov was. He makes Robert look like a fun guy."

"That's fiction again, Daniel. Eloise talks about operas, you talk about Dostoevsky. I'm trying to save her life. And you have to help me."

"If you ask me, Eloise has been looking for an altar to sacrifice herself on. If it hadn't been Robert, it would have been someone else. She's a willing victim. People fall in and out of love constantly without feeling the need to kill themselves. Most people move on from unsatisfactory relationships, build new lives, find other loves. But there are some characters out there who won't give up, who cling to the old romance, who wallow in the pain. You've seen them, I'm sure—the men and women who go around with bitter eyes and turned down mouths, the ones who never stop talking about their ex-husbands or ex-wives.

"I'm not saying Eloise is into pain exactly, but this is like the third strike for her—her mother, her father, now Robert. She doesn't want to build a new life and I don't think she wants to be bitter either. All she wants is to love Robert in her own way, to believe in that love. Look, Stacy. It's the age-old question. Can you save someone who doesn't want to be saved?"

"You can try. I can try."

"I don't know," he mused, looking up at his ceiling. "We might have had a chance if Eloise had been a true victim of brainwashing. Look at the Patty Hearst case. She experiences a trauma—the kidnapping. Then she falls in love with one of her abductors, espouses his causes, robs a bank with his gang; is on her way to being a full-fledged member of the SLA. She's been brainwashed. Then the police shoot her radical black boyfriend-stroke-captor in a stakeout, and the second trauma effectively negates the first. She emerges from the underground, rejoins society, becomes your run-of-the-mill wife and mother. Although she married her bodyguard, which also says something about her psyche. Anyway, what you need is to introduce a traumatic experience into Eloise's life. Which might shake her up enough to make her reconsider her belief in Robert."

"No." He shook his head. "It won't work. She's a willing participant in all this, that's the difference. We talked about brainwashing enough for me to know that she has *chosen* it. Funnily enough, she's the one with the power in the end. She knows exactly what's going on. In a way, she's manipulating him."

"Not if she kills herself, she isn't. She's giving him everything he wants."

"Yes, but what if he doesn't get what he wants in the end? What if he doesn't manage to wreck Sapphire's career? It's an off-the-wall plan of his. It won't work. And then where will he be? Being the psychotic he is, he might have to murder Sapphire, and once she was dead, Robert would have *nothing* left to live for, psychologically speaking. Eloise would have won, in a roundabout way."

"But Eloise would be dead. And for that matter, so would Sapphire."

"You've got a point there." He shrugged, gazing at me with a cool, appraising look. "It's good to have you back. Don't run away again, Stacy. It's unbecoming."

At work, sales reps from publishing companies were always trying to sell me on books, convince me to buy what they had to offer. My job was to pick the right titles and then persuade the customers to buy the titles I'd picked. But I wasn't always as cutthroat as I should have been. There were certain reps I had a soft spot for, people I'd buy lousy books from because they did such a good job of selling them, or simply because I liked them so much. There was one man from an arts books publishing house who made me laugh so much I'd always give him a good sale. Sometimes I took risks that paid off on obscure books by obscure authors, sometimes I took a dive on them. But I was practiced in the art of persuasion. I made decisions about which books in the store I'd put in window displays, which ones I'd face out on the shelves, which ones I'd hype to regular customers.

How, though, was I supposed to hype Eloise on life without Robert? How was I supposed to persuade her, sell her on herself? She'd been so resigned when we'd talked. Clearly, she wanted to stay with Robert even knowing what she knew. It was up to me to change her mind.

Daniel came with me to 74th Street. I needed him with me: I wasn't sure what step I should next take with Eloise and I *was* sure that I didn't want to be alone with Robert again, ever.

When we arrived, Sarah answered our knock and announced that Mr. and Mrs. Chappell weren't in. She had no idea where they were or when they'd be back. My bag was still sitting on the front bench and I grabbed it. I would prefer to wait at Daniel's until Eloise and Robert got back, so I asked Sarah to let Eloise know we'd visited, and to call me at Daniel's when she arrived back. "Make sure you tell *her,*" I said sternly. "Not Mr. Chappell. *Mrs.* Chappell." Sarah looked annoyed, then nodded.

Daniel and I then retraced our steps back to the West Side in a taxi.

"I feel like a yo-yo," he said. "Are we going to have to do this *again* as soon as she calls?"

"Yes," I replied curtly.

But Eloise didn't call. I waited two hours before I tried her, but Sarah answered and said they hadn't returned.

"I'll get her to call you when she comes in," she assured me. I waited another hour, pacing around Daniel's apartment, smoking and avoiding subjects such as where I'd been for the past nine months.

I called again and got the same response.

"Can't you find out where she has gone?" I asked.

"How am I supposed to do that?" Sarah was becoming increasingly irritated with me.

"Well, do you know if she has taken the limo?"

"I assume so." She sounded like a young Mrs. Danvers.

"Then let me have the limo number and *I'll* call her."

She gave me the number, but Eloise either wasn't in the car, or had switched the phone off.

"What do I do now?" I beseeched Daniel.

"You don't do anything," he answered. "There's nothing else you can do. Have your fiftieth cigarette of the day and I'll make us another cup of coffee. Want to watch Oprah?"

"No. I have to *do* something, Daniel. Where has he taken her? Why aren't they back? I don't like the feel of this."

"To tell you the truth, neither do I." Daniel came over and rubbed the top of my head. "But we can't call the police—she's gone somewhere with her husband, after all. And we know Robert wouldn't put a knife in her in the back of the limo. He's got to watch his ass, remember. There may well be an innocent explanation. Although nothing Robert does is entirely innocent, I'd bet."

I picked up one of the books on the floor. *Blind Faith* by Joe McGinniss. A true story about an upper-middle-class New Jersey man, pillar of the community, who arranges to have his wife murdered. A best seller. I turned on Daniel, fuming.

"Why do so many men murder their wives? Why do so many men *want* to murder their wives? What's wrong with us? Why do you all hate us so much?"

"Hey, nut case, it's just a fact of life. Men get tired of all the shit thrown at them, that's all. We get tired of listening to complaints all the time. So we dream about murdering our wives. And some of us do it.''

The telephone rang and I leaped to it.

"I don't care if it's a girlfriend. I'm getting it," I said. Hearing Sarah's voice on the other end, I sagged.

"Mrs. Chappell just called. She said to call you and tell you that she and Mr. Chappell were going out to dinner with friends—she'd forgotten she'd been invited to a dinner party. She's very sorry, but she wants you to make yourself at home here. I told her you were staying with Mr. Sterne and she said to send him her love, and wished you a wonderful night. She says she's sorry about missing the movies. She'll call you in the morning.''

"Thank you," I said, hanging up.

"Sarah says they're going to a dinner party," I told Daniel. "Eloise will call me tomorrow morning. Is it all right with you if I stay here?"

"It's fine by me, Stacy." He paused briefly. "But let's get something straight right now. I have no interest in being your friend. I have a big interest in being your lover. It's all or nothing. I don't want to bullshit around. It's boring.''

"Okay." Now I paused. "It's all. But I can't get into any passionate scenes tonight; my mind is on Eloise. Just be my friend tonight, all right? Afterward we'll deal with us.''

We went to the double feature at the Regency, Daniel substituting for Eloise. I had forgotten the plot of *Suspicion*. Joan Fontaine, the blushing young bride of Cary Grant becomes convinced, gradually, that he's

trying to kill her for her money. This was too much of
a coincidence, I thought as I sat in the dark. It was
terrifyingly similar to Robert and Eloise. Although in
the end, Cary turned out to be a devoted husband,
not a murderer. All the signs pointing to his guilt
were misinterpretations of the benign truth.

Was Alfred Hitchcock trying to tell me something
from the grave? I asked myself as we left the theater.
Had we all, Eloise included, misjudged Robert, read
the signs wrong? Did he truly love her after all?

"You know, Hitchcock *wanted* Cary to be a killer,"
Daniel told me as we walked up Broadway. "He shot
the ending with Grant as the murderer. I think he got
a kick out of suave, handsome Cary Grant being evil
underneath it all. Then the studios kicked up a fuss
and made him change it. As you know, Hollywood
isn't good at unhappy endings and Cary Grant had to
play a likeable guy. It's a shame."

Back at his apartment, Daniel watched the *Arsenio
Hall Show,* but I couldn't concentrate. Why hadn't
Eloise called me herself, I wondered. She knew Daniel's number—when she found out he'd been with
me, she could have called me. Maybe she was in a
hurry. Or maybe she wasn't going to a dinner party at
all, maybe she was lying and she didn't want to lie to
me directly—just as I'd chosen to write her that letter
about my world tour. If so, then where was she?
Where had she and Robert disappeared to? Anywhere
was the answer. He could have swept her off anywhere. I would have to wait until the morning to dis-
cover what was going on.

That night I curled up against Daniel, my head on

his chest, rehearsing scenes with Eloise; what I could say to her, how I'd say it. I would quit my job, stay with Daniel, see Eloise every day if need be. I'd protect her, make sure she wasn't drinking, make sure she got away from Robert as often as possible. I'd find her a good shrink, I'd accompany her to her appointments. I'd wean her away from Robert. She was my responsibility now; she *was* my sister and I'd fight to the end to get her life back on track. I wouldn't abandon her again, I wouldn't opt out and run away. For once in my life I was going to stay and fight for a person I loved.

22

DECEMBER 1990

The letter arrived at ten-thirty the next morning. I had called Eloise and been told that she and Mr. Chappell had not returned that evening and no one had been informed as to their whereabouts. A special courier rang Daniel's bell, and he made a crack about vacuum cleaner salesmen, but my heart froze when I saw the man at the door, holding out an envelope addressed to me.

"It's from Eloise," I said to Daniel. I stood in the middle of his apartment, turning the white envelope over and over in my hands. "I don't think I want to read this."

"You have to, Stacy." He looked grim, took my hand and led me to a chair, lit one of my cigarettes for me and put it in my mouth. "You have to read it."

"I don't want to," I said. I was crying. I was also shaking so much I could barely control my movements. Daniel sat in the chair beside me and waited silently.

"I know what's in this."

"No, you don't. You might be wrong."

"I'm not. She's dead. I can feel it. I've felt a sense

of doom since I woke up this morning. She's done it, Daniel. She's killed herself. I know it." I didn't bother to brush away the tears. "I fucked up. Jesus. I allowed this to happen."

"Read the letter, Stacy."

Dear Stace,

I want to apologize for breaking my promise to you. To be melodramatic, by the time you read this, I'll be dead. It's not your fault and I don't want you to feel responsible in any way. This is my decision, a decision I'm making for myself. I'm extraordinarily tired, Stace, and I'm not up to life. I'm the same age my mother was when she killed herself. I suppose the Freudians would think that was an important fact and I suppose it is.

You know what I hate? Having no memories of her. You'd think a three-year-old would have remembered something. The smell of her perfume —something. I know about the lilies only because the housekeeper told me. But I can't remember her kissing me good night, I can't remember anything about her at all. That's why I never had any pictures of her around. I wanted to remember what she looked like without any outside help. I wanted it to come from my heart, not a photograph. But all I know is this ache I've always had. A profound sense of loss.

When Daddy withdrew from my life, well, then I had too many memories. Restaurants he'd taken me to, the opera, always treating me like a special, grown-up person. So why did he stop thinking of me as his best friend? I'll never know, I can only guess. Because of me, my mother died. I was responsible for *his* ache, *his* sense of loss. He never talked to me about her, you know. And, as always, when someone avoids a subject, it's the most important subject of their life. His French mistress might have helped, but I bet she could never take the place of my mother.

I didn't fit in at boarding school. My fault. I kept to myself, was reclusive, didn't make friends. Our friendship at Barnard was such a wonderful surprise. It came as such a shock to me. I decided to live in a dorm because I didn't want to be in that house alone with the oh-so-occasional visit from Daddy. But I didn't think I'd make a friend like you. That was the kind of bonus I never expected.

Then, well, you had your life and I had whatever it was that amounted to mine. I'll never understand myself fully, never comprehend why it was I didn't go to graduate school. We make such strange choices that govern our future. But I thought that at graduate school the professors would find out that I really didn't know anything. Whenever I got good marks in a course, I'd think that it was just luck. Self-doubt is corrosive, and I had plenty of self-doubt. But you know all that.

I think I deliberately looked such a wreck in those days because then I could criticize myself before anyone else criticized me, if that makes any sense. If people dismissed me because of my appearance at least they weren't dismissing me because of my personality. Oh, Stace, I know I'm not making a lot of sense. I'm an outcast. Not because of the money—that's too simple. No. Because of my soul. I just don't belong.

I was like a nomad in Europe. I went from country to country and I never fit in anywhere. I couldn't be a jet-setter, but then I couldn't work at McDonald's either. Sometimes I wish I'd found out before about your divorce from Buddy. I might have come to San Francisco. We might have had a good time. But what am I saying? I wouldn't have met Robert then.

I'm not feeling sorry for myself—as I said, I've made the choices all along. I'm responsible for my own pain.

Robert changed all that. He came into my life and he gave me everything I've ever wanted—self-confidence, love, happiness. Everything. He even made me laugh the way you used to. We had a lot of fun—I mean it. Remember that Fred Astaire song: "They Can't Take That Away From Me?" Well, nobody can take those months away from me. It *was* real. Even if he was faking, it was real for me. That's another concept you might not understand, but try. Those months, those first months were worth it all. I mean it. I was completely, utterly fulfilled. How many people get to say that about any period in their lives? I consider myself lucky.

When it all began to collapse, I was miserable. And angry. There were times I wanted to kill *him*.

I've always been afraid of my own anger. But then I thought about it all rationally. He was obsessed with Sapphire, I was obsessed with him; for all I know, Sapphire might be obsessed with someone else who doesn't love her. It's a daisy chain of misplaced, mischosen love. It happens all the time. No one can guarantee that the person you love will love you back. It's a lottery. And I lost.

Give him up, you would say. Give him up and move on.

Do you know that he sleeps on his side with his head resting on one hand? Do you know that he buttons the last button of his shirt and then slips it over his head every morning? Isn't that a strange way to put on a shirt? Isn't it the most bizarre of reasons to love someone? I love his idiosyncrasies. I love his little hands and the piece of pencil lead that's still stuck in his palm from schooldays. You can see it just beneath the skin, lying beside his lifeline. He's got a short lifeline. That worries me.

Classic case here, Stace. I can't live with him and I can't live without him. Oh, I thought I *could* live with him, even knowing he wants me dead, but I can't. Why? Because he's killing something far more important. He's killing those first months—he is the only one who *can* take that away from me. Every time he barks at me, or every time he pours me a drink, he takes a little slice away from those first months; they become more distant, less real to me. I'm hanging on to them like a drowning person to the last plank of wood, but my grip is slipping. I'm tired. I want to die while there's still something left to die for.

If we could have had a child—well, that would be different. But Robert told me we needed time on our own before we had a child. Of course, he would never give me a child. No chance of that. No chance.

I think I should drown. I think that's the right way to die. But I'm a little worried about floating off to sea and being hooked by some poor fisherman. Not really fair, is it? Well, I'll figure something out.

So, Stace, there are only a few things left to say. I know about you and Robert having sex. And I don't blame you. When you wrote me that letter saying you'd gone off on a world tour, I called B. Dalton's to find out where you'd be on your first stop and whoever answered didn't have a clue what I was talking about. He said you were out at lunch but would be back shortly; that, as far as he knew, you weren't going anywhere. I called again two weeks later, just to make sure. I didn't call you at home because by that time, I'd started to figure everything out. You'd left Las Vegas so quickly, you'd avoided calling me, you'd made up some silly story.

Why? What reason could you have for avoiding me? If you didn't want to see Daniel, that was one thing, but why *me*? Why couldn't you even talk to me?

You've often accused me of being psychic. Well, I was then. It suddenly hit me. I just knew for a fact that it had happened. I was so hurt, Stace. So bewildered. My best friend and my husband. By that time, though, I was beginning to admit to myself that my husband wasn't—Robert wasn't in love with me. I can't recall the sequence of events too clearly, but I realized—I guess it was after reading Daniel's book—that Robert may have had a reason for sleeping with you, that it might not be just sex. He'd tell me about it someday. To wound me. Funnily enough, that was a real relief—that he slept with you because of *me* ultimately. Not because you were the woman of his dreams.

I should have called you to tell you I understood, but I was too involved in my own life and it took me a long time to forgive you anyway. I'm saying this now because I have forgiven you. You're right, you know. There are more important things than sex. You're my friend who made a mistake—I've made enough of them myself to realize how easy it is.

Poor Robert. He told me all about it on the way here. He was trying to paint you as the evil friend, out to steal my man. I'm getting better at being an actress, and I guess I managed to look really stunned and hurt. He won't be surprised when he finds my body. But I want you to show him this letter later. I want him to know what I've done for him. I want him to know I wasn't stupid. Maybe he'll fall in love with me again after I'm dead. I'm so tired I don't know if I'm being coherent, but trust me, Stace. It's all perfectly clear in my mind. Remember Nixon—"Let me make one thing perfectly clear . . ." And now we have Bush and maybe another war on the way and nothing changes that dramatically, does it?

One last thing. I've done something strange with my will. You'll find out soon enough. I did it last week. It's a little crazy but I feel good about it.

Don't feel sorry for me, Stace. You know how I hate that. Besides, I want to go home now. I want to find out where the taxi is going to take me. I want to see my mother again.

23

DECEMBER 1990

The moment I finished reading Eloise's letter, I called 74th Street. Sarah answered the phone. She could barely speak.

"Sarah, where is Mrs. Chappell? Do you have any idea? I need to know."

"She's dead," she sobbed. "They're both dead."

I thought I'd misheard.

"You mean Mrs. Chappell?" I said, my heart collapsing. "Mrs. Chappell is dead?"

"Mrs. Chappell, yes. She's dead. And Mr. Chappell. The police just called from the Cape house. That's where they were. Oh, what am I supposed to do? How can this have happened?"

"Are you sure?" I was beyond shock. "Are you sure Mr. Chappell is dead too?"

"Yes, I'm sure," she moaned. "The police told me. Mr. Chappell killed himself, they said. Mrs. Chappell was in . . . oh, God, she was in the bathtub. Drowned. They think it was a double suicide. They wanted to know if there were any relatives. I didn't know what to say. What am I supposed to do?"

"I don't know. I don't know. I can't help you. Oh,

Jesus." I hung up and turned to Daniel, Eloise's letter in my hand.

"She's dead. Robert's dead too. They were at the Cape. Robert's dead. They're both dead. They both killed themselves. Oh, Christ. Read this."

Daniel took the letter from my hand. I stood like a statue as he turned the pages. When he finished, he walked away from me.

"Daniel?"

"Yes, Stacy?" He reached his bookshelves and sat down on the floor, his back against a set of Shakespeare plays.

"Daniel, will you talk to me? Please?"

"What do you want me to say? That you're a fool? That you slept with your best friend's husband while I was what? Playing poker? Very nice."

"I was confused. I was . . ."

"Stupid. Gullible. Look, there's no point in me piling the guilt on you. You must feel it enough as it is. Eloise forgave you, I suppose I should. But it's not easy, Stacy. It's not easy at all."

"She's dead. He's dead. I don't understand. I don't believe it."

"Look. I'll get us both a cup of coffee. Sit down before you fall down."

I stumbled to a chair and Daniel rose, strode to the kitchen, the letter still in his hand. A few minutes later he reappeared with two mugs, handed one to me, and pulled a chair over to face mine. The coffee burned my tongue. I kept gulping it.

"Do you think we should go there—go to the Cape?" I asked.

"There's not much point in that. We could go see them in the morgue, but I don't think that's such a hot idea."

"She's dead," I said again. "She really is dead. Why didn't I stop her?"

"You don't have the monopoly on guilt on this one, you know. She came to me too. We had those talks. *I* should have done something."

We were silent. I began to cry. Daniel lit a cigarette.

"I don't get this double suicide business," Daniel said after he'd finished his Pall Mall. "Why would Robert kill himself? It doesn't make sense."

I could barely see him through my tears. "Maybe we all were wrong about Robert. Maybe when he found her body, he killed himself. Oh, God, what if he did love her and we helped convince her that he didn't. What if it's our fault. That stupid fucking book of yours."

"Do you honestly think that if he loved her he would have slept with you? *And* told her about it? Get real. And don't try to unload this onto my book."

"I'm sorry," was all I could say.

"Yeah, well, I'm sorry too. I care about Eloise too. If she's up in heaven, if there is a heaven, God's a lucky man to have her there."

"Daniel—" I found it difficult to complete a sentence. "Daniel—I know I shouldn't have slept with Robert. It was just after our fight. Oh, shit. I have no excuses that make sense. If it makes any difference, it was horrible."

"That fact doesn't make a significant difference to my life, no, Stacy."

He remained sitting, watching me cry.

"I think you should call Bobby. They might not have contacted him yet. He needs to know. Do you have a phone number for him?"

The practical element of this roused me from my tears.

"Yes. He's with Sapphire. I've got their hotel number. They're staying in L.A. The Bel Air."

"Good. Can you make the call or do you want me to?" His voice had softened, but only slightly.

"I will." It was 3 A.M. on the West Coast. Bobby's voice was groggy. When I told him the news, he was speechless.

"I think you better fly out here, Bobby. We'll have to make funeral arrangements."

"Jesus Christ. Dad. Dad killed himself? I don't believe it."

"I'm sorry, Bobby. But it's true. The police in Cape Cod told the maid in New York. I can't believe it myself. Maybe you should bring Sapphire with you. She might help."

"She had to go to some concert," Bobby said. "I'll be there as soon as I can."

"I'm sorry to have to tell you."

He hung up.

"He's coming as soon as he can," I told Daniel, avoiding his eyes.

"Okay. Now I think we should go over to 74th Street. We might be able to find out more, and we're the closest people to Eloise. To Robert too, for that matter. Bobby's going to need some support when he

arrives. We should help him with the funerals. Can
you deal with this, Stacy?"

"I don't know." I shook my head. "I guess so."

"We'll take the letter with us. The police will want
to see it."

My tears returned in a rush.

"Look—I know I've been tough on you. You've just
lost your best friend. You're probably in shock. I'll be
honest, this business with Robert and you has thrown
me. But I'll be with you while you go through all this.
I'll help you as much as I can. That's all I can do right
now."

"Thanks," I said.

Daniel shrugged.

The three days that followed are a blur. I remember
picking out coffins with Bobby and Daniel, deciding
where to hold the funeral, where to bury them both.
The Cape seemed the right option; a little cemetery
beside a church in Falmouth, looking over the sea.
But the logistics of the funeral arrangements were
mixed up with police visits. Two detectives came to
New York and asked us questions as to Eloise's and
Robert's state of mind. We handed over the letter.
Daniel made a point of finding out everything the
police knew about the case.

Robert and Eloise had gone to the Cape that Friday, right after Eloise had returned from her talk with
me. Edwin drove them, but the only information he
could offer was that it was Mr. Chappell's idea, that he
had wanted to celebrate their first wedding anniversary at Cape Cod. No other staff was there; Deborah

was scheduled to visit the house every Saturday morning, just to keep an eye on things and so Deborah was the unfortunate one—the one who found the bodies. Edwin was staying with a cousin who lived twenty minutes away.

Eloise was found in the bathtub with a massive amount of insulin in her body, enough to send her into a coma. It appeared that she had shot herself up and then climbed into the bathtub to drown. To save a poor fisherman from finding her, I thought. But why inject herself beforehand? Daniel agreed that this was strange, but if Robert had administered a fatal dose to her himself, the police reasoned, he wouldn't have shot himself afterward. He would have made it look like suicide and hoped for the best. Once we had handed over Eloise's letter, they were confirmed in their suicide theory.

Robert's time of death was three hours after Eloise's—approximately eleven P.M. The police concluded that he found her in the bathtub when he'd gone up to bed, and, overcome with horror and despair, snatched up his gun, lay down on the marital bed and shot himself through the heart. Double suicides were not that uncommon. There was no sign of a struggle, no forced entry into the house, no other conclusion to be drawn. Eloise Chappell had worried that her husband no longer loved her. She killed herself in a fit of depression. Robert Chappell found his wife's dead body, and, full of grief and remorse, took his own life. It was the obvious conclusion.

I told one of the detectives the story of Susan, but he didn't seem particularly interested. There were no known facts, no clear-cut evidence of Robert's guilt. Actually, it only reinforced the idea that Robert, feeling guilty for both his second and third wives' unfortunate deaths, would be inclined to shoot himself.

Daniel and I had to agree, but neither of us felt comfortable with the thought of Robert as a man with remorse. Then we found out a piece of information which changed everything. Robert's father had killed himself. He hadn't wasted away as Robert had told me, he'd shot himself. It was so symmetrical, it was uncanny. Eloise's mother drowns herself, Robert's father shoots himself. Both children decide to take the same way out.

"Poor Bobby," Daniel said. "What an inheritance."

After our trip to the funeral parlor, Daniel and Bobby went off for a long walk in Riverside Park.

"He's not a bad kid," Daniel told me when they returned to the 74th Street house. I'd been sitting in the living room on my own, studying the silver-framed pictures of Robert and Eloise. I couldn't bring myself to go upstairs and go through her closet, clean it of all vestiges of Eloise. I had hated picking out Eloise's coffin. The funeral director tried to hustle us into buying the most expensive model. I'd opted for a cheap one; no satin, no frills, and he'd intimated that Eloise would never be comfortable in the afterlife. It was a sordid business, and imagining Eloise stretched out forever beneath the earth, unable to bite her lip, twirl her hair—the finality of her death, the waste of it all— left me feeling bleak and hopeless.

Why wasn't Eloise here? How could I have let her down so badly? I should never have let her walk away from me in the psychological state she was in. Why hadn't I kept her beside me, never let her out of my sight? I had been fobbed off with that line about Cary Grant movies, I had laughed with relief and watched her disappear from my life. Her pain was more than I could handle, so I chose to believe that she would survive it. And as a result I had ended up with more pain than I had ever imagined I could experience. Life without Eloise seemed empty. Her death had ripped a hole in my heart.

"Bobby's bright and he's not as fucked up as I'd be in his shoes," Daniel continued. I wasn't concentrating. I kept looking at Eloise and Robert, arms around each other, smiling out from the photograph. Had he loved her? He might have hated womankind in general, but how could he hate Eloise? She would never have cheated on him, she hadn't wanted to control his life. Robert must have known that. Perhaps Eloise had been right in her letter. Robert could have fallen in love with her after her death. The final irony.

"He seems to believe that his father's suicide wipes the slate. That it proves Robert had feelings. Anyway, he's a nice kid. I'm going to take him out again tomorrow. It's a good idea for him to get of this house as much as possible. Once the funeral's over, I told him he should go back to UCLA and study like a fiend. Lose himself for a while in the books. And, of course, keep on with the shrink."

I wouldn't have minded getting out of the house myself, but I didn't suggest that I accompany them. The relationship between Daniel and myself was tenuous. He treated me like a friend, but not a close friend. He'd go back to his West Side apartment every night and I'd stay in the same guest bedroom I'd had before.

Eloise's death was affecting me in a myriad of ways. At various points during the day, I would suddenly become conscious that I was humming an aria. Arias from operas that she and I had gone to almost twenty years previously. Obscure ones that I had forgotten. Or, in the middle of conversations with Bobby, with Daniel, with the police, I'd remember specific meals Eloise and I had together. The first course, the main course, the dessert. The exact restaurant where we'd had that particular meal, our discussions during it. My memory was on overdrive. I was living in the past. With Eloise. One night I even had her dream. I dreamed I was Eloise, and I was dancing with Fred Astaire on a rooftop. When I woke up, I couldn't stop crying.

Very few people came to the two funerals. Edwin, Sarah, Frederick the butler, Bobby, Daniel, myself, and a man who introduced himself as Eloise's lawyer.

The two coffins were carried by professional mourners into the church, laid side by side. The minister, who knew neither Robert nor Eloise, spoke some words about the "tragedy" and read "Death, where is thy sting?" We sang the hymns, we prayed, we trooped to the graveyard and stood as they were lowered into adjoining plots. I placed some lilies on Eloise's coffin before it was covered with soil. I didn't cry.

Eloise had asked me, in that letter about her father's death, never to see her corpse, so I didn't. I had arranged that she be buried in the pink suit she had worn the day before her wedding. I thought briefly of Argyle socks, but discarded the idea quickly. The socks were a private joke between Eloise and me. God might not appreciate it.

Bobby loomed above us all at the graves. His hair had grown a little from the crew cut; he looked more like his mother that day; a little wild, definitely imposing. Sapphire had declined to come to the funerals; she told Bobby over the telephone that she thought her presence would be inappropriate. He agreed.

After the graveside service, the small group of mourners went back to the Cape house for sandwiches and tea. Bobby sat listlessly in the wicker chair staring out across the ocean. Frederick and Sarah looked ill at ease, not sure whether they should be passing the sandwiches around or behaving like guests.

Eloise's lawyer, David Lee, a preppie-looking man with wire-rimmed glasses and double-breasted pinstriped suit, approached Daniel and me as we sat on the sofa smoking.

"Do you mind if I speak to you both privately?" he asked.

We followed him into the study, off the dining room. When I walked through that dining room, I heard Robert's voice booming out. *Everyone should love me, I'm Lolita, remember?* And you've created as much mayhem as Lolita, I thought.

David Lee brushed some lint off the shoulder of his suit.

"As you know, I'm Eloise's lawyer. We can have a

formal reading of the will, but there are some irregu-
larities. To be precise, one irregularity. I thought I
should inform you now, because, well . . ." He
looked back and forth between Daniel and me, hesitated. "I'm not sure what the position is between you
two. You may want to contest a stipulation Mrs. Chappell made. It's very irregular. We could be facing years
of legal suits."

"What's the problem?" Daniel swept his hand
through his hair.

"I think you should sit down." David Lee motioned
us to two armchairs. He remained standing, took his
glasses off, replaced them. I found myself staring at a
portrait of Eloise's father hanging over the desk facing us. I'd never seen it before. He was young, probably in his twenties. Smiling. The same brown eyes as
Eloise.

"She changed her will a week before her death. I
would have said she was in sound mind and body, but,
of course, the suicide complicates that issue. Things
could get very messy indeed."

"Yes?" Daniel was tapping his foot. I kept staring at
Paul Parker's eyes.

"The gist of it is, well, she bequeathed a third of
her fortune to the Columbia University physics department. For scholarships, research work, and the
like."

Good for Eloise, I thought.

"That's fine." Daniel was impatient. "What's the
problem?"

"Another third—and I'm talking approximately
here, because we're involved in very complicated fi-

nancial structures—anyway, to simplify things I'll say the second third was left to Robert Chappell. Of course, since Robert Chappell is now deceased that will go to his son unless he made other arrangements in *his* will.''

Daniel lit a cigarette.

"I gather the problem lies in the last third."

"Right."

David Lee kept looking nervously at Daniel, then at me, rubbing his hands together.

"She left the last third to you, Ms. Carroll." I had reverted to my maiden name after my divorce. "With the stipulation, however, that you marry Mr. Sterne here. I tried to dissuade her, of course. This was such an unusual bequest. But she insisted."

Daniel put his head in his hands and began to laugh.

"I love it."

"This is crazy," I protested. "She said in the letter that she'd done something strange in her will. But this . . ." I trailed off. Daniel looked up at the ceiling, still laughing.

"Perfect. The romantic to the end. What incredible consistency. Jesus, Eloise. *Touché.*"

"Perhaps this is not the right moment to ask, but did you two have plans? I mean *do* you have plans to marry? It might simplify the issue."

"I don't . . . we don't. I mean . . ."

"Stacy is a little incoherent right now, Mr. Lee. As I'm sure you can understand. I think we need some time to discuss this. It wasn't something we had antici-pated."

"No. No. Of course not. Well, here's my card. You can contact me in New York when you've had some time. I'll do a little research, meanwhile. See exactly what your legal position is. When she made the will, I wasn't expecting an imminent death. I thought she might change it in time."

"Thank you very much." Daniel stood up and shook Mr. Lee's hand. "We'll be in touch."

I remained seated. Eloise. The Cupid from beyond the grave. Wielding a golden bow and arrow. What could she have possibly thought she was doing?

"Oh, one more thing. I said it was divided in thirds, but that's not strictly true. The Columbia University physics department doesn't receive quite as much, because she's made a cash bequest to someone named John McNeal. She didn't know his address. Do you happen to?"

"John McNeal?" I asked. He nodded. "I don't know any . . ." I stopped. "I think you'll find he worked as her chauffeur in the early seventies. The company must have a record of him somewhere."

"Thank you." Mr. Lee gave me a limp handshake and disappeared. Daniel laughed again.

"I give her points, I really do."

"Daniel. She's trying to bribe us to marry each other. I don't see the humor in this. I don't see the point."

"Oh, I do. Eloise decided she knew what was best for both of us and she was giving us a little kick up the ass because she worried we might not be able to see it for ourselves. We'd blow it. That's the point. If we agree with her, we agree with her and we end up rich.

If we don't, well, I'm sure you can contest it. Still. It's tremendously old fashioned. Henry James would approve."

"Are you saying that you'll forgive me for sleeping with Robert because you'll be paid to forgive me? That's absurd. It's awful."

"Listen, dunce. You always said Eloise was psychic. Well, maybe she guessed I'd find out about you and Robert, that I'd read the letter or you'd tell me in a fit of guilt. And maybe she knew how I'd react. Male pride. Jealousy. All that. And maybe now, with this, she's making me think about it. It's not just the money, although, of course, that's a factor. What it is is her certainty that we belong together—even after everything that's happened. *That's* what will make me think, you know. Make us both think. She cared so much. She wants us both to ditch our pride and uncertainty and live happily ever after. She probably thought it was worth a shot. Hell, it's worth it just to see Mr. Lee in such a sweat. I'm not too fond of preppie lawyers."

"Come on," He put his hand on my shoulder. "I think it's time we went back to New York."

The snow began to fall when we hit Route 195. A little less than a year ago, I reflected, Eloise had been playing in the snow with Robert. But it wasn't the same snow. It never would be.

24
DECEMBER 1990

Daniel suggested we go to a Knicks game the next night. He also suggested that I stay in his apartment for two weeks. He'd sleep on his sofa. We would be roommates and play things by ear. What we couldn't do was discuss Eloise's will.

"We need a little breathing space, Stacy. Let's hang out together for a while, try to pretend we're not under the gun. After two weeks, we'll talk. Does that make sense?"

"I guess so." I was still reeling from the suicides and the will, happy enough to let someone else make my decisions for me. Daniel called B. Dalton's, pretending to be my doctor. He told them I had had an acute attack of appendicitis and needed rest after my operation. Creative lying.

I slept a lot. We watched TV together. We went to a couple of concerts. We took walks. He began to touch me more, but in a strictly friendly fashion. The night before our two-week deadline, Sapphire Shannon called. She invited me to lunch the next day at her suite in the Carlyle. I surprised myself by accepting.

* * *

Sapphire answered the door wearing bright pink leggings, a pink skirt over them, a purple sweatshirt on top. Long purple boots which came over her knees.

"What happened to the blue jeans?" I asked.

"Time for a change," she replied. "Come on in, sit down. Have a glass of wine. Am I right in thinking we've declared a truce?"

"Sure." I settled onto a sofa. She poured me a glass of white wine. "Just don't break into my apartment again."

"It's a deal. Listen"—she sat beside me, grabbed my arm—"I'm sorry about Eloise. Really sorry. That was terrible. Fucking awful."

"It is awful," I said. "I miss her so much. I keep thinking about times we spent together and not believing we can't do it all again."

"Memories. They're killers, I can tell you."

The doorbell rang and Sapphire let in a room service waiter who was pushing a table with two tuna fish salads and some bread rolls.

"I hope this is okay. I didn't want us to be interrupted so I ordered early."

"It's fine."

Sapphire signed for the bill and the waiter, clearly a star-struck fan, exited reluctantly.

Sapphire came back to the sofa, turned her cloudy blue eyes on me.

"Tell me about her, Stacy. I'd like to know about Eloise. What she was really like. What kind of person she was."

I did my best to describe her. I felt compelled to do it well, as if I were giving an oration at her funeral. I hadn't had the strength to do it then, but with Sapphire's inquiring eyes on me the entire time, I gave what amounted to a testimonial to my best friend. At the end I told her about the suicide letter, leaving out the passage about my encounter with Robert.

"She must have written it as soon as she got to the Cape and then called one of those twenty-four-hour messengers, given him strict instructions not to deliver it to me until the next morning. I've been trying to work out the timings of that day. Eloise left me about eleven A.M. She and Robert must have left for the Cape about noon—Edwin said they arrived around six P.M. Supposedly she died around nine o'clock, so she must have written it between six and nine.

"There's something I don't understand, though. Why would she inject herself with insulin when she was going to drown herself anyway?"

"I'd say that Eloise didn't want to take any chances," Sapphire replied. "She thought if she tried to drown herself in the bath, she might stop at the last minute, but if she overdosed herself right before, then she could climb into the bathtub without worrying that she'd chicken out. It's a strange way to do it, I know. But she obviously wanted to go in the same way her mother did. Poor little thing. Shit."

"I guess you're right," I mused, amazed that Sapphire had come up with this plausible answer before I had.

"Where did the police find the needle?" she asked.

"The needle? Oh, in the bathtub. Her body had

kind of hidden it. I don't think I can discuss the details of this anymore, Sapphire."

"Sure." Sapphire nodded, tasting her wine. "That's fine. But you know, it occurred to me that if they hadn't found the needle, they might think Robert had given her the overdose and then put her body in the bath."

"Well, they might have. But then I had her suicide letter. And if Robert had killed her, why would he kill himself?"

"Yeah, right." Sapphire stretched her legs. "That's a problem. Want some salad?"

We sat across from each other in two chairs the waiter had set up and ate without speaking. Sapphire was preoccupied and I was wondering why she'd invited me to this lunch. We weren't exactly friends.

She speared an uneaten tomato from my plate.

"Some will, huh?"

I nodded.

"Bobby told me about it. Are you going to marry that cute guy in the baseball cap or what?"

"I don't know."

"You should, you know. There aren't that many cute guys around. It's a nice package—money and a man. And you're not getting any younger."

"Thanks a lot."

"No. Listen. I didn't mean to offend you. I'm not young either. We lose our options as we get older. That's all I meant."

I lit a cigarette.

"Smoking's not good for your face, you know. It makes the wrinkles multiply faster."

"Sapphire. I didn't come here for a beauty lecture. Actually, I'm not sure why I *did* come here. I think I should get going."

"Not now, Stacy. Not yet."

She stared at me. I could feel myself blinking wildly. Her face was even whiter than usual; the skin so transparent I began to think I would see through it if I could just stop blinking. I closed my eyes and saw Robert lying on the bed, shot through the heart. When I opened them I saw Sapphire was still staring at me. I stopped blinking.

"You know something, don't you? Something I don't know."

My eyes felt like heat-seeking missiles.

"I think you better tell me what you know," I said evenly. "Everything."

She leaned forward. So did I. Two conspirators over half-eaten salads.

"After you left on my plane, I started to think. Well, I know you may be pretty tough, but not half as tough as I am. You haven't been through the shit I've been through and you don't know Robert as well as I do. I figured you didn't have as good a chance as I did of stopping him. So I decided to get in on the act. I told Bobby I had a gig I couldn't cancel and I chartered a plane real early the next morning to New York. Meanwhile I got one of my trusty men to stake out Eloise's house on the East Side. So I knew that the two of them left together about noon, and my guy followed them, keeping me posted. When they arrived at the Cape Cod house, he phoned me in New York and I chartered another plane. He met me at Hyannis and took me to the house.

"By now we're talking 10 P.M. It's dark. My man has told me they're alone in the house, so I think, well, now's my chance. I'm going to make an entrance, I'm going to get this whole thing out in the open. I'm sick of all this shit. Ever since Bobby told me about Susan, well, I feel responsible, because I know that I'm involved somehow. There's all this unfinished business between Robert and me. I want to have it out with him, and I want to have it out with him in front of Eloise. Maybe I'm crazy, but I think it's the right thing to do.

"So I ring the doorbell, and Robert answers. Obviously, he's thrown when he sees me. Wants to know what the hell I'm doing there. Starts screaming at me immediately. Who the fuck do I think I am to come to his house unannounced, he's going to call the police, and so on.

"I say, 'Calm down, Robert, I just want to have a chat with you and your wife.' I walk into the house and plonk myself down on a sofa. He's got the TV on. Some basketball game. 'Where's your wife?' I ask. 'She's gone to bed,' he answers. 'She's tired.'

" 'Mmm,' I say. 'I bet she is. What is it you want from me, Robert? I know I'm at the bottom of all this shit with Susan and Eloise. Let's make it clean. Let's get this over with once and for all between you and me.'

"He goes into the kitchen, then brings back a bottle of champagne, pours me a glass. 'Fine,' he says.

And I think, well, maybe I'm getting somewhere, maybe this was a good move after all.

"Then he starts. The tirade stuff. The same old bullshit he used to do night after night. What a cunt I am, what a slut, how I fucked up his life, his career, how I humiliated him.

"I sit there and take it all and he rants on and on and he's beginning to scare me because he's even worse than he was before. I mean his rage is like some thick, smothering oil slick. He won't stop talking, he won't stop calling me names. He's telling me he's going to destroy my life, he's going to make me suffer and there's nothing I can do about it. He's got this brutal look in his eyes.

"Meanwhile, I'm thinking I want Eloise to see this. Maybe she's never seen this side of him. He won't be able to control it now. She has to see this.

"I say, 'Robert, I've got to pee. Where's the john?' He's so immersed in his own anger and bitching that he hardly takes any notice of this—he just says, 'Upstairs,' and I promise you, he keeps on talking, keeps ranting on—even while I'm walking upstairs I can hear him. Pacing up and down that living room muttering. I'm looking for Eloise now. I'm going to wake her up and get her downstairs with me. She has to see this, and after she sees it, well, maybe I can sweep her away. My guy in the car is waiting outside. I can bundle her into it with me and take her away. I can save her like I got saved.

"I go into what turns out to be the master bedroom —it's the first door I find and the light's on and nobody is in the bed, but there's a note on the pillow.

It's a real strange note, as if she were writing it for a medical examiner. She's talking about insulin, blood sugar levels—all this technical stuff. But it's a fucking suicide note, that much is for sure. And in the end she says she's going to give herself an overdose so she won't chicken out, and then climb in the bathtub, because she wants to drown like her mother. I read it real quick and I realize what's happened and I see a door that must lead into the bathroom. I stand there for a second wondering whether I have the guts to go in, but then I think maybe I can save her, maybe she's not dead yet. Maybe I can drag her out of the bath and get the insulin pumped out of her body or something. I don't know. I'm not feeling very calm at this point.

"But I walk in and there she is floating in that tub like something out of a horror movie and there's no fucking way she's not dead. I vomit. I'm close enough to the john to be sick into that and while I'm being sick, I start thinking fast. Very fast. As fast as I've ever thought in my life.

"She's killed herself, she's written a note, the whole thing's kosher and Robert's won again. I'm not going to let this happen. I look around wildly for the needle, you see. Check the medicine cabinet, the floor. I figure if I can get the needle and somehow get Robert's fingerprints on it I can set him up. I run into the bedroom and stuff the suicide note in my bag, but I can't find the fucking needle."

"Then I hear Robert coming up the stairs and I freeze. He comes into the bedroom, looking around for Eloise. I point to the bathroom door. 'In there, Robert,' I say. 'Go look at what you've done.'

"And then you know what happens? He goes into that bathroom and the next thing I know, he comes dancing into the bedroom, singing: 'Heaven, she's in heaven,' like everybody did when Fred Astaire died, and suddenly he stops and says, 'She loved me that much. She really loved me. She loved me enough to die for me. Isn't that great?' Like he's just won a war or something.

"I say, 'Not as far as I'm concerned, Robert.' For some reason I'm calm now. I'm watching my ex-husband standing there triumphantly after he's seen that godawful sight and *I'm* standing very calmly. Because there's no way I'm going to let him win. It's between me and him, now. One on one, like the old days. But I've changed. That's the kicker—that's what he doesn't know. I've got that suicide note in my bag and I'm still calculating how to make him take the rap for this. I even do a few quick fantasies of him in jail getting buggered, when suddenly he goes real quiet. He sits down in a chair in the corner of the room and he stares at me.

" 'What are you going to wear tonight?' he asks.

"I don't answer this weird question. His eyes are real narrow and he's not moving an inch.

" 'Who are you going out with tonight?' he asks again.

" 'I'm not planning on going out on the town tonight,' I say finally, because he's beginning to look like that guy in *Psycho* and I'm beginning to get scared. I think I should play along with him.

366

" 'Well, I can't move, can I? I can't take you out.'

"Now I start to back away. I don't understand what's happening here and there's this body in the bathtub and I want out.

" 'Don't move.' He reaches into the top drawer of a dresser by his chair and he pulls out a gun. Well, this definitely stops me. 'Don't even think about moving.' He waves the gun at me. 'You ignore me and you ignore our son and you think you can get away with it.'

" 'Robert. That was all a long time ago and I just saw Bobby yesterday. I'm not ignoring Bobby.'

" 'You never cared how he did at school. Never paid any attention to him. Left us together like two heaps of shit you didn't want to step in.'

" 'I wouldn't put it that way,' I say. 'You're the one that made *me* feel like shit.'

" 'That's rich,' he smirks. 'You think that you can junket around being successful, going out every night, torturing me, and I won't fight back. You want me to kill myself, don't you, so that you'll be rid of me finally. Well, it's not going to happen that way. I'm going to kill you, and then my son and I can live peacefully together.'

" 'Listen,' I say. 'Calm down. Put the gun away. Eloise is the person who has killed herself here. Don't you think we should call the police?'

" 'Eloise?' He looks confused. His head kind of snaps back.

" 'Robert, put the gun down, will you?' I sit down on the bed very carefully. I have to sit down, I'm shaking so much.

" 'Amy'—he stands up now, moves toward me still pointing the gun at me—'you look beautiful tonight. I love you, you know. I've always loved you.' He comes up to me and he starts to kiss me, but that gun is sticking in my ribs the whole time. He pulls me to my feet and he's kissing me and he begins to dance with me, humming that Shirley Temple song."

" 'The Good Ship Lollipop'?" I asked.

"Right, how did you know?" Sapphire nodded. "He's got his left arm around me and the gun is in his right hand. Pointing straight at my heart. We're dancing. And this is the really sick part. I mean the whole scene is sick, but this is the worst bit. I start to fall for it. It's unreal. It's as if we'd been sent back in a time machine and suddenly I'm dancing with the man I love. That song—that song was the first song he ever sang to me. He came to my house and he serenaded me. It was so beautiful.

"I know you're not going to understand that. You were never attracted to Robert, so you wouldn't understand. But I did love him. That's what's so awful. Even when I left him, I loved him in a way. Everything I've done since I left him, my whole act, all the sexy stuff, everything—it was aimed at him. I wanted to get to him, hit him where it hurt. Robert had this hold over me—there's no other way to put it. In a way, well, he always had a gun pointing at my heart.

"Anyway, it's like an episode of *Twin Peaks*. There's Eloise in the bathtub and there are Robert and I dancing like the old days, except he's got the gun. But he smelled the same, Stacy. I swear he did. The way he used to. I always loved his smell. And that voice. When he wanted to, he could be so charming, so romantic. And kind of helpless. Like a little boy. That's what it felt like when we were dancing. I remembered the good times. Everything else melted away. I must have been in shock.''

Sapphire fell silent, bowed her head.

"What happened then?" I prompted her.

"He asked me if I loved him. He said: 'Amy, do you love me?' ''

Sapphire whispered the next sentence.

"What?"

She looked up at me.

"I told him I did. Can you believe that? Can you believe how fucked up I am?"

I didn't respond.

"Anyway, as soon as I said yes, he stepped back and eyed me. Up and down. Like he was trying to figure out whether I was lying or not. 'Prove it, then,' he said. 'Show me.' He went and lay down on the bed. He placed the gun right beside him.

" 'What do you want me to do?' I ask. I'm figuring sex, of course. I'm so far gone. I'm ready to climb into bed with him. I'm nineteen again. Do you know what it's like to feel nineteen again?

" 'Amy. Amy.' he says. 'You do love me, don't you? Because I love you. I'm thinking of what's best for you. How much longer are you going to last? What's going to happen in your future? You'll have to watch yourself being replaced by younger singers, younger stars. Tell me this: do you see yourself playing Vegas when you're sixty? Do you?'

" 'Are you going to prance around the stage in

your blue jeans belting out all your old hits for the geriatric crowd? You won't like that, will you?'

"He's lying on the bed, propped up on one elbow. He's speaking very softly.

" 'What are your options, Amy? A facelift? Yearly visits to the plastic surgeon to keep yourself up to par? You'll be running like an Olympic racer just to stay in place. You'll be looking over your shoulder, frightened the whole time. Terrified that you've lost it. Or will you retire gracefully, slip into obscurity without a battle? Become one of those reclusive female stars who don't go out. I'm worried about you, you see. I'm concerned. It's not as if you had any solid relationship to help you through all this. Those boys can't be good for you. They're using you, aren't they? For their own purposes. Everybody's using you. People will do anything to get a piece of celebrity.'

" 'And, let's face it, you're not a mother. You may establish some kind of relationship with Bobby, but you'll never be his mother. You lost out on that, didn't you? One of the greatest human experiences and you missed it. So what's left for you now, Amy? Where do you go from here? What do you have to look forward to?'

"He's staring at me with this very *kind* look. He takes my hand and squeezes it.

" 'I don't know, Robert.' I feel like I'm about to cry. 'I've got an album coming out at the beginning of next year.'

" 'Oh, Amy,' he sighs. He gets that disappointed look. 'I mean, what do you *really* have to look forward to? Your life is empty, isn't it? You're living a charade.

Be honest with yourself for once. Where can you possibly go from here except downhill?' Now I can see that he's crying. We're both crying. I'm feeling like a wall has just fallen on top of me and I can't dig myself out from under the bricks.

"I remember my last meeting with my PR people. They're trying to tell me what to wear for the cover of my album and they're laughing about it. They're in hysterics about what stupid over-the-top pose I can come up with next. It's like a huge joke. At my expense.

"I don't know why, but I reach over and I pick up Robert's gun and I hold it. I'm like a car with four flat tires, but this gun makes me feel better. I play with it, pass it back and forth from hand to hand. It's nice and heavy. Robert's not saying anything, he's watching me. He's still crying, but he's got a smile on his face as well. He looks so handsome. I remember riding around Providence in his Mustang, my feet up on the dashboard. My happiest times. I hold the gun up to my face, rub it against my cheek. I think of that Beatles song: 'Happiness Is a Warm Gun.' I think of John Lennon getting blown away and how the whole world mourned him. I think of Marilyn Monroe and James Dean and all these people who never had to get old and fade away.

" 'Life hurts, Amy, doesn't it?' Robert says, and he reaches out and puts his fingers on my lips.

"I'm resting my head against this gun. Robert's still smiling. Then I see something out of the corner of my eye. I see a framed picture of Eloise on the bedside table. She's smiling too, holding a bunch of lilies. She

371

looks so sweet she could be an angel. I stop picturing myself as an old has-been. What I see now is Eloise's face in that tub. I imagine Susan in a hospital bed, all these tubes attached to her. Everything comes back in a rush. My brain is screaming, 'Close call, you stupid fuck. You almost bought it.' And I know then that Robert's not going to let me walk out of that house alive.

" 'Yes, Robert,' I say, 'life hurts.' I lean over and kiss him on the lips. Then I point the gun and I pull the trigger. I blast him right through the heart.

"His smile evaporates. His chest heaves a couple of times and then stops. I sit there staring at his body, holding the gun, wondering what the hell to do next. I keep expecting him to jump back up at me. Then I wipe the gun clean of my fingerprints and put it in that little right hand of his, curve his arm around, so it looks like he was pointing it at his chest.

"I do the whole schtick—wipe my fingerprints from everything I might have touched, including the toilet, but I shield my eyes from Eloise's body. I go downstairs and wash that glass of champagne I had, then stuff that in my purse. I see Eloise's suicide note in there. I think of going back, putting it on the bed, but I can't face seeing Robert again. He came so close.

"I get rid of the note later—tear it up into little pieces and stuff it in a trash can outside a McDonald's on the road back to New York. I figure the police will think Robert killed Eloise and then himself or that they both killed themselves. There's no reason to suspect me because there's no reason to suspect a murder. It's his gun, his fingerprints. Eloise is in the bathroom beside him. What else could they possibly think?

"Of course, the next day I gave the guy who drove me a promotion and an expenses-paid vacation to Europe, and he's so grateful he's not about to spill any beans about my little trip to Cape Cod. Later on, if he puts everything together and thinks about blackmailing me, I'll tell the police my story. It was self-defense in the end. If a jury doesn't believe that, well, I'll have to start giving prison concerts. Release a cover version of Johnny Cash's 'Folsom Prison Blues.' What a media splash."

She sagged back in her chair, waving smoke away from her face. We sat in silence.

"Why did you tell *me* this, Sapphire?" I finally asked.

"You weren't happy with that double suicide bit, were you?"

"No," I admitted, "I wasn't."

"So you see? You needed to know the truth. That's why I told you. As a favor to you. Your friend Eloise ended up saving me. I owe her and she's not around. So you're the closest I could come. Besides, I had to tell *somebody*. It all seems like a dream. Telling you makes it real. I can deal with reality."

"I'm going to have to tell Daniel, you know."

"That's all right. He looked like a guy who knows how to keep his mouth shut. But don't tell Bobby. I'm trusting you not to tell Bobby. That's your favor to me."

"I won't. I promise."

"Good. Now"—she stood up, stretched—"I've got

some meetings. I'm playing Madison Square Garden next Tuesday. You want some tickets?"

"Sure." My thoughts were frenzied. I wanted to get out of there, have time to think her story through by myself.

"Fine. I'll arrange it. Maybe we'll see each other again sometime. What do you think?"

"Maybe." I walked to the door, my hand was on the knob. "And Sapphire? Take care of yourself."

"I plan to, babe. I'm not dead yet."

25

DECEMBER 1990

"I hope Sapphire doesn't have to tell that story to the police." Daniel was tilting on his chair, balancing on the back two legs.

"Me too."

"It's much better if Bobby never knows."

"Right." I nodded.

"Although I'm not so sure it changes the verdict. It's still double suicide as far as I'm concerned."

"What do you mean? She pulled the trigger. She killed him."

The chair landed upright. Daniel scratched his head.

"The man put the gun down, Stacy. He knew it was loaded and he let Sapphire pick it up. What does that tell you?"

"It tells me that he thought she'd kill herself. He deliberately played on all her weak spots. He was waiting for her to shoot herself."

"I don't think so. He might have seen it another way. When she pulls that trigger, shoots him, it links her to him forever. It's another kind of power. That's why he was smiling at the end. He knew she wouldn't go through with killing herself, but that she *would* kill him. He may have hated his mother, but he may have loved her too. There was such ambiguity in Robert. He knew how to sweep women off their feet, so he had to have some kind of insight into what women want. A sympathy of sorts. He was dancing back and forth between madness and sanity; maybe somewhere in between he identified with his so-called victims. Maybe he wanted to be a victim again himself. It's possible.''

''I suppose so. But I don't agree.''

''It's not in your interest to agree.'' Daniel smiled. I got up and made a cup of coffee in his kitchen, wondering what he meant by that. I was sure it had something to do with my sleeping with Robert, but I hated thinking about that afternoon and I didn't want to go over it yet again. Or consider what effect it had on my future with Daniel.

A phrase in Eloise's letter kept haunting me. *No one can guarantee that the person you love will love you. It's a lottery.*

When I went back into the living room, I could tell Daniel was well into one of his silent moods. I drank my coffee and thumbed through a copy of *Harper's.* Our two week deadline was up, but I wasn't going to remind him. Every night he slept on the sofa, I felt him slipping away.

Daniel suddenly roused himself, sprang from his chair, grabbed me by the hand, threw me my coat and bundled me out of the door, down the stairs, onto the street. We walked to the subway, got on a train downtown. To the World Trade Center. I kept asking him what was going on, but he wouldn't answer. He bought two tickets for the Observation Deck and we traveled up with a horde of tourists. The day was just on the point of turning into night, New York City was lighting up beneath us, as Daniel guided me to a glass bench. We were sitting in a sculpted-out hollow, inches away from the glass windows.

"This gives us a certain perspective, don't you think? I come here on my own quite a bit. It's a good place to think."

Looking down was breathtaking. It was also terrifying.

"Do you remember when Philippe Petit crossed to the other tower there on his tightrope? That has to be the most astounding feat of the century. Can you imagine the nerve it took? The wind up here is always tricky. To keep his balance must have been close to impossible."

"I remember," I replied.

"Now. Since we're talking high wire acts, I think we better address the question of our future. What's the game plan, Stacy?"

"I don't have any game plan, Daniel."

"Well, I have a few plays mapped out. But I've got a problem. Do you know what will happen the minute we get the money? My ex-wife will up the alimony payments through the roof. I'll be paying for swimming pools, châteaux in the South of France. She'll probably want to buy the Plaza Hotel off Ivana Trump."

I laughed, but I knew I was about to cry.

"Was that a proposal, Daniel?"

"Of course, nuthead. Christ—if we don't get married and take the money I'll have to finish my back book."

The tears were taking their time, but they were getting there.

"Oh, hey, Stace—" He put his arm around me and squeezed my shoulder. "Don't look so stricken. If you really think I'm marrying you for the money, you can say no. I figure Eloise is right. We love each other, always have, but we've made some mistakes along the way. You're the one who has made the most glaring mistakes, and I'll have fun reminding you of them over the years."

I disregarded all the signs and lit a cigarette.

"But if you don't marry me, I'll throw myself through this window and splat on the street," he said. "How about that? Is that romantic enough?"

"Daniel. These windows are designed so you couldn't do that even if you tried."

"Well, sure. I know that. But it's the thought that counts, right?"